KARL SCHROEDER

ASHES OF CANDESCE

Virga | BOOK FIVE

A TOM DOHERTY ASSOCIATES BOOK TOR™ NEW YORK

This is a work of fiction. All of the characters, organizations, and events portrayed in this novel are either products of the author's imagination or are used fictitiously.

ASHES OF CANDESCE: BOOK FIVE OF VIRGA

A Tor Book
Published by Tom Doherty Associates, LLC
175 Fifth Avenue
New York, NY 10010

www.tor-forge.com

Tor® is a registered trademark of Tom Doherty Associates, LLC.

ISBN 978-0-7653-2492-4

First Edition: February 2012

Printed in the United States of America

0 9 8 7 6 5 4 3 2 1

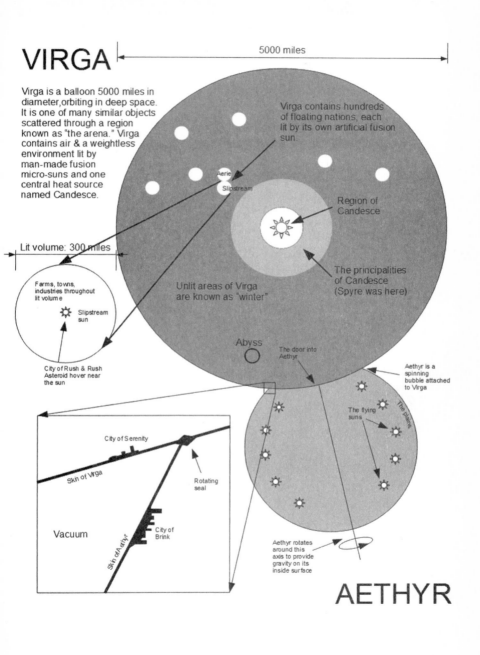

VIRGA

5000 miles

Virga is a balloon 5000 miles in diameter, orbiting in deep space. It is one of many similar objects scattered through a region known as "the arena." Virga contains air & a weightless environment lit by man-made fusion micro-suns and one central heat source named Candesce.

Virga contains hundreds of floating nations, each lit by its own artificial fusion sun.

Aerie
Slipstream

Region of Candesce

Lit volume: 300 miles

Farms, towns, industries throughout lit volume

Slipstream sun

City of Rush & Rush Asteroid hover near the sun

Unlit areas of Virga are known as "winter"

The principalities of Candesce (Spyre was here)

Abyss

The door into Aethyr

Aethyr is a spinning bubble attached to Virga

The flying suns

The plains

City of Serenity

Skin of Virga

Rotating seal

Vacuum

City of Brink

Skin of Aethyr

Aethyr rotates around this axis to provide gravity on its inside surface

AETHYR

ASHES OF CANDESCE

Prologue

DARKNESS, AND A rope road.

"Champagne?" asked the flight attendant. Antaea Argyre raised her hand to wave him away, then turned the motion into acceptance of the helix glass. It wasn't as if she was on duty, after all. She sipped the tart wine from one end of the glass coil that surface tension held it to, and watched the undulating rope ravel by outside the window.

None of the other passengers were watching. In knots of two or three or five, they preened and posed, drank and laughed at one another's jokes. The gaslights of this passenger ship's lounge lit the space brightly, highlighting the gold filigree around the doorjambs and the deep mazelike patterns in the velvet of the cushioned pillars. Everything held sumptuous color and texture, except the floor-to-ceiling window that took up one entire wall. This was black, like the uniform Antaea wore. She was the only passenger close enough to touch the cold glass; the only one looking out.

The last hour had somehow managed to be tedious and nerve-racking at the same time. The lounge was full of diplomats, military commanders, politicians, and newspaper reporters. They were all attentive to one another, and all were adept at negotiating today's social minefield.

They had all stopped talking when Antaea entered the room.

Even now she felt eyes on her back, though of course, nobody would have the courage to actually approach her.

She took a bigger drink of the champagne, and was just regretting not having started in on it earlier when the doors to the lounge opened and a new knot of officials sailed in. They caught various discreet straps and guide ropes and glided to a unified halt just as the distant drone of the ship's engines changed in tone.

"Ladies and gentlemen," said a bright young thing in a sequined corset and diaphanous harem pants, "we've arrived."

There was a murmur and polite applause; Antaea turned back to the window. As her hand felt for the railing, it fell on someone else's. "Oh!"

"Excuse me." The voice was a deep, commanding rumble. It came from a man with the craggy features of an elder statesman and silver hair tied back in a short tail. He was dressed in a silk suit of a red so dark it was almost black. He seemed quite relaxed in the company of so many powerful people; but his accent pegged him as a foreigner.

He'd shifted his grip and she put her hand on the rail next to his. Only then did she notice that they were still the only ones at the window; everyone else was listening attentively to the government delegation. Of course they were. They couldn't very well ignore their hosts.

The rope that their ship had been following through the weightless air of Virga ended at a beacon about a mile ahead. This was a heavy cement cylinder with flashing lamps on its ends. Right now their flickering light was highlighting the rounded shapes of clouds that would otherwise have been invisible in the permanent darkness. Without the rope and the beacon, it would have been impossible for any ship to find this particular spot in the thousands of cubic kilometers of darkness that made up Virga's sunless reaches.

"We thank you all for coming with us today," the young thing was saying breathily. "We know the rumors have been intense and widespread. There've been stories of monsters, of ancient powers awakened in the dark old corners of Virga. We're here today to help put any anxieties you might have to rest."

"There." The man beside her raised one hand and pressed his

index finger against the glass. For a second she was distracted by the halo of condensation that instantly fogged into existence around his fingertip. Then she looked past and into the blackness.

She saw nothing there but the ghostly curve of a cloud bank.

"For some months last year, our nation of Abyss felt itself to be under siege," the spokeswoman continued. "There were reports of attacks on outlying towns. Rumors began to circulate of a vast voice crying in the dark. Ah! I see by the expression on some faces that some of our visitors from the warm interior of the world have already figured out the mystery. Don't tell! You must understand how traumatic it was for us, who live here in the permanent dark and cold near the wall of the world. Many of the things you take for granted in the principalities are never seen out here. Maybe that makes us provincials, I don't know; but we had no reason to expect the kind of attack that really did happen."

The man next to Antaea removed his finger from the glass, leaving a little oval of frost behind. "You don't see it, do you?" he asked in obvious amusement.

She shrugged in irritation. "Behind that cloud?"

"So you think that's a cloud?"

Startled, she looked again.

"The crisis culminated in an attack on the city of Sere," the spokeswoman said. "There was panic and confusion, and people claimed to have seen all manner of things. The hysteria of crowds is well known, and mass hallucination is not uncommon in such circumstances. Of course, the stories and reports immediately spread far beyond Sere—to your own countries, and I daresay beyond. A deluge of concern came back to us—inquiries about our safety, our loyalties, the stability of our trade agreements. It's become a big mess—especially because we long since sorted out the cause of the problem, and it's been dealt with."

The officials from the Abyssal government moved to the window, not too far from where Antaea and the stranger perched. "Behold," said the spokeswoman, "the Crier in the Dark!"

She gestured dramatically, and floodlights on the outside of the ship snapped on. The thing Antaea had at first taken to be a vast cloud blinked into view; at least, part of it did.

There were shouts of surprise, and relieved laughter; then, applause. "A capital bug!" someone shouted.

The spokeswoman bowed; behind her, the (entirely male) group of officials were smiling and nodding in obvious relief at the crowd's reaction. Their backdrop was a cavern of light carved by the floodlights out of an infinite ocean of night. The lights barely reached the gray skin of the city-sized beast that hung motionless and dormant in the icy air. Antaea could see a rank of tower-sized horns jutting from beyond the horizon of its back. In a live bug those horns would be blaring the notes of a chord so loudly that no ordinary form of life could survive within a mile of the thing.

Everybody was talking now, and the reporters were throwing questions at the Abyssals: *When did you discover it was a capital bug? Why is it silent now? How did you save the city from it?* The stranger next to Antaea shook his head minutely and his lips quirked into a faint smile.

"The gullibility of people never ceases to amaze me," he murmured.

Antaea realized that she'd bought this explanation, too, and frowned now in confusion. "You think it's a lie?" she asked quietly.

He gave her a pointed once-over—taking in, she assumed, her uniform, though not without a slight pause here and there. "You tell me," he said. "I'm sure the Abyssal government doesn't tie its collective shoes without the permission of the Virga Home Guard."

Rather than answer that, she pointed to the obvious. "They do have a bug, don't they? Capital bugs aren't native to this part of Virga. It's too cold for them. So if one strayed this deep . . ."

"Oh, yes, if one strayed this deep." He shook his head. "But I happen to know that a bug that's been living on the fringes of Meridian for years disappeared about a month ago. There were witnesses said they saw ships circling it in the evening sky—heard the sound of artillery being fired. Now, tell me: those horns there. Do they look intact to you?"

She did think she could see dark pits in the giant horns, now that he'd mentioned it. Behind her, one of the men from the government was saying, "It took weeks for it to cool down enough to fall into a dormant state. We didn't really have to do anything, just keep it away from the city until it finally began snowing in its body cavity. Now, as you can see, it's in hibernation."

Antaea frowned at the frost-painted hide, more landscape than flank, that curved far beyond the range of the ship's floodlights. She had to admit, she wanted the monster to have been something ordinary like this. It would be so much simpler; so reassuring.

If she thought this way, though, how much more so would the officious, conservative bureaucrats who ran Abyss these days? Monster was not a column heading in their ledgers. So, would they invent an answer if they couldn't find one? Of course they would.

She shot her companion a sour look. "Are you going to mention your little theory to our hosts? And how did you hear about it anyway?"

"I pride myself in listening well," he said; then he put out his hand for her to shake. "Jacoby Sarto."

That was definitely a name from the principalities of Candesce, thousands of kilometers from here. "Sayrea Airsigh," she said as they shook, and she saw his eyes widen minutely. He noticed her noticing, and grimaced.

"Excuse me," he said. "You look like another Guardswoman of winter wraith descent . . ."

Had he seen a photo of her somewhere? That wouldn't be unusual, what with her notoriety after recent events in Slipstream. "Well, there's more than one of us in the Guard, you know," she said, and then added icily, "and I'm told we all look alike."

He refused to be baited. "So the Virga Home Guard agrees with

Abyss's official story, that the monster was a capital bug all along? —
Even though there are dozens of Guard cruisers patrolling the
sunless countries even now?"

"Are there?" She didn't have to pretend her ignorance; this man
seemed to know details of the situation that Antaea had only been
able to wonder about.

He gazed at the pebbled hide of the capital bug. "Some of us are
keenly interested in the truth of the situation. Of course, as a member of the Home Guard, you know everything already. That being
the case, I really have no reason to give you my card"—and here
a small rectangle of white paper suddenly appeared between his
fingers—"nor tell you that I'm staying at the Stormburl Hotel, on
Rowan Wheel."

Damn him, he had her figured out. She opened her mouth to say
something dismissive, but his gaze flicked over her shoulder and
back; she quickly snatched the card and palmed it before turning
to find that two Abyssal cabinet ministers were closing in on her.
"Gentlemen," she said with a gracious smile.

"It's a magnificent beast, isn't it?" said one of the two. Antaea
glanced over her shoulder; Sarto was gone.

"Yes, beautiful," she said. "I've seen them before, but never up
close, of course. Their song kills."

"Yes." He nodded vigorously. "We trust that the Guard is, ah, in
agreement with us that the disappearance of the outlying towns,
the battle with the sun lighter—these were all caused by this one?"

The battle with the sun lighter. She'd heard about that; well, practically
everybody in Virga had by now. Hayden Griffin was fabled for building a new sun to free his country from enslavement by the pirate
nation of Slipstream. He had been constructing another sun for a
client here in Abyss when the monster interrupted his work. The
stories had him pursuing it to its lair and incinerating it with the
nuclear fire of his half-built generator. Antaea hadn't really believed
this part of the rapidly mutating legend, but here was an Abyssal
government official, offhandedly confirming it.

She belatedly realized he wanted some response from her. "Um—sorry?"

He looked impatient. "Do you think this explanation works?"

"Oh. Yes, yes, of course. It's very, uh, convincing." She gestured to the bug. "Especially having the actual bug to show. A nice touch."

He relaxed. "The response has been good, I think." Around them, the guests were chatting animatedly, and some of the reporters had left with a steward to find a good vantage point from which to photograph the bug. "I think we can finally lay this incident to rest." The official hesitated, then said, "But we'd understood that we had the Guard's consent to do this. It was a bit of a surprise to see you here. Was there any problem . . . ?"

"Oh! No, no, I'm just observing." She gave him a sphinxlike smile. "Everything is just fine."

"Good," he said, as he and his companion nodded to one another. "That's . . . good."

They bowed themselves away, and she watched them go with mixed contempt and bemusement. Then she turned back to examine the bug.

This was indeed a clue. Maybe she should rent a jet bike from one of the wheelside vendors back in Sere, and slip back here to check the thing out herself. Those horns did look shot up—though the Abyssal navy would have targeted them first if the creature really had been threatening the city. No. Any evidence she might find here would be inconclusive. She would need more if she was to disprove the government's story.

Even assuming that she did, what then? Clearly, whatever was going on, the Home Guard knew about it. What could Antaea do here but satisfy her own curiosity?

Well, there was one thing. A life to save, maybe. She should focus on that; this bug, and all the furor around it, was just a distraction.

With a sharp nod she turned from the window. Before she left the lounge to join the photographers in the fresh air on the hull, she looked for Jacoby Sarto among the crowd. She didn't see him;

and by the time the dart-shaped passenger liner had finished its tour of the capital bug, she had put him and his cryptic comments out of her mind.

BY THE TIME the streetcar deposited her in front of her hotel, Antaea was exhausted. She had been in Sere a few days now—long enough to have gotten over any residual nostalgia from her college days. The city was the same as always, after all: locked in permanent darkness, its mile-wide copper wheels lit only by gaslight. Rings of windows turned above her head, and the streets soared up to either side to join in an arch overhead; nothing unusual there. Each window, though, spoke of some isolated room, some tightly constrained human life. There were thousands of them.

It was raining, as it often did here. Rain was something that happened only in town wheels, and she'd used to think it was a wonderful novelty. The wheel cut into a cloud, and droplets of water that had been hanging in the weightless air suddenly became little missiles pelting in almost horizontally. They were cold, though. The novelty wore off fast; so she hunched her shoulders and trotted across the verdigris-mottled street to the hotel, where the permanent fans of light and shadow had faded the paint in the entryway, and thousands of footsteps had worn a gray smear in the once-red carpet.

The boy behind the desk sent her a covert, hostile glance as she walked past. It was the thousandth such glance today and she ignored it. They might hate her kind, but as long as she wore this uniform, no one would dare lay a hand on her.

In the elevator she pulled back her black hair and wiped the rain from her face. The dimly lit car thumped at each floor, monotonously counting its way up to her room. No one else got on or off. When it stopped, she fumbled for her key as she counted the doors to hers, and, in a state of nonthinking exhaustion, slid the key into the lock.

Antaea just had time to realize that the lights in the room were on before iron fingers clamped onto her wrist and yanked her arm behind her. She automatically went with the motion but before she could finish her recovery somebody'd kicked her leading foot out from under her, and then she hit the floor and the wind went out of her.

Some heavy body was sitting on the small of her back, holding her wrists against the floor. She snarled, furious and humiliated.

"Just like I thought," said a familiar male voice. "She's wearing it."

"Crase?" She craned her neck and saw a small forest of black-clad shins and boots. After struggling to breathe for a few seconds, she managed, "What are you doing here?"

"Today, I'm chasing down an imposter." Lieutenant Anander Crase of the Virga Home Guard knelt to look into her face. "You've no right to wear that uniform. Not since the trial."

She hissed. "All I wanted to do was come home. Without the uniform, I'd have been arrested by now, or strung up by some vigilante gang. You know how they feel about winter wraiths here."

He'd been looking her in the eye, but now that she'd highlighted the racism they both knew was common here, his gaze slid away. "Why did you come back, then?" he asked sullenly. "If there's no welcome here for you?"

"It's not up to me to justify returning. It's up to them to justify keeping me out. Let me up," she added to whoever it was that sat on her back.

Crase looked up, shrugged. The pressure on Antaea's back eased, and she rolled into a crouch.

There were six of them, all men, only their standard-issue boots betraying that they were Home Guard. They'd tossed her room efficiently and ruthlessly. She almost smiled at the thought of how disappointed Crase must be at finding nothing.

He went to sit in the small suite's one chair. "You almost make sense," he said, "but not quite. You lived here for a while, but Abyss isn't your home. You grew up on the winter wraith fleet."

"—Which I did not want to return to. They're the most isolationist people in Virga, even if it's for good reason because normal people are always trying to kill them . . . Crase, where did you expect me to go? I have no home anywhere. The Guard was my home. Without that . . ."

"You have friends here?" He was skirting very close to the truth, but she had no option now. She nodded.

He leaned forward in the chair. "Then where are they? And why did you use your *disguise*," he nodded to her frayed old uniform, "to wrangle your way onto a government-sponsored expedition today?"

"I'll tell you that if you tell me why the Guard is lying about the Crier in the Dark."

He exchanged a glance with another of the men. Then he stood up and walked up to loom over her. "I want you out of here on the next ship," he said. "None of this concerns you. You're not Home Guard anymore."

She could probably have put him and his friends on the floor, if she'd been training the way she used to. As it was, she had to stand there and take his intimidation. She hung her head, and consciously kept her hands from balling into fists.

Crase shoved past her, and he and his goons clotted the doorway. "You know what happens to people who pretend to be Guardsmen," he said before closing the door. "You got off lucky this time."

The click of the door locking itself surprised her into motion. Antaea went to her bags and began assessing what they'd done. Crase really had let her off easily; imposters usually disappeared. And though they'd gone through her luggage with trained efficiency, they hadn't taken anything. When she was sure of this, she sat down on the edge of the bed and let out a heavy sigh. Her chest hurt, and her arm. There would be finger-shaped bruises there later.

Crase might have stayed to interrogate her further, but they had a bit of a history. He knew her well enough to suspect that she was tougher than he was. She half-smiled at the thought, then reached into her jacket for the item that, if they'd frisked her, would have told them why she'd come here.

She hadn't lied about this being the only place where she had ties—it was just that those ties were almost impossibly thin, and left to herself, she would never have come back because of any of them.

The letter in her hands was so worn from travel and folding and refolding that it was practically falling apart. Still, she smoothed it carefully onto the bedspread. She didn't have to read it; she just needed the reassurance of knowing it existed at all.

Dear Antaea, it read.

My name is Leal Hieronyma Maspeth. I don't know if you remember me, I studied with your sister at the academy. We had supper together, the three of us, one time. Your sister once told me she wanted to join the Home Guard and I told her it was a myth. I guess I was wrong.

She *did* remember Leal Maspeth; she'd been her sister's timid, academically minded roommate when Telen went to college here in the city of Sere. Maspeth was one of the few people in the world who'd known of Telen and Antaea's plan to track down the supposedly mythical Virga Home Guard and join up.

I'm writing you, Maspeth continued, *because we have a problem, and the government refuses to admit to it, and they refuse to let the Home Guard in to investigate. I don't know who else to turn to, so I've asked the Guard to bring this letter to Slipstream and maybe they can get it to you.*

There is something in the dark.

Antaea stood and walked to the window. It looked out over Rowan Wheel's main street, providing an unchanging vista of lit windows and deep shadow. No sun ever rose here. No one born and raised in Abyss should be afraid of the dark.

Nobody will talk about it. Officially, things are fine. But people have been disappearing—whole town wheels! They're outlier communities, fringe places whose people only show up to market once or twice a year. Now they're not showing up at all. Far as we are from any sun, the darkness has always seemed normal. You know, you grew up here. Lately, though, it broods. I believe something has awakened in one of the cold abandoned places of the world. It is picking off the weak and those who get separated from the group and it is growing bolder.

If you make inquiries no one will admit to anything, so don't even try! I know I'm asking a lot, but you must trust me. We need someone who has experience with this world's mysteries, Antaea. We need a hunter.

Nobody cares about Abyss. We're all like you and Telen, as far as the sunlit countries are concerned: just winter wraiths of no account. Maybe you no longer care about your old home, either, in which case I shall never hear from you.

But if you do care—if you believe me even a little—please come home. I don't know who else to turn to.

—Leal Maspeth

Once, the darkness hadn't bothered Antaea, either. There had been a time when she wondered what waited there—oh, not in the unlit cloud banks and fungal mists beyond the lights of Sere, but beyond: past the iceberg-choked walls of Virga itself, in the vast universe that bounded and, lately, threatened this little world. Telen had wondered and had found out, and been more than killed for that knowledge. Antaea had chased her, too late to catch her, and didn't know what it was that she'd found other than that it was horrible.

Leal Maspeth was missing, too. The government wouldn't talk about it; the officials Antaea had spoken to acted like she should already know, and she'd been afraid to push lest they begin to question her authenticity. So far, though, Antaea had learned that somehow, impossibly, timid little Leal had gotten to know the famous sun lighter and adventurer Hayden Griffin, and then . . . The rumors spoke of murder and of the Crier in the Dark, and then she was gone.

Antaea unbuttoned her jacket, aware with each twist of her fingers that she would never be putting it on again. She'd kept it out of sentimentality uncommon for her; it was time to let it go. She dropped it on the bed and forced herself to turn away.

Then, she dressed herself in civilian clothes, slid knives into the boots still hidden under her trousers, and added one to the back of her belt.

Crase wasn't going to make her leave. She'd failed to save her own sister from the dire mystery that pressed upon her world. Walking the streets here was about to get much more dangerous for her, and the ministries and offices she'd been able to enter as a Home Guard member would be closed. From now on, her appointments would be in the alleys and at the docks. It was going to be hard.

She would find Leal Maspeth.

Part One | THE OFFER

1

"LEAL, HURRY!"

Leal Hieronyma Maspeth took a look back to see how close their pursuer was and felt the scree under her feet give way. Suddenly on her knees and then her side, she began to slide. She heard shouts, and half-visible hands reached for her. Darkness opened below and, in desperation, she grabbed for a half-glimpsed jut of rock.

She swung, suddenly and shockingly, above open air. The gravel made a trickling sound as it sped past her, but she couldn't hear it land. It just disappeared.

"The rope's just to your left, Leal, can you see it?"

"No," said Leal. "That's okay. I'm going to reach for it now. Tell me if I . . ." She forgot words as she stretched out her left hand, and felt her right slip another inch. Now she was hanging on by just her fingertips.

She had an awful moment then. The thing that was following them was close. If it caught up to them, if it was the one to rescue her—for she was sure it would neither kill her nor leave her in this predicament—would she regret not having just let go?

Should she let go?

"Leal!" That was Piero Harper's voice . . . She blinked; something brushed her face. "Grab the rope!" He was only a few feet away, but above her.

"You've got to keep going!" she hissed at him. He shook his head.

"This'll only take a second. Take hold, ma'am."

Damn his politeness. She flailed for the rope and met empty air. Her fingers slipped, were about to lose it—

Something tapped her knuckles, and then she felt cool fibers coil around her fingers. With relief Leal let go of the rock, but again there was that damned gravity pulling her straight. Stretched and jolted, she yelped with pain as, in jerks and yanks, she rose rather than fell.

Rock banged her shoulder and she felt herself being dragged over the lip of a rough ledge. "Are you okay?" said Piero as the rope unwound itself from her lacerated hand and slithered back. It was visible now in lantern light and she watched in abstract amusement as it inched and twisted its way back into the body of the large, four-footed creature standing next to Harper.

"I-I'm fine. Thanks," she said to both of them. Once again the emissary had taken a hand in saving her life. The emissary! She brought up her hands to touch her shoulders. "Are you there—"

"Yes," said a tiny voice near her ear. She felt little pulls on the cloth of her collar as a small doll regained its accustomed seat on her shoulder. "I fell down your back," it said, "but hung on."

"Good." She wilted with relief. "We've lost too much of you as it is . . ." The doll was made of junk: A coiled wire made up its left arm, a couple of broken pencils its right. Its head was the porcelain knob from some electrical device, with bright screws attached that moved uncannily like eyes. Its mouth was the reed from a ship's horn.

There was no magical spirit animating these random pieces, but fine, hairlike threads of something the emissary called nanotech. This body—this doll, so unlike the ones Leal had collected back when she lived in Sere—was part of the alien. It was the part that she spoke with, and could cup in her hands and so treat, if only for moments at a time, as a being like herself.

She fully intended to start moving, but for a long moment remained at the edge of the cliff, staring downward. She'd seen faces as she dangled: of poor Dean Porril, huddled in permanent mourning behind his great iron desk in a wind-rattled office deep underneath the university; of Easley Fencher, who could never keep his lanky elbows and knees from sticking out, nor his equally awkward thoughts and attitudes. Of her friend Seana, in the bright metal exoskeleton that kept her upright in the unfamiliar gravity of the city. Of fire, bright and orange and frantic, as it consumed Easley's home with Easley in it . . .

"We'd best get going," said Piero quietly. The rest of the group had already moved on—predictably, with the limping silhouette of Eustace Loll, high official in her country's government, in the lead.

"For somebody who's half-lame, he sure moves," she muttered; Piero saw where she was looking and grinned.

They made to catch up, unspeaking. There was no sound for a while then, but for the muttering of the breeze and the distant crack of glacial ice falling from the wall of the world. Their pursuer had stopped yelling for them to stop, wait, just hold on a minute and talk to it. It must know it was going to catch them now, so why bother talking?

They'd had a seemingly insurmountable lead when they set out this morning. Leal had stood on a promontory and scanned the steep, seemingly infinite slope below their campsite. Far down there, barely visible in the gray light that only indicated a sky, something was heaving itself across the rocks. As usual, somebody had been watching it at all times, as the rest of them slept. She'd taken her turn, and she could see that it hadn't gotten very far since then.

They'd walked on up the slope, reassured. And then, an hour ago, she'd heard that familiar voice again.

And here it came again, from only a few hundred yards back: "*Leal! Wait, please!*"

As if in agreement, there came a deep grumble of sound from far above. At first, as they'd toiled their way up steeper and steeper slopes, those occasional bellows of thunder had seemed familiar. Leal had waited to see lightning, but there never was any. Gradually, she'd come to realize that she wasn't hearing storms. Thunder here meant something different than it did at home.

"*Leal, come back! I can help you!*"

"Come on, what are you waiting for?" she snapped at the little group of men whose faces were painted by lantern light in shades of worry and doubt. "All we need is a big overhang. We'll be fine."

She'd slipped because there was as much ice up here as rock. Generally you could tell the difference, but not always. She'd been careless; now she stalked on, head down, fiercely focused on the uneven tumbled stones ahead of her. Piero walked next to her; in another time and place, he might have gallantly demanded that she rest, but they had no time for that.

Another man had been walking beside her when they'd set out on this journey. He was gone now. He wouldn't be back, despite her doubts, despite the promise of that distant voice that followed her through her waking hours and even into her dreams. She shuddered and tried to bring her attention back to the tilted, broken slabs of the ancient roadway under her feet.

This worked for a while, but then a series of cracking sounds, like distant gunshots, echoed from far overhead. In the silence that followed, Leal and her men met one another's eyes; then somebody said, "Move!"

Everything was tilted at an absurdly steep angle here, but luckily gravity had been lessening as they climbed. It was easy to balance on the narrowest of ledges or blades of shattered pavement, and she could jump distances she would never have considered on the day-lit plains they'd come from. Like fleas on some vast monster's back, they popped from stone to stone, trying to get away from what was coming.

The whole slope shuddered and slid down a few feet. Leal stumbled, luckily, as something slashed through the air just above her. Clattering and pattering, splinters of shrapnel ice shot from the point where some glacial mountain had hit the rocks behind them. Distant booms signaled the landing of other house-sized chunks of hail.

"Maybe it's a seasonal thing." Piero's voice sounded very small in the sudden quiet.

Leal shook her head. The icefalls had been increasing in frequency for days. Something was peeling away the great glacial sheets that built up above the rock line. Up there, the world's wall was black and smooth, a fine weave of carbon nanotubes that was only a meter or two thick. Thin as it was, it transmitted the chill of interstellar vacuum from the other side. Water—and even air—froze to it. The glaciers that resulted would normally split and fall away in their own time, but they were hurrying now, as if they sensed the presence of intruders coming from below.

The only door home from this strange and perilous world was past those glaciers, at the very top of the wall. Leal and her companions had no choice but to come this way if they were ever to see their countries and people again.

She eyed the silhouette of Eustace Loll, who had fallen back from the lead and was watching the skies fearfully. The politician had branded her a traitor, and though he'd promised to lift that accusation if they ever made it home, he couldn't be trusted. If she ever walked the copper streets of Sere again, she feared it would be as a paraded prisoner, in chains and spat upon by the countrymen she had tried so hard to save.

One foot ahead of the other. Just keep walking . . . She ignored her pounding headache and the ever-present knot in her stomach. She had a job to do.

They'd gone about a mile when Piero held up his hand. "Wait," he said. They all stopped, and in the new silence Leal heard it: cracks and pops and splintering sounds, layered over one another in an almost continuous grumble. This was like the sound that presaged the fall of a glacier, but stretched out, as if not just one berg but an entire sky full of bergs was about to come down . . .

Piero swore, and Loll stumped back to blink at them both. "What do we do?"

The little junk-doll suddenly grabbed her ear. "There!" It stood up, pointing past her eyebrow at something . . .

Miles above, a little string of lights broke the total darkness. It was impossible for them to be there—Aethyr was an empty world, and nowhere was as desolate as this long treacherous slope—and yet there they were:

Windows.

THE SOUND OF children playing faded as Keir Chen took the down stairs three steps at a time. He didn't have much time; recess would be over in fifteen minutes.

The stairwell was pitch black, and he had no light; to guide him, Keir relied on the little cloud of buzzing dragonflies that accompanied him everywhere. They were his second set of eyes, and they did pretty well in low light. Now they showed him the knapsack he'd stowed here yesterday. It was heavy as he picked it up—stuffed with food, clothing, and other supplies. He'd carefully spent months accumulating it all, taking his time so the others wouldn't see the pattern.

He wanted to run, but even if the gravity was low here in the city of Brink, he couldn't risk a fall. Some of these stone stairwells plummeted for miles through the foundations of the city. It took too many seconds to pick his way down, so when he reached the bottom he began pelting at full speed through a succession of dark, empty corridors and chambers where his footsteps were the only sound. His dragonflies had been gamely trying to catch up, and when he reached one particular side chamber and finally stopped, they came to zizz around his head angrily.

This little room had two doors, one leading inside where he'd just come from, the other letting onto a balcony. There was a spot next to the entrance where he'd stood a few times; he went there now and put his back to the wall. Then he knelt and picked up a sharp rock that lay by the door. When he straightened with his back against the wall, he lifted his hand to scratch it behind his head.

Keir lowered the stone, his eyes fixed on the black-on-black doorway that led outside. *"Don't worry about such things,"* Maerta had told him when he'd revealed his suspicion to her. *"You're a kid, Keir. Why don't you just enjoy being a kid?"*

He took one more deep breath, squared his shoulders as he'd seen some of the older men do, and stepped away from the wall. He turned around and, summoning his dragonflies, peered at the latest mark he'd made. There was at least a half-centimeter gap between it and the last one he'd made.

There was no doubt about it.

He was getting shorter.

He'd talked to the other kids, and he'd been watching them. They were all growing up; but he wasn't. They were learning new things every day, a fine layering of knowledge on knowledge that was taking them all to adulthood.

Keir knew that he knew less than he once had, not more.

He stepped out onto the balcony, and turned around to look up.

From this little balcony the city was visible only as black piled up on black, its cornered intricacies lost in permanent shadow—all save for that one ring of windows in one high tower. With the aid of his dragonflies' eyes, he could see the city's overall shape, and size. Their vision gave him a little courage, too, when the distant winds sighed like voices from the empty apartments, and when he fancied he saw movement in the blackest shadows of the stone gardens. They let him see and verify that, no, nothing ever spoke here, and nothing ever moved.

—Which was good. He couldn't afford for anyone to find what he'd been doing on this little parapet, half a mile from the inhabited halls.

He took a deep breath and stepped up to something that sat swaying slightly on the parapet, all folded angles and parchment-like planes. "Are you ready?" he asked the ornithopter he'd been growing. "Tell me you're ready."

"Not ready," it said in its mindless monotone. "Feed me."

"You said you'd be ready!" he burst out. "You said you'd be ready to fly!"

"Yes. Can fly. Cannot carry."

"That's not what I—!" He punched its wing. It shuffled aside. Keir stepped back, clutching his knapsack and nearly in tears. He couldn't go through with his plan today, but Gallard was going to catch him for sure if he went back, and then he'd never get another chance. Or maybe he could be extra sneaky; maybe he could pretend to be a dutiful student for another few days. He could hide feedstock for the ornithopter, maybe make it down here one more time to feed it . . .

With a curse at his own indecision, he stalked back into the tower. He hadn't brought anything to feed the aircraft, because stealing feedstock was risky and anyway, he'd thought it was ready. But there was another potential source of the stuff here . . .

He waited for his dragonflies to catch up and when their eyesight supplemented his, he could see what he was after in one corner of the room. He hunkered down and shuffled toward it.

A tiny pinprick of light suddenly glowed there, then another, then a dozen. Little gleaming midges flew up from the experiment he'd begun here a week ago. A pipsqueak voice sounded in his head: "*I am the mighty Brick! Tremble before me, mortal!*"

"That's okay, it's okay," he said in a soothing tone as he reached slowly for the half-open bag of feedstock lying next to the brick. His fingers were almost touching it when the little midges dove at his hand. "Ow!"

The air was suddenly full of dragonflies, and little dogfight battles erupted all over the room, complete with the pittering sound of minuscule machine guns firing and tiny smoking death spirals. "*Do not defy the mighty Brick!*" cried the brick. Keir ducked under the aerial battle and snagged the bag of feedstock. Then he ran from the room before the brick was able to bring its little howitzers to bear on him.

He'd had some compelling reason for making a minitech AI think that it *was* the brick. It had been some sort of reminder to himself, he knew that. But the details . . . they were gone, like so much of what he'd done and intended lately. All he had left was a terrible feeling of apprehension, a certainty that if he didn't get out of this place, and soon, something terrible was going to happen.

Shakily, he went out to the balcony again and dumped the bag of feedstock in front of the ornithopter. As it eagerly scarfed down the mixture of metals, silicates, and rare earth elements, Keir leaned on the balustrade, looked out, and sighed.

This world had suns—dozens of them—but they were too far away to provide even a hint of radiance to the sky. The city was as invisible as it ever was, its cornered intricacies lost in permanent shadow. Only that one ring of windows in one high tower betrayed habitation.

Brink crested above that and over itself, in wave after frozen wave whose dark caps faded into obscurity in the heights. The near-infinite wall to which the city clung rose at an eighty-degree angle. Farther down, the angle decreased to a mythically distant, sunlit plain, while above it steepened to the vertical so far away that all gravity would cease by the time you got there.

Giant knuckled slabs of glacier and stone were the city's only companions at this height. Paths wove from one patch of scree to another, avoiding the perilously slick black skin of the world's wall whenever possible. Eyeless goats brayed from their rock perches, and fungi and meatshrooms blossomed from cracks in the stone. He could hear booming sounds from distant avalanches; those had increased in frequency lately, sometimes shaking Complication Hall with the power of their passage.

He'd thought about just walking off down that slope, but if he were to try it he'd surely be killed by icefall before he got ten kilometers; and anyway, *down* led only to the realm of the oaks, who had filled Aethyr with grasslands and forests that were prowled by strange predators, and sometimes by the oaks themselves. He'd hoped his ornithopter would take him high enough that they'd become weight-less, and then it would have been easy to cross Aethyr to the wild but free worlds of the arena. Wild, free—and in their own way, far more dangerous than any encounter with the oaks.

If he and the ornithopter sailed off to the arena right now, no one would see him go. Of course, there would be no one to see him crash on the steep slopes below the city, break a leg or a collar-bone, and slowly freeze to death. Even if they noticed his absence right away, they wouldn't know where to look for him.

He should have tried the other door, the one that led to the one world he knew would be safe for his kind. The door to it wasn't even closed. —No, not closed, merely guarded by monsters.

Keir hugged himself, feeling miserable. He scowled down at the darkness, and one of his dragonflies soared away from the miniature battle in the room, spiraled into the air over his head, and spotted something.

In the dark below the city, a cluster of lights wavered.

They were fantastically small pinpricks, hovering on the very edge of visibility, but now the rest of his dragonflies could see them, too. Kilometers down the gradually decreasing curve of the world's wall, something had carved a little cave of illumination out of the dark.

"Hey," he said to the ornithopter, "are you ready to carry me yet?"

"Need to digest," it said. "Two hours."

"Hmmpf." He stared at the little lights. Who could that possibly be? Nobody from the Renaissance ever went out on the slopes; the constant avalanches made it too dangerous. There was nothing down there but blind goats and unstable scree, anyway. Visitors came to Brink occasionally—but they only ever came by air.

Whatever those lights were, he had other priorities.

—Although, if somebody had wanted to sneak up on the city, coming up from below like that would certainly be the way to do it.

"Not my problem," he said to the ornithopter. It turned its camera eyes to him, then resumed munching the feedstock.

"The grown-ups can take care of it," he continued.

It said nothing.

He stood for a while looking down at the faint lights.

"Could you fly down there and back?"

"Yes," it said. It didn't move.

Keir opened his mouth, closed it, then, cursing his own curiosity, ordered one of his dragonflies to clamp itself to the ornithopter's foot. "Go on, then," he said. The mechanical bird dropped the feedstock bag, bunched up its wings, and leaped awkwardly into the air. Startlingly graceful once aloft, it swooped away and disappeared into the gloom.

A minute later it returned, and as it collapsed in some sort of mechanical relief onto the flagstones at his feet, Keir received a download of images from the dragonfly that had ridden with it.

The people down there weren't part of the Renaissance. Some dozen or so of the climbers looked human, though with them were things that had the unmistakable air of morphonts: artificial lifeforms that built bodies for themselves from strands of nanotech. These morphonts walked on legs, and they had heads. They also twined together, forming something like a mobile fence, and they stayed downslope from the humans, a sort of living guardrail.

The humans looked ragged and half-starved, and some of them were limping. The morphonts were clearly friendly, and morphonts meant the sophistication and resource-rich worlds of the arena; but the humans seemed neither sophisticated nor rich. He'd seen photos of people like them—telephoto images taken through kilometers of air. Keir's recent memories were fuzzy, but he did remember the pictures: of a people who lived in permanent weightlessness, building rotating cities for gravity and flying chemical-powered aircraft in a world where only the most primitive of technologies worked.

But it couldn't be. *They* couldn't be *here.*

He scowled and barked a laugh and walked to the edge of the balcony to get a look at those lights with his own eyes. They were still there.

He heard the gunshot cracks that signaled an avalanche—they went on and on, signaling a big fall this time. Squinting, he thought he could actually see something way up the wall above the city, like a vast pale hand reaching down. Keir turned all his dragonflies to that view, and now he could make it out: a veritable continent of ice peeling away from the slope ten kilometers or more overhead.

He called up his scry, the collection of processors, communications systems, and interfaces that helped him keep up with the multilayered, surreal world the adults of the Renaissance had built. He tried to call the nannies, then anybody else in Complication Hall; but it was too far away.

This far up the world's slope, gravity was less than half a standard g. He looked up at the majestically bowing facade of ice, then down at those wavering, faint lights below the city; and he asked his scry how long it would take before the one landed on the other.

The answer came back almost instantly; but then Keir stood there frowning for long seconds, as his breath frosted in front of him.

Then he cursed and ran inside, down two halls, and out to another stairway. His instinct was to hesitate, but he'd set a timer in his scry telling him exactly how long he had before the ice reached the slope below. So he tested the top steps and, when they held him, leaped down the rest recklessly, accompanied by a cloud of watchful eyes. Soon he was standing on the round parapet of a minaret, and in the upper right corner of his visual field, the timer was still ticking down. He went down this next staircase, but in the darkness it took much longer than he'd hoped. When he emerged from an outside doorway to stand on unworked rock, he was sure it was too late.

This slope lay in the shadow of Complication Hall's lights, but it wasn't completely dark. A faint red glow permeated the air from the far distance, and this gave just enough light for him to make out tumbled stones and a nearby goat path.

Here he made the mistake of looking up. With the help of the dragonflies he could plainly see a ceiling of white, kilometers wide, lowering toward the city.

He could see the strangers' lights—they were close at hand now—and, very close by, the entrance to a tunnel that doubtless ran into Brink's foundations. It was clear the people with the lanterns couldn't see that archway, because it lay above them and behind some tall boulders, and their little lights could only reach a few meters anyway.

"Heeeyy!" He jumped and waved his arms, but nobody noticed. The strangers were picking their way one step at a time, heads bent and focused on their task. Yet they must have heard the cataclysmic cracking of the ice sheet; must know that even now it was silently bearing down on them.

Now that he was close enough Keir tried to hail the newcomers through his scry. It didn't register them at all. And according to his timer the ice would be here in a matter of seconds.

He swore and began leaping down the rocks toward them.

Now the orange-lit ovals of their faces turned in his direction. They all stopped walking and he could see them talking—verbally— among themselves; there was a sudden flurry of movement and, just as he half-slid down the last few meters, four of them produced odd, compact handheld devices and pointed them at him. Keir's scry identified these as weapons—but the idea that they might threaten him more than what was approaching was simply laughable.

"Run!" He pointed in the direction of the entrance he'd spotted, which really was invisible from here. "Ruuuuun! There!"

One of them stepped forward. She was pale-skinned, her features oddly mis-composed, as though she'd never taken the effort to adjust her bone structure or skin type. "Who are you?"

"Never mind! Run!" And, because his timer had about fifteen

seconds left to it, he bounded past them, making for that other entrance. "Come on!"

"Why?" she shouted after him. "Is it—"

"The ice!" Belatedly, they began to move. With eight seconds left, Keir made it to the archway. Two blind goats were cowering in the entrance, but beyond them, it ran back into indeterminate blackness.

Eleven seconds, and the first of the strangers reached the arch.

Thirteen, and the strange goat-railing creatures scrabbled up; one was carrying a man on its back.

Fifteen seconds and the rest of them were in. Nothing happened, and the last of the strangers—including the woman—were only meters away.

A new silhouette appeared in the doorway. It looked like a man, but when the woman saw it she screamed. One of the men raised something that looked like a primitive weapon and shouted, "Keep back!"

"Let me in!" shouted the stranger. "I just want to talk."

Keir jumped at a loud bang and the silhouette staggered back. The woman ducked her face in her hands, the others were standing, shouting, and—

Whump! The stranger disappeared behind a wall of white. The entire slope bowed under the impact of something gigantic. A roar beyond sound, a physical wall of noise, hit Keir. He was tossed about the tunnel, hitting wall and ceiling and floor as the thunder went on and on, and outside the cave mouth all that was visible was a churning chaos of grinding and hammering snow.

Gradually that vast cry, like the thunderous rage of a giant, dwindled to ordinary thunder, then to grumbling and sighs interspersed with pattering and sliding sounds. Though the floor still swayed and dipped beneath him, Keir staggered to the entrance to look out. Towering thunderheads reared to all sides, their bases rooted in the world's slope. Yet for a dozen or more meters to every side, the rocks were clear of ice.

Keir found he was trembling. He'd known the tunnel would survive the avalanche; the metropoloid that called itself Brink had built itself strong enough to withstand the occasional glacial fall. Yet it was terrifying to be so close to the avalanche that he could feel its wind on his face, and taste the flavor of ancient ice.

His ears were ringing and he was sure the others were half-deaf, too, but a little deafness wouldn't stop scry. As she picked herself up and dusted herself off, Keir tried pinging the woman again; when there was no response, he tried the others. There was no reply from the humans, but an icon cloud rose from the backs of the strange, trunk-to-tail-entwined guardrail goats. A glyph of men fencing appeared in the upper left corner of Keir's vision as his scry did a handshake with theirs. The humans remained dark to data; they didn't even seem to be able to see the data cloud he was emitting.

The shaking subsided; the thunder and hammering echoes rolled away and away, and a great slow sigh of icy air wafted into the tunnel, causing the survivors to huddle together.

"Thank you," shouted the woman. Keir barely heard her; his ears were still stunned.

He pointed at the entrance. "But why did you shoot that man?"

"That wasn't a man." She walked among her people, touching each in turn and speaking to them. Some nodded; some shook their heads. Keir estimated there were about a dozen of them, an impossibly tiny party to deploy for the purposes of scaling a world's wall.

She returned and now gave Keir a frank, head-to-toe appraisal. He wanted to ask more about the incident with the gun, but she spoke first. "Where did you come from?"

"I—I live here," he stammered; and in the pale light of the strangers' lanterns, he took in her archaic, hand-sewn apparel, the tightly drawn-back hair and her intriguing, imperfect features, and knew that his earlier guess had been right. "Are you from *Virga*?"

She nodded, then shot him a suspicious look. "But you're not. Who are your people?" Then, in a somewhat dazed tone, "We saw lights."

"That's Complication Hall. Where I live."

Another man, red-faced and mustachioed, came to stand next to the woman. They exchanged a glance, and she shrugged. Behind him, several of the others were moving outside, presumably to look for the one they had shot. Keir knew it would be futile, that the ice would have scoured him away to nothing.

"Do you have water, and a place to sleep?" asked the red-faced man.

Keir shrugged wryly. "A whole city's worth of guest rooms. None ever slept in. I—"

"I'm not sure we can pay," she said quickly.

Keir thought through these words, and he had to smile. "Nobody's ever offered to 'pay' me for anything before," he said. "I think that would be . . . amazing. What is it you pay with?"

"Forget I mentioned it," she said, frowning quizzically. She put out her hand and Keir gingerly took it in his own to shake. He'd never actually performed this particular ritual before, but again she didn't seem to notice.

"I'm Leal Maspeth," she said. It took him a moment to realize she'd given him her name, since the words were just a garble of sound buried in her accent. She swept an arm to indicate her companions. "We were stranded on the floor of Aethyr, some weeks ago. We're walking back to the axle of the world, so we can get back to Virga with some important information."

"Really?" His scry had finished handshaking with the goats' and subtitles were starting to appear under Maspeth's chin when she spoke. A sizable cloud of tags hovered over her party now, so Keir no longer needed to pester her with questions, which would be rude. He'd review their records as they walked.

The men who'd gone to look outside returned, shaking their heads grimly. They could all return the way Keir had come, but there might be straggler avalanches; better to take this tunnel back to one of the central stairwells.

Keir commanded his dragonflies to explore the tunnel. They'd been clinging for dear life to his jacket and now wafted off of him in a little cloud. The Virgans looked startled at this sudden motion. After a short sortie the dragonflies reported that the tunnel was clear, and so Keir began walking up it.

"Um . . ." said Maspeth. After a few moments he heard her and the others following him, whispering among themselves.

According to the scry, Leal Hieronyma Maspeth was from a country called Abyss. These people really were from Virga! Maybe they knew a way back there, and now that he'd saved their lives, maybe . . .

"Uh," Maspeth said again, hurrying to catch up to Keir. "What's this place called?"

"Brink," said a pipsqueak voice issuing from somewhere around her shoulder. She craned her neck to look at a little doll-shaped figure sitting on the ragged felt of her coat. Keir hadn't spotted the little man-thing before, but its presence didn't surprise him; it was obviously a bodily extension like his own dragonflies.

"How do you know what it's called?" she asked it in irritated surprise.

"Keir Chen has given us guest citizenship in his scry," said the golden doll. "I'm reading his records now."

Belatedly, Keir realized that since she herself couldn't read his scry, his silence might not seem polite to her. "Brink," he said, spreading his arms to encompass everything above the tunnel's ceiling. "Looks like a city, but it's not. We're the only people living here. Only people who ever lived here."

She looked puzzled. "How many of you?"

"About a hundred."

"What do you do here?"

He might have intended to run away today, but even if he had, Keir wouldn't have told the truth at this point. "We're trying to find new patterns of meaning in the metropoloid's architecture," he said smoothly as his scry supplied him with a plausible story. "They could be the genes for a new urbanoid."

She gave him a look so eloquently uncomprehending that he

almost regretted having lied to her. "We're city breeders," he clarified. Maspeth blinked, then shook her head.

She batted distractedly at the air. "Damn bugs," she said. "Never seen any until now."

She was actually trying to swat his eyes! Keir ordered the dragonflies to stay away from the Virgans from now on.

"We were following a road," said Maspeth urgently. "Does it continue up past the city?"

Keir shook his head. "I've looked, believe me. The slope's too steep to keep the rock on it up there. It's bare carbon-nanotube weave, smooth as silk. It's impossible to climb beyond this point."

She gave a stifled wail and stopped walking. Keir blinked at her in surprise; she looked for all the world just like he often felt. "Then—" She fought to say or not say something. "Then where does this damned road go?!"

"It goes no farther . . . but it does come here," he said gently.

"Yes . . . yes, it's not a total loss maybe." She had fallen in beside him. "You took a huge risk coming down to warn us," she said suddenly. "I want to thank you on behalf of all of us."

Suddenly shy, he looked away.

Why had he done it? The whole episode was so totally out of character for him, and yet while he had been racing down here, no other course of action had been conceivable. It was as though some side of himself that had always been in darkness had suddenly lit up; and, in fact, he felt somehow that he'd acted this way before—selflessly, and foolishly.

"Yes, thank you!" Somebody was pushing his way up from the back of the group. He was stumping along using a stick like a third leg. He was lank-haired, with a chin that seemed to have been designed for a larger person, and small darting eyes. The guardrail introduced him as Eustace Loll, a "cabinet minister" in the archaic control system Abyss called its "government."

Still faintly embarrassed, Keir said, "Think nothing of it, Minister Loll," and at the sound of his name Loll nearly fell over. Leal

Maspeth steadied him, and Keir now saw that one of Loll's ankles was bundled and bound with pieces of wood and cloth. Keir looked for a tag cloud in his scry but of course he had none—and that was when Keir realized with horror that the man was nursing an untreated injury.

"Tell me, how is it that you spotted us?" asked Loll in an innocent tone. Keir was too shocked at his obvious pain to organize his thoughts; luckily his scry was popping up plausible explanations. After a few awkward seconds he said, "I accidentally dropped something on that path yesterday. I'd finally gotten a chance to come down and look for it when I spotted you."

They seemed to accept this explanation, so he led them on, to a round chamber from which a spiral stairway led up. As their lights supplemented his dragonflies' vision, Keir saw that the wall behind the steps was covered with carvings of eyeless goats.

Before he could stop himself he burst out laughing; even to himself, the sound had a slightly hysterical tinge to it. Maspeth looked at him with wide eyes, which just made him laugh more. "Sorry, sorry," he gasped. "Sometimes I can't tell whether the city's just recording what it sees, or whether it has a sense of humor." He shook his head, embarrassed again, and added, "I'm a little out of myself . . . after what just happened. I didn't mean to laugh."

To his surprise she nodded. "Nobody's going to fault you," she said. "We've all endured some big shocks lately, and people react . . . well, however they react. So—do we go up now?"

He nodded. "Yes, up . . .

"To Complication Hall."

2

KEIR'S SCRY HAD begun lighting up even before they reached the Hall. Startled emoticons fluttered around his head, and colored glyphs appeared in his peripheral vision. The glyphs signaled an epic battle between the various agendas and schemes of his own subconscious mind, and those of his compatriots in the Renaissance. Maerta and his teachers kept telling him he should pay close attention to this sort of interface-fencing. Power and privilege were measured by how well one navigated the shoals of personality and ambition, after all.

Keir marched to his own personal soundtrack, even when it was bad for him; everybody knew that. The other kids could never tell what he was going to do next, and lately he'd realized that the grown-ups had a similar wariness of him—though where they might have learned that, he had no idea. Sure, he liked to play practical jokes; he invented strange devices in class and set them loose in the hallways at night. But that alone hardly explained their caution. Right now the glyphs showed wild speculation on the Renaissance's prediction market. He assumed it was because of the strangers, until he realized that the stock that was alternately crashing and soaring was his. The tone of the trading could almost be translated into words: words like, *Keir's done it again!*

Enveloped in this invisible storm of consternation, he pushed open the great iron doors and said to his guests, "Welcome to Complication Hall."

Tired as they were, he still saw Leal Maspeth and her friends react to the sight. He knew what was visible here, the fabs, Edisonians, lab benches, and work areas; but he couldn't be sure what they actually *saw*—and he knew the other members of the Renaissance were wondering the same thing.

Some of the objects scattered around the floor would be recognizable to anyone living in Artificial Nature. There were the usual microrefineries, ecosyms, Edisonians to imagine new designs, and fabs to build anything you might want. Most of these were in turn made out of black utility fog that had taken these forms only temporarily.

Standardization didn't exist outside Virga; it was a primitive thing, a signal of the inefficiencies of pre-Edisonian manufacturing. Keir had been learning lately that things were different inside Virga, though: There, they still had factories, and things called *designs* that told you how to duplicate a machine you'd already built. *Designs* could be read and understood by human beings—an extraordinary idea.

If Maspeth and her people looked around Complication Hall they could easily see dozens of identical devices and objects, many of them showing signs of having been put together by human hands. They might see these things, but would they recognize how unusual they were? To have more than one of something, *and to be able to build more yourself* . . . in Keir's world, these were astonishing, even frightening anomalies.

But no—as Keir entered with his refugees, it was other details that caught their attention. People began popping out from behind partitions and curtains scattered around the place. He was disappointed to see that nearly all of them were second bodies; what kind of invasion did they think he was mounting?

Here came Maerta, conspicuously in her own stocky, dark-skinned body. Her clothing was shuffling, watching pupil dilation and other indicators in the visitors as his own had on the hillside. In short order it had adjusted itself into conservative garb that would seem neutral, if not familiar, to these people from Virga. Some of the other people were undergoing similar transformations, but those encased in glittering exoskeletons or half-visible under swirling dragonflies had no hope of looking familiar. Sure enough, the Virgans stumbled to a halt, closing ranks and muttering in alarm as they were surrounded by dozens of shambling, dancing, or plodding figures of various degrees of humanity.

"Don't be alarmed," said Maerta, striding forward with her hand outstretched and a welcoming smile on her face. "I'm afraid you've caught us in our work clothes today." She shook Maspeth's hand, and then, as the man stepped in between them, Eustace Loll's. "Keir warned us that you're tired and hungry. I've got a nice stew on the boil over here, why don't you come and sit down?"

They didn't take much persuading, especially when Maerta made shooing motions at the others and they mostly retreated back to their workstations. With Keir's reassurance that nothing dangerous was happening, the bigger exoskeletons retreated and those wearing them sent proxy bodies in their stead. Soon the floor was empty of all but human-appearing people. The Virgans slumped with relief onto some benches behind one of the material partitions, and Maerta began serving soup.

"It's lucky that Keir spotted you," she was saying; as she said this out loud, she glyphed a message at Keir's scry: *Why weren't you in class?*

"Just lucky, I guess," he said with a grin. "I'm often looking in the wrong direction at the right time."

Maerta's own smile faltered, and behind her he noticed a couple of the other grown-ups exchange glances. What did that mean? He'd just been making a joke.

Maspeth said, "We owe him our lives," and the look she sent Keir wiped every other consideration out of his mind. "We were at the end of our strength," she went on, "and with the avalanches . . . we wouldn't have made it to the city without his help."

Maerta looked pleased, and for a tiny moment Keir thought that things would end here. But—"There he is!"—he turned and here came Gallard, who was the kids' designated teacher, and as humorless and unforgiving as any adult he'd known.

Gallard's face had all the anonymous perfection of his people; he was from the inner reaches of Vega, where the virtuals ruled and body-swapping was common. As usual, he was surrounded by a cloud of glyphs and emoticons, so many of so many types that Keir could never tell what he was thinking. "Where did you get to?" he asked as he strode across the stone floor to glower down at Keir. "—I know, I know, you were on the slopes. But what conceivable reason could you have had for that?"

Keir's scry flashed all kinds of red warnings, but they didn't stop him from blurting, "Better company?"

Gallard's face didn't change, but his icon cloud scowled at Keir. He appealed to Maerta. "He's out of control. You see what I have to put up with?"

Keir found his ears becoming hot as he realized that Leal Maspeth was watching this exchange with interest. "I'm sorry," he said, trying to be adult about it all. "It won't happen again."

"You've said that before. Maerta—"

She held up a hand. "I'll talk to him, Gallard. Maybe some discipline is in order. For now, I'm grateful that he helped these travelers. It was something he didn't have to do, especially if he knew how you'd react."

Gallard glanced over at the Virgans with disinterest, then turned back to Keir. "Come on. You have a simulation to finish."

"Maerta—" But she shook her head at him.

"Go on, Keir. We'll discuss your absence later."

Even more acutely embarrassed, he snuck a glance at Maspeth, who was actually grinning! "It's good to see that some things never change," she said. Then she added in a sympathetic tone to Gallard, "I'm a teacher, too."

"Come, Keir." He strode away without acknowledging Maspeth's comment. Keir shrugged at her, ducked his head to Maerta while firing a cloud of apology glyphs at her scry, then hurried after his tutor.

"REST, PLEASE," INSISTED the woman Keir Chen had introduced as Maerta. "You're safe now." She was matronly, of apparent middle age, but Leal had learned lately to be wary of appearances in the world outside Virga. Maerta's twin sister was handing out bowls of broth to Leal's men, who sat or lay in various exhausted poses on a well-lit stone floor.

"Thank you, but I'm not sure we *are* safe," Leal said. She was aware that she was shifting from foot to foot, looking around herself nervously. They might well have gone from the frying pan into the fire; Keir Chen's people didn't all look human. Some were huge and hulking, with hydraulic lines and metal spars intertwining the flesh of their arms. Others were whiskered and coiffed with silvery antennae that turned and swerved as they looked about. Some were entirely metal, and multi-armed. And now that she was noticing things, she realized that Maerta and her sister were not the only twins in this huge room. She counted at least five other pairs in her first glance around.

Keir Chen had called this place Complication Hall. Apparently it was the only inhabited spot in the city. The Hall was a cathedral-sized space, built in a cross shape and complete with a vast, backlit rose window at its far end. Its pillared sides rose seventy meters into the architectural insanity that may have given the place its name: a frozen explosion of arches, cornices, footings, and crenellations all toppled over one another in a narrowing gyre whose ultimate ceiling was lost in mazey detail. At least the floor was level. Its polished surface hosted heaps of boxes, sleeping and living areas behind partitions, and many strange silvery forestlike growths of machinery. For Leal, only the brown stone floors, the pervasive shadows, and the smell of cooking food were familiar.

Maerta smiled knowingly now and nodded up at the strange ceiling. "Brink is immune to avalanches," she said. "In the five years we've been here, not one roof has broken."

"It's not avalanches I'm worried about." Leal bit her lip, unsure of what to say; then she blurted, "We were followed."

Maerta's eyes narrowed. "By what?"

That was telling: she had not asked by whom. "He was my . . . one of our former companions," said Leal. She couldn't afford to describe John Tarvey any other way; it was too painful. "He was taken by one of those, I think the word is 'river,' and when he came back to us he'd . . . changed." She looked at the floor.

Maerta stared at her in wonder. "You really are from Virga, aren't you?"

"Yes, and I promise to tell you all about how we got here, but first we have to make sure that the thing that's, that's *wearing Tarvey like a coat* can't get in!"

She'd said that too loudly; her men were all staring at her. Eustace Loll limped over. His lips pursed into an expression that might have been concern, or might have been disapproval. "You've been through a lot, Leal. You should rest." He bowed to Maerta. "On behalf of the government and people of Abyss, I'd like to thank you for rescuing us."

Leal wanted to tell him to shut up, but in this place, surrounded by so many people, she no longer had the power. Loll had been waiting for such a moment, she realized: for a time when he no longer had to defer to her.

"You're welcome," said Maerta. "We'll send some bodies down to patrol the city's lower entrances."

Loll raised his eyebrow. "Thank you. However—though I appreciate Leal's anxieties—I don't think that will be necessary. The man was swept away by the avalanche. He won't be back."

"He will be back," said Leal; but she abruptly felt very dizzy. Piero Harper was suddenly at her side, helping her sit on a strange blocky thing that sculpted itself to her shape as if it were alive. "It will be back." Tired and defeated, she stared around at the strange people, the extra bodies and odd machines. "Unless its purpose was to drive us into your arms. Are you like it?"

"They are not," said the junk-doll on her shoulder.

Leal shrugged irritably. "But why is that boy walking around in a cloud of bugs?" She glared at Maerta. "Why are there two of you?"

"We'll explain," she soothed. "Or your morphont companion can tell you. But for now, you must rest. You're at the end of your strength, and your physiology's not been augmented to support the restoratives we'd like to give you."

"What's that supposed to mean?"

"Just rest."

Leal leaned her chin on her hand, and closed her eyes. She could sense Eustace Loll moving about, though she could neither see nor hear him. Her suspicion was like Hayden Griffin's fabled *radar*, telling her that he must be speaking to Maerta and her kin, ingratiating, lulling. There were two sides to the story of how Leal and her people had come to be here, and Loll would never let her version go uncontested.

She should be defying his story with her own, but she hadn't the strength. When someone put a bowl in her hands, she ate, and then she lay back and the couch/chair accommodated her and was very comfortable; and she slept.

IT WAS TWO hours before Keir could convince Gallard that he'd finished all his work—that, indeed, he'd done it before ducking out earlier. Pleading exhaustion at the adventures of the afternoon, he swore that he would go straight to his room and not venture forth for the remainder of the day. Fuming a scry cloud of virtual sighs and annoyance glyphs, Gallard agreed, and Keir headed out.

He knew the way, of course, but walking these corridors would never become familiar. If the city of Brink had possessed an air of abandonment, he might have been able to imagine that he was investigating someplace lost and mysterious—disturbing the ghosts of people who might have once crisscrossed these bleak gothic corridors in previous lifetimes. But Brink had never been inhabited. It wasn't strictly a city at all, rather a variety of morphont called a *metropoloid*. Its ancestors had been true, inhabited cities, but Brink was part of an evolutionary offshoot that had lost some of the defining traits of a true urban space. Traits like plumbing, and lights, and elevators with doors.

The blank facades and grasping towers didn't sum to a place at all, but to a wilderness, one that he was desperate to escape from.

He hesitated in the doorway to his oddly angled room. This was definitely not where he wanted to be; but he didn't know where else to go. He sat at the desk.

He stood.

He walked to the sartorius, which proffered clothing, exoskeleton parts, and other extensions as he approached.

Turning away from that, he fell backward and let the bed catch him. For a few minutes he just lay there as his dragonflies zipped in a restless cloud from door to ceiling to floor and back.

The sounds of distant conversation filtered in through the chamber's narrow windows—echoes of voices from the Hall, including Maspeth's anxious tones. He sat up, wrapped his fingers around his skull, and bent his head over his knees.

A gentle knock came from the doorway. He wanted nothing more than to tell whoever it was to go away, but instead he heard himself say, "Come." Maerta stepped in, in her second body, and came to sit on the bed next to him. Her scry was muted, only a few faint glyphs twirling near her ears. She was carrying something heavy, and now she moved to set it on the floor by the bed.

It was the brick—the Mighty Brick, now stripped of its agencies and protective devices. "Ah," said Keir, gazing at it mournfully. "You killed it."

"We found it near a rather grouchy ornithopter. That one claimed you were starving it to death."

He shrugged, but he couldn't look her in the eye. He'd drawn his own scry all the way in, leaving him bare of context.

"Keir," she said softly, "what were you doing with these things?"

His restless fingers tangled together. "I—I don't know." Now he did look at her directly. "I mean that. I know I made this," he pointed at the brick, "but I don't know what it is."

"That I can answer," she said. "You and Gallard were studying embodiment a few weeks back. To have a body is, well, almost a sacred thing, no? —To us, I mean. It's what separates us, and our allies like the oaks and the morphonts, from things like the creature that was chasing Leal Maspeth and her friends." She nudged the brick with her toe. "Having a body, even if it's a block of dumb stone, anchors the mind and its values. We're fighting to keep our anchors, all of us, and none more so than the people who live in Virga. Even if they don't know it.

"I'm pretty sure you made the Mighty Brick to remind yourself of these things."

"Then why did I forget?"

She shook her head. "I don't—"

"Stop lying to me! You *do* know."

She was silent for a moment, and he felt a small sense of triumph at having scored a point in their ongoing argument—because, before today, he hadn't even been sure himself that something was wrong. Now he had proof, in the form of those lines scratched next to the door a kilometer below the Hall.

"Keir," she said slowly, "why did you grow that aircraft?" He looked away, but she put a hand on his shoulder. "Where were you going to go?"

"I don't know."

"You didn't have someone in specific you were going to look for?"

That was an odd question; he looked at her for the first time. "No. Who would I have to look for?"

"Sita?"

He didn't recognize the name, and shook his head, confused. Scry gave no hint as to who this Sita might be, either. Somehow his incomprehension satisfied Maerta, who took away her hand and sighed.

"I'm not a real boy, am I?" he asked her. "The other kids are growing up, but I'm growing down. Getting shorter, stupider. Forgetting things—like, like this Sita whoever. Why? What's happening to me?"

She looked him in the eye. "Keir, you have to trust me when I say I can't tell you."

"Can't tell me? Or won't?"

"Can't. Because I made a promise that I wouldn't."

"To who? You're the leader here, aren't you? Who could you possibly have to make a promise to that you'd have to keep?"

Maerta stood up, clasped her hands, and walked to the door. Then she turned and said, "I can't betray my promise, Keir; and I'm sorry, but for now, that's how it has to be."

He just stared at her, tears starting in the corners of his eyes. Maerta came back, her hands hovering over him. "Oh, no, no, I'm sorry, Keir. It's for the best. You'll understand when it's all over and it'll be fine, fine. You'll see. We would never do this to hurt you, we love you."

"Do what?" He was crying as much from frustration as disappointment or fear. "What did you do?"

"You'll see in time, and it'll be all right, I promise." Briskly, she went on: "Now I have to ask you something, and it's very important. Can you be honest with me? Did you tell the Virgans anything about what we're doing here? —In Brink? Anything about who the Renaissance are?"

He shook his head bitterly. Now he wished he had.

"Good. Good. We don't know them, Keir. They might be spies. They might be dangerous, do you understand?"

He nodded sullenly.

"And Keir, the flying machine . . ." She was silent so long that finally he was forced to look at her.

"When the time comes," she said, "you'll be able to leave Brink, and go anywhere in the universe that you want to go. But just hang on a little longer. Your time's not yet, Keir."

"Not yet."

"MA'AM?"

Leal turned to find Piero Harper at the doorway; there was concern written on his wind- and labor-aged features. She smiled warmly at Hayden Griffin's loyal crewman, and raised her hands to show off the room. "Isn't this nice? It has a roof! I'd forgotten what those were like."

Piero smiled and ducked his head. "It's no fun, ma'am, camping out under gravity."

"The things you learn." This chamber they'd given her was huge—but then, there was no lack of space in this city-that-wasn't-a-city. Before letting herself be walked here last night, she'd had to wait while her bed was constructed—extruded, actually, from one of the odd half-animal, half-machine things they called a *fab*. The things had squatted and huffed and beeped and squelched out chairs, tables, and cupboards, each one to order and each one slightly different. Maerta and her people had demonstrated what they called exoskeletons, which hoisted the finished goods on their backs and hauled them—a roomful of furniture per person—up stairs and ramps to these chambers. It would all have been wonderful to someone who wasn't half-dead with exhaustion. As it was Leal had slept like a stone for what must have been twelve hours; in this permanent gloom, it could have been six or two days. Now she felt like she could barely lift a limb. The lethargy was good; her mind had been gloriously blank for much of the day.

"Are they actually doing it?" she asked.

Piero nodded, and she shook her head with a wondering smile. Keir Chen's people were being outrageously generous. Leal, Piero, and some of his more trusted crewmates had spent part of the morning sitting around another strange device, the one Maerta called an Edisonian, discussing how they might rescue Piero's master Hayden Griffin and the rest of the airmen trapped on the lower plains. While they talked, the Edisonian listened; and then it thought a little bit; and then it began showing glowing images on its side, of the complete design for a flying machine of a type Leal had never seen before. The thing had big ungainly bags attached to it, and stiff wings, presumably to catch the wind. Neither of those were features of Virgan airships, but they made sense in the context of the pervasive gravity in Aethyr. "How long will it take to construct these?" Leal had asked Maerta.

The woman had shrugged. "A couple of days."

"They *are* being generous," Piero said now. She waved him in and he shut the door (also new, also made last night while they watched), but didn't advance any further into the room. "Ma'am, it's not that I'm ungrateful . . . but I can't help getting the feeling they want to get rid of us."

"Y-yesss," she admitted. "But not in a hostile way. You know the old saying, 'Fish and visitors stink after two days.'"

He grinned. "They're like monks, aren't they? Very serious and studious. But I can't for the life of me figure out what they're studying."

"Keir said they're studying the city."

"The boy. You believe him?"

She shrugged. "No. Look, what does it matter, if we get our airships in two days? We can go *home*, Piero."

He stood there uncertainly until she shook her head and said, "Oh, do sit down!" He lowered himself into one of the armchairs—becoming, she realized, the very first and maybe the last human to use it—and clutched its arms uncomfortably.

"Beggin' your pardon, ma'am, but if it don't matter, then why were you standing in the window when I came in, just starin' at nothing and sighing?"

She scratched the side of her head. "Mm, well . . ."

"Somethin' about this place is bothering you, ma'am. What is it?"

"It's not these people." She looked down, summoning her thoughts and her courage to express them. "Piero . . . how old were you, when your country was conquered?"

This was obviously not the question he'd expected. "Wha— Well, about fifteen. Old enough to know what I was losing."

"And what is that like?"

"Ah." Crow's-feet gathered around his eyes as he smiled. "You think you've lost Abyss forever?"

"Haven't I? Piero, I've been branded a traitor! Bringing Loll with us was a mistake, I know that now. We'll never win him over, and when we get home and he's among his old cronies and the power-brokers of Abyss, he'll turn on us. I know it, no matter what he says. He'll have me arrested if I return."

He nodded, but then said, "You suppose that his word is all that matters there now? Ma'am, Slipstream took over my beloved Aerie, and I lost my home. It's a terrible thing, being lost like that. But I got it back. Aerie's a nation again, thanks to Mr. Hayden Griffin and the sun he made. And you'll see, when all this is over, Abyss will take you back with open arms. All'll be forgiven when they realize you saved them all."

She looked away. After a moment she murmured, "Maybe it's not enough for them to forgive me; after all, I've done nothing wrong. What I keep asking myself, after what's happened, is whether I'll ever be able to forgive *them*."

Piero frowned.

"And if not," she continued, "where will I ever find a new home?"

Piero stood and came to lightly touch her hand—reticent, always-polite Piero, who had always treated her like some upper-class client, like the professor she'd wanted to be. She clasped her own hand over his and blinked up at him. "Ma'am, you'd be queen of

Aerie if I had any say in it," he said fiercely. "And a citizen, surely, there or in Slipstream or any nation that learns the treasure you're bringing and what you had to sacrifice to get it."

Tears blurred her view of him. She hadn't cried since the night her friend Easley had died, because in order to survive, she'd had to choke the old, emotionally fluttery version of herself. These tears were different than the old Leal's would have been, though—more hard-won, and with vaster depths of feeling behind them.

"Thank you, Piero," she said. "Still, I feel like a bird lost in an ocean of air. Where can I set my feet, Piero? And when can I fold my wings, and sleep?" She closed her eyes. "Sleep like I used to sleep."

"Tell the people back home what you learned out here, ma'am," Piero asserted. "And then you may be surprised what becomes possible."

3

"I KNOW IT doesn't look like much right now," Maerta was telling Leal Maspeth, "but in a day or two it'll be able to fly."

Keir hung back, in the shadows, watching the grown-ups inspect the new flying machine. This one was different from his ornithopter—naturally, since the Edisonians evolved each object from scratch.

"What are the air bags for?" Maspeth asked. With her were Minister Loll, Piero Harper, and several other "airmen."

Maerta frowned. "I don't know. —We often don't know the inner workings of the devices the Edisonians make. You could ask one of them, but they might not know, either; since they merely evolve the designs, they don't need to comprehend them."

"Lift," said Keir without thinking. They both turned to look for him, and he reluctantly stepped out of the shadows.

"The bags will probably hold hydrogen," he said, "which is lighter than air. So they'll carry you up, at least until you reach the freefall zone."

"Keir knows something about flying machines," said Maerta with no trace of irony or malice. "He has one of his own." And she nodded to where his ornithopter sat preening its metal feathers in a distant corner of the courtyard.

"Oh, do you fly?" asked Harper. Keir regretted having spoken, and shuffled his feet.

"Not yet," he said curtly.

"You're wise to start slow." Harper grinned. "Flying under gravity's no mean feat. We learned that the hard way."

Keir's scry was telling him to disengage from this conversation. That was probably Maerta's fault; she didn't want him to socialize with the strangers, even though he'd saved their lives and they were clearly grateful. Keir knew his own scry was registering his anger to her and the other Renaissance people nearby, but he kept his face composed as he bowed to the Virgans. "Yes . . . if you'll excuse me?" He walked away.

"We'll be able to ferry the rest of our men up from the surface in these?" said Leal Maspeth behind him—but she was watching him go. He could see that through his dragonflies.

He wondered what his scry would tell hers if she had it; it was frustrating that she had none. Scry was useful, because it made explicit the implicit. It interpreted your unconscious thoughts and motives, and communicated those to the scry of the people around you. This took the guesswork out of social relations; or at any rate, Keir's tutors said that was its original function. Like anything else that actually survived in the real world, it had evolved.

Scry was said to predate Artificial Nature. If that were the case, then the original scry technology had been *thought up* and *designed*, maybe even by human minds. Some idealist, perhaps, had believed that human society would function more efficiently if people's unconscious minds coordinated their efforts.

Feeling isolated and lonely, he went to his ornithopter and knelt next to it. "How are you?" he asked it.

"Ready," it said. Keir sighed in annoyance and stood up again.

"Ahem." He looked around to find the Virgan government minister, Eustace Loll, standing a polite distance away. Maerta's bots had fixed his broken leg, and he'd seemed pathetically grateful, as if he hadn't expected such a basic courtesy from his hosts.

Of all the Virgans, only Loll seemed to sense the scry around him. He couldn't actually see the emoticons and assessment tags that hovered virtually around everybody and everything here—but he somehow acted like he could. Maerta and the others had warmed up to him very quickly, yet Keir's scry told him that Maspeth didn't trust him.

Maspeth, however, wasn't anywhere to be seen. None of the Virgans were in the courtyard anymore, except for Loll.

He bowed. "Keir Chen, may I talk to you for a minute?"

"Certainly, Minister. I'm done here anyway." Keir didn't know what a "minister" was, but the title came attached to Loll, so he used it.

Loll appeared to like being addressed this way. He peered up at the black sky above the courtyard, then smiled and shook his head. "I confess, I find it strange that your people claim not to understand the very flying machine they're building for us."

Keir shrugged. "Nobody *understands* machines. We just use 'em. And if we're not careful, we get used by 'em."

Loll's laugh was rich and comradely. He reached out to pat the ornithopter's wing. "So who uses who, in this particular relationship?"

"Oh, it's not very bright and it doesn't think for itself," he said.

"Yet it does what you tell it to?"

Keir nodded. "You can command it, yes. Or use the hand controls, but I still haven't got the hang of it."

Loll mused, rubbing his large chin. "Yet, I should think I'd feel guilty, ordering such a creature around. It may only be a beast of burden, but . . . perhaps I can sympathize with it on that level."

"How are you a beast of burden, Minister?" he asked after a conspicuous and awkward silence.

"Oh! Well, I've had to carry heavy loads before. Mostly policy, you know." Loll shrugged. "And responsibility. I don't know how it is in your world, Keir Chen, but in mine we have to take individual responsibility for the welfare of people we may never meet. That's what I've done all my life. It's a calling, really. I help care for people who may not have the resources or information to make certain kinds of decisions for themselves. That's what we call 'government.' I gather you don't have that here."

"Government? No. Responsibility? Sure."

"Ah, then maybe you'll understand my . . . distress . . . at the current situation."

"Your being stranded here? I guess you've got people waiting for you back home," he said, a little enviously. "A family?"

Loll shook his head. "A city—actually, a whole country whose fate may rest on my ability to reach them in time with a warning."

"Is that why you were out here?"

Loll looked uncomfortable. "Yes, though—it pains me to say this—we've been told not to talk about the details to any outsiders. By that creature Professor Maspeth calls the 'emissary.'"

"The morphont?" Keir's scry was trying to read Loll by the man's stance, blood perfusion, eye movements, and so on. It wasn't having any success—no extra emoticons were floating around Loll that weren't already obvious from the tone of his voice and expression. Either he had fabulous self-control, or he was telling the truth. "It looked like a servant," said Keir. "When I saw it on the mountainside, it was just helping you stay on your feet."

"It wouldn't show its other side to you, naturally." Loll looked grieved. "It's a creature we know very little about. You've seen that little rider it has perched on Maspeth's shoulder? It's impossible to talk to her without it listening. Impossible for her to say what she really means without it hearing, as well. It's using her as its mouthpiece and it wants to get that mouthpiece into Virga to deliver an ultimatum to my people." He glanced around. "We can only tell you this now because, for the moment, it's elsewhere."

Keir hid his surprise and sudden curiosity behind a noncommittal "Hmm.

"It's a morphont, though," he added, "so it could hide any sort of mind in its bodies. You can't judge them by how they look, so I guess I can't tell you what to expect, either. If you're asking us to help you in any way regarding it, I'm not sure what we can do."

Loll gestured impatiently at the half-grown aircraft. "You have power! It seems to me that the people of this world can do anything you want." He rubbed his forehead. "Sorry. It's just the strain of this march we've been forced to undertake. —Make no mistake, we all want to get home, and as quickly as possible. We don't even mind the emissary delivering its message. But our people need to be warned in advance. They need to be prepared. And all this time, as we've walked and walked in its company, it seemed impossible that we could send anyone on ahead. Until now."

Keir glanced at a scry summary. "The airship will be ready in a couple of days—"

"And when it is, it'll carry all of us," insisted Loll. "All of us—including the, the morphont. We need someone to go *ahead* of it."

Keir finally realized what the man was asking. "You want to take my ornithopter!"

Loll looked chagrined. "If there were any way to return it . . . And maybe there will be. We have many friends and allies in Abyss—in my nation. If you could see it in your heart to lend it to us—this is our chance to break away from the emissary's watchful eye . . ."

First Maerta impounded it, and now this outsider wanted to borrow it! And Keir himself was never going to get to use the thing. "No, you can't," he said quickly—and a little loudly. "I made it, I should get to use it!"

"I understand," said Loll in a soothing tone. "But . . . will they let you?"

What had he heard? Maerta must have told others about Keir's plans to leave. Suddenly she didn't seem so wise, or nearly as caring as she pretended. Keir pictured her laughing with her friends while she told them about Keir's folly.

He decided. "I get to use it first. But once I'm done, I can send it back here. It's smart enough to find its way."

The Virgan minister nodded. "And where are you going with it, if I may ask?"

Keir shrugged. "It's a . . . private matter. But I do intend to start as soon as I can." He thought about the timetable for completing the new airship, and suddenly realized what he was agreeing to. "Maybe even tonight . . ."

Loll nodded.

Suddenly not at all sure about this, Keir stepped away, looking around at who might be in earshot or scry distance. "You know," he mumbled, "once I go, the others will, um, kick up something of a fuss. About my being gone. It's important that you stay out of their way and say nothing. I can't guarantee that they won't catch and confiscate the 'thopter when it returns, so you'll have to set a watch for it and be ready to jump in the moment it lands."

"I understand," said Loll. "It's the best we can do under the circumstances. Thank you very much for indulging me in this, Keir Chen. If there were any way we could pay you back . . ."

He shook his head. "Just keep this secret."

Loll laughed. "Since you've told me nothing about your destination, that should be easy."

After the Virgan walked away Keir stood for a long time staring at the ornithopter. It seemed uncomfortable under his gaze, finally shuffling around to face the other way as it stretched out its wings and landing gear. Keir barely noticed.

He was thinking about the black air beyond the city, and about what it would really mean to launch himself into it. It should have helped that he knew now of two destinations up there: the exit to the arena, at the far end of Aethyr, and, much closer by, the corresponding door to Virga. Before he'd known about that second door, the arena had been his only hope. Now he could picture himself flying to Virga instead, and yet, from what Loll had said, that door was guarded, too. When he landed there, they would ask where he came from. They would investigate, and probably send him back here.

He clenched his fists and glared at the pavement. "But you're getting *shorter*," he whispered.

The ornithopter angled its sensors as though pondering how to reply, and Keir turned and began walking away—only realizing, midstep, that he was doing it because of subtle hints from his scry.

No—not his scry. One of Maerta's annoying overrides had just kicked in, shoving his own emoticons and hints into the background, making him think he should head to his room.

Why would they want him there? He raised his hands and his dragonflies fountained up and away in every direction. And now he saw it—

—Human figures running up to Leal Maspeth and her people; lumbering mechs shouldering their way out of stone niches where they'd slept ever since the Renaissance arrived here; Maerta herself, pacing down the stairs along with her double, both equally grim-faced.

The usual scry map of Complication Hall and its environs had been edited down to a small set of corridors and rooms—the kids' spaces. A cold prickling feeling washed over Keir as he realized that Gallard had called everyone together and he was using scry to herd them somewhere safe—somewhere high up.

The searchlight of Maerta's attention landed on Keir for an instant, and he gulped and started walking again. He couldn't defy her, or any of the adults. He was going to his room. That didn't mean he couldn't find out what was going on, though.

On the way to the stairs he passed one of the blocky Edisonians. The kids learned early how to make queries to these devices—to ask for things. Along with your earliest lessons in dealing with an Edisonian, the Renaissance grown-ups taught you ancient stories about mythical beings who could grant wishes. Beware what you asked for, these stories cautioned. If your request was not worded exactly right, calamity might emerge from triumph. In one such story, King Midas wished that everything he touched turn to gold, and so his food, his dog, and finally his own wife and children all became statues and sculptures.

On more than one occasion, Keir had asked an Edisonian to

extend the communications range of his dragonflies, but Maerta or Gallard or someone had anticipated this, and the Edisonians invariably replied that it was forbidden.

Keir had lately discovered that he had a bit of a talent for thinking around such problems. Actually, it was kind of a big talent for asking the right question. Everybody in the Renaissance had it to one degree or another, but for Keir it seemed to come easily. So, a few weeks ago he'd done something most of his people wouldn't think to do: he'd *designed* a solution to the range problem.

"Form a chain," he told his dragonflies as he took the steps two at a time. "One end by me, the other end by . . . by Maerta."

The dragonflies formed a whirling cloud, which suddenly unreeled in the direction the grown-ups had gone.

Now he issued a second command he'd designed. "Lip-read," he told the lead dragonfly just before it disappeared through a distant archway. Then he had to turn his attention back to his main body, because as he went up one flight of stairs, Maerta and Leal Maspeth were going down another. The confusion of directions caused him to nearly fall flat on his face when he reached the top of his own flight.

He rubbed his shin; but the pain didn't dampen his enjoyment of the moment. He'd never really had cause to use the signal-chain idea before, but it worked perfectly. It was amazing the things you could do if you chose not to use the Edisonians to solve all your problems.

Maerta and Leal Maspeth were talking, and Keir's dragonflies relayed their words back along the chain, along with full visuals.

"—showed up about ten minutes ago," said Maerta.

Maspeth was shaking her head, twisting her hands together as she half-ran down the steps. "But how did he survive? I saw him get washed away by, by a thousand tons of ice!"

"That body probably *didn't* survive," said Maerta. They burst into one of the chambers just below Complication Hall. This place was normally dark, being just beyond the last storage rooms the

Renaissance used. Keir had only ever seen it through the night vision of his dragonflies, which was probably just as well: the place was one of the city's follies, a chamber whose walls and ceiling looked like they were in the process of toppling in on you. Its menacing stone stalactites and leaning walls were lit bright as day by hovering light globes.

The globes, and the smoldering, lightly vibrating mechs, and a few of the older members of the Renaissance, formed a half-circle around a single figure who stood in the center of the room.

Keir didn't know this lean, bald man's face, but he guessed that he'd seen his silhouette before, in the mouth of the tunnel under Brink. He'd reached out one hand and asked them to let him in, and Piero Harper had shot him, driving him into the teeth of the avalanche. Now, once again, he had one hand out in an appeal.

"Leal." A smile of pure joy lit up his face as he saw her. He took a step forward, and one of the mechs moved to block him. The smile faltered.

Maspeth had stopped at the room's entrance, seemingly unsure of what to pay attention to—the looming catastrophe of the ceiling, the hulking metal warriors on either side of her, or the man standing alone on the flat stone floor. Her right hand had gone up to her throat, and she steadied herself momentarily against the doorjamb. Then her expression hardened, and with no more hesitation, she stepped into the room.

"Why have you come here?" she snapped.

The man bowed, a sad half-smile on his face. "Leal, it's me, John."

"John Tarvey drowned. I saw it happen."

He nodded. "And, if this were Virga, that would have been the end of it. Surely the emissary explained it to you?"

The doll riding on Maspeth's shoulder must have said something, because she tilted her head toward it and there was a pause; but Keir's dragonflies couldn't read its lips, because it had none. He was sitting on his bed by now and smacked the mattress in frustration.

"Your enemies, yes, yes," she said to it. "I still don't understand." To Tarvey she said, "They raised you from the dead, or so you say. But this one says no." She curled one hand up to touch the junk-doll's tiny shoulder.

John Tarvey scowled at the little morphont. "It should know better than anybody how expendable bodies are! It wears them like gloves, you've seen that. Leal, I don't understand you. I might almost say you were being, well, hypocritical." He wouldn't meet her eye as he said this. "You keep that thing as your companion knowing full well that it's not what it looks like, that it has no body of its own. It doesn't bother you when it loses one, like it did in the river or in the landslides. It just builds another one or consolidates itself into what's left. But when I do it, you treat me like a monster."

Maspeth shook her head in confusion. "It was meant to be what it is! You weren't. Maybe the emissary's people can come back from the dead because they don't really die to begin with. But people die. You died! I saw you die."

"I didn't die, I became post-physical." He shook his head angrily. "Look, the only reason the people of Virga die is because we don't have allies to rebuild our bodies. I didn't know that before, none of us did. It was dumb luck that I drowned in an area where post-physical scouts were working. They revived me and made me an offer." His half-smile was back.

Maspeth looked very pale and small now, standing half in shadow by the door as though ready to bolt up the stairs at any moment. "What offer is that?"

Tarvey held out his hand. "The same one I'm making to you now. The offer of immortality."

Maspeth shook her head rapidly and sat down on the bottom step. "What does he mean?" She stared up at Maerta, who had stood with her arms crossed through the whole exchange. "Are you like him?"

"No," said Maerta. "We're not." She put herself in between Maspeth and the shade of John Tarvey. "I think you should leave now. She's not ready for your offer. None of them are."

"That's not for you to say, is it?" He walked up to her, looking her up and down. "What exactly are you, anyway? Why are you here, hiding in the darkness next to Virga's wall? Such an odd place to live. I'm sure my friends can tell me what you are; I'll know soon enough. What I wonder, though, is whether you've told her." He nodded at Maspeth.

—Who stood up and stepped past Maerta to glare into his face. "You are not who you say you are; that's all I need to know. Now leave!" She pointed to the black archway opposite the stairs.

He slouched for a moment, his mouth a moue of disagreement; then he turned on one heel and strode away. "The offer stands," he tossed back. "For all your people." He disappeared through the archway.

Maspeth put her face in her hands for a moment, and Maerta stepped forward, maybe to console her—but Maspeth looked up quickly at her, and Keir could see she was furious.

"Explain this!" she bellowed. Keir's lip-reading software rendered the words in as flat a tone as it had everything else so far; he dearly wished he'd heard her own voice at that moment. Clearly, her tone was electric; even the mechs shifted in some analogue of unease.

Then the doll on her shoulder said something. It spoke at length, while she held her head tilted to listen. Finally she shook her head and stalked to the stairs.

Keir called his dragonflies back, and images and words from the confrontation whirled through his head as he let himself fall back on the bed. He understood it on one level: certainly the virtuals could bring someone back from the dead, it probably happened all the time in areas where they held full sway. It was just that . . . why was Leal Maspeth so upset by it? And why the strange dynamic between her and Tarvey—why this "offer" that Tarvey talked about?

Something was going on there, some adult political game he couldn't fathom. Yet he felt he *should* be able to understand it.

He thought furiously for a while, and then startled himself with a new idea. Maspeth and her people came from a place where transformations and extensions and metamorphoses just didn't happen. In Virga, people were born people and kept their one body all their lives. If part of it broke, like Eustace Loll's leg, that was it—it was broken. Nobody had second bodies or morphont extensions like his dragonflies. So, for Maspeth, a resurrected John Tarvey must have seemed impossible, even an abomination.

He barked a laugh at the ceiling. Yes, that was it . . . or part of it. The apparent urgency of Tarvey's "offer" was still a mystery, but . . .

Keir flipped over and raised his head to glare at the silent door. He'd never given much thought to what it was actually like in Virga. The important thing about the place was the technological bubble that sheltered it from Artificial Nature; beyond that, he'd just thought of it as a realm of boring backwardness, where primitive humans scrabbled for survival in a state of ignorance and helplessness. Yet, if Virga was also a place where transformations and metamorphoses were impossible . . .

He sat up, examining his hands—hands that were smaller, weaker, and smoother than they should be.

Eustace Loll had asked Keir where he would go, if he left Brink. At the time, he'd had no idea; he just needed to get away. Now, though, the answer was obvious.

Somehow, he needed to convince Leal Maspeth that, when she returned to Virga, she must take him with her.

4

"IT'S UNDENIABLE! YOU can't deny it!" He wasn't going to stop or listen to what she had to say; so for what felt like the hundredth time since she'd met Eustace Loll, Leal found herself shaking her head and walking away from him.

The promised airship would be ready tomorrow. She had to hold on to that fact. Soon, very soon, they would be free of this world of oppressive gravity and strange threats. The free airs of Virga were close; but the closer they became, the more strident Loll became in his preaching.

"Someone told him of your encounter with John Tarvey," said the emissary, which rode her shoulder today in the form of the little junk-doll. "Yet you told none of your own people."

She waved a hand irritably. "He makes friends. It's what he does. Maybe he talked to one of the mechs, I don't know."

Loll had opinions about yesterday's encounter, and today he had cornered Leal to demand that she listen to them. It was the same old stuff, though: how could she trust the emissary, this shape-shifting, clearly nonhuman entity that built bodies for itself from nano-stuff and whatever trash might be lying about? It had threatened their home, the city of Sere—had built monstrous forms to gibber and scream at the citizens, and had then fled into the dark, pursued by the fabled sun lighter, Hayden Griffin. Somehow, it had convinced Leal Maspeth that it was benign, and yet—

"And yet humanity already has allies in the greater universe," Loll had said, nearly shouting, as he stood before her in the remote corridor where he'd found her. "Our true allies! Human, like us!

And more than that—immortal! I told you we should heed Tarvey's words the first time he came back to us, but you fled. Leal, you're still fleeing, but from what? The mere chance that you might be wrong?"

Just thinking of those words made her pick up her pace, and she would have been half-running now if the gravity in Brink were not so low. Each step she took lifted her off the floor for a couple of seconds, and the delay frustrated her attempt to act out her mood. After a few minutes she had to laugh at her own petulance, and she came to a stop in the intersection of several black-mouthed corridors.

This area was still within the precincts of Complication Hall. Tarvey's shade couldn't reach her here, if indeed it still prowled the city. By itself the darkness didn't frighten Leal; she had grown up in a sunless country, after all. So, after getting her bearings, she set off determinedly down one of the less-traveled ways.

"Where are we going?" asked the emissary mildly.

"Maerta told me there's a room where you can see stars."

"Ah." It said nothing more, and she quirked a smile in the dark. The junk-doll often said "ah" when it encountered human behavior that it didn't understand. The less of its nanomaterial there was in one of the emissary's bodies, the stupider it was. At least the doll could speak, though, unlike many of its constructions.

It had taken Leal quite a while to realize that the buildings of this "metropoloid," Brink, weren't just anchored on the skin of Aethyr—many of them penetrated that skin, so that above they clawed at the sky, and below, airtight galleries and inverted towers hung like icicles in the actual vacuum of space. All she had to do was find the lowest level of the Hall and locate stairs that continued down . . . search down some curving corridors, walk yet more stairs, and pace through some dark arches . . . and there it was.

She took a deep breath and tentatively stepped out to stand on a glass floor, above a canyon of immeasurable depth, its walls the hulls of Virga and Aethyr. Far below her feet, tiny pinpricks glittered in their uncountable thousands.

She let the sight of them fill her eyes, and murmured, "I may never get another chance to see stars, you know. How could I explain to my grandchildren that I missed my last chance?"

"Or they may become commonplace for you," said the doll.

She sent it a sharp look. Would she ever leave Virga again, once she made it back? It was doubtful, but anything had become possible for her—which was the problem. Her future was a frightening blank, and the closer she got to delivering the emissary's message to her people, the larger that uncertainty loomed.

She plucked the doll from her shoulder and set it on the floor. "I'd like to be alone for a while, if you don't mind." She made a shooing motion, back in the direction of Complication Hall.

It looked around itself, then said, "Are you not worried by what Minister Loll said? He threatened you."

"Did he? I don't think so." Loll's next-to-last words to her had been "I'm giving you one last chance to see reason, Leal! Say you'll at least listen to what John Tarvey has to say. You can't deny that he's offering us a kind of hope that your 'emissary' never has!" He'd made to grab her arm, and Leal had pulled back; but she'd never felt physically threatened by him.

"Loll relies on others to do his violence. Himself, he wouldn't hurt a fly. No, I'll be all right, I just need some time to think. Tomorrow—tomorrow we return to Virga, and then things will get . . . busy." She made the shooing motion again, and with obvious reluctance, the doll walked away.

Leal knelt and gazed for a while at the quiet stars. She tried to fill her eyes and her mind with them, yet her thoughts kept circling around to that blank in her future. She could not picture a future where she was happy.

She hated the weight of responsibility that lay on her shoulders. Of all her people, only Leal had visited the emissary's realm. She'd spent several weeks there and learned much about the weird and chaotic reality that reigned beyond Virga's walls. Except for Loll, her human companions were ordinary airmen caught up in an adventure they'd never sought. Harper and the others had literally been cast without warning from the familiar airs of Virga onto the plains of Aethyr. None had even guessed that Virga—the five-thousand-mile-diameter bubble that they mostly just called "the world"—had a Siamese sister, that the two worlds were joined like two soap bubbles floating through space. Leal had found a door in the wall between the two bubbles; alone, she had traveled from Virga to Aethyr and beyond. She had chosen to do so. She had seen stars. The others had not.

The emissary's people were eloquent, and their arguments convincing. The emissary itself . . . was not so good with human language. When they returned to Virga, it would lose its mind, as it had when it first visited there. The responsibility for delivering its message to all the nations of Virga lay entirely on Leal's shoulders. And that was terribly unfair.

The silence here was so perfect that she heard the scuffing footsteps from a good hundred feet away. Suddenly certain that the emissary had been right and Loll was after her, Leal straightened and looked for shelter or escape. If she ran, the other would hear her footsteps, too, and anyway, running was impractical in this gravity. There were places to hide, though, so she hunkered down behind one of the room's buttresses. There were stars below her feet and at her back, but the buttress itself was of solid metal, so it should hide her.

Keir Chen entered the gallery. He was only really visible as a silhouette, but she didn't know anyone else who walked around in a swarm of glowing bugs. He didn't glance at the starscape or pause in stepping from white floor to glass. Then he disappeared through an exit in the glass wall that Leal hadn't spotted earlier.

He had been friendly toward her; he was no threat. The temptation to follow him was too great, so, she did.

Chen could somehow see through his dragonflies, so Leal hung well back. Everybody had assured her that the wild city was empty; Keir's people spent almost all their time in and around Complication Hall. So where was Chen going?

The reason she hadn't spotted the passage he was taking now was because it was a simple glass tube that arced out into the darkness for an indeterminate distance. Born as she'd been in a world of freefall, Leal had no trouble with the illusion that she was walking on air (or, she knew, in empty space). There was none of the sense of crushing cold that you felt at the walls of Virga or on the slopes of Aethyr; at least here, Brink had remembered to insulate its chambers. Keir Chen walked on darkness a few hundred feet ahead, and Leal padded steadily behind him.

Once she glanced back, and saw that they had left the icicle-like hanging towers of Brink far behind. This corridor was some kind of road connecting the metropoloid to another location, one that lay well outside Aethyr's walls. The road crossed a kind of cavity between the curving shells of Aethyr and Virga—and though she'd never thought about it, she realized she'd assumed that the space between the two worlds would be empty. Yet in the distance, starlight gave ghostly outlines to complicated silvery shapes, some of which must be miles long. Dozens of widely separated objects, like pieces of a shattered city, seemed to be swooping down and under her with grand, almost imperceptible slowness. This was an illusion: It was Aethyr, and of course her corridor and Leal herself, that was turning. Those glittering mountains were fixed perfectly still in space, apparently attached to neither world and so sovereign in some way.

The glass tube Chen was leading her through hung from almost invisible cables that were suspended from somewhere overhead. Leal could see other mechanisms way up there, where the worlds converged to finally touch.

She was so distracted by these sights that it took her a few seconds to notice the dragonfly that was buzzing a foot from her nose.

Should she run? She didn't think Chen or his people were any threat—but if he were dangerous, there was no way she could have evaded his dragonflies here. His physical body stood fifty feet away, a black-on-black figure now turned toward her.

"I was curious," she said. The dragonfly didn't reply, and Chen didn't move, so Leal swept her arm to indicate the wonders encircling them. "It's so strange. There's all this *stuff* out here! And we were taught that the space beyond Virga's walls was just empty. What are all these things?"

The dragonfly began drifting away in the direction of Chen. That was an obvious invitation, so Leal followed it. "No idea what they are," said Chen. "An armada, I suspect, awaiting its orders to invade Virga."

"Oh!" After everything she'd recently seen, Leal should have come to that conclusion herself. She knew there were things outside her world struggling to get in. But to actually *see* them was suddenly, profoundly upsetting. "Do they know we're here?"

"I hope not."

"And this road . . ." He hadn't resumed walking, now that she was standing beside him. She looked ahead to where the glass angles of floor and wall converged, miles away. Something was there, a vague hulk hinted at by starlight.

Keir said, "What if I told you that it runs to Virga?"

"*What?*" She stared at him. He appeared completely serious.

"I'd say you're lying," she said after a moment's thought. "This world rotates. Virga doesn't. The only place you could make a door between the two would be, well, where the door we're trying to get to is—at the axle, where the two worlds are attached."

Even as she said this she realized it wasn't necessarily true. Her city, Sere, was composed of a dozen giant iron-and-brass wheels, each one a mile or more across. You could board a flea car on the rim of one and be tossed to the rim of the next in line—handed off by the giants, one by one, until you reached the farthest wheel. Maybe some similar mechanism joined Virga and Aethyr.

"But then why didn't you tell us?" She was raising her voice.

"Why let us languish here while you build us an airship to reach the axle door, when we could have just walked home?"

He looked away. "If leaving were that easy, I wouldn't be here now."

This was no answer, so she waited. After a moment he shrugged and said, "Yes, this way does lead to Virga. No, you can't take it. The way is blocked."

"By what?"

"By them." He nodded at the indistinct shapes he'd called an armada. "Or their cousins, at any rate. Things live in the walls of Virga. They would eat you or incorporate you before you got ten meters."

"Then why were you going there?"

He looked up the long glass hall, appearing to weigh what he should tell her. "I come here sometimes," he said, still not looking at her, "and think about leaving Brink."

"For Virga?" She was careful not to sound too surprised; she wanted to encourage him to say more.

"Virga would be safer than . . . back there." He nodded the other way, past Brink, at the many worlds of the arena and beyond. Well, that made sense, she thought; the emissary had told her much about the strange alien worlds of the arena—that volume of space that included Aethyr and Virga and, apparently, many other artificial worlds—and she wouldn't have wanted to visit them alone.

Here, though, was an apparent door to home, tantalizingly within reach. "The Edisonians build anything for you," she pointed out. "Couldn't they make something to get you past that door?"

"Maerta has forbidden them to make me anything more complicated than my experiments."

"Experiments?"

He shrugged. "Toys, I guess. I ask questions about the world. I make things to find out the answers."

Now he began walking, but back the way they'd come. Leal stared ahead at the hint of escape in the distance, and fell into step with Keir Chen. "So you're a prisoner here? Or do you just feel like you are?" She indicated the dragonflies hovering around him. "Are those your jailers?"

He laughed. "No, they're just eyes." He raised his hand and one of the little bugs came to land on his fingertip. "I evolved them and I guess I . . . grew used to them. I'd feel blind without them now."

Then he frowned at her. "No, Maerta and the others aren't keeping me prisoner. They're just watching over me."

"Why do you need watching over?"

He seemed to struggle for an answer, then shrugged. "Because I'm a kid."

"You look like you'd be a man where I come from."

Keir didn't reply and she realized she might have embarrassed him. Eventually, as they came to the gallery again, she said, "Isn't there another world somewhere that you used to call home?"

"Oh, yes. I'm from Revelation." She raised her eyebrows encouragingly, and after a moment he said, "Ah. It's a planet in the inner system."

"I don't know anything about Vega's planets," she said. Leal had known there was a wider universe outside Virga, but like most people she'd been raised to think of it as an empty place, of no relevance to civilized human life. She'd learned differently when she met the emissary, but even it knew little about worlds other than its own.

Chen smiled slyly. "I'll tell you about Revelation, if you tell me about Virga."

Leal did an imitation of the scoffing sound her father used to make. "And I'll tell you about Virga if you tell me what you people are really doing in this godforsaken place. How's that for a deal?"

He laughed, sounding genuinely delighted. "I like that! And why not? I have nothing to hide." His face suddenly fell. "Less and less as the days pass, it seems."

Leal thought about her confrontation yesterday, and about Loll's reaction when he'd heard. "I've asked everyone I know from this world—your Maerta, the emissary, I even spoke to one of your Edisonians—but I still can't get a straight answer about something."

He looked amused. "That doesn't surprise me at all. What was the question?"

"What's so bad about immortality?"

He stopped, cocked his head, and said, "It assumes that there's some part of you that is, or could be, impervious to change. There isn't." He started walking again.

"Oh, but—" She caught up. "But this, this offer. You probably don't know, but yesterday something happened—" He held up a hand.

"I was kind of listening in," he said. He shrugged at her shocked expression. "Sorry."

"Then you know what happened. To my friend."

"He died and was revived by one of the factions of Artificial Nature. It happens."

"The virtuals, yes? But what are they? What is he now? And what is this offer he's talking about?"

Keir frowned. "He's become a part of the system that we're here to oppose. The virtuals want to dissolve the boundaries between everything physical. They want every physical object in the universe to be a potential host to Mind. They didn't so much revive your friend John as upgrade him. They loaded his consciousness into a network where it can live virtually, without reference to the physical world. There's trillions of consciousnesses in Artificial Nature, and more and more of them are leaving reality behind for these fantasy-realms."

"Oh. But—but that isn't how the emissary works, is it? The emissary claims it's also an enemy of these virtuals."

"Yes, your friend is different. It's a shape-shifter, yeah, but it's always embodied in one way or another. Have you noticed that its personality changes depending on what body it's built?"

"Yeessss . . . It's rather annoying, actually."

"The morphonts—your emissary's people—allow themselves to be changed by their bodies. They don't pretend to be disembodied, pure software agents, like the things that upgraded your friend. Those—well, they're a nightmare."

"But why?"

"The virtual use physical bodies like puppets, but the problem is, either they were once physical beings like your friend John, or they never were. If they were, their whole consciousness is designed to fit a certain kind of physical being. Without that to anchor them, they go mad. I'm sorry to say this, but your friend either already has, or soon will. The only way to prevent it is to give him a virtual body or download him into a new physical one.

"The ones that never did have bodies never had any anchor to the physical world. They hate and despise it as a realm of dumb matter that shouldn't exist. Freedom for them means the ability to change not just their bodies, but their emotions, their minds, their memories . . . they have no stable identity. They're a kind of force, one that's steadily aligned itself against the embodied—the *real*—throughout history."

"And they hate Virga . . ."

"Because Virga," and here he turned to gesture at the vast wall of darkness behind them, "is the last refuge of the fully embodied. The very last place where reality is not just what you say it is."

Very gradually, without really realizing it, they had come to a halt in the middle of the glass passageway. Now Leal rubbed her chin musingly, and nodded at Keir. "That's why your people are here, isn't it? You're trying to figure out how Candesce defends Virga against A.N."

He looked startled, then nodded sheepishly. "We're doing something humans used to do thousands of years ago. It's called *science*. You've probably never heard of it."

She laughed. "Of course I've heard of it. What kind of science?"

"Um. Experimental physics?" He looked at her as if he was expecting some outburst from her: laughter? Awe?

"Of course," she said.

Thoroughly deflated, he merely nodded. "That's no surprise," she told him mildly. "It sounds like everyone outside of Virga wants to know how the sun of suns works. How it is that it's able to keep Artificial Nature at bay. We kind of figured you were doing something like that. The question is, who are you doing it for?"

"For the embodied, because the virtuals are trying to absorb all of us. Most of the time they just move in and take over. Some of us, they makes their 'offer' to." He opened his mouth to continue speaking, but suddenly stopped dead.

At first Leal thought her words had stung him overmuch—though she fully intended them to sting. But Chen's head was tilted, his eyes focused on nothing as though listening intently to something.

"Don't panic," he said—not to her, she judged. "No, no, I mean I'm pretty sure I know what that was. Oh, stop it! I'll explain when we get there."

He began walking, then stopped again. "Yes, *we*." He turned to Leal, his mouth twisted in annoyance. "It seems I've offended my brethren again. They beg me to stay, then get angry when I do."

Chen hurried ahead, his fireflies practicing formation flying over his head. "Um," she said as she followed. "What did you do?"

"The ornithopter I built—my flying machine—it's missing."

"Missing? But who could have—?"

Even as she spoke, Leal realized who it must be. They'd reached a T intersection; without another word to each other, Leal turned right while Chen went left.

When he was out of sight she began to bound along as quickly as the low gravity would let her. Rounding a final corner, she entered the chambers the Renaissance had given her party. For a moment, everything looked fine: Piero was playing cards with two of the airmen, while two more were trying on new shoes that the

Edisonians had customized for their feet. They all looked up in surprise as she bounced to a halt in the doorway.

"Ma'am?" said Piero. Leal counted heads, and her suspicion was confirmed.

"Where," she shouted, "is Eustace Loll?"

5

MAYBE THIS INSTITUTIONAL mint-green paint had once made the offices of the Abyss Ministry of the Interior inviting. Now, cracked and begrimed by the ages and lit only by flickering gaslight, it was merely depressing.

"It's an honor, truly an honor," the midlevel official behind the desk was saying. (Was he a subminister? An attaché? After so many referrals and re-referrals, she couldn't recall.) "Always an honor to meet a member of the legendary Virga Home Guard, Ms.—?"

"Argyre. Antaea Argyre." She had promised Crase—not to mention herself—that she wouldn't use that name, or this uniform, again. It was a measure of Antaea's desperation that she was here today, smiling and shaking the hand the subminister (or attaché) held out. She'd skulked here through alleys and understreet tunnels, and changed into the uniform in a downstairs washroom; still, Crase might yet discover that she was continuing to impersonate a member of the Home Guard. For that reason, and because this was her last lead, she would have to leave Sere after today.

The subminister gestured for her to sit, and for a moment there was silence punctuated by the clatter of typewriter keys in the outer office, and the rumble of a passing trolley in the street below. Then he held up the forms Antaea had filled out in the other room.

"Let me tell you, it's always a delight to meet a member of your race, Ms. Argyre." She did not return his smile this time.

"I'm just a little surprised," he went on.

"Oh?" She kept her expression neutral, and leaned forward indulgently.

"Well, I only mean," he said with a shrug, "that when your compatriots, ah, visited us a few months back, they demanded—I mean, requested—all our records pertaining to the incident you're referring to. The one in which the fugitive, this 'Leal Maspeth,' was centrally involved. You already know everything we know," he finished. Then he steepled his hands and smiled at her again.

"Maybe," she said to buy time. "But our copies have flown halfway around the world by now. It would take me months to lay my hands on them, and, well, I'm *here*, aren't I?"

He sighed. "I'd like to help, really I would. But it's not up to me. Your request is unusual enough, and, frankly, sensitive enough that it will have to be vetted at the highest levels. I can send it on—" He paused at a knock on the door. "Pardon me." He stood and went to open an inside door a crack. Gaslight shone off his bald spot as he bent to say, "What is it?"

Someone started to explain something through the narrow opening, but the subminister interrupted with a scoffing sound.

"What do you mean, Loll's back?"

There were more mumbled words; then, with sudden energy, the subminister turned and said, "I'm sorry, Officer Argyre, I'm going to have to cut this meeting short. Something's come up. If you will—?" He indicated the other door.

"Ah," she said. "Of course. Thank you for your time."

He ducked through the interior door and Antaea heard him talking to someone on the other side. She leaped out of her chair and put her ear to the door. *Loll.* That name had come up again and again in connection with Leal's case. He was an important man, by all accounts, and he'd disappeared at the same time as she had.

The thick imported wood of the door muffled the voices; she couldn't hear what was being said. They seemed to be moving away. There was no keyhole through which to peek; she couldn't just risk following them.

She eyed the window. It was narrow, there more for ventilation than the view, which meant it opened. She pushed it up and verified that there was a ledge outside. With only a glance back, she climbed out onto it and edged along to the next window.

Antaea didn't glance down, but even if she had the view wouldn't have daunted her. She was used to the yawning vistas of gravity-free air. Even if a fall from this ledge would be fatal, she had long ago become conditioned against a fear of heights.

She knelt carefully, holding the slick bricks with her fingertips. Now she could hear the voices better.

"—a city, he says." That was the voice of the man who'd interrupted the subminister. "Two hundred miles from the Site."

"And he was alone? What about the ships—and the Home Guard escort?"

"Something's not right," continued the subminister. "That was a Home Guard inspector in my office just now! Asking about Maspeth. Haven't they debriefed Loll themselves?"

"He slipped by them! Got himself smuggled through the Site on one of our regular supply ships. He was flying some little one-person aircraft, seems he was able to sneak on to one of our cruisers without the Guard noticing."

"Well, obviously the Guard suspects something. And all of these resources he's asking for?" scoffed the subminister. "TC-34s? And he's fast-tracking the gravity ships? How are we going to pay for all this?"

There was a pause. Then the other man said, "Would you rather ignore the request? See what happens?"

The subminister cursed, and then Antaea heard the scraping of chairs against the floor. The voices continued but were moving away again.

A glance through the glass showed that this smaller office was now empty. Antaea climbed back through the window she'd come out of, and left the subminister's office by the correct door. She was thinking hard, and ignored the gaze of the secretaries in the outer office as she stalked past them. No doubt there would be whispers once she'd left, or maybe even loud conversation: a *winter* wraith had visited them! Who cared; she had more important things to think about.

She didn't forget to change out of her uniform in the main-floor washroom. People in the lobby stared, but no one accosted her as she passed them. She kept her eyes forward and acknowledged no one.

She was out of options. All her money was gone, and her only possessions in the world were the clothes on her back, and the jet bike currently parked at Rowan Wheel's dock a mile overhead. All manner of revelatory conversations and events might be taking place in the offices above, but she had no access to any of them. There was only so much ledge-balancing and skulduggery a girl could do on her own.

She stopped at the taxi stand to think. The ragged remains of protest posters hung in strips from the lamppost next to it. The secret service had been by again, evidently, but the poster-printers kept just a step ahead of them. Although the crudely printed papers were gone, she—and everybody else in the city—knew what they said. In big bold letters, they asked, "WHY IS THE GOVERNMENT LYING TO US?"

There was no proof that the Crier in the Dark had been destroyed, the broadsheets went on. No proof at all. If the government remained incompetent to deal with the clearly still-existent threat, then it should be replaced.

That made her smile, and then, after a glance around, she walked away from the taxi stand. Two blocks up the curve of the wheel she paused again, under the velvet-draped entrance of a grand hotel she could never have afforded to stay in, even when she did work for the Guard. The doorman scowled at her as she brought out the card she'd been thumbing in her pocket for days. As she made up her mind and walked up to the door, he put his arm out to block her.

"Are you sure you have business here?" he asked in an all-too-familiar tone.

"Is this the Stormburl Hotel?" she asked sweetly.

"It is, but—"

"Then I have business here." She pushed past him and into the building.

"I'm sorry, miss, but I'm afraid I'm going to have to ask you to—"

"It's all right," said a voice behind them. "She's expected."

The clerk ducked his head; and Antaea turned, and there stood the man she'd met on the airship.

Jacoby Sarto smiled and put out his hand for her to shake. "I was just on my way to dinner. Would you like to join me?"

THE RESTAURANT WAS located about a mile from Sere's biggest town wheel. It was an ornately carved wooden centrifuge about a hundred feet across. It rotated slowly to produce just enough gravity to make dining pleasant in the gaslit gardens that paved its inner surface. You could watch the kitchen workers pick and clean your fabulously expensive vegetables and herbs; if the duck Jacoby ordered was killed on the spot, too, they did it somewhere out of sight. It was the greens that mattered, because in a sunless country like Abyss, most vegetables were imported.

He watched Antaea watch the city. She was beautiful in a striking and unsettling way; he'd been unable to keep himself from glancing surreptitiously at her as they flew here. Her ears, nose, and chin were tiny, but her eyes were huge. Jacoby had heard of winter wraiths, those members of a genetically engineered offshoot of humanity whose features were designed to mesmerize ordinary humans. Antaea Argyre was certainly mesmerizing, but he had done his research since their meeting at the capital bug; he knew she was a capable and ruthless killer.

Now she turned back to him. "I'm not really sure why I'm here," she admitted.

"You're here because you think I may know things," he said

with a mild shrug. "Maybe I do, and maybe I'm willing to share. How's that for a start?"

She eyed him warily. "But what's the price?"

"Well, there may not be one," he admitted, "if your interests are as aligned with mine as I think they are."

"Explain."

He suppressed a smile at her imperious tone. He was used to dealing with people who assumed command the way she was attempting to. His reply was to lean forward and spill a sheaf of photographs and reports onto the tabletop.

"I was born, raised, and spent almost my entire life in the nation of Sacrus, on Spyre," he said as he slid the pictures around with one finger. Argyre showed no sign of recognizing the name, so he tamped down on his irritated pride and explained: "Spyre was one of the ancient places, a metal cylinder twelve kilometers across and twenty long. Open at the ends, of course; it flew in the airs near Candesce, at the center of the world. Its inner surface was sown with countries like Sacrus—some small as a building, some miles in extent. All of them thousands of years old. Older than any of these places." He waved contemptuously at the rust- and verdigris-rimmed wheels of Sere.

"One day," he continued, "a woman from this outside world drifted in and miraculously survived her fall onto Spyre's inner surface." His fingers continued to move the pictures, but he was no longer looking at them. "Shortly after Venera Fanning's arrival—" He pretended not to notice as Argyre started at the name, nearly spilling her drink. "—Spyre fell apart. Literally. Sacrus, its ancient neighbors and rivals, all of them were ripped asunder and scattered to the six winds."

Antaea Argyre leaned back, obviously considering what to say. "From what I've heard of Venera Fanning, that doesn't surprise me in the least."

"I lost my home—my whole nation," Jacoby went on. "I'm an

exile now, forced to make my living by means that are, frankly, sordid compared to what I once was."

"If it's revenge you're after," said Argyre, "all I can say is that I have no way of getting you close to Fanning."

Sarto crossed his arms and glowered at the photos. "I was born and raised to believe in the sanctity, not to mention the necessity, of revenge," he admitted. "But revenge against whom? Or, in this case, what?"

"Ah."

"Venera Fanning trampled all our traditions and values, and then blew up the world," said Jacoby as he handed some of the pictures to her. "But I'd be lying if I said those traditions and values didn't heartily deserve to be trampled. The world's a better place now that Sacrus is gone, and that's probably true for the rest of Spyre, too. —What do you see?" he said of the photos.

Jacoby watched Argyre's mounting puzzlement as she shuffled through the images. "What is this: an eye?" She held up a photo that showed nothing but a white circle surrounded by black.

"That," said Jacoby, "would be entirely visible from where you're sitting, if this godforsaken country had a sun to light it. It's a photograph of the outer skin of Virga, an area only a hundred miles or so away from this very spot. The picture was taken through a telescope by . . . a friend of mine. That circle is a span of Virga's outer wall. This picture was shot in infrared, so the cold parts are black."

"Then . . ." She frowned in confusion. "This circle is an area of the world's skin that is *warm*?"

He nodded. "It's hundreds of miles across. And in the past few months, practically the entire Home Guard fleet has converged on a spot right at its center."

She blinked at him rapidly—a disconcerting sight given her huge eyes. "Really." She turned the other pictures over. "This?" Blurred and speckled with distance was an image of square block-houses encircling a ragged black patch. "Is this . . . a hole?"

"I wouldn't speculate on that," he said. "But that's what's at the very center of the circle. You can see there's ships clustering around that spot like flies on—"

"Yes, I can see that," she said. "But—" Her fabulous eyes widened even further. "The Site," she muttered. "He said he'd come from the Site . . ." She glanced up guiltily, but it was plain he'd heard her. Jacoby watched her struggle with a decision.

"A local cabinet minister went missing a while ago," she said. "During the monster scare. Now he's back. Back from somewhere on the other side of 'the Site.'"

"Ah . . ." Jacoby smiled as the waiter set down their appetizers. "I came here because I'm chasing the ones who are ultimately responsible for the destruction of Spyre. Care to tell me why you're here?"

She bit her lip, but they both knew there was no going back now—and he already thought he knew, from the research his spies had done on her.

"I'm looking for a friend of mine," she said. "Her name is Leal Maspeth; she was being groomed to become dean of the university's history department when she suddenly disappeared. The official reports say she defied the government over something to do with the monster. She supposedly stole state secrets and—this is utterly unbelievable—burned one of her coworkers to death in his own home. Then she fled into the arms of the monster itself. Well, maybe it's true. Maybe she went somewhere . . ." She paused, a forkful of salad halfway to her mouth, and gazed at the photo lying between them. "Two hundred miles . . ."

Jacoby nearly dropped his own fork this time, and damn her, she noticed. "What's that?" he said irritably.

"I overheard a couple of clerks talking," she said. "One said that Loll had come from some kind of city that was two hundred miles from the Site."

Jacoby tried to act nonchalant as he dug through the papers, but he was sure his eagerness must be obvious as he brought out a different picture. "Look at this one," he said, tossing it down in front of her. Argyre snatched it up.

While she examined the picture, he scowled at the flamboyantly lit towers of Sere. "There's a certain kind of self-delusion particular to people who've lived in peace for too long," he said, half to himself. "Right up until the day that the enemy swoops in to torch their wheel, they think that their problems are the biggest problems in the world, and their power the biggest power. I've spent my whole life looking into the eyes of those people after I had taken away everything they had . . . and then, quite suddenly, I lost my homeland in exactly the same way. Spyre, Sacrus, and even Virga itself . . . they're just pawns in a larger conflict, aren't they? I know that now. You know. But who else really understands? It seems to me that Leal Maspeth does—or did."

Argyre held up the photo. "This is some city somewhere? What's the connection?"

He nodded. "The ancient city of Serenity. A dead place now, choked with icebergs, frozen into the outer wall of Virga like a corpse in winter . . . and right at the edge of that mysterious warm circle." The image showed dark towers on a flat plain, ensnared by rivers of ice. "In fact, it's precisely two hundred miles from the Site."

"Aha! So maybe this is the real place, then—the monster's home . . ." She stopped as she saw Jacoby shaking his head.

"My people have cruised by the place several times. There's no ships docked there, no signs of life at all. The Guard haven't gone near Serenity. It may be that they don't even know it's there, it may be that they're just distracted by whatever it is they've found at the center of the circle."

"Maybe they're about to become interested," she said.

"You'd think. It's strange, though—my men spent much of the morning watching the rest of the Abyssal fleet set sail. Their trajectory will take them straight to what you've called the Site—the center of the circle. If this cabinet minister came from Serenity, why aren't they going there?"

"How many men do you have, anyway?" she asked with a little smile.

"Oh, a few."

She snorted, then turned her attention back to the photo. "We could speculate about this all day," she pointed out. "Or we could go to this city of Serenity, and find out."

Jacoby picked up the photos and shuffled them and the rest of the papers back into the file folder. "There, you see?" he said. "It turns out our interests align after all."

6

KEIR SAT IN his room, hands folded in his lap. His knapsack lay on the bed, but he'd pulled the clothes and rations out of it. With no means of escape other than walking, it just seemed pathetic to keep it ready to go.

Maerta had spoken to the Edisonians and forbidden them to evolve any kind of vehicle or personal transportation device for him. She didn't trust him, clearly—and he didn't blame her. The need for escape burned so brightly in him that he could no longer think about anything else.

And yet . . . he could have done what Eustace Loll actually did; he could have taken the ornithopter himself and flown away. There'd been no guard on it, only his promise to Maerta that he wouldn't use it. If he wanted to get away so badly, why had he given her his word that he wouldn't; and why had he kept it?

Maybe for the same reason that, until today, he hadn't delved through his own scry to look at his memories from more than six months ago.

Because there weren't any. He remembered school. He remembered a mounting anxiety, a feeling that these happy days with the other kids, the lessons, the comfort of elders in the morning and evening—that these were a mask of some kind, covering . . .

He stood up and started to pace to the door, but caught himself, and sat down again. That was how it had been: whenever he'd actually started to think about his situation, terror had bubbled up overwhelmingly, and *escape* became the only option. So he'd walked the dark corridors of the city, explored it end to end, and fantasized about being anywhere else. It had worked to stave off the panic, but only because it was a distraction.

And then, Maerta had said the name *Sita*.

There was no one in the Renaissance named Sita. His scry couldn't locate any reference to her, and when he'd asked the Edisonians they'd simply sat there like dumb blocks of stone. Yet Maerta thought he should know the name.

He looked down at his hands, where two of his dragonflies perched, then up at the forlorn knapsack. What he should have done was go after Maerta, demand that she explain. Or he should have talked to the others. That was something, in fact, that he should have been doing from the start. Why hadn't he cornered another of the adults, forced them to tell him what had happened? Surely they all knew.

The panic was rising in him again. He couldn't help himself; he had to stand and leave the room. This time, though, he swore, he wouldn't take one of those dark archways and disappear into avoidance and solitude.

His mouth set in a determined line, he headed for the plaza where the new airship was being built.

He passed Gallard on the way down the stairs. "You were supposed to be in workshop this morning," Gallard commented, though not in a scolding tone.

"Not now," said Keir, and he kept going.

As he reached the bottom of the steps a nagging little voice in the back of his mind said, *Why didn't you confront Gallard?* Gallard was something of a friend; at least, Keir trusted him.

But something had been done to Keir, and Maerta had promised someone that she would not tell him what that was. Who was that someone? Could it be Gallard? It could be anybody. Anybody in the Renaissance.

He picked up the pace a bit until he reached the entrance to the plaza.

Maerta was taking a walk around the airship with Leal Maspeth.

An Edisonian remote was lumbering beside them, trying to explain in its halting way how the ship worked. Leal was shaking her head.

He shouldn't interrupt them. Of course; he'd wait until they were done and then speak to Maerta alone.

No. No, he wouldn't.

She was *right there*. Yet he knew he couldn't do it. The panic had taken over, and he stumbled back into the shadow of the archway, covering his eyes with his hands.

He could still see through his dragonflies, and they had fanned out into the plaza; so that's why he once again became the one to see something no one else was looking for.

In the featureless, unchanging black sky above the plaza, a little orange spark had appeared. His misery kept Keir from wondering about it until it had grown into a dot with a truncated tail—and then it came to him that it was moving *fast*.

"Look out!" He didn't know why he was running into the plaza, but as Maerta and Leal turned, he shouted, "Up there!"

Maspeth turned to look, and her eyes widened in shock. She grabbed Maerta's arm and began to run for the colonnade at the plaza's edge.

Maerta pulled back. "What is—"

"Missile!" Leal pulled all the harder, and now Keir took Maerta's other arm. The Edisonian took a ponderous step, then aimed its blocklike head at the spear of fire. "Perchlorate oxidizer," it observed. "Evidence of a conical gas expansion device to exploit law of equal and opposite reaction."

"Run, you stupid . . ." Keir had no word for it. Anyway, they'd reached the colonnade and fell together behind one of its vast, dark pillars.

The Edisonian reached up as if to catch the missile, and the orange streak hit it with an overwhelming flash. What followed wasn't sound, but a hammer blow that picked Keir up and flung him against the wall.

Dust and grit whirled, and pieces of the airship tumbled in the plaza. Most of the lamps that had lit the space were out, but a few were bouncing around like terrified lightning bugs. Weird shadows capered after them, but the whole scene was oddly silent except for a kind of long throbbing note. Keir helped Leal Maspeth to her feet, and although her lips were moving, she wasn't making any sound.

His dragonflies had been scattered, but they could still see; and he realized that their vision was much better than that of his own eyes. He sent a couple through the dust to check if any of the plaza's entrances had collapsed, and shot another one up and up to loft finally out of the spiraling cone of dust.

Another red spark appeared, and in the flash of its birth he glimpsed the thing that had fired it: a cylindrical craft of some kind, its prow narrow and surmounted with an ornate ram. On its sides and at its rear were engines of some sort, all pointed down and laboring to keep it aloft.

It fired a third missile. "Come on!" Keir pushed and hauled Maerta and Leal in the direction of the nearest stairwell. They came readily enough and all three made it into the archway just before the second missile hit. This time, as the flash happened, they crouched as one and braced themselves.

This time it was scry that he saw first. The Renaissance was lighting up with frantic messages and queries. They all boiled down to one question: *What's going on?*

"We're under attack!" he projected. "Some kind of airship."

Glyphs of astonishment and outrage flooded the air. Maerta, however, was projecting only confusion. As the shock of the second explosion passed, the three of them hurried farther down the stairs with Leal in the lead, and Keir saw that Maerta was flinging questions at her back. Maerta had forgotten that Maspeth didn't have scry.

They reached a landing. Though the walls shook to another thumping explosion, they seemed far enough away now to be safe.

Maerta grabbed Leal by the shoulder and whirled her around. She was shouting, and past the buzz and pain in his ears, he faintly heard her words: *"Who did you bring here?"*

Leal shook her head and said something. Keir didn't hear the words, but her mouth shaped a name he recognized.

Loll.

Scry had done a head count, and nobody had been hurt. Except that, as Maerta pointed out, she, Keir, and Leal had damaged eardrums.

"Come up to the Hall," somebody said. "We'll fix you up."

Maerta shook her head. "Evacuate the Hall. One of these bombs would obliterate it. Everybody needs to get into interior corridors and rooms that are behind Aethyr's skin."

Leal was flailing around frantically. After a moment Keir realized that it was entirely dark down here; she couldn't see. Only he could, apparently, through his dragonflies. Keir grabbed her hands, and she shouted something. He made out the words "my people" behind the ringing drone.

"Does anybody know where the Virgans are?" he interjected.

The walls of Brink faded, replaced by a wireframe map where everybody's location was indicated. He tapped both of the women on their shoulders, then took their hands and began guiding them through blackness to the empty depths of the city.

THEY'D FUSSED AROUND her ears for a minute, and now Leal had something icy cold in each one. Her junk-doll was standing on tiptoe, its hand in the left canal, which felt simultaneously odd and comforting.

Running people and single-minded machines swirled around her as she sat on a crate that had just been brought into this long chamber. Keir's people looked panicked, but they acted in perfect synchrony, stacking supplies in precise locations, avoiding one another with uncanny accuracy. Piero Harper and the other Virgan airmen looked calm, but they were all over each other in their attempt to get organized.

"How do you hear now?" asked the junk-doll. Surprisingly, the ringing had stopped.

"Uh, fine. It's like normal." The ice seemed to be penetrating deep into her skull, twin spikes on either side. She felt they should be visible, like antennae or headlamps.

Piero knelt down and looked at her with concern. "You're sure you're okay?"

"She will be fine, thank you," said the doll. Leal couldn't help but smile.

"Was it Loll? Did you see?"

She shook her head. "It was too dark. But it must have been. Though I didn't think Abyss had ships that could come so deep into gravity . . ."

"They've had time to experiment. Probably just clamped extra engines onto something until it stayed up. But," he added, glancing up at the stone ceiling, "I doubt they can land."

"They don't have to. They can pummel the city into dust from above."

He stood up again. "I don't think they can. Or will. Listen." Now that she could hear, Leal realized that the only sounds she heard were from the people and machines here. The assault had stopped, at least for the moment.

"If it's Loll, he knows he don't have to kill us," Piero said. "He's sending a message, to you."

She had to nod. And she knew what the message was: *The door to Virga is closed.*

"He'll have spun some story about being the only survivor. I bet we're all dead, or the emissary's taken over our bodies. But would he go so far as to strand his own countrymen down on the plains?"

"If he can convince the Guard to give up on rescuing them?" Piero snorted. "In a heartbeat. Beggin' your pardon, ma'am, but I never trusted him. Why did we bring him along?"

She sighed wearily. "Because we're compassionate people, I guess. It's a flaw."

Leal stared at the polished floor, where maybe no human feet had trod before hers. She gradually became aware that the others were gathering around. She looked up and did a count; nobody else was missing, at least.

"We can't go back, can we, ma'am?"

She opened her mouth to agree, the words like stones in her heart—and then saw Keir Chen walk by in the background.

Leal stood up. "Not that way," she agreed.

"But there may be another.

"Keir!"

7

"REEL IN THE hulls!" shouted Jacoby Sarto. He turned to Antaea Argyre, his face only half-visible in the light of the few oil lanterns that hung from the ship's rigging. "I'm turning off our gravity. It's safer at this point."

She nodded. Behind Jacoby, the crew was hulking silhouettes, their half-seen hands reaching up to clutch and drag at the gravity ropes.

Antaea heard a quiet clatter—Jacoby's teeth chattering—and she smiled. "Finding winter too cold for you, Jacoby? You're from the principalities, after all." Her breath fogged as she spoke.

They stepped down from the railing as Jacoby's ship, the *Torn Page of Fate*, began to sway. Half a mile overhead, the faint lights of the ship's other hull faded in and out of view as clouds obscured it.

"Time for the winter gear, I suppose," Jacoby agreed grudgingly. "I shall be back." She watched him walk to the forward cabin, bouncing slightly in the lowering gravity. Then one of the men shouted something and she turned and squinted, watching the airman's lips move as he held up a lantern.

"Ice!"

Antaea spun around in time to see a pale boulder, smudged with darkness and the size of a house, glide by off to starboard. Jacoby had given the order to draw in the hulls just in time.

She made her way to the bow, using her hands as much as her feet for purchase. Lines creaked overhead and the men began greeting their companions in the other hull, whom they hadn't seen in days.

They would be passing more icebergs soon enough—and perhaps, other things. When the first of the vast, dark lanterns had loomed out of the darkness, Antaea had half-believed it was a mirage. She'd spent her childhood and much of her adult life in these frozen regions, far from the light of civilized suns, and there should be no man-made constructions here—other than the walls of Virga itself.

The lantern had been a hundred feet across, clenched together out of rusted girders and huge, bowed sheets of glass. Those glossy panes were dark; once this lamp might have been visible a hundred miles away. From one of its corners, thick cables twisted away into the dark. It was moored to the skin of the world somewhere, but if the photos from Jacoby's magic telescope were right, it was just an outrigger. Once, she imagined, the city the lantern pointed to had been its own beacon, a glittering jewel nestled in a forest of bergs on the world's wall. All lost to the dark now.

The cables had kept the lantern pointed in one direction. That heading had confirmed Jacoby's inertial map, and so they had followed the dark lamp's lead. The *Page* had eventually come to another lantern, then another.

Antaea's feet left the deck. She grabbed some rigging to stabilize herself as the ceiling of the second hull lowered over her. By splitting the hull of the spindle-shaped *Page* down its midline they could let the two pieces out and spin them around a common axis. The result looked a bit like two ancient gravity-bound ships of the sea, attached mast-to-mast and pinwheeling together through the sky. In this way, they had enjoyed gravity throughout most of the journey. Now, with a set of muffled thuds, the *Page*'s two halves closed over one another and what had been exposed decks were now the inside walls of a single hull.

Antaea watched as Mauven, the first mate, took reports from the men in the other hull. To her surprise, she felt a sigh of relief escape her at being enclosed by the hulls—cut off, finally, from the necessity of having to feel the wintry airs of Virga's outer reaches.

She'd hoped never to have to come here again. This place was the realm of the Virga Home Guard—of precipice moths, and strange beasts like the eaners; of icebergs that coated the world's wall like stucco; of myths and darkness and dreams. It had also been her home as a child, and for much of her adult life with the Guard.

She remembered this darkness lit with fire. Battles had been fought here in the days following an incident now referred to as the *outage*: a brief time when Candesce's shield against the monsters of the outside world had failed. Antaea and her sister, Telen, had been members of the Home Guard then, and they had joined ranks with the fearsome precipice moths to beat back an incursion that followed the start of the outage so closely that the two must have been coordinated somehow. Scheduled.

Antaea herself had been an "extraction specialist"; she specialized in rescuing people from sticky situations such as jail and imminent execution. Ironic, then, that she had ended up in a Guard prison herself after the events following the outage.

She'd become caught up in circumstances beyond her control, forced to kidnap Admiral Chaison Fanning of Slipstream under the threat that Telen would be killed if she did not. Antaea had been emotionally shattered by the discovery that her sister had died long before, and after the triumphant return of Fanning and the fall of Slipstream's pilot, she had left civilization entirely. For months she had flown through the near-infinite depths of Virga's skies, visiting countries she'd never heard of and basking in the light of nuclear-fusion suns glowing in every color of the spectrum. She'd been running as much from herself as from the Guard; but in the end, the Guard had found her.

She waited now for a few minutes until the warmth of the ship drove away the memory of ice. Then she flew to Jacoby Sarto's cabin and knocked. "Come," he said curtly.

He had taken off his jacket, and the white linen shirt emphasized his barrel chest. He held a helix glass of amber liquid, and as he saw it was her he gently lofted it over to her. Antaea took a cautious sip, and as the liquid slipped into her mouth, she almost coughed. It was rum, and very strong.

"Good, eh?" he said with a quick grin.

He'd found all sorts of ways to divert her attention over the past few days: with preparations, with plans, with the details of sailing the *Page*. Antaea had begun to relax around him, and he, it seemed, around her. She decided it was time to be blunt. "When I first asked you how an exile like yourself could afford this ship, you told me that you'd taken over Sacrus's international network after the fall of Spyre."

"Yes," he said. "What of it?"

"Your crewmen," she nodded at the door, "are little more than pirates. They're the cheapest of a bad lot. Hard to imagine you'd be buying men at bargain rates if you really had access to your country's assets."

He wound some liquor from a small cask into another glass. "I didn't lie to you," he said before taking a sip. "I *did* take over the network. Briefly. Long enough to extract those men who were loyal to me—and a goodly amount of money, to boot."

"What happened?"

Jacoby tilted his head, frowning at her. He was obviously considering how much truth to tell her—so Antaea said in exasperation, "I can hardly run out on you now. We're at the walls of the world."

He grunted, and looked down. "The Sartos were one of two great ruling families in Sacrus. The other was the Ferances, and they were in charge when Spyre broke up. My cousin, Inshiri Ferance, was the ruler of Sacrus—and never was born a more vicious, morally distorted human being."

Antaea raised an eyebrow. "Worse than Venera Fanning?"

"Venera's a good person." He shook his head. "Inshiri has . . . hobbies. That you wouldn't want me to describe. Sacrus's product—what we traded to the world—was expertise in the art of manipulating people, and nobody's better at it than Inshiri. One of her protégés was her niece, Margit, who had a little run-in with Venera and came out the worse for it. Venera got the better of Margit—but Inshiri would eat Venera alive. Maybe literally."

He said this so matter-of-factly that Antaea couldn't doubt it was true. "You're afraid of her," she observed.

"That's because I know her. And, because I know her, I didn't try to fight when she demanded that I give back control of the network. I cut my losses and ran."

"I get it," she said, nodding. "This expedition we're on—you're doing this because it's the furthest thing from your cousin's interests you could find. You're staying out of her way."

Now Jacoby sighed heavily. "Oh, if only that were true. I'd be able to sleep a lot better if it were."

"What do you mean?"

"Before Spyre fell, Inshiri made a political pact with an outsider—and by outsider, I mean an ambassador from beyond Virga. The same people—if you can call them people—who killed your sister, and who've been trying to take down Virga's defenses . . . they're supporting Inshiri now."

"Supporting—! Why didn't you tell me this before?"

He laughed. "You wouldn't have signed up if you thought I had any connection at all with Artificial Nature."

"Do you?"

He shrugged. "I met one of their ambassadors once. He made Inshiri look like an amateur, not because he enjoys torment and terror the way she does, but because he doesn't seem to consider human beings as, well, human at all. But I don't know how much involvement he and his kind have with Inshiri. All I know is that *she* has plans."

"To do what?"

"I don't know!" He glowered at her. "All I know is that this friend of yours, Leal Maspeth, has Inshiri and her friends running scared for some reason. They're so afraid of her that they're stretching the network to its breaking point, sending spies and

diplomats and courtesans to all the great nations. They're proposing alliances . . . making friends. Getting ready for something."

Antaea thought about this for a long while, and Jacoby watched
her. The creak of the hull, the rumble of the *Page*'s jets, and the
distant murmur of the crew were the only sounds.

"When were you going to tell me this?" she asked finally.

"When I had some idea of what they're up to," he said. "That
may be once we've had a look at what the Guard is doing at the
center of that ice-free area.

"Anyway," he added as he tossed off the last of the rum, "I
didn't know how far I could trust you."

"Captain! City's in sight!" Jacoby and Antaea looked at one another, then both bolted for the door.

"I TOLD YOU," Keir insisted. "That way is too dangerous."

"Did you see those missiles?" Piero Harper crossed his arms
and glared at him. "We have to get home."

The Virgans had him surrounded—or thought they did. Actually
it was Keir's second body they were looming over. He was able to
watch the confrontation from thirty feet away, in his real one.
Still, he felt the intensity of their desperation, and it struck a chord
with him.

"Where does this other door actually go?" asked Leal. "You just
said it went to Virga."

"It's a city on the Virgan side," he told them. "Beyond that, we
don't know much."

"And the inhabitants of this city? They're hostile?"

"There are no inhabitants. It's like Brink, empty, except for
guards that the virtuals put there. Those will tear you apart before
you get ten meters."

"But not," said Piero, "if we were suitably armed?"

"Sure, but I—" He'd been about to say *I'm not allowed to evolve weap-*

ons. And of course that was true; Keir had never had any means of equipping himself to fight the guardians of that gate.

Not four meters away from where his main body stood, two Edisonians were vomiting weapons onto the floor.

Piero Harper had seen this activity, and now he walked over to the members of the Renaissance who were outfitting themselves there. "Pardon, but this is our fault," he said. "There ain't no need for any of you to get hurt if they come down here."

Gallard shook his head. "We can send our second bodies in," he pointed out. "We don't die if they're destroyed. Can you say the same?"

"We're willing to take that risk. And this is our fault."

Gallard cocked his head and narrowed his eyes. He was consulting with the rest of the Renaissance. Keir tried to remain silent and small, willing them to trust the Virgans. Of course, the weapons could be remotely disabled at a command from the Renaissance; there was no danger these people could pull a coup.

Gallard gave a sharp nod. "All right. Equip yourselves. And good luck."

As the Virgans picked up the new guns, Keir broke out of the shadows and joined his second body. "Surely we can't just abandon these people?" one of the airmen was whispering.

"They'll be fine," he said. "They know the city. And now that they're forewarned, they can build weapons that can eliminate another attack from a hundred kilometers away."

Keir saw Maerta approaching from the far end of the hall. If she realized what they were planning . . . But before she got within voice distance, a deep rumble shook the floor under them.

"It's a second attack!" Suddenly everybody was running again.

Maerta turned to talk to somebody.

"This way! Now!"

Keir ran with both his bodies, hoping that in the chaos, nobody would wonder where they were going until it was too late.

AS THE SHIP'S searchlight played over the ice-choked domes and spires of the lost city, Jacoby felt an unnerving sense of doubt. The frozen towers were clutched by the fingers of a glacier that encircled most of the world. Yet on one side of the city, they stopped. The wall of the world that underlay them was swept clear here. A black plain, it stretched away into obscurity, utterly empty of any feature the eye could use to judge its scale. Two hundred miles away across that flat blackness, a hundred Home Guard ships were building a base of some kind.

These lightless windows in empty facades, the grasping iceberg wall—even to Jacoby, this place looked like nothing so much as a gateway to the afterworld.

The city had never known gravity, so its buildings grew out of Virga's wall at all angles. Black glittering windows corkscrewed around the towers and swept in spirals and whorls across the vast gray domes. Girdered docking gantries stood into the air, faint whiskers in the distance. No ships were berthed on them.

The pastel airs of his home were far away, veiled behind more than two thousand miles of air. The influence of the sun of suns itself was barely felt here; nothing grew, and not even the poorest or most desperate souls would try to subsist in this place. What mad impulse would lead a people to colonize such empty desolation?

"Captain?" said Mauven from behind him.

Jacoby blinked away his distraction. "Yes, yes," he said, then cleared his throat. "Locate an area that's clear of ice and has a view of the blank area. Forget the docking gantries, we'll lash the ship directly to whatever building we choose to camp in. That'll make for a speedy exit if we have to."

Antaea was waiting at the main hatch with a sizable crowd of airmen. They were all holding the straps of packs that were bigger than they were—carrying tents, heaters and stoves, gas supplies, guns big and small, ammunition, food supplies, extra clothing, blankets, and personal items. They looked ready to settle in for a long stay; good.

"What's that for?" Antaea pointed at two men who were struggling with a huge reel of rope.

Jacoby grunted. "When we triangulate the direction of that nest of Guard ships, we'll unreel that behind us as we go, to make a road back. We're bringing black cloth to make a blind we can hide behind when we get close enough to watch them."

"Ah. Clever."

"We wouldn't have to be clever if the Guard trusted you better," he said. "Then you could have just asked them what they were up to."

She scowled at him. With one last look at the readiness of his men, Jacoby swung out the hatch and into the darkness of the lost city.

The air smelled of stale ice. One by one the others left the warmth of the ship behind, gathering in a knot around Jacoby. There were already several crewmen out here manning searchlights and telescopes; the telescopes were aimed into the black-on-black geometry of the city, but the searchlights were roving over the tower that they had stopped next to. This was cylindrical, with one band of glass windows that spiraled around it from its base to its crown. The windows were unbroken, and Jacoby had seen no wreckage drifting in the air. Whatever ancient event had caused its citizens to abandon the place, it seemed not to have been a war.

"Find a way through that glass," he said. "If you have to break it, then break it. I want this tower thoroughly searched and secured within one hour." Then he turned to Antaea. "Can you fly a bike?"

"Mine is in the hold, remember?" He heard the eagerness in her voice, and smiled.

"We have six. Break 'em out, boys!"

The bikes were simple: wingless jet engines with a saddle and handlebars. Each was capable of accelerating hard enough to knock its rider off, and cruise fast enough that the headwind would snap your neck if you poked your head out from behind the windscreen. Jacoby had no special ambitions for them today, of course; they were convenient for reconnoitering the ruin. He and Antaea each took one, and some of his men doubled up on the other four. They growled and grumbled into the grasp of the towers, listening to echoes murmur back from dead walls.

One of the men quickly spotted a set of big square doors gaping at the base of the docking gantries. He swung his headlight in, "Sir? Can we?"

The boys were nervous, and that was making them dare one another to go farther. Well, Jacoby could play that game, too. He turned to Antaea, who expertly straddled her bike a dozen feet away. "Shall we?"

"You brought rope?" He nodded. "Then let's not waste time," she said. "Remember, the Guard may be on its way here."

They lashed the bikes at the base of the docking gantries, and left the icy air of the outdoors for even colder inside air. One of the crew whistled as he played his little magnesium lantern around the walls.

From the maw at the base of the gantries, the passages and veins of the dead city corkscrewed away like the inside of a nautilus's shell. From the first long curving chamber—like the inside of a hollow horn—large openings like the maws of great arteries branched away. Other smaller ways branched and rebranched into impossible complexity like some system of capillaries. All the open spaces were crisscrossed by cables that one could swing or jump from. Doors and windows were scattered over the walls in patterns; great dark lamps hung like dead jellyfish in the open air.

And everywhere, there was debris. It clotted the dark air, flicking into visibility as the lantern's light found it: chairs, books, picture frames, wicker storage balls full of china plates—the whole inventory of a living city, vomited into these spaces and left to drift and assemble in strange clouds. Spiderwebs and skeins of fungi held some of the collections together.

They moved in, casting their lights in side passages as they went, but keeping to the main way. This corkscrewed but maintained a steady direction, heading toward Virga's outer wall.

"I saw no town wheels," said Mauven after a long silence. "Nothing to spin at all. What did these people do for gravity? . . . Sir? What's that?"

He looked to where the first mate had aimed his lantern. At first this artery seemed like the others they'd come through—but no, Mauven had spotted something affixed to one wall. It looked like nothing so much as a great fist, made of a substance disturbingly like cuticle or horn. The thing was eight feet across, and it clenched the wall so strongly that the ancient metal surface was furled and torn.

Jacoby swung his own lantern around and looked back the way they had come. His heart sank as he saw that they'd already passed a number of the things, but had missed them in the jumble of junk that choked the round corridor.

"I hate to say this," said Antaea, "but those look like eggs."

One of Jacoby's men swore suddenly and loudly. Jacoby followed the light of another lantern and felt a prickle of shock down his spine.

The lamplight played across a galaxy of corpses, all hanging in perfect stillness in the center of the passage ahead of them.

The sight was paralyzing, but as soon as Jacoby saw how it had stunned everyone else into silence, he shook himself and forced himself to take a more dispassionate look at what they'd discovered. The bodies were frozen, many showing huge and distressing cuts and slashes; beads of frozen blood hung in the air next to them. They were dressed like airmen, in a style he hadn't seen since he last visited some of the more backward nations of Spyre.

"So now we know why no one comes here," he said heavily. "But who did this? I don't like it; we'd better get back."

They had been drifting down the middle of the corridor, but now they all tried to stop themselves by grabbing ancient pedestrian ropes or wall rings. Mauven, however, was in the middle of the way and had nothing to grab on to; he kicked his feet into the stirrups of the spring-loaded wings mounted on his back, and they flapped once. The burst of wind caught the cloud of bodies, and the corpses began to move languidly. Less massive, the frozen beads and balls of blood began colliding and spinning away. The passageway filled with a strange, rapid-fire clicking sound as a wave of movement spread through the blood cloud.

Jacoby heard himself say, "Let's get out of here," and there was no disagreement. But as they turned to go back the way they'd come, the clicking sound was suddenly drowned out by a dry crackling noise.

One of the ominous growths that lined the wall was rocking. It was thirty feet up the corridor—in between them and the way out—and just a gray outline in the penumbra of their lanterns' light. It shook again, and then with a shattering sound it burst, and bright metal and splintering crystal flew through the air. Something scrabbled out of the wrecked cocoon and in seconds the passageway was filled with screaming and the sound of gunfire.

8

MAERTA WAS WAITING in the glass-walled gallery. Both her bodies were here, and six other large multi-armed shapes hovered in the dimness behind her. "Keir, what are you doing?" she asked.

The Virgans all stopped, looking around uneasily. Keir stepped up, meeting Maerta's gaze with a level look of his own. "This is their only way out," he said defiantly. "If they can break through the cordon on the other side, they'll be home-free. The guard bots won't be able to follow them into Candesce's field."

"I understand that," she said gently. "That's not what I asked. What are *you* doing?"

He swallowed, feeling the panic starting to return. "I'm leaving," he said; then, realizing that he hadn't yet talked to the Virgans about it, he turned to them. "If you'll have me."

Leal and Piero glanced at one another. "We would," said Leal, "but it's not for us to decide."

Maerta shook her head. "It's too soon, Keir. There's no telling what will happen to you if you enter Candesce's influence before the process is complete."

"What process?" He wanted to tear at his hair in frustrated anger. "What's happening to me," he demanded, "and who did it?"

Maerta opened her mouth, closed it, and for the first time, looked genuinely distressed. "Keir," she said hesitantly. "You're . . . Dear, you're de-indexing. And . . . you did it to yourself."

De-indexing? He polled scry, but the data was inaccessible—doubtless one of Maerta's "child-proofing" locks. He shook his head in confusion.

"I don't understand! None of this is making any sense." He backed toward the glass passage that led out of the city. "But you can't keep me here. I won't stay."

"It's suicide!" Maerta appealed to the Virgans. "Hasn't he told you what's waiting on the other side of the door? Stay here, we'll keep you safe until we come up with a better option."

To Keir's relief, Leal shook her head with a frown. "I have to deliver my message. I'm overdue."

Maerta took an angry step in Keir's direction; he backed away. "What message could be so important that you'll risk your own lives to bring it back to Virga?"

Leal just stared at her in disbelief. From the look on her face, Keir expected some outburst from her, but what she said was "I've been wondering something ever since we arrived here, Maerta.

"How is that you and your people are still human?"

Maerta said nothing.

"You're not from Virga," Leal went on. "Keir said he's from a planet named Revelation. Are you as well?" Guardedly, Maerta nodded. "And is Revelation within Artificial Nature?"

Another nod.

"Yet you fled here. You're *hiding* here. From what? What happened on Revelation?"

Maerta looked at Keir, then away. Finally she said, "Revelation was . . . a little bubble of humanity in the larger universe. Outside of the arena, you understand, where truces hold between the various forces that contend inside A.N. Then . . . the balance of power shifted, several years ago. Revelation's protection evaporated. The planet . . . fell.

"We came here because Brink was an obscure place, a secret place, and right next to Virga."

"You came to study Candesce," said Leal.

"Yes. To try to find a way to defend ourselves."

"Then let us go," Leal commanded, "because you are not the only ones with this goal. And if *I* succeed, *I* may be able to give you direct access to Candesce, to study it from the inside. —And besides," she added, "if you can rescue the rest of our people from the plains below the city, they can stop this assault. Half of them are Home Guard people, anyway; if the others try to land they'll put a stop to whatever lies Loll's told to incite them. Take care of them, and I promise you, we will take care of Keir Chen."

Maerta looked at Keir. Again he held her gaze defiantly. Her shoulders slumped. "Then go," she said. "And yes, Leal, we'll find your men."

Keir turned and, without a look back, raced up the crystal passage that led from Aethyr, Brink, and Complication Hall to Virga.

FOR A FEW minutes, Leal thought they would make it. Yet as the mysterious blockhouse that hung in the precise black between the worlds came nearer, she heard muttering among her companions; Piero and the other men were slowing. Leal peered ahead, and she, too, faltered.

John Tarvey was waiting for them at the end of the crystal tunnel.

The lads were drawing their guns, both the ones they'd brought and the new ones Keir Chen's people had made for them. Tarvey just stood there, his hands up and his face half-turned aside—not a gesture of surrender, but a pose that said *hear me out*.

Keir had come abreast of Leal and now he sent her an uneasy frown. She guessed what he was thinking. They could go back; he could summon his people to help. She shook her head minutely. If the firepower they had with them wasn't sufficient to deal with this thing that had taken on the shape of her friend, whatever force would be enough might also be enough to shatter the crystal tube, and kill them all through exposure to the vacuum.

She brought her party to a halt about thirty feet from the creature. "We shot you before," she shouted. "What makes you think we won't do it again?"

"I'm absolutely sure you will," he said. Still with his hands up, he continued, "But I'm not out to stop you. I can help."

The lads exchanged suspicious glances; then their eyes turned to Leal. She moistened her lips and thought about what to say. "What do you mean?" was all she could finally summon.

"We can end that primitive bombardment that's threatening your friends," said Tarvey. "It's just chemical weapons, after all— primitive airships. They could be swept aside in seconds. All I have to do is make the call."

"Make the call?" She shook her head, uncomprehending. "To who? Who's this 'we' you're talking about? I thought *we* were your friends."

A look of distress flickered across his face then, to be quickly erased by the uncanny serenity that was so unlike the John Tarvey she knew. "You know us as the virtuals," he said. "We're a vast and ancient civilization—the inheritors of humanity's original spark of consciousness. And we want to help you."

"We don't want your help!" shouted Piero Harper. He raised his pistol. "Stand aside. Now!"

Leal touched her hand to Piero's wrist. "Wait," she said. "Tarvey, we don't need the help of the virtuals right now. But we could use *your* help."

Tarvey tilted his head to one side, minutely. "What?" he asked.

"You said that all you have to do is make the call." She had some notion of what that meant: there had been telephone stations on some street corners in Sere. You could pay the vendor and shout into the staticky roar of the handset, and with luck make out the gist of what the person on the other end was saying. Here, where Candesce's influence was barely felt, such long-distance communication must be easy. "Do you mean to say that you *haven't* yet told this civilization of yours what's happening here?"

Now it was Tarvey's turn to look suspicious. "They know I've been following you. They know about Brink."

"But do they know about this?" She nodded at the blockhouse behind him.

Tarvey looked aloof. "I can't find any record of this door, but—"

"Don't. In the name of the friendship we had, John, I beg this of you. If it's in your power to hide this door from your . . . friends . . . if you can do that, then you can help. You. Not Artificial Nature, John. You."

He slowly lowered his chin, and she could see he was troubled. "All I want," he said, "is that you not die. That we can be . . . together."

Leal felt a prickle down the back of her neck at the sudden realization of what he was offering. When John said *not die*, he meant *never die*. —And that would have been the most wonderful of offers she could ever have heard, were it not for one thing: his reasons.

"John," she said with quiet sadness, "I can't help you now."

He looked up again, and she saw it in his eyes: the prospect of an eternity outside of Virga, of outliving his friends, his family, his country and even the language of his birth. The loneliness of the image made her shudder. If such loneliness was possible, Leal didn't want to be immortal.

"Please," she said again. "Do this for us. For what you once were. And for what we still are."

John Tarvey crossed his arms and, with the slightest push of his toe against the crystal, drifted to the side. Leal and her lads filed past him, until all that was left to him was silence.

IT LOOKED LIKE nothing so much as a bush made of knives. It even shone as if it were made of metal, but it moved as though alive—and as it advanced on Jacoby and his men, its blades fanned open like deadly flowers.

Jacoby grabbed a pedestrian rope and drew his sword. "Maybe

we can . . ." But his men were diving away through the bodies; Antaea looked at them, looked at Jacoby, shrugged; and followed the others. To buy time, Jacoby drew his pistol and fired it at the center of the shapeless jagged thing that was advancing on him.

Jacoby's shot struck the knife thing in its knotted metal heart, but it simply pulsed like a steel jellyfish, jetting backward, then opened up multiple arms and came on.

A jumble of bodies and whirling lanterns ricocheted down the passage. His men were shouting to one another and somebody kept on firing, the bullets narrowly missing Jacoby as he struggled to catch up. Behind them, loud cracking noises signaled the birth of more of the dagger-balls.

In the tangle of the corridor Jacoby had to jump from rope to rope, or bounce his shoulder or hip off the walls, then plow through clouds of debris. The dagger-balls simply cut through the lines and batted any obstacles aside.

"Wait, maybe they're friendly!" Antaea shouted, then she laughed wildly. But she was hanging back, waiting for Jacoby. "Come on!" She let go of the lantern she was holding and extended a hand to Jacoby. The lantern spun lazily, sweeping shadows across the bladed thing on Jacoby's heels. They weren't going to get away from it.

In desperation he kicked the lantern. It sailed straight into the snicking complex of blades and exploded. He and Antaea dove away from it; they'd made several jumps from rope to rope before Jacoby realized that the burning thing wasn't following.

"Hold." He grabbed a line to steady himself and looked back. The dagger-ball hovered motionless in the center of the passage, its brothers crowded behind it but unable to get past. "Did we kill it?"

Antaea shook her head. "I think it's too clever for that. Look!"

In zero gravity, fire needed moving air to sustain it. Even as Jacoby realized what the dagger-ball was doing, the globe of flame enveloping it exhausted the available oxygen, flickered, and went out.

"Hell!" They fled as the monsters surged forward again.

A hundred feet on and Mauven had stopped dead. He was waving his lantern in frantic puzzlement at a branching of the passage. "Which way?" Antaea shouted.

Jacoby cursed again. "Just pick one!" It was too late as scything blades filled the air between them. "Fall back!" he shouted, but Desick, his boatswain, drew his sword and leaped at a monster. Desick had fought in three wars and was the best swordsman on the *Page*, but he couldn't parry the six blades that found him and he tumbled backward, silent and trailing red beads.

The dagger-balls had split the party, with Jacoby, Mauven, and Antaea on one side and the others on the other. There was a passage open to each group, so Jacoby yelled "Go!" across the bladed air and dragged Antaea with him into the dark way.

"MY MIND WON'T be able to go with you." It was the little golden doll speaking from its perch on Maspeth's shoulder. "The interference from Candesce will drive me mad again."

Maspeth nodded. "We knew you'd have to leave us before we got home. I guess it's good-bye?"

"I can supplement these weapons so that they are more effective," it said. "Would that be helpful?"

"Oh!" She smiled, almost bashfully. "That's a great idea."

"Ach! Come on, then," said Piero Harper. "Everybody up and at 'em." He turned to Keir. "By your leave, sir, show us the way to Virga." Keir nodded; his second body was already on its way to the door. "Come on."

"What are those?" Harper was pointing at the faint glitter of the distant ships that sat silently in the space just outside Virga's hull.

"Keir called it an armada," said Maspeth. "I believe that is what you came to warn us about," she added, speaking to the doll.

Keir saw it nod. "Those ships would be powerless inside Virga. Candesce's suppression field is fatal to the technologies they rely on. They're waiting for the field to fail, as it did a couple of years ago."

"Gods, I hope Hayden never hears about this," she muttered.

They had been bounding along the transparent bridge tube that led to the place Keir called the Glass Jaw. It had been very difficult to discern that they were making any headway these last several minutes; but now a long shape began to resolve out of the darkness ahead. The bridge terminated in the side of this.

"That's where we're going," he said. "The door to Virga."

Harper frowned. "Doesn't look like much. It's not even connected to Virga, I can see that. Is there another bridge on the other side?"

"Can't be," said Leal. "We're turning, Virga is not. How would any sort of bridge connect a still object to a moving one?" She turned to Keir. "What's this all about?"

"There's no bridge," he said quickly, "it's something else. You'll see when we get there."

"What do you mean?" she said, suddenly suspicious.

"It's not like any door you've ever seen."

What they had come to was a vast blockhouse, forbidding and dark, its metal sides devoid of windows or running light. The whole structure—which must have been two thousand feet long and half that in height—hung at the bottom of a set of half-visible gnarled buttresses that must have been dozens of miles long. They rose up into dizzying perspective, ultimately disappearing within the chaos of machinery that sealed Virga to Aethyr and allowed one of those worlds to turn against the other.

"It's like a big version of Complication Hall," one of the airmen said about that ceiling, just before they passed through the round entrance leading into the blockhouse and what little pale light there was vanished.

There was a pause while lamps were switched on. Keir took the opportunity to send his dragonflies ahead and make sure that everything was normal in the Jaw room. Then he said, "This way," and led them past side passages and rooms he'd never explored to Virga's door.

Various hulking robot forms waited in the darkness. Some of these were guardians, Keir knew, heavily armed and keyed to wake once an hour. The rest of the bots were sensing devices the Renaissance was preparing to send through the Jaw. Scry showed all of this detail, but of course the Virgans couldn't see it. "This is it?" somebody muttered as flashlight beams roved to and fro. "It looks like a theater."

"Except they won't be puttin' any plays on in this one," said Harper. As Keir knew, there was no stage, nor any screen facing those tall seats—just a blank wall. Many of the seats had been torn out of the metal flooring and now lay jumbled against their neighbors or broken against the back wall. The remainder looked as though they'd once been deeply padded, but the material was torn out in clumps and strewn about the floor. "Looks like some angry monster chewed on these," Piero joked.

"That's about right," Keir agreed. They all looked at him.

"Sometimes things come through," he explained, "from the Virga side. Agents of the virtuals, sort of advance scouts for the armada you saw a minute ago. They're barely able to survive Candesce's radiation, and it makes 'em a bit rabid. These bots put them down when they climb through."

"Climb through," said Leal. "From where?"

Keir pointed at another door on the opposite side of the chamber. "When this door is open, that door is closed, and vice versa." He checked his scry; it was almost time. "We've got about ten minutes. We have to check these chairs, make sure that there's enough secure ones for all of us. What we're going to do is sit down in them and wait."

"And then?" Harper asked.

"There's two cities, one on the Virga side and this one on our side. Each has a room like this. The rooms can move. In about ten minutes the cities are going to exchange their rooms."

Harper looked puzzled. "But—we're turning; compared to Virga, this whole city is going . . ."

"About four hundred miles per hour," Keir admitted. "Which is why you'd better hope that these seats can withstand the strain when we're suddenly accelerated up to speed."

He put his head back against the rusted metal seat frame and waited. That was enough time for him to wonder about what he was about to lose—not metaphorically, but literally—by entering Virga. His dragonflies were perched about the room. He'd had them to see with for most of his life. They were as much a part of him as his two native-born eyes.

He turned his head to the left, saw Leal Maspeth. She raised one hand to her shoulder, briefly touching the chest of the little doll on her shoulder. Did she feel the same as him?

The silence was absolute, and it stretched out for one minute, then another. Then somebody giggled. "Is anybody else starting to feel foolish?"

Something hit the back of Keir's chair. The room didn't seem to be moving but he was suddenly being crushed into the seat with tremendous force. A buzzing vibration rolled in waves through him from its metal frame.

He heard a sharp crack and a shout, then a tumbling crashing noise as one of the other chairs flew backward. Then, with shocking suddenness, the pressure disappeared. Keir had been bracing his body against it and in the sudden absence he flew forward out of his chair.

The others were doing the same in a chaos of flailing limbs and shouts. They were weightless—naturally, he'd known they would be, but it still felt like falling.

Part of that feeling was visual: his dragonflies were tumbling to the back wall, and as they fell, their vision went out. He could see one twirling toward him and watched himself reach out and grab it from the air.

There was silence, and in the feeling of falling, some steadiness. Things began to drift.

Several loud bangs rang out, shocking and sudden in the darkness. Keir couldn't see, couldn't feel his dragonflies at all anymore. "Who's shooting?" shouted Piero Harper.

"Not us! It's coming from there!"

Keir tried to look around himself, failed, and then forced his head and eyes to turn. It was an unfamiliar gesture, the sort of movement you reserved for those times when you wanted to make eye contact with people you were speaking to. There were the other chairs, a cloud of silhouetted people and weaving flashlight beams—and orange flashes from the black rectangle of the room's suddenly open other door.

"We're in Virga!" he shouted—maybe unnecessarily, maybe they knew it better than he—but something was out there.

"Quiet!" It was Harper again, and as the clamor of voices fell away Keir heard others shouting—and someone screamed.

Then someone appeared in the dark doorway, for just a moment, but fully lit by flashlight beam. Without the competing vision of his dragonflies, untagged by distracting scry, her image burned into Keir's mind:

An oval face, its fine, perfect features dominated by two gigantic eyes. The face framed by hair in a black pageboy cut that held its shape even in freefall. Her garb, black leather that made her limbs disappear—though he could see her toes sticking out of the half-shoes she wore. She was staring straight at him, lips in an O of surprise.

Something flashed over her shoulder and she whirled, raising something—a sword—and sparks flew as it struck something. The force of the blow knocked her right through the doorway.

The thing that tried to follow her was made entirely of metal. Lacking any tags or annotations, it was all movement and eerily smooth metallic sheen. The absence of any tags made Keir's hackles rise—as if the thing had moved in some perfect silence, as though it had stolen his ability to understand what it was. All knives, saws, and swords, it gripped the doorjamb with three of four bladed limbs and twisted this way and that as if looking for something.

It had struck at the woman's spine but the blow had been absorbed by the battered leather satchel slung over her shoulder.

The others seemed paralyzed at the sight of the dagger-thing, but the sheer terror of seeing an untagged machine moving on its own made Keir pull out the weapon the Edisonians had built. He'd had no time to learn how it worked, but it had been evolved for human use and it felt satisfyingly solid in his arms. His finger found a trigger right where one should be, and he pulled it.

The *bang!* was deafening. He was suddenly blind in a whole new way. Afterimage lozenges were smeared across his vision and so he groped for the sight of his dragonflies, but they weren't there. Suddenly panicked, he kicked away from the doorway and the thing that had been there.

"Help us!" It was the woman. He heard Harper shout something, then a tumble of motion around him. The shocking report of the new guns crashed and roared through the room—but now, it was coming from beyond the door.

"Are you okay?" Long fingers touched his hand, then his face. He flinched.

"Just the flash. I'll be all right." He blinked at her, saw a jacketed shoulder and pale fingers around the fading afterimage. The smear of light was oddly reassuring; it made her look as if she were tagged in some way that he couldn't quite focus on. "Did I get it?"

She laughed, a bit wildly. "It's not there anymore, if that's what you mean."

Her accent was thick from the centuries of Virga's isolation. She smelled of sweat and leather and lamp oil. "Can you shoot?" she said suddenly. "If not, give me the gun."

He squinted, shook his head, gave up, and handed it to her. "Careful," he said. "It's a lot more powerful than you're probably used to."

"I saw," she said. "Don't worry, I'm experienced with firearms."

He could see well enough to show her its operation and did so; then they pulled themselves through the doorway and into a rapidly subsiding firefight.

Knotted in the center of a long gallery was a large group of Virgans, all dressed in piratical glory compared with Keir's utilitarian coverall. They were firing enthusiastically into a cloud of knife-drones, splintering and exploding them. The drones responded by whirling at high speed and throwing blades at the men; Keir saw that several were pulling shrapnel out of their forearms or hips. Several more were drifting, ominously still.

The leather-clad woman aimed and fired. Keir shut his eyes just in time. She barked in triumph and aimed again. The new guns were making quick work of the drones, and quite suddenly they were all ruined—the last one sparking from multiple gunshots as it tumbled away.

There was silence, then a ragged cheer.

The woman turned to Keir. "Where did you come from? We couldn't get the other door open."

"It was locked on your side," he said. It would just take too long to explain what was beyond it. "But what are you—" He stopped, and so did she, with a laugh: they'd spoken simultaneously.

"—doing here?" he said. "Mine's a long story. What about yours?"

She tilted her head, considering. "Long," she said. "Forget it. Can we go your way?"

"The door won't open again for another hour," he said. "I don't think those drones will leave us alone that long."

A man's voice, clear and sharp, cut through the gabble of voices. "Listen up! Who are we all? There's two groups here. Will somebody from each introduce themselves?"

Everybody looked at the man who'd spoken. He bowed in mid-air. "I'm Jacoby Sarto of Sacrus. We're docked at the edge of the city. We're here on . . . Home Guard business."

Leal moved out of the doorway. "I'm Leal Maspeth of Abyss," she said. "We—"

"*Leal?*" The huge-eyed woman gave a shriek. "It is you!"

"What—? A-Antaea?"

Suddenly they were hugging, laughing wildly, while the men all looked at one another in confusion. Keir shrugged at the leonine Jacoby Sarto, who scowled in return.

"I got your letter," Antaea was saying. "We came to find you!"

"Among other things," Sarto pointed out.

"But I never in a million years would have expected to find you fighting monsters in a . . . a place like this! How did you get here?"

Now Leal's expression became cautious. "It's a very long story," she said. "But what it boils down to is, I'm here with a message for the people of Virga, and these men have risked their lives to help me bring it here."

"I . . . see." Antaea and Jacoby Sarto exchanged a look, and then so did Leal and Piero Harper. This bizarre tension was interrupted as someone shouted, "Incoming!"

Flashlights swirled around and their light pinioned a door on the far wall of the gallery. The three men who'd suddenly appeared there blinked at the lights. "Uh . . . Captain Sarto?" one of them said hesitantly.

Sarto laughed. "You made it!"

"Yes, but those things're right behind us, sir."

"Then we'd best save the stories for later," said Sarto. "Who's got a clear idea of how to get out of here?"

One of Sarto's men put up his hand. "I do."

"Come on, then. Let's form up. We need one of those special guns you brought," Sarto said to Leal, "aimed at each of the six directions. We'll bunch up so they can't cut us off from each other like last time. Is everybody ready?"

"What about . . ." Two of Sarto's men were cradling the bodies of their dead comrades.

"Bring them, then," said Sarto brusquely. "But don't fall behind."

Leal Maspeth looked around until she spotted Keir, then she flew over. "Are you sure you want to come?" she asked. "You still have time to turn and go back."

He hesitated. The plan had made so much sense just a few hours ago—but that had been before his dragonflies had died and left him half-blind. "I don't know what to—" He shook himself. "Seems I have no choice but to go with you. If you'll have me."

"Of course, but how are you going to get home again?"

He shuddered. "Brink's not home."

"Let's go!" shouted Sarto. The big-eyed woman—Antaea—was leading an unruly flock toward one of the black entrances. He should really get the weapon back; on the other hand, he'd never fired any sort of gun before today. Maybe it would do more good in her hands.

He and Leal followed the rest. Two of her people took up the rear, one moving forward, the other clutching the back of the first one's belt. He let his comrade tow him while he faced backward. "Pull me like that?" Leal asked Keir.

Keir wanted to say no—he couldn't see properly, freefall was making him nauseous, and there weren't even any scry tags on the people or things here—but in the end he nodded. It would be better to let Leal watch for danger coming up from behind, because he was beginning to doubt whether he would be able to see it if it came. He would just keep his two remaining eyes fixed on the backs of the people ahead of him.

What followed was chaotic and terrifying and seemed to go on forever. They bounced, toppled, and flew up small passages like capillaries, large ones like arteries. Hissing whispering things awoke as they passed, and the darkness behind filled with the angry drone of pursuit. Startled shouts and gunshots erupted at random moments; once, everything dissolved into screaming and orange flashes and bangs for long minutes, and then Leal's hand found Keir's wrist again and pulled him onward.

He did his best. He'd expected to lose his extra senses in Virga; it was just that he hadn't counted on the terrible feeling of help-lessness that came with that loss.

His scry had gone out for the first time in his life, and too late he was realizing that he'd relied on it far more than he'd known. Half-blind, half-deaf, he held the hand of a stranger as they fled together through a city of monsters.

Only when the pursuit had faded behind them did he begin to feel the sharp pain in his left hand and realize he was tightly clutching something in it. He raised it in a stray beam of lantern light, and stiffly opened his fingers.

One of his dragonflies nestled, half-crushed in his palm. Suddenly it seemed infinitely precious and he regretted leaving its brothers behind. He tenderly teased it out, and slipped it inside the pocket of his coat.

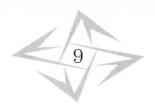

9

THE ICE-CHOKED CITY of Serenity fell behind, and with it the constant edge of anxiety that had become so familiar to Leal that she hardly knew it was there anymore. In the first minutes of the flight she felt a huge *lifting away*, as though some immense weight had lain on her heart; over the next hours that lifting continued, combined with a growing revelation that really, they were safe.

In the little hold where the refugees from Aethyr had been put, Leal watched her lads celebrate with something like maternal affection. Their initial backslapping and cheering had faded to grins, but now they were starting to tell each other stories about the ordeal they'd been through together—stories they all knew, but were delighted to hear again.

The biggest surprise was Piero, whom Leal had known for a few months now. She'd met him on Hayden Griffin's yacht, one black-skyed day when they'd been beset by monsters in the dark, and she'd told him a ghost story to distract them all. Now he was surprising her. "It's not so much that I think she'll be frantic with worry," he said about the wife Leal hadn't known he had, "as it's that I'm afraid she'll have remarried by the time I get back to her."

The other lads variously grumbled and joked at that; one smacked Piero lightly on the back of the head and said, "As it is, she's not going to recognize you with all that weight you've lost." They all laughed—except for Keir Chen, who was half-curled into a silent ball on the edge of the discussion.

Piero pressed his stomach with tentative fingers. "It's muscle," he protested; but Leal had turned away from the discussion. One of the ship's crew had appeared at the edge of the lantern light and was gesturing for her to follow him. Harper flew over to perch next to her. He looked where she was gazing, and nodded.

"If this Antaea Argyre really has had some kind of falling-out with the Guard," he said, "then she may not take us to them."

"All I can do is ask," said Leal. She was still astonished that her halfhearted appeal to Antaea had actually been answered. The Guard had accepted the letter from Leal, but had made it very plain that they had little intention of bringing it to Antaea herself, since they considered her a traitor.

Leal shook her head. "Maybe she'll remember my friendship with her sister." She kicked off lightly and, following the airman who'd come for her, sailed up the center of the ship.

She was traveling the length of two decks that visually made a floor and ceiling, but which were both rigged as floors. The ship must split lengthwise, probably so the two sections could spin around a common center for gravity. The portholes were open, letting in cold air and revealing only blackness. Leal knew the ship was running at speed with its headlights poking as far ahead into the darkness as they could—but that was not far, and their airspeed was not great.

"Haul it in, boys!" Up ahead, one of the big starboard hatches was open. Some airmen were pulling on a rope, and to Leal's shock a dagger-ball bounced into the ship. It was securely netted and unmoving, but still her hackles rose at the sight of it.

The older man, Jacoby Santo, was there, directing the airmen. "It's playing dead or something," he said. "Better clip those knives just in case."

Leal saw an opening. "Not playing dead," she said as she flew over. "Really dead—or dormant, at best. Where did you find it?"

"Clutching the hull with a death grip," said an airman, making a clawing shape with his own hands. "Gave me the fright of my life when I saw it."

The commander looked at Leal again, then frowned at the airman she had been following. "Where were you taking her?" he asked the man.

"Lady's orders."

"I see." He drifted himself over and stuck out his hand for Leal to shake. "Jacoby Sarto. Welcome to my ship, the *Torn Page of Fate*."

"Leal Maspeth. My men and I are very grateful that we met you, Captain Sarto. I didn't relish the notion of fighting our way out of the city on our own."

"Hmmpf," he said. "Neither did we. The thanks go both ways." Sarto glowered at the knife-ball. "It's dead, you say? Why?"

"Because we're well inside the walls of Virga now. Under the spell of the sun of suns, you might say."

To her surprise he nodded as if this made perfect sense to him. "So you know something about these beasts."

Leal half-smiled. "I've recently become something of an expert in monsters."

Sarto rubbed his chin, then flicked a hand at the men who were securing the dead dagger-ball. "Carry on. You," he said to the airman who'd been guiding Leal, "back to your duties. I'll take it from here." He began rappelling his way up the ship's central core, slowly enough that she could fall in beside him.

"So you know Antaea Argyre," he said. Leal nodded.

"It's been many years," she admitted. "But tell me, how did you come to find me?"

"We followed the trail," he said, "of a man you may know."

She laughed grimly. "Loll!"

They had come to a set of tiny cabins built under the forward compartment. Sarto rapped on one door, and Leal heard Antaea's voice say something muffled. Sarto opened it.

The moment was strangely powerful, because in this lantern light, cleaned up and dressed in something like her old style, Antaea looked much as she had back in Leal's college days. For a moment their surroundings vanished and Leal saw her leaning on the doorjamb of the tiny apartment her sister had shared with Leal.

Always the active one, Antaea rarely sat down, often paced, usually with a bottle in one hand. Her sister, more quiet but more self-assured, would interrupt the stream of Antaea's monologues to divert its direction, but rarely to stop it.

Antaea blinked, said nothing, and then unexpectedly she opened her arms. "Oh, Leal," she said, her voice cracking, "she's dead."

Leal hugged her. "I know," she murmured, but really, until that moment, Telen's death had just been a fact to her, a piece of news from a distant land that she'd thought about, but not really come to grips with. Her old life had been busy and selfish. But Antaea had something of Telen's scent to her and suddenly it was real: Leal found herself blinking away tears.

"How did you find me?" asked Leal as she disengaged herself. Suddenly awkward, Antaea floated back to the hammock that stretched from floor to ceiling. She steadied herself against the empty rope cocoon and shrugged.

"Eustace Loll," she said. "He made something of a splash when he returned to Sere, calling up the navy and Guard to help him with something. We were both there for"—she shot Sarto a look—"different reasons. Jacoby here had heard of Serenity, and we thought he'd come from there."

"And you?" asked Sarto. "What in the world were you doing in that hellhole?"

"Just passing through. On my way to speak to the Guard, actually," she said.

Antaea and Jacoby exchanged another glance, and Leal scowled in exasperation. "I'm a bit tired of politics," she said. "My message is too important to be restricted to just one audience. I came to deliver it to the Guard because they seemed most likely to be able to act on it, but after they bombed Brink I'm not so sure."

"Bombed Brink?" said Antaea.

"What message?" said Sarto.

She decided that describing Brink would just take too long. "A message from some of the people who live outside of Virga," said

Leal, "and it's simple: Stop bickering amongst yourselves and form a united front, or Virga will be destroyed—probably within the year."

She'd seen this reaction in Hayden Griffin's airmen: both stared at her for a moment in shock, then simultaneously opened their mouths to argue or question. Leal held up her hand and turned her head away. "No," she said. "I'm tired of explaining myself to gatekeepers. The Guard are swarming around the door to Aethyr because of me and my message. A thousand ships are mustered because all they know is that Virga is threatened. I alone have the answer to their panic."

She'd allowed some of her impatience to creep into her voice and stance, and she could see they were both taken aback by that sudden hint of ferocity.

Jacoby Sarto raised an eyebrow. "So what would you have of us?" he asked with heavy irony. "That we deliver you to the Guard? The legends say they're based at the Gates of Virga." Antaea nodded as if this were common knowledge.

"That was my original plan," Leal admitted. "But on our way here I thought about it, and I don't believe they'll listen to me now. My intention was to confront them with the witnesses who accompanied me up from the plains of Aethyr, but Eustace Loll was one of those men, and he's had plenty of time now to poison them with lies. If we go to the Gates, I'll just be arrested again and my message will never reach the ears of those who need to hear it."

Sarto's ironic look slipped as he saw that she was dead serious. "You say that you alone have the answer to their panic. But," he pointed out, "I can't see that you've brought any proof with you. Or have you?"

Bitterly, she shook her head. "The Guard knows much of what happened, and with my witnesses I might have convinced them—if Eustace Loll hadn't gotten to them first. No, I have no direct proof of my claims."

"Then why should any of us believe you?"

"Oh, you don't have to," she said with a grim smile. "Nobody has to, at this point. But I do have a way of getting all the proof I need, if you'll drop me and my men at a particular port."

"And where would that be?" asked Sarto.

Leal looked at Antaea. "I need to talk to a man I think you know," she said. "Bring me to the city of Rush, in the nation of Slipstream, that I may speak to Admiral Chaison Fanning."

After Antaea flinched back and swore, Leal said again, "Take me to him.

"And then things will start to happen."

Part Two | THE CHEETAH AND THE TREE

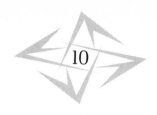

10

"WHAT ARE YOU doing?"

Keir had to turn his head to see who'd spoken. It was Leal Maspeth, but she seemed somehow transformed—younger. Part of that was freefall, he knew, which took years off you. But she seemed radiant from some other cause as well. A glance around was all it took to know what that was.

He shifted his position slightly, allowing her to climb onto the mast beside him. "I feel less blind out here," he said in answer to her question. He'd been riding on the outside of the ship for the past hour, as light slowly emerged from the dark sky ahead of them.

He opened his hands to show her what he'd been cupping in the ship's headwind. "A dragonfly?" she asked.

He nodded.

Inside the ship he was constantly reminded of the vision he now lacked. He kept hitting his head on unexpected obstacles, and rapping his knuckles on invisible objects in the dimness. It was upsetting. So he'd come out here.

He pointed past the gray prow of the ship, to where a triangle of mauve and peach-colored sky beckoned past flocks of black cloud. "What is that?"

"That," she said, obviously savoring the sight, "is a *country*."

"Your country?"

She shook her head. "My country has no sun. No—that should be Slipstream, in the Hadley cell called Meridian."

Keir realized he'd been waiting for something to happen—waiting for his scry to update him on her recent activities; her alliances and distances within the group. But the intricate small-group politics of the Renaissance didn't exist in Virga. Some other kind of complexity did, and he couldn't figure out how it worked.

"So . . . how are you?"

His question sounded utterly inane to his own ears, and it must have to her as well, because she simply smiled and said, "Antaea said this was yours."

She handed him the gun he'd given Argyre. As he took it from Leal she gripped the spar between her feet and casually, gracefully back-flipped through the ship's open hatch and out of sight.

"Oh, but I—" *Don't need it.* He sat there dumbly holding the weapon for a few seconds. There was no helpful advice from his scry about what she'd really wanted, or what he should do. After an awkward pause he clipped the gun onto his belt and turned back to the view.

Had he not been half-blind already, he surely would have retreated inside soon after, because as the light welled up the terrifying scale of this ocean of air became visible. Keir couldn't remember much about his life before Brink, but he knew he'd grown up on a planet. He was used to skies that had, if not a visible boundary, at least some end to their cloudscapes. He was used to sky being framed by ground. In Virga there was only an infinity of cloudscapes spreading to all directions—tolerable, when it was dark, but a staggering assault on the imagination when its vast depths were sketched by light. It was exhilarating, magnificent, and far too big to take in no matter how much he stared.

The ship wove its way between mountain-sized clouds, making a steady sixty or eighty kilometers per hour. As it did the light from ahead brightened, becoming a broad region of canary-yellow sky cupping an intense red dot at its center. Though it must be hundreds of kilometers away, that red dot was the visible radiance of a man-made sun, a nuclear-fusion reactor of mightily primitive but practical design. This eternally falling drop of air, this world of Virga, was clouded with such suns—hundreds of them. Keir had never seen one with his own eyes, for bright as they were, the devices could only carve small spheres of day out of the dark. —With one exception, of course. Candesce, the sun of suns, immolated the whole middle space of Virga, and dozens of civilizations orbited it like birds wheeling around a lighthouse.

Far to the right was another crimson dot, this one smaller—another nation, remote, half-eclipsed by its neighbor.

Long minutes passed and Leal didn't return. Keir watched the dawn open like a flower, a sun not rising but emerging. And with it, at last, came details.

First to become clear were this nation's heavy industries. They skimmed the shell of the spherical domain carved by the light: factories, complicated snarls of metal like vast seashells gouting smoke and grit and poisonous clouds into the dark. Any farther out, and these places stood to lose sight of their sun altogether—and could thus be doomed to wander the blackness unless by luck they found another country. Any further in, and they would pollute the agricultural spheres.

These came next as the Page sailed on—as the light became brighter, Keir saw that some of the clouds around him were not white, but green. On an individual basis those specks were potato and corn, rice and millet and oats; gathered together in wave upon wave of ever-greater scale, they became cirrus and cumulus, nimbus and stratus—entire clouds of life.

The Page passed a streamer of tomatoes. Keir watched a small knot of them sail by, five plants with their roots tangled around a common clod of dirt. Aphids and midges swarmed around the little world, and some sort of songbird trilled from inside the foliage.

They passed schools of giant, fire-colored fish that showed obvious signs of being genetically engineered: their fins were huge, like diaphanous wings, and they had eyelids; one flew next to Keir for a long minute, blinking at him dumbly, before turning back to its fellows.

He'd heard that many of the people who lived in Virga were unaware their world was artificial. He found this hard to believe.

In the agricultural sphere, the sky shaded from deep blue behind the ship to bright yellow ahead; the predominant color was a kind of mauve. Here were the first wheeled towns he'd seen, and they were as pretty and delicate as he'd imagined they would be. They appeared first as faint circles drawn on the sky, then gradually resolved into wood-and-rope hoops, very thin and fragile, their narrow inside surfaces crowded with buildings. Like the tomato plants, they were surrounded by swarming life, in this case, ships, winged human figures, and drifting cargo nets. He saw flights of saddled dolphins, these not genetically engineered but wearing fin extenders.

Inside the thick shell of farming communities was another volume of sky, this one speckled with towns and private dwellings in all shapes and sizes. Here the air was blue, the clouds white and the sunlight yellow. The Page passed double-hulled, majestically spinning yacht-houses that defied definition as either building or vehicle.

Now that the agricultural clouds no longer occluded the view, Keir could see something strange about the sky ahead. Contrails pierced the vista like the threads of some gigantic spiderweb. Some converged on the sun whose light now felt hot on Keir's face—but the vast majority drew lines at right angles to it. Squinting, he saw that dozens—maybe hundreds—of giant ships were jetting in the direction of that other sun he'd spotted earlier. Alerted to the movement, he could now see that some of the town wheels were inching in that direction, too—rolling, as it were, through the sky. He squinted, holding up his hand to block the light, and thus caught his first glimpse of the city of Rush.

Rush's iron town wheels spun in quartets, each mile-wide circle bannered like a twirling paper lantern. The city hovered in the long shadow cast by a forested asteroid, in white, water-saturated air that trembled with heat. Here the ships and jets and flying contraptions flocked in the thousands, contrails and rope roads stitched the air, and the mansions of the wealthy and powerful flocked as thickly as the fish had earlier.

He heard a banging sound and turned to see a hatch opening on the *Page*'s hull. Leal Maspeth's people started boiling out, laughing and turning their faces to the light with grins of relief and pleasure; and when one of them swore, pointed, and shouted something to the others, they suddenly began cheering as one.

Maspeth's head poked out after them. She appeared as puzzled as Keir by the vision of her men shrieking and howling. One of them bounced right off the hull in his excitement and only the quick reflexes of a friend kept him from sailing off into the sky.

Keir hand-walked toward them along the netting draped on the side of the ship. Maspeth's friend Piero Harper had appeared now, and he, too, was grinning like a fool.

Keir stopped next to Leal, who nodded coolly at him, as if this were their first meeting today. One of her eyebrows was cocked in bemusement. "They're happy to be home?" asked Keir.

"This isn't their home," she said. "These men are from Aerie; this country is Slipstream."

"It's today! It's today!" one of the airmen was shouting. Another was weeping openly, his tears flicking away like jewels in the ship's headwind. "We made it in time!"

Harper laughed. "Freedom Day!" he shouted. "We did it!"

Leal's eyes lit with understanding. "Oh! Look!" Keir followed her pointing finger.

Now he saw that there were two colors of banner and crest on the airships and town wheels. Those of Rush were gold and red. On the ships that were now arrowing toward that distant second sun, the crests were green.

"Slipstream invaded and conquered Aerie a decade ago," Leal said to Keir. "They destroyed Aerie's sun so that Aerie's people would become utterly dependent on them. It was the Pilot of Slipstream who gave the orders, and no one could oppose him at the time.

"These men," she gestured at Harper and the others, "built a new sun for Aerie; you can see it burning there." She pointed at the distant second point of light. "They gave Aerie a new sun, and with the Pilot dead, Slipstream has given the citizens of Aerie their freedom. But even though they lit the new sun two years ago, most people haven't moved into its light yet. It's been going through testing and safety trials."

"And now," shouted Harper, "they're done! Our sun's been proven stable. We can all go home!"

Freedom Day. Keir pictured two Virgan nations: each was defined by a vast sphere of light inside of which were all its agriculture, its towns, factories, and mansions. A country could be destroyed if its sun was snuffed out. Its people would become refugees, desperately fleeing to whatever lit airs they could find. Even worse, one nation could simply move into the space occupied by another, assimilating its sun and cities and people directly, like one amoeba swallowing another. Evidently Aerie had proven too tough a foe for this latter strategy, but with their sun gone, they'd been helpless. Slipstream had swallowed all their towns and farms, making them all dependent on Slipstream's own sun.

The great iron wheels of Rush surrounded the *Page* now. Keir could clearly make out the rooftops, chimneys, and streets that paved their inside surfaces. Also visible were clouds of people swarming around a wheel whose inner surface was one continuous building—a sumptuous place of gardens and balconies, towers and towering halls, all wrapped into a ring and spun like a giant's toy. The crowds—men and women and children flapping spring-loaded wings or pedaling saddled propeller-fans—were gathering at the central space around which this beautiful building turned.

Harper nodded at it. "The Pilot's palace," he said. "Hey,

look!" he added, turning to his men. "Whose face is that?" He laughed.

Keir could see that some of the biggest banners had been printed with the image of a man's face. He seemed young, with angular features and pale eyes. Now Harper and the others began pumping their fists in the air and chanting, "Sun lighter! Sun lighter! Sun lighter!"

The crowd and the banners formed a rough arc around a crimson disk that hovered in the air next to the palace. Huge mirrors aimed sunlight at this, and as Keir watched, a small group of people (little more than dots at this distance) began drifting into the focus of the light.

"Who's that?" he wondered aloud.

Leal Maspeth crossed her arms on the edge of the hatch, and smiled in self-satisfaction. "I believe those are the very people we've come to talk to."

"Really? And what are we here to talk about?"

Now she laughed. "Why, we've come to tell them the whereabouts of the one man who's missing this party—the man responsible for building Aerie's new sun."

"And who would that be?"

She pointed at the image on the distant banners.

"Hayden Griffin. The *sun lighter!*"

TO EVERYONE'S SURPRISE, when they hove to at a mooring station high on the axle of one of the grand cylinders, Jacoby Sarto refused to dock the ship. "Belay that!" he'd shouted at the crewman who was about to toss a rope to a boy waiting at the metal lip of the docking cylinder. "We're unloading passengers only."

They'd all been gathered at the open door of the ship's little hold anyway, and now Antaea turned to Sarto. "Why?" she asked.

He laughed brusquely. "*You* ask *me* that? What do you think she'll do to you when she finds out you're here?" He shook his head.

"Don't get me wrong, give her my best when you see her," he added to Leal. "But I intend to be over the border before she knows I've been here."

Nobody argued; they all knew who she was, either personally or by reputation. So, Leal found herself admiring Antaea's courage when, two hours later, they stood in an outer office of the Slipstream admiralty, and Argyre said calmly, "Oh, he'll know me," to the uniformed secretary.

Leal glanced around the austere office, idly wondering if this wasn't a more dangerous gambit than taking her message to the Guard. If so, it was far too late for second choices.

She and Antaea had argued long and hard about this choice; oddly, it was Piero Harper who had been the deciding factor. "Hayden's from Aerie," he'd pointed out, "and we left him trapped on the plains of Aethyr. He's Aerie's native son, our hero. Take us to the new Aerie government, they'll fall all over themselves to get him back."

They might, she'd agreed; yet Aerie's government was still a government-in-exile, located in the city of Rush while they awaited the shakedown of Aerie's new sun. All power in the region still rested with Slipstream. It was Slipstream that had the navy, Slipstream the disciplined intelligence network, the money and resources to mount a rescue effort. And more: it was Slipstream that had the international clout to make agreements and alliances stick, right now.

"We're taking our message to Slipstream," she had insisted.

This little office was not in the palace wheel. That vast edifice was visible outside the window to the secretary's left. Currently, the fireworks there were causing banging echoes to rebound throughout the city. The Torn Page of Fate was arrowing for the border as Sarto had promised, but most of Piero Harper's men had gone straight from the docks to the independence ceremony—and part of her longed to be there, too, writing it all down, as it was indeed a historic day.

She would have to content herself with simply saying that she was here for it—later, when she wrote her memoirs. The rebirth of a nation and the division of two peoples like the fissioning of a cell would have to be footnotes to a chapter dealing with this smaller place; this room, and the meeting that was about to start.

The secretary went into the inner office and could be heard speaking to someone. Beside Leal, Antaea cleared her throat and shifted from foot to foot. She half-wished that Jacoby Sarto had come with them, because without even opening his mouth, he had a way of attracting attention and deference like a magnet. The doormen and lackeys who'd only reluctantly let Leal's party through would have leaped to their feet when they saw him coming, even though they had no idea who he was. He simply *looked* important. It still seemed odd that he'd fled from the wrath of Venera Fanning.

The secretary slid around the door to the inner office and quickly shut it behind himself. "The admiral has appointments today," he said in an arch tone. "He's aware of your petition, and will contact you at your hotel," he glanced down at the paper Leal had given him, "when you actually have one."

Leal felt her stomach flip over in an old familiar way: she was being shunted aside *again*. The feeling lasted for just a second, and then she laughed.

"What are the odds," she said to Antaea, "that Admiral Chaison Fanning would put off seeing *you*?"

She turned to the secretary. "All right," she said with a nod. He went to sit down, and as soon as he'd rounded his desk, she stalked over to the inner door and yanked it open. "Hey!" he shouted as Leal walked through.

The old man wobbling on a rolling ladder next to the bookcase said "Oh my goodness!" and would have fallen had she not steadied him. He blinked at her over oval pince-nez glasses, then smiled. "What can we do for you, my dear?"

"I'm looking for the . . ." Leal forgot the rest of the sentence as she saw the state of the small room. If it even *was* a small room—it seemed perfectly possible that architecturally, the place was much larger, but had become the repository of so many books, charts, and blueprint tubes that its original walls were hidden, perhaps yards behind the new facades of paper. There was one desk, mounded with paper and parchment with one tiny clear corner (this open space obviously made possible by the growing pile on the floor beside the desk).

It was breathtaking.

"A-Admiral Chaison Fanning?" Leal asked the old man. He laughed.

"Oh my heavens, no." He put a finger to his lips. "I'm not even supposed to be here." He turned and finished jamming a book into the bookshelf—a futile gesture considering that the tomes themselves had become shelves for volumes resting atop them, squeezed in around them, and even (in some cases) hanging off the shelf by opened covers pinned under them.

"Please leave!" the secretary was saying. "Do you know where you are? I can have a dozen naval officers in here in a minute and simply have you thrown off the wheel."

"No doubt," Antaea said dryly.

"Have you seen the admiral?" Leal asked the old man brightly.

He waved at another wall, and after some peering Leal realized there was a door there, half-hidden behind some hanging charts.

"Now don't you tell him I'm in here," he said as Leal picked her way through the maze of books. "Just, sometimes, I have to tidy up a bit."

She put her hand on the half-hidden doorknob, paused, looked back, and asked, "Does he ever notice?"

"All right, I'm calling security," said the secretary, and Leal pushed through this door, too, with her companions behind her. She found herself in a long, wood-paneled hallway with infrequent doors leading off it. Starting to feel a bit ridiculous, she hurried down it.

"Ah!" That had been a woman's voice. Leal stopped.

"Heh heh," chuckled a man. The voices were coming from behind one of the doors. He seemed to be panting, she thought—laboring at something.

Her voice: "Huh-huh-huh-huh!"

He growled in response.

Leal crossed her arms and looked back at Antaea, who suddenly seemed profoundly embarrassed. "Maybe we should come back," said the former Home Guard extraction expert.

Leal thought about everything she'd gone through to reach this spot. "No," she said. She rapped loudly on the door and opened it.

The chamber was large, brightly lit by tall windows, and floored in golden lacquered wood; it looked like a dance floor except that large geometric shapes had been painted on it.

A man and a woman circled each other in the center of the room. He was compact and wiry, with a face that, while somewhat weather-beaten, still managed to convey the mild impression of a civil servant or clerk. He wore naval dress clothes, without the jacket. The woman had raven-colored hair and pale skin, and was dressed in courtly silks that were entirely inappropriate for what she was doing.

"That's a yellow card," the man was saying. "This is sabre: there is a right of way."

She sneered at him. "Advance!" he snapped, and raised his sword.

She seemed to begin a lunge but instead stamped one foot on the floor loudly; he'd twitched, starting a defensive move, and now she skipped in place and then hopped forward. She sent a vicious cut at his head and he dropped onto his hand while his sword arm shot out, placing his blade right at her sternum.

"Appel!" he said as he straightened up.

"—And passata-sotto," added Antaea, clapping slowly. "Nicely done."

The woman snarled in frustration and turned. "Who—" She stopped, gaping at Antaea. Simultaneously, the man noticed the women and almost fumbled his own blade.

"You!" they said as one.

Antaea nodded coolly. "Chaison."

At that moment there was a clattering at the door as six or eight soldiers made their presence known. "Admiral," came the secretary's voice from somewhere behind them, "they barged past me before I could stop them—"

"It's all right, Idosh," Chaison Fanning called out. "They're friends."

As the soldiers backed away, he turned to the visitors and crossed his arms. Venera Fanning came to stand beside him, looking Antaea Argyre up and down as she did. "Ah, Chaison, it's your little friend from before. Antaea, isn't it?" Antaea's momentary cockiness had vanished; now she just nodded guardedly, and Venera gave her another once-over. "I must say, I like your clothes. Where did you get those flying leathers?"

"The principalities," blurted Antaea. "It's a little shop in Gehellen—"

"We don't like Gehellen," interrupted Venera. "Or, at any rate, Gehellen doesn't like us."

Leal cleared her throat impatiently. "My lord, my lady, I am Leal Maspeth of the nation of Abyss. I've come to you with important news, and I've brought this woman, whom you know, to testify on my behalf."

Chaison looked down his nose at her; it was a rather priggish motion, but the sabre hadn't moved. "The last time I met Antaea Argyre, she trussed me up like a festival bird ready for the oven."

Patience, patience. The sun lighter Hayden Griffin had only praise for this admiral, Leal reminded herself—and he had told her that Venera Fanning was one of the most dangerous people he'd ever met. Coming from a man who had spent his adolescence among pirates, that was a recommendation to be borne in mind.

"My name is Leal Hieronyma Maspeth," she repeated. "I am a historian from Abyss, which is one of the sunless countries. Recently

I spent some time outside of Virga, and the . . . people I visited have news and an offer of an alliance for the people of Virga."

She'd said it all matter-of-factly, but how else was she going to do it? Months of rehearsal had yielded no better words.

And they seemed to have taken hold: Chaison Fanning was staring at her, his blade quite forgotten, and his wife was frowning, looking from Leal to Antaea and back again.

"Who are these people and what is this offer?" The admiral walked to a side table and poured himself a glass of water. He did not offer his guests anything, a tiny but pointed warning.

"There is a force that we sometimes call 'Artificial Nature,'" said Leal. "One of its factions is trying to gain access to Virga—actually, it's trying to get to Candesce at Virga's center. Lord and Lady Fanning, you have both had direct experience of its tactics and amoral nature." Chaison Fanning had been kidnapped and tortured by an agent from A.N.—a being that had taken up residence in the body of Antaea's sister, Telen. Venera Fanning had fought against another agent of A.N. inside the sun of suns itself and had later been pursued through the principalities by others. Neither could know—no one in Virga seemed to know—that there were factions within A.N. The emissary's claim that it was the virtuals who were responsible for the attempted incursions would be news to the Fannings, and vitally important news.

"The virtuals are preparing an all-out assault on Virga," Leal continued. "As long as Virga keeps A.N. out, our world stands as an example to others who resist final assimilation by their system. Those resisters have banded together, and they want to ally with the humans of Virga to defeat the virtuals, or at least to push them back."

Fanning squinted at her. "Interesting . . ."

"Not to mention preposterous. And why tell us?" Venera was swishing her sabre at her side in an unconscious but dangerous way. "Isn't this a message for the Home Guard?"

"It would be, yes," said Leal. "That would be why we're here."

Chaison put down his glass and walked up to Antaea. "Would that be why you're here?" he asked her.

She nodded. "The Guard has been deceived by the virtuals. It's not the first time—"

"How do we know it's not you who's been deceived? You come to us with offers of an alliance—with who? If they're friendly, why are they sending messengers instead of coming to us themselves?"

"The morphonts did come to us," said Leal. "Virga proved to be too toxic for them to survive here. That's why I had to leave, to visit them in their own airs. Anyway, if you don't believe me, maybe you'll believe Hayden Griffin?"

The Fannings exchanged a glance. "How's he involved in this?"

"He can confirm my story," said Leal, "he and a few top-ranking members of the Guard he's currently trapped with. Even if I'm wrong, I'm offering you the chance to rescue Griffin, which alone would be a feat with great propaganda value to Slipstream. . . . Considering your new relationship with Griffin's country, Aerie."

Antaea tilted her head, looking puzzled. "Which begs a question. Why are you two here, and not at the big party?"

"We'd be a bad memory," said the admiral with a shrug. "Can't say I disagree. . . . What do you mean, rescue Griffin? Trapped? How's he trapped?"

"That's a very long story," said Leal.

"Let's hear it."

Venera tapped Chaison's ankle with her sabre.

"Well," said Leal, "I suppose it all started the day a great voice began crying in the darkness beyond the city lights . . ."

Venera rapped Chaison's shin again. She made to do it a third time, but his blade was suddenly in the way.

"*Dear,*" said Venera sweetly, "why don't we invite the nice people over for *dinner?* I think that would be the best time for lengthy stories, don't you?"

"No," he said, "I want to hear this now—"

Venera's sabre slid along his and nearly disarmed him.

The Fannings took a step away from each other as their swords came up.

"Really," said Chaison, "if this is as important as it sounds—"

She lunged and he bounced away. "Venera . . ."

"They've come a long way," she said, punctuating her words with casual cuts at his head, "and they're very tired. It would be impolite not to offer them some food and refreshments." She broke off, turned to Leal, and said, "Shall we say six o'clock? The admiralty staff can direct you to our apartments."

"Six o'clock would be fine," said Leal as she, too, backed away.

"Now really—" Chaison moved to intercept Leal, and Venera interposed herself, blade up. The two began to circle one another warily.

"Until six, then . . ." Leal waved for Antaea to follow her— Argyre was staring at Chaison Fanning—and she drew her out into the hall and closed the door even as the sound of clashing blades started up in earnest.

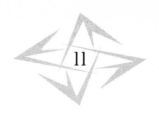

11

"YOU'RE TELLING ME that this terrible news is not true?" Antonin Kestrel, the unlikely prime minister of Slipstream's new government, glared up and down the table. "That it's a lie?"

Leal Maspeth nodded at the prime minister, who sat at the head of the table in Chaison Fanning's surprisingly small dining room. "He was alive when I left him," she said. "The stories out of Abyss are simply untrue."

"But why should we believe you, and not the government of Abyss?"

"Because," she said with a winning smile, "I know where he is. We can pick him up and you can ask him yourself whether he's alive."

From its position ringed by empty dishes, water jugs, and bottles in the center of the table, Leal's now-inert doll watched Kestrel curse and rub his lean chin.

Leal kept glancing at the doll while she talked—whether in embarrassment, or in hope that it might rise and speak, Keir couldn't tell. It faced Kestrel as a strange kind of centerpiece; flanking Kestrel down the sides of the table were Leal, the Fannings, Antaea, and Keir, who felt as out of place as the doll.

Part of that was feeling underdressed; they'd had only a day to prepare for this meeting, and so he wore the livery of a junior naval officer, minus any badge of rank or affiliation. The admiral himself was in a white dress uniform that looked carved rather than sewn. Antaea Argyre, whom Keir had seen before only in leather and trousers, was displaying her cleavage in a gold gown. The dress was gorgeous, but she obviously wasn't comfortable in it; here, Venera had her outclassed. The admiral's wife had squeezed into a long slinky black number made of a material so thin that Keir found his eyes drifting despite himself to trace every muscle and curve of her glorious body. She awoke something buried in him, a startling excitement; but he had no time to think about it right now.

Compared with the other women, Leal Maspeth looked dowdy in brown slacks and a white top. Dresses and skirts were admittedly rare in Virga (in some countries, he'd heard, only prostitutes would wear an article of clothing that was so revealing in freefall). While Slipstream clearly allowed them, Maspeth was just as clearly not used to seeing them, much less wearing one. She, too, kept surreptitiously goggling at Venera and Antaea.

Chaison Fanning half-rose. "Mr. Prime Minister, I know this is a lot to take in, and my apologies again for dragging you away from the opera. We've only just learned many of these details ourselves; in fact, we're not done yet, but the conversation had gotten to a point where I thought it best to bring you in." The delay had cost them an hour, but Fanning had been insistent that they wait. With no safe topics of conversation, the time had dragged as they sipped their coffees and stared at one another—but Chaison had kept them in line, glaring around the table like a disciplinary father.

"Here's where we stand," he said now. "Item one: We have learned that foreigners have made the offer of an alliance to all the humans in Virga."

It was Leal Maspeth's tale that had convinced Fanning to call in the prime minister. Granted, her story alone would have been enough to bring the house down in any decent theater, especially the revelation about the existence of other spheres like Virga. It had been hard for her to drag the Fannings past that realization, and now the admiral demanded that she do it again for Kestrel. When she finished, Kestrel steepled his hands, scowled at her, and said only, "You're telling me that they brought this to us first, instead of taking it to the Guard?"

Maspeth raised her chin defiantly—an admirable posture she was clearly unused to. "Good," said Kestrel. "Go on."

Venera Fanning was nodding. "If you'd gone to the Guard you would have been placing yourself at their mercy. I wouldn't have done it."

"Item two," Fanning said now; he looked every inch the bureaucrat as he ticked off another finger. "The Guard seem to be divided about what to do. Even worse, they seem to have been caught napping by the offer."

Now it was Antaea's turn to throw in what she knew about Jacoby Sarto's serpentine cousin Inshiri, and her apparent alliance with forces from outside Virga. Kestrel looked skeptical, but surprisingly, Venera sprang to Antaea's assistance. "I can vouch for this," she said. "My own people have seen increasing civilian traffic to the tourist center at the walls of Virga, and also to the place where the Gates of Virga are supposed to be. Some kind of high-level governmental liaison is going on between certain key governments in Virga and the Home Guard."

"I've heard nothing of this," said Kestrel, clearly disturbed.

"Slipstream would be the last place they'd include in their consultations," Antaea pointed out. "Sarto was quite clear about it, though; he told me they're visiting pilots and kings and presidents and making them some sort of proposal. I don't think it's the same as the one Leal's beasts are suggesting."

"What my people are seeing," ventured Venera, "is consistent with the view that the Guard's traditional allies outside Virga are putting political pressure on both the Guard and the ruling class of Virga itself."

"Pressure about what?" asked the prime minister.

"This is where we'd gotten to when I decided to bring you into the conversation," said Fanning. "Keir Chen? Can you show our guest what you showed us?"

He hopped up from his chair, nearly knocking it over. Damn—he still wasn't used to the gravity in Rush. Stepping around the main table, he went to a side table under a window, where a white table-cloth draped Exhibit A. "On our way into Virga," he said to Kestrel, "we ran into some of these." With what he hoped was an appropriate flourish, he pulled the tablecloth away, revealing the inert knife-ball that had fixed itself to Sarto's ship. Kestrel swore and did knock his own chair over as he stood up.

"What the hell is that?" He came around to look at it, and as he did, Keir described the gigantic invasion fleet waiting in the frigid blackness just beyond the world's skin. "These are the tiniest motes compared to those vessels," he pointed out.

"You found these in an abandoned city, you say?" Kestrel ran his fingertip along one of the thing's blades. "I know that traditionally, monsters hang around empty places for no apparent reason—and I've always assumed that the lack of a decent food supply in crypt clouds and abandoned town wheels explained why said monsters are not more plentiful. But you say they guarded a door. If these things were scouts—pickets waiting for a signal . . ."

Antaea was nodding. "After the outage, my sister and I fought beasts a lot like those ones," she said. "There's all sorts of eggs and seeds and dormant dragons slumbering among the icebergs of the world's wall. The Guard and their precipice moths patrol the wall, rooting them out where we find them. Where *they* find them . . . Candesce keeps them at bay, so when the outage happened, thousands of them woke up, and they came in. The dagger-balls at the city aren't just aimlessly hanging around there; they're waiting for an opportunity . . . waiting for another outage."

"And that," said Fanning, "means we have an item four: Some enemy of our world is waiting to pounce if we let our guard down." He glanced at his wife and said, "In large part, this current crisis is my fault. In order to win a local war, I sent Venera and Hayden Griffin into Candesce. They caused the outage, which allowed me to win an important battle. But what we didn't know was that it also opened the door for the monsters Antaea and her people had to fight. And it seems to have encouraged those monsters. They've started trying different tactics to get in. This latest one seems to be diplomatic."

"—Backed up by an invasion force," Venera pointed out.

"Yes, yes," he said impatiently. "That's how diplomacy works."

"And anyway," Venera went on, "it wasn't our fault. We were manipulated by that bitch, Aubrey Mahallan. It was her idea to shut down the sun of suns—and she came from outside Virga."

"So." Chaison Fanning stood with his arms crossed; except for Kestrel, who was still examining the knife-ball, the rest of the dinner party was still seated.

"Item five," said Fanning, "and it's the most significant. *We have little proof of any of these things.* Worse, although there's rumors and wide-eyed legends galore about recent events, almost nobody in Virga has heard anything like the stories we've just traded. Most people still don't even know there's a universe beyond our own walls."

"My people don't believe it," agreed Maspeth. "They think Virga *is* the universe, and that it's always existed just as it is. They'd never believe in a threat to the whole world, especially one from outside."

"Yes," said Kestrel as he returned to his seat, "and while your story is interesting, Ms. Maspeth, I'm not compelled to believe it, either, on the strength of your word and this—" He leaned forward and plucked up her doll from the table. "—this figurine that you claim talks, but only to you, and only when you're conveniently outside of the world . . ."

Maspeth glared at him. "Proof is easy to get! Just send a ship to Serenity. The rest of our men should have been rescued by Keir Chen's people by now. And with them is Hayden Griffin—"

Kestrel held up a hand. "I'd be a fool not to at least try to verify your story. So the admiral will be sending the ship—although the logical thing to do would be tell the Guard about the situation at Serenity and go in there together."

"Ah," said Venera. "But how do we contact the Guard? They stay in the shadows. Antaea is the one and only Guardsman we've ever met, and even she's a pariah to them now. Mr. Prime Minister: Since you've been in power, has the Guard contacted *you* in any way?"

With obvious reluctance, he shook his head.

The admiral smiled slightly. "They might sit up and notice if we were to rescue not just Griffin, *but their own men from Aethyr.*"

"A public handover would humiliate them," Kestrel pointed out. "I wouldn't do that—"

"—but we might threaten to," finished Venera with a smile.

Antaea shook her head. "They won't respond well to threats. You try to blackmail them and they'll make you disappear. They have the forces to do it and mop up the witnesses afterward. How do you think they've remained a legend all these centuries? Few people who've seen them ever tell."

"This isn't their problem anyway," Maspeth burst out. "The offer I'm carrying isn't for them, it's for the people of Virga!"

Antaea nodded. "Hear, hear!"

"We need to approach them, so we will," said Fanning. "But at the same time it's risky to keep what we've learned secret."

"So I say we don't."

Kestrel frowned.

Fanning seemed lost in thought; but after swirling his coffee for a moment he shot a rakish grin at his dinner guests.

"If Sarto's cousin Inshiri is doing diplomacy on the sly, and the Guard know no other way of doing it, then what we need to do is turn all this civilized backroom dealing into a public fight—and as nasty a one as we can manage. *We* hold a grand colloquy, to which we will invite all the heads of state, ambassadors, newspaper reporters, and gossips of Virga. We will accuse the Guard of outrageous things to draw them out. And at this colloquy, we will reveal all that we know.

"Twice in five years, some force within Artificial Nature has tried to gain entrance to Candesce. We're already at war. Let's bring that war to the doorsteps of every man, woman, and child in Virga—or at least, threaten to."

Kestrel's eyebrows had shot up, and he looked around the table in bemusement. Antaea was grinning openly, but that came as no surprise; but Venera Fanning was also nodding, as was Leal Maspeth. It seemed, for the moment, like Fanning's idea would carry the day.

"There's just one problem," Kestrel said loudly, "even assuming we find the proof you claim is out there. The problem is you can't control what people will do when they find out. What you're proposing is to let go completely of any control of the situation we might have had!"

Fanning shrugged. "And how much is that?" he said. "Next to none, right now."

Kestrel growled, but then nodded slowly. "Your plan has an interesting edge to it, anyway. So as our chief strategist, what do you propose we do next?"

The admiral clearly had a love for ticking things off his fingers, as he did it again now: "One, we gather our proof, which means recovering Hayden Griffin from Aethyr and establishing better contact with Leal's new friends; two, we gather Slipstream's allies, call in favors, and make outrageous promises." He turned to Venera. "Dear, that will be your job. And three, we shake the Guard out of its den and demand a public accounting of what they're up to, to be given at a time and place of our choosing.

"We have two advantages right now," he went on, "that we can't afford to go to waste. Firstly, we have a secret door into Aethyr, and contact already made with allies there. And secondly, we have a way to prove that the Guard is lying, if we can return Hayden Griffin. He's a hero to the people, and the story out of Abyss that he's dead has taken all the wind out of the celebrations here."

Kestrel shrugged. "The backlash will be so much stronger when they find out they've been lied to."

Fanning fixed Antaea, Keir, and Leal in turn with a fierce look.

"You've each undergone terrible experiences," he said, "in the course of bringing what you know to us on this day, in this place, and for this decision. I want you to understand that everything that's happened prior to tonight—the outage and the battles around it, the betrayals and deaths, our loss of loved ones and the ruin of Spyre and the fall of civilized life in Abyss—all these were just scene-setting. They merely laid the groundwork for what is to follow, and when history looks back on these years they will be footnotes; because what's really important is what's *about* to happen. —What *we* are about to do.

"If you're right about the scale of the threat we face, then what we thought were the adventures of our lives have merely been training, if you will, for our real tasks. Therefore, we will go forth from here, each in our own directions, to gather what we need in order to keep our whole world from vanishing the way that our comfortable lives, our illusions, our families and cities have already gone. We've lost so much, but can we even imagine what it will be like if we lose Virga itself?

"We'll go our ways, and gather information, proof, power, allies, and weapons. We will rendezvous back here in two months, and the grand colloquy will be called. And then, everyone who has been conspiring behind the backs of the people of Virga will be exposed. Then, the real history of our time will be made."

He folded his napkin neatly on the table and stood up. "I think that's it for dinner, then."

THIS CLOSE TO Slipstream's sun, nights were warm and evenings always sultry. As the sun's eight-hour maintenance shift approached, the sky dimmed through purple and mauve to pink and peach, and the vast cloudscapes became a mandala of shifting colors—endless tunnels of hue and sheen receding in any direction you looked.

There were various places around the Fanning estate where one could pause to watch this fabulous display unfold; one was a tall recessed window, half-curtained, at the end of the attic corridor containing the guest apartments. Keir sat in the window box, his arms wrapped around his drawn-up knees. Fireworks were starting now that the light was dim enough. The crowds—thousands of black dots on the air—had not lessened, and in fact as night came they were turning into stars: each person or family group had brought its lantern and they were now lighting them.

Keir had sat down here because it was a private spot and the view was pretty (he had no comparable view from his guest apartment). As he watched the festivities, however, he caught himself musing that Slipstream's government had somehow managed to turn the return of freedom to an unjustly conquered vassal state into some sort of national triumph. The thought was intrusive—alien—and somehow disturbing. He shifted uncomfortably, as if his own body was a puppet, and he'd suddenly felt someone else tug on the strings. That thought about the cunning of Slipstream's government . . . it was as if somebody else had thought it, using his own brain to do so.

He buried his face in his knees for a moment. It must be some effect of the de-indexing, or just shock from losing his dragonflies and his scry. Ever since he'd entered Virga he'd been having these strange flashes—thoughts that were somehow louder than his own thoughts; memories that felt like his but could not be. For instance, these skies felt familiar, as if he'd been in Virga before.

Maybe he had been.

It was hard to remember things without the help of scry, but he clearly recalled Maerta, at the door to Virga, telling him that he'd de-indexed himself. The term had a familiar ring to it, and normally he would simply query scry and the answer would pop into his head, as naturally as if it were his own thought. Scry was gone; so what did his primitive biological memory tell him about de-indexing?

He was racking his mind for clues when he heard voices. Cautiously, he drew himself farther into the window well. The sounds came from down the short flight of stairs that led off the attic; it was Chaison and Venera Fanning speaking.

He: "With all the excitement today I neglected to sign the papers commissioning some new officers. It's important for them, so I'm just going to walk up to the office and do it."

She: "All right, dear. I need to brief my agents on their new assignments, so I'll be in the lounge if you need me."

He: "Bye!"

She: "Bye."

There was a very long pause, during which Keir's thoughts drifted. The clouds outside reminded him of other sunset skies, mauve and pale green, of streaked clouds and a band of orange spanning half the horizon . . . some planet's dusk sometime.

What was there, locked in his mind?

Quiet footsteps padded up the stairs, paused at the top, then moved down the hall. Keir peeked around the curtain and saw that it was Chaison Fanning, in his dress uniform, skulking.

Fanning paused at one of the doors, raised his hand, hesitated, then cursed under his breath and knocked. In the pause that followed he put his hands behind his back and leaned back to glance up and down the hallway. Keir ducked back and so did not see who answered the door, but he heard her gasp, and it was Antaea Argyre's voice.

The door thudded softly shut. Keir frowned out the window, but the frown kept twitching into a smile. His feelings hovered between embarrassment and an alien—but very dry—feeling of amusement. He thought about what would happen if Venera Fanning were to come up here now, and found that alien mind intruding again. This time, it clearly held one idea:

This is not a good place to be right now.

At the far end of the hallway, a small set of steps led up to another door; he'd presumed when he saw it earlier that it led to the roof. Keir unwound himself from the window well and moved to it. As quietly as he could, he tried the latch. It opened.

Warm night air coiled around him; to his surprise, as he stepped onto the roof, he found himself among trees and flower beds. Though Slipstream's admiralty wheel was a pretty utilitarian place, the Fannings had managed to find space for a garden between two sloping roofs. Keir was grateful now for the night air and relative silence, and the feel of a warm breeze on his face.

The garden was lit by window and city light—the sky was a glittering tapestry of pinpricks and glowing squares. The air felt wonderful, so like that of a planet . . . were it not for the subtle tug in his inner ear that told him he was slowly turning over and over with the whole admiralty wheel. He strolled through the garden, letting his fingers trail through the fronds of living things. He closed his eyes, and flashes of imagery came to him of things he could not remember ever having remembered: plains and forests; sun on his face; and the water of lakes and streams swirling around his ankles, his waist . . .

"Stop." He opened his eyes and saw that he'd strayed close to the edge of the roof. City lights and dove-gray scraps of cloud raced by below him.

He turned to find Leal Maspeth looking up at him. She was sitting on a verdigrisy copper box that jutted up out of the carefully tended flowers. She frowned at him. "It looked like you were about to walk off the roof."

"Maybe I was, Ms. Maspeth," he said ruefully. "I don't have a very good sense of where I am—without my dragonflies, you know . . ."

"Call me Leal."

"Leal . . . I was just enjoying the feel of grass."

"Yes, you're from beyond the world," she said. "I guess you wouldn't have touched grass before."

Surprised, he laughed. "Of course we have grass. On planets . . ." He paused, troubled, then said, "But we make worlds, little ones, you know, and spin them for gravity. Ten kilometers across, a hundred . . . lots of room for trees and forests."

She smiled. "Of course."

There was a quiet pause. He looked around for someplace to sit, but Maspeth had the only available perch. Noticing what he was doing, she bumped over a bit and patted the surface next to her. "There's room."

Keir flushed, hoping she couldn't tell in the darkness. Sure he'd hesitated too long, he sat down and found the only way to stay on the box was to be thigh-to-thigh with her. She didn't seem to notice their hips touching, but leaned back, putting her hands behind her. He turned so he could continue to see her, and found her invitingly close.

She'd seemed old when he'd first met her, but maybe what he'd been seeing had been the weight of responsibility burdening her at the time. She was definitely older than he—maybe by ten years—but at dinner he'd caught himself exchanging glances with her that, at times, had the feel of youthful conspiracy to them.

Pinioned by her frank gaze—and acutely feeling the lack of helpful suggestions from his scry—he struggled for something clever to say. Finally he noticed that she was holding a thick, old-fashioned book made of the flat leaves they called "pages." A quill pen jutted out of it. "What's that?" he blurted.

She waggled the heavy volume. "A navigator's log book. I'm writing down my story, at last! I wasn't sure I would ever get to."

She sat up and he took it from her gingerly. The thing was floppier than he'd expected, and he nearly dropped it. The pages were all blank, except for the first few that were covered with fine, looping handwriting in black ink.

Keir had seen such things in sims and other virtual entertainments, but he'd never held an actual book in his hand, nor traced actual handwriting with his fingers. He did so now and found that his touch was reverent. This object had awoken some deep feeling inside him, a surprising respect.

"You learned all you know," he said, "from these."

"Oh, don't put it that way!" She laughed. "I'm already intimidated enough at the thought of writing my own."

He returned it, and smiled at the glittering night. "You must be glad to be back."

"Well." Now she frowned. "I'm not exactly 'back.' This place isn't my home."

"But it's Virga."

"If I threw you to some star across the universe, could you say you felt at home because it *wasn't* Virga?"

"No, but—" He saw her point, but continued, anyway. "If Artificial Nature was there, it would feel much the same as anywhere else I've lived."

"Why? Is it really all the same everywhere?"

He shrugged. "Seems so . . . The admiral wants me to go back. Says I should 'liaise' with the Renaissance when they pick up the rest of your men."

"Oh, that's good. So are you happy to be going home?"

"I told him no." Her eyes widened, but she said nothing. At this moment his lack of scry was a powerful ache, because he really didn't know how much or how little to tell her. "I can't go back," he heard himself say. "Something was happening to me there— something awful . . . I, I don't feel right, like this isn't my skin . . ." He pulled at the flesh of his forearm. "I think I lost my memory, but I seem to think I was once older . . ."

She looked startled. "Older?" she asked. There was surprise in her voice, but concern as well, and he relaxed a bit. "Was it during what we call the outage?"

"No, we came here after that." He realized he shouldn't have said that, but it was too late.

"That's not very long ago." She leaned back again, her lips pursed and brow furrowed. "You've only spent the last couple of years of your life in Aethyr. Which means you spent most of it somewhere else. Are you telling me you don't remember any of that?"

"N-no . . . the memories are there. They're just not in . . . what do you call it? Chronological order. They're jumbled up, like those spy's photos Venera threw on the table." And there were far too many of them, too; but he didn't say that.

"Keir—you said you were once older. How old do you think you really are?"

He shook his head.

"You look somewhere between sixteen and nineteen," she said. "When I met you I thought you were younger. You look like you've put on a year or two since then."

"I was getting shorter!" He'd jumped to his feet and started to walk, but there was nowhere to walk to in this tiny garden. He paced to the stairwell, then back to the edge of the roof. "The day I met you, I'd proved it. I was getting shorter." He raised a shaking hand to wipe at his eyes. "What was that? What's going on?"

"Did you tell the admiral about this?"

Her voice was quiet and steady. He turned to find she was still seated, but leaning forward, book on knees, all her attention on him. Keir shook his head.

"Did he insist you should go back?"

"Y-yes. But I can't." He scowled at the pretty night. "I'll run away first."

She stood up. "I'll speak to him. He wants me to go, too—to bring his diplomats to the emissary's people. I told him he didn't need me and that anyway I'd done my part. He insisted until I pointed out that if he lost me, he'd lose his only connection to them." She held up the book and grinned. "I said, better that I stay here and write down everything that happened, so at least there's a record. The emissary's perfectly capable of guiding its people to their home without me. So that's what's happening."

Leal walked to his side and put a reassuring hand on his shoulder. "You see, all things are possible."

Keir took a deep breath, and let it out. He smiled at her. "Thanks." She nodded, half-smiling.

"I'm still a stranger here, though." He looked down, past ledge and shingle, down the sheer walls of the admiralty to where on any world-bound building, grass or stone or soil would begin. There was only air, and soaring clouds half-lit by the city glow. "I can't even read your letters."

"How lucky for you, then," said Leal, "that I'm a teacher currently lacking a student. I can teach you to read."

"I don't want to be a burden."

"Hmm." She tapped her chin with a fingertip. "Well, then, why don't you tell me everything you know about Artificial Nature? And the Renaissance? I'll add it to my book. You may know more than you think; and what you know could be more useful to us than you realize."

The first rule of the Renaissance was to keep what they were doing secret. —Then again, he'd already given most of it away before they'd even left Aethyr.

He smiled wryly. "It's a deal."

12

DAYS PASSED IN a flurry of dispatches, expeditions, and consultations. The prime minister took their case to his cabinet, and the decision was made—for now—to indulge Chaison Fanning, just in case it turned out that Leal's story was true. The very first order of business was to verify that, and so a small flotilla of ships made for the sunless countries the very next day, charged with finding Serenity, establishing a safe bridgehead at the door, and entering Brink. Maerta had promised Leal that she would try to rescue Hayden Griffin and the stranded Home Guard airmen from the plains of Aethyr. With luck, they would be able to return the Guardsmen to their people and win some allies there.

In case the rescue didn't happen or the rescued Guardsmen were hostile, Chaison had a Plan B for contacting the Home Guard, and it involved sending Antaea Argyre on a journey to the principalities of Candesce.

That expedition was arranged; meanwhile, Venera's spies went into overtime, tracking the movements of a small set of people who were nominally stateless refugees, but who certainly didn't act like them. The name Inshiri Ferance came up again and again; it began to seem like she had visited every sun in Virga—just, not Slipstream's.

Chaison and Venera Fanning worked together almost without consultation (though that might go on under the covers at night, as some speculated), he organizing the logistics of a new diplomatic network, she calling in favors, sending out invitations, and frankly spying on everybody.

Leal's message to the people of Virga had not yet been announced, but the ripples from its impact were already spreading.

"THE SIMPLE FACT is, you can't worry people into acting," Admiral Fanning had said at the crowded strategy session. Keir remembered him shrugging. "No matter how much truth you have on your side, and no matter how compelling your arguments, people simply won't move if they don't have to." He had taken a piece of chalk and drawn a white slash through the words "Artificial Nature" written on the chalkboard behind him. Next to it he'd written one of many curious new words Keir was learning lately. This one was "velleity."

"That's our true enemy," he said. "Velleity means 'having a vague desire to do something, but not enough will to actually do it.' If we take our message of urgent action around to the nations of Virga, that's what we're going to get: a vague interest, some desultory waves of the hand, and no commitment.

"So, our first tool will be outrage and excitement."

Keir saw little of that today as he strolled the iron pavement of Rush, Slipstream's capital city. He did see a lot of rushing about in Quartet Two, Wheel One—but that was because the merchants were still making out like bandits from the Freedom Day tourists, many of whom had stayed to enjoy a rare heat wave cooked up by Slipstream's sun controllers. There were plenty of stalls in alley mouths, a few street performers on the odd corner, lots of traffic on foot and in man-powered jitneys, and many smiling faces. The headlines in the newspapers were in small type these days. In more than one sense, a new summer had settled on Slipstream.

"There's the shop," Leal said. "You go on—I'll see you back at the palace."

He grinned at her. " 'Back at the palace.' I like that."

They'd just been clothes-shopping, since he couldn't wear his Brink-made apparel without attracting attention, and the boy's clothing he'd borrowed from a mate on the *Torn Page of Fate* had apparently shrunk. That was today's excuse, anyway; Leal had been dragging him out into the streets every day since they'd arrived. He had to admit it was helping him gain his bearings.

She sent him a luminous smile and turned away. He paused at the beveled-glass door to the bookstore and glanced back, in time to see her raise her face to a beam of hot sunlight from the nearby sun. Of course, Slipstream was as exotic to her as it was to him. He smiled and hauled on the heavy door.

Doors that didn't open for you automatically; gaslight in the evenings; no screens, no scry—it was all bewildering and wonderful, but there was a kind of beauty to life here that he was starting to appreciate. Beauty like these books! He stood by the door, breathing in the scent of the paper for a moment and gazing around in wonder. The walls were lined with leather-bound folios, and most of the floor space was taken up with shelves. The amount of actual information here was infinitesimal—his scry implants could have carried a billion bookstores' worth—but that hardly mattered. Each book was a thing, the care and material going into making it announcing to the world that this knowledge or this story, however small, was a treasure. He flipped through a few of them in delight as the bemused shopkeeper watched.

"Anything I can help you with?"

"Well, maybe." He let his accent shine through. The paper bag containing his clothing would help with this role, but Leal had told him severely, "No pretending. Be what you are: a foreigner." So he didn't hide his hesitation at finding a spot to put down the bag; and he looked around carefully to make sure they were alone before saying, "I hear there's a book I can't buy from you."

The shopkeeper's open expression became veiled. "Don't know what you mean. We have a free press in Slipstream, since the Pilot's death."

"Well, it's not officially banned, but I heard the admiral bought up the whole print run."

"I really don't know—"

"Oh, come on! Do I look like a spy?" —Which was the worst kind of thing to say if you really were a spy, of course, but he was going to obey Leal's instructions to the letter. "You're my last chance; I'm leaving for home tomorrow."

The shopkeeper sighed heavily. "Listen, son, if a book's been banned—officially or not—do you really think you'd be likely to find a copy here?"

"Well, exactly. So . . ."

The man leaned over the counter. "Where's the last place you'd expect to be buying books?"

"Oh, I don't know. The docks? The butcher's?"

"There's a cheese shop two blocks spinward," said the shopkeeper innocently. "That's pretty much the last place I'd look."

"Huh. Thanks, I'll bear that in mind." Keir left the shop, and five minutes later he walked out of the cheese shop with a brand-new copy of Antaea Argyre's controversial new autobiography. It was, of course, buried in the bag under his new clothing.

The book had been produced in record time. Keir had stopped by while Antaea was still dictating it to the bank of ghostwriters Admiral Fanning had attached to her. Dangling one leg over the velvet arm of the chair she was slumped in, idly swirling a wine-glass in her hand, she had been answering yet another question about her mad dash across the airs of the world. The writers were typing madly at their baroque cast-iron "type writers"; torn and crumpled pages forested the floor of the admiralty office where this secret activity was taking place. Keir had shaken his head at her, and she'd rolled her eyes in reply.

Fanning had driven his authors like pack animals, and so the book had hit the printers in a little over a week. Announced in a flurry of press releases and newspaper articles, it was immediately suppressed (though all the copies reputedly destroyed by the admiral were actually winging their way to neighboring countries, to there be sold as rare surviving editions).

All copies were supposed to be going to the public, since Keir and all the others already knew the story. Still, the admiral had started giving him an allowance, and it was up to him how to spend it. This copy of Antaea's book was his.

For a while he strolled the boulevards, enjoying the mad energy of a Virgan city. Without scry and all the other distractions of the outside world, the people here maintained a fantastic focus on their immediate lives. They were passionate in a way that nobody in the Renaissance could ever be. They reminded him of another place . . . when he'd . . .

He stopped, scowling. He'd almost caught that one. The memories were there, but without the order imposed on them by scry, he had to recover them manually, as it were. This was what *de-indexing* meant, he'd concluded: erasing, not memories themselves, but one's artificial aids to retrieving them. Maerta had acted like de-indexing was some sort of death sentence, and he supposed that in a way, it was—to someone born outside Virga.

These people, though, had never used artificial augmentations to their natural memories, and they were hardly suffering. In fact, they seemed happier than any people he'd ever met.

Was this his home now? He supposed it could be, and the thought made him shake his head in wonder at himself, for having had no plan beyond leaving Brink. Had that recklessness been courage, or youthful folly? He'd literally had no idea where he would go, but it hadn't mattered. He might not be done wandering yet, but for the moment, he didn't care.

So much for worrying about the future. Leal Maspeth had been shocked and appalled at John Tarvey's offer—but what was his sort of immortality, after all, but a photograph of life, preserved but not living. By contrast, the embodied people of Virga—who lived entirely in their flesh, and died there, too—had the better deal.

The rumble of a trolley sounded behind him. He glanced up to watch it go past, loving its crude mechanical beauty. A machine, *designed* and *built* to *plan*. Wonderful!

The machines of the city charmed him. Maybe he could become an engineer, and design and build the way people had thousands of years ago. To create something like that streetcar from nothing but your imagination and knowledge of the world! That one trolley made the evolved wonders of the Edisonians seem cheap.

Except that one woman didn't seem to see the thing coming. She was waving at a friend and stepping across the tracks as the trolley bore down on her. Keir felt a funny knot in his stomach—was this normal?—and the huge vehicle eclipsed her and he heard screams.

He just stood there, bag dangling from one hand, as people began running from all sides. Where were the medical remotes? The morphonts? First-aid nano? Why should all these strangers be converging on the screeching, braking streetcar whose passengers were toppling and grabbing one another now as the driver swore and swore?

Horror nearly drove him to his knees as he realized that there *was* no help coming.

Dropping the bag, he ran to the front of the trolley where what had been a woman in a green coat was now half-mashed under its prow. There was blood everywhere. The woman's friend was kneeling next to her and her screams were unlike anything Keir had ever heard.

He found himself reaching out—issuing commands to scry to summon help, to launch first-aid programs—but his hands grasped empty air. There were verbal commands to scry and to the Edisonians and fabs and he choked them out, but everyone ignored him as the driver staggered out of the trolley crying and shouting words in no language. The crying, shouting, and screaming echoed off the buildings and it must be climbing the canyon of the city like a pyre, a smoke of words and regrets rising to vanish in the light of the suns.

The crowd pushed Keir aside and he put one foot in front of the other, and again, feet ticking step by unsteady step up the curb, down the street, but going nowhere now.

THE LIGHT FROM Rush's sun made a circuit around the room, once every fifty seconds. Leal had timed it. The town wheel turned over, silent and perfect as a clock, and the parallelogram of yellow-white slid slowly down the wall, across the floor, up the farther wall, and back along the ceiling. You could keep time by it—if its cycle lasted a full minute, which it didn't. Somewhere, fluttering deep inside her, was resentment that the wheel's build-ers couldn't have given it a one-minute rotation. At least then she would have known how long she'd been sitting here with her hands clutched in her lap.

There was a commotion in the admiralty's foyer, then a junior officer stepped into the room. "They've found him," he said.

Leal jumped to his feet. "Is he—"

"He's fine. Doctor says he suffered some sort of shock, but physi-cally, he's fine."

"Ah. I—can I see him? Please?"

The officer stepped out and conferred with someone, then re-turned. "This way."

Chaison Fanning's admiralty building was huge—so big that its floors curved with the town wheel itself. She shouldn't have been surprised to discover that it contained an entire hospital, apparently for veterans. The officer handed Leal off to a nurse, who led her through a succession of pea-green rooms to a curtained nook where Keir sat. He was staring past the curtain when she got there. Leal looked where he was looking, and saw an old soldier basking in the same sunlight she'd been watching a minute ago. The man was missing a leg and a hand, but otherwise seemed perfectly normal.

The nurse frowned and twitched the curtain closed. Keir blinked and looked up, noticing Leal for the first time.

He said nothing. Heart in her throat, Leal sat down next to him and took his hand.

What to do? She bit her lip, then, impulsively, said, "I've seen that look before."

He cocked his head just slightly. Encouraged, she went on. "My friend Brun went looking for the emissary and found it. He and his men had no idea what they were getting themselves in for. We found him half-dead from exposure, alone in the weightless darkness. He was trapped in a drop of water; the stuff kept condensing onto him, and though he'd push it away it kept coming back. Once he slept, it was going to cover his mouth and nose and suffocate him."

Why was she telling him this? The last thing Keir needed to hear right now was one of the horrors she'd seen. Yet, she heard herself continue. "We got him back, revived him, but something in him . . . was broken. He wasn't the same after that. Keir, please tell me that something inside you didn't break today. Whatever it was, it was nothing. Nothing!"

"A woman died," he mumbled. "I saw a woman die."

"Oh." She supposed, coming from where he had, that he'd never had such an experience before. "Oh, Keir, I'm so sorry you had to learn it like that. People die, they die." She sat next to him, pulling his head into the curve of her neck.

"Not where I come from," he said. She tensed, remembering Tarvey, but then he said, "We de-index, and we neotenize. I'd forgotten what those things were, but now I remember. They're an alternative to death. We live immensely long lives, Leal, and when we weary of the world, we . . . forget our lives. Start over. We grow down, so we can grow up again and discover everything anew."

Stunned, she froze, and for a long minute neither of them spoke. Then: "Sita," he said, "was my wife."

"Was . . ." Leal tried to think past her confusion. "Before you came to the Renaissance?"

"I don't know. But I do know that she lost her life. I also know that she didn't die. Not the way that woman today died."

They sat there for another long time, while Leal hunted for something to say that would make sense. "Our world's not evil," she said finally. "Just different. Brun—if you'd seen what he saw in the dark, you'd have laughed it off. To him, meeting the emissary was like . . . what you saw today is to you. Not that I would ever laugh off a death, I don't mean that."

He shut his eyes tightly and grimaced. "I was just starting to think that I'd found paradise—like I'd been living in some shadow world my whole life and only just now woke up. And then . . ."

She nodded against his thick hair. "There's this ancient story that I came across while I was researching the emissary—back when the rumors were that it was a worldwasp, one of the builders of Virga. The story's about a prince who builds a machine to travel outside of Virga. He's been maddened, see, by grief at the death of his wife, and has decided to visit the country of the dead to bring her back. The country of the dead is what lies outside Virga. The story goes that he builds a vast black orb, bigger than a town and sealed with tar and bound in iron. Somehow, he pierces the outer skin of the world and then he sails his mad vessel into the blackness there."

Keir leaned away from her. He still looked haggard, but that awful stare had gone, at least for now. "And then what?" he said.

"Well," she said, crossing her legs and clasping one knee. "That's where the legend ends for most versions of the story; but over the centuries some authors were unsatisfied with this cliffhanger, and here this one added a dramatic return, that one a cryptic message in a bottle, and another, a great voice shouting from the dark . . ." She smiled at him. "But it's as the story says—the walls of Virga separate the land of the living from the land of the dead. Only now I see, which I never did before, that whichever side you come from is the land of the living, and whichever side you end up in, is . . ." Suddenly realizing how awful this notion must sound, she stopped; but he was nodding.

"There's a choice to be made," he said. "Immortality or death. Sita is still alive—in some sense. But what happened to her—what

I think happened—well, immortality and death are equally terrible."

"There's a third choice, though," she said. He nodded, and then to her surprise, sent her a rueful, and very old-looking smile.

"How neatly symmetrical." His words were dry, even cynical.

He shook away her hands and stood up. "I'm fine," he said. "I'll be fine." Then he looked around his feet. "I lost the bag."

"Don't worry about that. Let's just get out of here." He walked out of the infirmary with her hand on his arm, and, twenty minutes ago, Leal would have imagined no better ending to the episode. Yet his face was a mask and she now knew that it had been from the start—that she had a long way to go before she met the real Keir Chen.

WHEN VENERA FANNING learned what had happened, she frowned, thought for a minute, then strode into the guest quarters and said, "Where is he?"

She came to stand over him as he sat ashen-faced in a lounge by the window. For a while she sized him up, noting the length of his arms, the muscles in his thighs. He looked back at her mildly; across the room, Leal watched the strange assessment with alarm.

Then Venera turned her attention to Leal. "You. What are you doing?"

"I'm . . . writing my memoirs."

Venera narrowed her eyes. "Smacks of procrastination to me." Then she nodded sharply. "Both of you. The naval dockyard, pier fifteen, tomorrow morning. Nine sharp, don't be late."

She stalked to the door, then noticing their astonished expressions, scowled at them both. "Well," she said as if it were obvious, "you might as make yourselves useful."

She turned on her heel and left.

"THEY DO NOT want me to talk about this. But why not? The truth belongs to all of us."

The sky here was glorious. Fully six suns were cradled by the weightless air, at varying distances that filtered their light from bright blue-white (for the closest one) to bloodred (for the most distant). The spaces around them were shaded every possible hue and, like a faint mist, uncountable cities and towns, farms, lakes and clouds receded through and past them, seemingly to infinity.

It was Candesce that most strongly lit the few pages of notes that Antaea had brought with her. The sun of suns hung directly over her head, and it outshone the lesser lights of the principalities by orders of magnitude.

She cleared her throat, nervously shuffling the pages. About a thousand people had come out to listen to her story; the numbers were growing with every stop she made. People loved to hear the tale of her betrayal, her kidnapping of an admiral and the incursion of a precipice moth into the palace of that infamous pirate nation, Slipstream. She'd spent an hour on it tonight—but it was just the teaser, the bait to bring them here. Her real message would be harder for them to swallow—was not, in fact, meant for these people at all.

In the front rank of the cloud of people, her agent gave her an encouraging thumbs-up. She smiled gamely back, and continued.

"Our societies are only as just as our technologies allow them to be," she said. "In Virga, our governments have to use bureaucracies to manage all the information needed to run a nation. That's important to remember, because when we are oppressed it is not by monarchy, capitalism, absolutism, or whatever 'ism' might cling to the top of a given society's pyramid. Tyranny is shaped by the command-and-control mechanisms that are available—and not by the specific class that tries to use those means. So, in Virga, we are doomed to live lives straitjacketed by bureaucratic governance."

She took a deep breath and proclaimed, "Their individual

character doesn't matter! They may be churches, armies, democracies, or 'people's republics'; whatever they are, they all use the same tools, and it is the limitation of those tools that keep our societies in primitive and unjust paralysis.

"The Virga Home Guard knows this. Yet they refuse to act."

Whenever she reached this part of the talk, she half-expected a bullet to strike at her from some unwatched direction. For two weeks now now her talks had been drawing crowds up and down the principalities of Candesce—the most thickly populated volume of Virga. It was part of Chaison Fanning's plan that she be seen, very publicly, to be rebelling against centuries of secretive tradition by revealing the inner workings of the Guard, by speaking of its foibles and its failures. "It will draw them out," he'd said. "You'll see."

Well, it might—but what form would their reaction take? She was risking her life with these words; she hoped he appreciated it.

"The Guard protects us from what lies outside our world," she said, swinging an arm to indicate the indigo depths opposite the bright suns. The citizens of the principalities had an almost unreasoning fear of the darkness that lay outside Candesce's sphere of radiance. The very fact that Antaea was a winter wraith—born and raised in the sunless countries thousands of miles beyond the principalities—helped her draw crowds. Her presence was titillating to the decadents of these inward-turned civilizations, but some of them also heard and responded to her real message. There were rumors now of some secret meeting that was to take place in the pirate nation of Slipstream. Some alarming thing to do with the fabled Guard.

Her next words had not been written by Chaison's ghostwriters. They were her own thoughts, committed to paper in long evening reveries, as she'd thought about Leal's message, and what they'd come to call the Offer. "The Guard protects us, because what lurks outside Virga is another kind of tyranny. There, Artificial Nature makes new kinds of society possible—of course it does, and that's what makes it attractive. But its miraculous technologies also make some ways of life impossible. Some of those ways are the very ones we prize most highly.

"So what are we to do? Accept the tyranny of the system we've got, or bring in a new, different kind of tyranny on the theory that any change will be an improvement? The Guard has always refused to make that choice for us—and this is because they recognize that they do not have the right.

"The Guard's correct not to make the decision for us," she shouted out to anyone who would hear. "For it is our decision to make. It is time for us to take collective responsibility for our situation, and decide: do we accept that we will only ever be able to use those few primitive technologies that Candesce permits us to use? Will we command the Guard to throw open the Gates of Virga and let Artificial Nature into our world, thus changing it irreversibly? Or is there some middle way? Maybe we can send our youth to study in the outside universe, let them return wiser and more knowledgeable than we can be. Maybe we should stop isolating ourselves, and begin asking for news of that wider universe. Allow immigration, emigration, and the transit of ideas even while we use Candesce's power to maintain Virga's technologies as they are.

"Maybe," she said, and now her smile was genuine and confident, "maybe we have other choices."

The talk wound down but now it was all theatrics and calls for action, and when it was done Antaea bowed to the usual applause. The message had been sent, her gauntlet thrown down. Now all she had to do was wait.

She signed books and chatted with people for a while as the crowd slowly dispersed. One of the suns was going out for local night, and in a formerly dark quadrant of the sky, another was coming alight. Antaea yawned as the last autograph-seeker flapped away, and eyed Candesce, which was the sun she set her watch by these days. It blazed as brightly as ever, but she knew it wouldn't be long until it shut down for the evening as well. Then, this unbelievable sky would reveal a sight even more beautiful than the fine colors that reigned now, as millions of windows and running lights lit up across hundreds of miles of clear air. She could go to sleep in the embrace of a measureless galaxy of home and city light. When she closed her eyes, some nights that light remained in her dreams.

"Time to retire, my lady," said Richard Reiss, her agent. She turned and smiled at him.

"What did I say?"

"Nothing." She shrugged. "How was our take tonight?"

"Respectable." He held a thick satchel. "Best get to the drop-off before someone tries to mug us for it."

They shared a smile. There were few people alive who could best Antaea in a fair fight. The money wasn't the bait for their trap, anyway. She'd already laid that out.

Now, as the purple light of Candesce's evening began to wash across the principality skies, she climbed into their twin-engined aircar and took the satchel from Richard's hand. Slipstream's former ambassador to Gehellen was proud to turn his wine-stain birthmark to the light these days; notoriety, he'd discovered, suited him as well as respectability once had. His knowledge of principality fashions and customs was invaluable to Antaea during this junket—as he'd known it would be.

He settled into the cockpit. "Our hotel? Or a good restaurant. I know of one," he said.

"I'm tired," she admitted. "Maybe the hotel tonight." He nodded and turned to his controls, and she reached out to shut the hatch.

"Excuse me." A large figure blocked the outside light. "Are you Antaea Argyre?"

Her hand shot to the little pistol at her belt. "Sorry, show's over," she said quickly as she hauled on the door handle.

A large hand reached up and the door wouldn't move. Antaea pulled out the pistol and aimed it straight at the silhouetted man's chest, her own heart suddenly pounding. "Let go or I'll shoot!"

"Shooting will be quite unnecessary," said another, familiar-sounding voice. A slim silhouette moved into the light, and Antaea's grip on the door eased. "Captain Sayrea Airsigh, of the Home Guard's Last Line," she said. "I believe we met four or five years ago, at the Gates of Virga? —At least, I gather I made an impression on you, since I hear you've been using my name as one of your aliases, lately."

Damn Crase anyway. He'd obviously reported her presence in Sere. She smiled anyway. "Yes, Captain, it was quite a party, and I do remember you. It's good to see you."

"And you," said Airsigh in a sincere tone.

"Apart from catching up on old times, though, I've been instructed to invite you to a small meeting my people have organized. We'd like your opinion on something—or rather, someone."

"Do I have your guarantee that I'll be let go again safely afterwards?"

Airsigh took the question seriously. "You do."

Antaea glanced at Richard, who shrugged. "What do you mean, you want my opinion on some*one*?"

"The Last Line has a visitor—from outside."

"Outside? You mean—"

"The First Line have sent us an ambassador from beyond Virga, and we don't know what to make of him.

"We'd like you to help us answer a question. Is he—"

"—a monster?" Antaea nodded grimly. "Yes.

"I can do that."

13

"KEEP UP" WAS all Venera Fanning said. So they tried.

Five countries in five days: that had been Keir's first week with Venera. Her viciously thin yacht, the *Judgment*, would scream from destination to destination while Venera stood up from its hatch to hold out her hand to men on passing jet bikes, like a falconer waiting for her bird to alight on her wrist. What the passing hands exchanged with her was letters. Outbound, she sent announcements (or, perhaps, warnings) of her imminent arrival at this or that palace or pavilion; inbound, she received cautious, fawning, or stiffly cool acknowledgments.

A very public campaign was under way by ambassadors and senior public officials of both Slipstream and Aerie; they, too, were fanning out across the world, visiting capitals and city-states everywhere from the principalities to Virga's cold outer reaches. They brought reminders of the two incursions into Virga that had occurred within the past several years, and proposed that all concerned heads of state send delegates to a grand colloquy, to be held in Aerie's new capital city, Aurora. The Virga Home Guard were invited as well—though whether the semimythical organization would show up was anybody's guess—to give an accounting of their own actions to the people of Virga.

Venera's mission was not so public. Her extensive spy network had spent years researching vulnerabilities and finding the skeletons in everybody's closets. For those nations and cities which proved reluctant to attend the colloquy, she was acting as a discreet second strand of persuasion. It was a process that was fascinating to watch.

As they approached the mauve or peach or lime-colored airs of the next nation on their itinerary, Venera would order one of her men out to hang gay banners off the more wicked-looking of the yacht's fins. Twirling Slipstream's colors, they glided into port like some fabulously long-lived firework. Then, the fast-and-furious game would begin.

Keir usually watched that game from a distance.

"What is she telling them?" Leal Maspeth hissed now; she was craning her neck to see the head table at tonight's banquet. The nation was Unduvine, the city Greydrop. More than that, Keir didn't know, except that they built their town wheels of iron and asteroidal stone, and that this great hall whose corner he and Leal sat in was ancient.

He glanced over his shoulder. Venera Fanning had leaned forward, across the table, and was putting most of her weight on the dinner knife she'd plunged into the oak tabletop. The ambassadors, admirals, nobles, and members of parliament seated with her were to a man cringing back in their own chairs, for all the world as if Venera were radiating some force field.

Suddenly Venera put her hand next to her temple and splayed open her fingers, said something short, and brayed with laughter. The entire table broke into howls of mirth and, as she sat down again, they leaned forward, even more relaxed than they'd been before her tirade.

"I believe," Keir said somberly, "that Venera Fanning just told a joke."

"Well, at least they're having a good time," muttered Leal. She and Keir had been introduced as minor members of Venera's ambassadorial staff, which meant they had to sit in waiting rooms, or stand in the hall, or, as now, eat at what Leal insisted on calling "the kid's table" far to one side of the real action.

"I told you to bring your notebook," he said as he tucked into the dinner. "You could have been writing your book all this time."

"They'd think I was spying," she countered; then she frowned at his plate. "And what exactly are you doing?"

Keir looked down and realized he had, once again, dismembered and dissected his dinner in such a way as to lay out his main course's bone structure for examination. "Sorry," he said. "I've just never seen birds like these. I keep trying to figure out how they fly."

"Birds don't fly," she said with an air of great patience. "Flying is something you do under gravity. Virgan birds swim. Like fish. Or people."

"Ah. I suppose." He grinned at the little skeleton.

Leal eyed him. "You're having the time of your life, aren't you?"

He shrugged. "I really don't know, I haven't had a moment to think about it." It was true; he was starting to feel safe again here in Virga—if not feel at home—and Venera kept him too busy to brood about the past. "I just . . ." Now he did frown.

"What?"

"I hope I remember all of this later, that's all."

"And why wouldn't you?"

Because scry used to be my memory, and now it's gone. But he didn't say that, firstly because she wouldn't understand; and secondly because increasingly, he was realizing that he *could* remember things without using the neural implant system.

This whole whirlwind diplomatic mission, for instance: it seemed every instant was indelibly printed in his mind. The curling mists that enwrapped the frozen city of Seasory were as vivid to him now as when they had arrived there. Mostly what he remembered about Seasory was Leal—Leal emerging from her cabin to breathe deep the brisk air of one of her own country's major trading partners; her craning her neck at the city's sights—its tenements made of ice that loomed over cleated iron streets, the men and women like feathered pillars in their coats, gliding to and fro in the mist.

Throughout their visit she had seemed under some spell caused by the permanent darkness and cold; once, Keir had seen her dance a few steps to an inaudible tune when she stood in shadow and thought no one could see her.

He remembered the mechanical back-and-forth of Venera's hips as she stalked straight to the palace of Seasory's satrap to bow here, bow there, give gifts, kiss barons on the cheeks and baronesses on the hand, and then, swaying tick tick tick, leave just as quickly. "Next stop, Aeolia," was all she said as Keir and Leal (confusedly looking back at the bright palace where they'd only been for ten minutes) followed.

And he remembered Aeolia. In Aeolia, the skies sang. Rather than single big town wheels, the Aeolians spun thousands of small ones, each boasting a dozen or so buildings. They begrudged their ancient genes that required they spend some time in gravity, so everything of value that they built soared in the weightless spaces between their wheels. Most important of all these creations were the symphonicads: gigantic assemblages that filtered wind through thousands of pipes and horns and across the strings of countless harps and dulcimers. The symphonicads sang, but it was no random clitter-clatter such as a wind chime might make. Their design was so cunning that they improvised melodies and harmonies of entrancing beauty and complexity. The Aeolians staged plays and built brilliantly lit tableaux around them. They hooped wires to catch water, touching a single drop of oil to the stretched surfaces, and built vast intricate cities of quivering rainbow transparency, disguising their town wheels behind bouquets of silvered color.

They feted Venera on a single giant spinning hoop of golden silk. It undulated in the air, turning only as quickly as necessary to keep the tables and chairs in contact with its inner surface. Keir bounced, delighted on this pliant surface whose outer edges rippled in the wind; jugglers and tumblers rolled onto and off the ribbon, the symphonicads chorused like angels, and Venera earnestly declared Slipstream's eternal pledge to defend Aeolia.

The Aeolians laughed. No one attacked them. They were too beautiful.

"No one has ever *yet* attacked you," replied Venera. "But they will. And soon."

The Aeolians laughed again, but, when they left the next morning, Venera carried with her a sheaf of gilded documents bearing the Aeolian seal. Keir hadn't seen who had given them to her—but then, he'd not had the stamina to stay up half the night talking and drinking as she had.

"Next stop, Emperaza," Venera had said. And in the *Judgment's* lounge, she added a green dot to the giant chart that half-filled one wall.

"Memory . . ." Keir said now. Leal raised an eyebrow expectantly. "Where I come from, all our experiences are recorded by devices like my dragonflies. Stored in perfect faithful detail. We only use our biological memories to find those records and then we replay them, instead of remembering in full the natural way."

Leal thought about that. "I don't get it," she said after a minute. "How would you remember this dinner, then? Wouldn't you have to sit through the whole damn interminable hours-long grind of it again? Wouldn't it take longer to remember things that way?"

"Oh! No, you see, scry builds emblems for us." She looked puzzled. "An emblem is a collection of perceptual moments that registered as important to us at the time," he said. "Scry builds a little tableau or mini-scene, usually just a second or two long, out of those elements. But you can focus on any one of them and spin it out into as much detail as you want, right up to slowing down or stopping time so you can thoroughly explore any given second."

Leal leaned across the table and pushed at his forearm. "And you said you were human."

"I'm serious! I had that, and I've lost it."

Instead of concern, he saw a mischievous look bloom across her face. "You know, we have something like that, too—and so do you. It's called *imagination.*

"—Oh, wait," she said suddenly. "Someone's coming."

A diminutive page appeared at the tableside. He was not more than ten years old but crammed into a starched black uniform. "Lady requests your presence," he said solemnly to Keir.

"Mine? Oh." He glanced at Leal, who shrugged; so he wiped his lips on the napkin and followed the boy back to the head table.

"See?" said Venera, putting out her arms in a span to show Keir off to the others at the table. "This is one of them."

An elderly woman in fine silks frowned skeptically at Keir. "The boy is from Artificial Nature?"

Keir bowed, as Venera had coached him.

"Come on, then," prompted the man next to the frowning woman. "Prove it."

Keir looked at Venera.

"He's not a dancing raven," she snapped. "He doesn't do tricks."

"Well, then . . ."

"Excuse me," interrupted Keir. "Perhaps if I knew what it was you had been debating?"

"No, that's—" Venera began, but the frowning woman said, "What is Artificial Nature?"

"Ah." Venera glowered, and he imagined she had just spent a few minutes trying to explain that on her own. "Artificial Nature is technology that is employed by and for nonhuman ends, including the ends of plants, animals, and even other technologies."

"But why is it called Artificial Nature?" the lady pressed.

Keir eyed Venera, who nodded almost imperceptibly. "Well," he said, "what is technology?"

The lady looked confused. "Why, it's . . ." She frowned.

"This fork," said her companion.

"Suns," said someone else.

"Guns."

"Clocks."

Keir made sure to bow again, and Venera began to relax. "Those are all individual cases," he admitted. "But what is technology as such?"

There was silence. Keir nodded. "It is not so obvious. Technology is any natural phenomenon harnessed for human use. —Clothing, for instance, harnesses the phenomenon of insulating air layers to keep us warm; our suns harness the phenomenon of nuclear fusion to light our skies."

They all went *ahh* and smirked at one another as if it had been obvious all along.

"Outside of Virga," Keir continued, "we have a situation where natural phenomena are harnessed for nonhuman use. In fact, harnessed for nonliving, nonsentient uses . . . Is such a thing still a technology?"

Venera was smiling at him now; encouraged, he said, "Out there is a world of natural phenomena employed by other natural phenomena. Some are employed for a purpose; others are controlled by systems that have no purpose—that are just technologies run amok. It's a wilderness. Chaos. A state of nature, built with and by and for what we would call technologies. Out there . . ." He suppressed a shudder at a flash of memory he'd not known he had. "Things look like they are designed, look like they have a function, look like they're being used by someone for some purpose . . . when they're not. They appear to be technologies, but they are in fact just natural phenomena, distilled to their essences, and running wild."

Something in his tone had silenced the entire table. Their general expression was one of alarm—all save Venera, who appeared quite satisfied. "Thank you," she said, waving a hand brusquely. Keir bowed, and backed away as she'd taught him.

He was trying to catch that elusive memory as he sat down across from Leal. Something about a garden, and a house—and a woman who didn't remember Keir's name.

"—went all right?" Leal was asking. Keir shook his head.

"Yes, I think I gave them exactly the answer Venera was asking for."

"About what?"

He told her, and they talked on; but for the rest of the evening, Keir felt as though his mind were somehow divided in two. Part of him was at the table, basking in golden gaslight in the exotic palace of a Virgan kingdom. The other part was casting here and there, overturning the furniture of disused, natural memories in search of something elusive that suddenly seemed hugely important.

EVERY TEN SECONDS, the room flipped over. Antaea ignored the stomach-flipping effects of artificial gravity in such a small wheel as Airsigh indicated she should sit down opposite her. Along with them, the long and slightly curved conference table accommodated some other Last Line officers—but none of especially high rank. This, Antaea found especially interesting.

She looked from Airsigh to the other faces. "All right," she said, "what the hell is going on?"

They exchanged a few glances. "We're not sure ourselves," said a gray-haired captain. "We're told there's some new accommodation with the outsiders. A new alliance. But it's the First Line who're telling us this, dictating to us like we have no say in the matter. It's . . ."

"Disturbing," said Airsigh. "Look, Argyre, I'll be blunt. Our senior officers don't seem concerned, but those of us on the lines, we're hearing conflicting stories, and we want to know . . ."

"Who's right and who's lying?" She twined her fingers together on the tabletop. "I'm afraid I can't help you with that."

The older man shook his head impatiently. "Your friends in Slipstream think there's a threat to Virga."

Airsigh nodded. "And the First Line followed what it thought was that threat into Aethyr, where it crashed some of their ships. At least, that's the official story. But we know there's another side to it—this claim that somebody out there was trying to make contact with us and it all went wrong."

Antaea blinked in surprise. "You heard that?"

Airsigh tapped a sheaf of papers Antaea hadn't noticed before. "Something out there has continued to try to make contact. It calls itself a 'morphont' and claims that some history dean, Leal Hieronyma Maspeth, was its intermediary." She shot Antaea an intent look. "Do you know anything about these morphonts?"

"I know they're not sapient like we are," Antaea said. She'd made the same objection when Leal had told her about the emissary. "They wear consciousness like clothing—they don it and shed it as needed. How can the interests of creatures like that possibly align with ours?"

Airsigh gave that question some consideration. "They might if we faced another, bigger threat," she said finally. "'The enemy of my enemy' and all that. Maybe they don't think the way we do, but they can calculate odds just as well as us. Anyway, we don't know, and this is why we're trying to investigate further."

Antaea frowned at this unsatisfying answer.

"The problem," said the older Guardsman, "is that the First Line has declared the matter closed and refuses to talk to the morphonts. At the same time they're receiving all these new visitors of their own. It's as if some other faction has gone into high gear. We know there were already some ambassadors among the First Line."

"So you don't have any reliable information about what's going on out at the high command?"

Airsigh laughed. "Oh, we have plenty of information! It's just hard to make sense of it. Like, take the 'emissary' or 'monster,' for instance. We've seen reports from the lone survivor of its attack, and they corroborate the First Line's story."

"Who's this survivor?"

"He's a cabinet minister from the same sunless country as the professor. Name's Loll."

Leal had told Antaea all about Eustace Loll, of course, and had painted him as an untrustworthy mosquito of a man. There was no way Antaea could admit to these people that she knew anything about him. "What's his story?"

"That the white filaments making up the morphont's body had taken over the other survivors of the crash one by one, turning them all into horrible extensions of itself. He spun quite a tale— and he ended it by warning that anybody else who went down to the plains of Aethyr was likely to meet the same fate. Convenient. Our senior people believe it."

"Wait a minute!" Antaea looked from face to face. "There is no plan to look for other survivors?"

"None," said Airsigh tersely. Distractedly, she tapped the papers with one fingertip. "Then the First Line sent us him." She nodded at a closed door that led to another section of the tiny house wheel.

"Who is he?" Antaea asked.

"Why don't you meet him," suggested Airsigh, "and then maybe you can tell us?" She made to rise, causing the two men on her left to shuffle out from behind the table to make way for her. Suddenly apprehensive, Antaea followed her to the door, where she knocked discreetly. "Come in," someone said.

He was extraordinarily good-looking, and would have stood out in any Virgan crowd despite his attempt to wear nondescript, even slightly shabby clothing. He bowed, a little awkwardly, as Antaea entered the parlor where he'd been waiting. "I'm Holon," he said.

"Antaea Argyre."

"Ah, yes! The adventuress. I've heard so much about you."

His name was vaguely familiar, but she couldn't quite place it. Something Leal had said . . . "They tell me you're an ambassador," she said cautiously.

He shook his head. "Not really—oh, I should explain. I was an observer sent from my people as part of an exchange with your Home Guard. When the incident at Aethyr happened, I was stranded with the Home Guard ships on the plains. I managed to return to my people, but I'm afraid the rest of that expedition was lost. —Except, I hear, for Minister Loll."

This Holon was as charming as he was handsome, but Antaea remembered where she'd heard the name before. She nearly said, "You tried to convince the Guard to kill Leal Maspeth," before remembering that if she admitted she knew that, she'd be giving away Leal's return, the existence of another door to Aethyr—essentially everything. "How is it you survived?"

"I walked away," he said with a shrug. "The Guardsmen and the other humans from Virga wouldn't have survived the journey. But I," he raised his perfect hands, "have augmentations that allowed me to survive until I could contact some of my people."

"But by then the rest of the survivors were dead?" He nodded. "Killed," pressed Antaea, "by . . . what?"

Holon crossed his arms and frowned out the parlor's window. "We call them morphonts. They're creatures of Artificial Nature; they come in as many varieties as there are stars in the sky.

"Oh," he said suddenly. "You caught me as I was eating. You don't mind if I—?"

"By all means." She saw that a small buffet had been set up under the window.

He noticed her interest, and smiled. "Would you care to join me?"

Silent, she piled her plate high with cold cuts. Standing next to this foreigner, loading up on food—it was a very strange experience, but she barely noticed. She was thinking about Leal's conviction that the emissary was a friend, while at the same time, she'd insisted that it wasn't a conscious being like herself. The contradiction had been glaring the first time Antaea heard it. Over the weeks it hadn't become any less so.

Holon frowned at the fare, which was mostly meat. "It's difficult grazing for a vegetarian here."

"You're a vegetarian?" She watched as he picked through the food.

"Don't get me wrong, I love meat," he added as he piled up a plate. "Back home, I eat it all the time. But then, we've got other things besides meat and vegetable matter to eat—and whatever meat I eat is vat-grown."

She nodded, remembering the Home Guard fortress at the Gates of Virga. "I've had it. A perfect steak, every time."

"The mere thought of eating the flesh of something that once had a brain horrifies me," he continued. "I know you Virgans are a bit more ruthless that way. I suppose you have to be. But my conscience won't allow me to harm another sentient being."

Antaea put down her plate. "But you're happy to kill the morphonts." He shrugged. He sat at the parlor's little table, arraying his food around him.

"Tell me more about the morphonts," she said. "They're not aware like you and me, you say. How then are they a threat to anyone? Wouldn't they just be like plants, if they have no minds?"

"It's hardly a secret who they are or how they work—"

"Oh, but it is. Your people never told us about them," she interjected. "I was in the Guard for many years. I even traveled outside Virga—"

"I'm sure we told you," he said with sudden irritation. "Maybe you didn't understand us."

"Fair enough." She held up a placating hand. "And forgive me if you've been asked this twenty times already. Indulge me—what do you believe the morphonts are?"

"A mistake," Holon said curtly. "One that's taken over much of the universe, at the expense of conscious beings like you and me.

"Imagine that your tools could think—even anticipate your needs. Back in the early days of our expansion into space, we humans created machines like that. At first, we had to tell them what to do. They obeyed our orders—did what we said, but not always what we *wanted*. They didn't understand us the way we understood each other. So some wise idiots decided to give them the capacity to understand our needs, as well as our commands.

192 | KARL SCHROEDER

So they could anticipate what we would want, rather than having to be told."

Antaea frowned. "And this was a mistake?"

He snorted. "Well, it's not as if there hadn't been countless stories written by then about what would happen if you let your machines understand you that well. —Problem is, they were all wrong. They all assumed the machines would take over—remove our free choice, disobey our orders in order to give us what we needed instead of what we wanted. Ridiculous, of course. They never ceased to follow orders."

"Then what went wrong?"

"We'd given them the ability to perceive purpose. Many of our researchers thought that purpose—or values, intentionality—was an illusion of our human perspective. Turns out it's not; it's an emergent feature of the universe, as real as water and rock. And it's not just humans that have it."

"Purpose . . . You're talking about *meaning?*"

Holon nodded. "The Moderns who built the first artificial intelligences didn't really believe our minds were a part of this universe. They were still saddled with ancient religious beliefs, but they didn't know it. They thought meaning was some kind of local human illusion, or the gift of a god. But everything that lives, wants, and to want is to give meaning to things. —To say *yes,* or *no,* even if it's just about whether some speck is food.

"Once our machines could see that, they could no longer see the distinction between us and any other living thing. Of course, we didn't realize it at first. By the time our ancestors figured it out, some of our machines had started taking orders from nonhuman— and nonthinking—kinds of life."

"You're saying they started working for . . . what?" She laughed. "Trees?"

But Holon wasn't laughing. "We *recognize* each other. We see the spark of life, of awareness, in one another. It's so easy for us that we never even considered that it might not be easy for an artificial intelligence. But they are not us. They cannot recognize that spark in us, the way we see each other. Other than its shape, and the fact that one can give verbal orders and the other can't, what's the *real* difference between a human and a tree? Or a dog. Or a lion?"

She didn't know what those last two things were, but the implication was clear—and unbelievably strange—to Antaea. But she remembered some of the weird things she'd seen when she'd visited the realms of Artificial Nature. There had been odd machines—giant crystal spheres encapsulating little miniature ecosystems, surrounded by a retinue of guard bots and helper machines. She'd seen one plow down the center of a street, humans and virtual life-forms hopping out of its way, but none protesting or trying to stop it. She'd asked what they were at the time, but had not understood the answer. "You're saying we gave away our technology to . . . nature itself?"

Holon nodded. "Exactly. One way to put it would be to say that we accidentally created a universal interface for our entire industrial and intellectual legacy—an interface that anything that can *want*, can use."

"But why not simply go back to the way it was? Make machines that only obey orders from something that looks like a human?"

"Oh, we do. Now. But the machines that chained their own purposes to those of nonhuman life-forms proliferated; they took their own will to survive and reproduce from the species they allied with. Some became fierce beyond all human control."

Antaea was shaking her head. Holon said, "Look at it this way, then: an artificial intelligence doesn't come with its own will to live. That's something separate from the ability to think, it has to be added on. You don't notice this until you start to build tools that can act on their own—when you stop using them directly. The greater the distance between your guiding hand and the actions of the machine, the more it has to develop its own sense of who 'you' and 'it' are. The best way to get such an autonomous machine to work for you is to design it in such a way that it thinks it *is* you. It studies your desires and needs the way your brain studies the needs of your body; it identifies with you entirely, and has no desires of its own. It isn't even aware of itself. But a machine that can do that can just as easily identify itself as a flower, or a crow, or any other creature. It could identify itself as a rock, I suppose, but rocks have no needs. A machine that did that would just stop. But imagine one that, for one reason or another, has no human to imprint on. It searches for things like humans—and let's say it finds a crow. Once it understands some particular crow, it comes to think of itself *as* the crow—and has access to the entire history of human ingenuity and industry, to aid in obtaining what that crow wants . . .

"So nature rebelled, first on Earth, then all her colonies. Except in one place, where our technology couldn't reach."

"Virga." She thought about it. "So who are you, in this new world?"

He looked ruefully at his plate. "We're mice in the walls. You know, all things being equal, human beings aren't that competitive—I mean, as a species. But things haven't been equal for the past hundred thousand years. We've had technology, society, and the ability to plan. Other life-forms haven't. Artificial Nature gives all those things to anything that wants them. All things are equal now."

"Look, Argyre, there's no 'us versus them' thing happening here. *They* don't really exist. The morphonts are just mindless forces that have been given an industrial base. Something we made got away from us, and we're starting to get it back. The only question that's of any relevance is whether you're on your own side here, or on the side of blind forces that are against you. Your choice."

Antaea looked down, her arms crossed, then said, "Thanks. Enjoy your meal."

She made to leave, and he said, "Talk to me any time. I'm not just here for the food."

"I WISH I could tell you who to trust," she told Airsigh, "but I'm as confused as everybody."

The Last Line captain seemed to accept this. As she flew Antaea back to her hotel, however, she said, "What about Slipstream?"

Antaea pretended to think about the possibility. "I have ties there. I know they're deeply concerned about the same issues . . . If you'd like, I can set up a meeting between some of your people and the admiralty."

"That would be good. I'll give the address of our drop box."

As she climbed out of Airsigh's little jet and watched it soar off into the flocking traffic of the city, Antaea knew she should be feeling a sense of triumph at how things had turned out. She'd made exactly the contact Chaison had hoped. Why, then, was she so troubled?

And, of course, she knew why: Holon. He'd not been what she'd expected. She remembered the blank thing her sister had become after being possessed by something from outside of Virga. Holon wasn't like that.

If anything *was* like the monster her sister had become, it was this emissary Leal claimed as her friend.

Deeply disturbed, she flew to her hotel to tell Richard that she'd been successful.

ANOTHER COUNTRY, ANOTHER palace, and another dinner party. They had long since blurred together in Keir's mind, yet he found himself smiling tonight as he, Leal, and Venera made their way back to this city's dockyards. Their military escort saluted and left them on the inner curve of the cylindrical dock. Leal waved to the soldiers, but Venera dismissed them with a sniff and, in the microgravity, bounded in long slow steps in the direction of their ship.

A cowled figure waited in the shadow of the yacht. Leal saw it only when Venera suddenly stopped and put her arm across Leal's chest. As Keir bumped into Leal, Venera reached for an absent sidearm; they'd been required to leave their weapons on the yacht. "Please, I'm a friend," said a woman's voice. The gray-cloaked shape bobbed through the dock's minuscule gravity to perch before them, and as Venera said "Who—" it threw back its hood.

Leal recognized the face; this young woman had been at the banquet. She'd been seated at the first table to the right of the main table, which meant she was a person of high standing. Leal carefully bowed, and didn't quite have to kick Keir in the shins before he did, too. Venera held her head high—but of course, Venera bowed to no one.

They all stood in half-shadow, but the young woman clearly thought that this wasn't discreet enough; she windmilled her arms and sailed a few feet back, into the darkness. "Please, I can't be seen here," she called softly.

Venera glanced up at the well-lit main hatch of the yacht. "There's another way in," she said curtly. "This way." She led them under the belly of the yacht. To the left were the lights, gantries, and piled crates of the docking ring that rode at the central axle of the town wheel; to the right was a sheer drop-off, and night skies.

Venera fished a key out of her belt, then reached up into blackness. "Keir, give me a boost," she said. He knitted his fingers together and she stepped up to push an unseen door aside. She clambered in, and a moment later let down a rope ladder.

When they were all inside—in the yacht's cramped storage locker, as it turned out—Venera turned to the stranger and said, "You can speak freely in front of my companions. What is this about?"

"My name is Thavia. I'm the satrap's niece." She eyed Leal and Keir suspiciously, but then found a perch on some boxes and without further hesitation said, "You are not the first to come to us with talk of an invasion from the outside universe. The viziers made a big show tonight of sending a delegation to your grand colloquy, but according to my father, our government has already committed our loyalty to a different faction."

Venera scowled. "Who were they?"

Thavia described two foreigners who had visited court. She had been pale-skinned, pale-haired, her lips a red slash across her beautiful face. Her name was Inshiri Ferance, and though Thavia had never heard of her, the mere mention of her was enough to make the satrap and his viziers turn as pale as her. Thavia had always feared the viziers, who were known to be capricious and judgmental, and she had never seen them afraid. They were afraid of Inshiri.

She offered the satrap power and new riches if he would ally with her against that upstart pirate sun, Slipstream. The Slipstreamers would arrive soon, spreading their lies, and Inshiri advised the satrap to imprison them at once. Her friends would be grateful if that were to happen. But as she spoke, she kept her head turned, ever so slightly, in the direction of the silent, bronze-skinned man who had accompanied her here. He was never introduced, but merely stood in the background with his arms crossed and watched Inshiri's performance. No one in the room, Thavia swore, had doubted who was really in charge here.

"They made a deal," Thavia told Venera. "I wasn't party to it, but whatever it was, my parents were supremely uncomfortable with it. After they left, I was told I was being sent to some city named Fracas, as a 'special ambassador' of some sort. I don't want to go . . ."

Venera stroked the scar on her chin. "Fracas? Would any of the people there recognize you?"

"Surely not."

Venera smiled. "In that case, I have a plan."

JACOBY SARTO CLOSED the door to his hotel room, and then had to lean on it heavily as a wave of pain and nausea overtook him. He looked up and down the hall, but there was no one to see his weakness. With a muted curse he walked carefully to the stairs, keeping his head high despite the almost overwhelming urge to simply lie down and curl around his maimed hand.

She had left his hotel room half an hour before. Theirs had not been a romantic rendezvous. The least of it had been the interrogation she'd subjected him to. He'd expected that, of course; how could she know he could be trusted, since she didn't even know where he'd been and what he'd been up to since they had parted ways.

That had been humiliating, but nothing compared with what had happened next. Inshiri still didn't trust him; she needed a guarantee of his loyalty.

"Fool," he muttered to himself as he leaned on the doorjamb to the stairwell. As Sacrus's representative on Spyre's grand council, he'd had a legitimate claim to all of Sacrus's remaining assets after the destruction of Spyre. He could have fought Inshiri for them— should have taken it down to a contest of loyalties and cunning then, when she was vulnerable. He had all of Sacrus's foreign operations in his hand, since he'd been able to act days before any of the surviving members of the ruling families thought to try it themselves.

But with the reins of true power in his hands at last, Jacoby Sarto had lost his nerve. Now he looked at the blood-soaked bandages wrapped around his left hand and said, "You've got no one to blame but yourself, Jacoby."

Unused to wielding power for his own sake, he'd found he had no idea what to do with the resources he'd acquired. He would never admit it to anyone else, but he'd been terrified to be saddled with the responsibility it all came with.

Inshiri Ferance hadn't had to threaten him. At the first opportunity he'd turned the foreign services back over to her, and he'd flown away from his chance at real power with haste and a terribly unmanning relief.

Inshiri knew he'd blinked, and though she'd allowed him back into her inner circle, she treated him with contempt. The guarantee she'd taken from him tonight was minor for her, but calculated to make him aware, every day for the rest of his life, that he was and would always remain a servant.

He put his good hand on the railing and stared down the stairwell, which seemed to be tipping slowly over—whether due to this wheel's rotation, or the delirium of pain he was in, he couldn't have said.

"Sane people put their docks up top," he said, then laughed at himself. He was talking to no one! Anyway, it was true; at the axis of a wheel there was no gravity and you could moor or unmoor at leisure. The engineers at Kaleidogig were stupid barbarians, though, and they liked to live dangerously. He slowly descended the steps, leaning on the wall to guarantee that he knew up from down.

When he entered the Kaleidogig docking galleries he shook his head in fury: how was he going to make it across this jumble of half-built jet bikes, stolen taxis, and decommissioned military catamarans, all of them swinging off hooks like fresh-caught game? The floor under them was a minefield of big hatches that could be thrown open by the pull of a lever—and might fall out from under you if you stepped on them. Even as he leaned there trying to pick out a safe route, the lamps in the long, upward-curving room flickered as one of the hatches banged down and a puff of wind rushed through the place. A courier who sat astride his bike above this hatch reached up, casually unclipped the chain suspending him, and he and the bike fell through the opening and into the hundred-mile-per-hour headwind made by the town wheel's spin.

A dockhand approached, wiping his hands on a greasy rag. "Yer all right, sar?"

"Fine. I'm fine." He hid his left hand behind himself, and wiped away the sweat on his forehead with his palm. "I'm expecting someone," he added curtly.

"If yer say so. Just don't go near the cats." The hand nodded at the bigger military craft, which hung nodding behind a yellow rope.

Jacoby pulled himself into a more dignified posture and forced himself to walk steadily over to the entrance hatches. These looked similar to the exits, but he knew that below, on the outside of the town's hull, each was partially sheltered by a ramp-shaped windbreak. There were lookouts down there waiting to open the hatches for incoming craft. That must be cold and lonely shift work, he thought, and he felt a momentary kinship with the men down there.

A hatch thirty feet away fell open without warning, and a small tornado of air blasted Jacoby, making him stagger. Like a strange jack-in-the-box, an airman on a bike popped up out of the hatch. He was standing up in his stirrups, holding up a hook, and at the top of his bounce into the hangar, he clanged the hook over one of the overhead rods. Then he sat down heavily as the bike swung, engine roaring, in the vortex of air that was howling through the hatch below him.

He cut the engine as the doors to the hatch laboriously inched shut. When the last crack had been sealed, leaving only the ominous whistle that all the closed hatches made, he pulled off his leather flyer's helmet and dismounted the bike.

Jacoby recognized him. They met just in front of the bike, whose round maw showed a still-spinning maze of teeth. "Sarto," said the man with a barely respectful duck of the head.

Jacoby took a shuddering breath and said, "Were you seen? Did anyone question you?"

"Naw, it's black air out there, I took the last fifty miles at a hundred 'n fifty miles an hour. Have to be crazy to follow me." He grinned, obviously still exhilarated at his daredevil stunt.

"Good, but you'll have to leave the same way." Jacoby couldn't help but glance around to see if there was anyone but the dockhand working here. If he were Inshiri, he'd put a watch on Jacoby Sarto—and maybe she was about to do that very thing. He had to put his plan in motion before it became impossible for him to contact his own men without her noticing.

He fumbled one-handed in his jacket, then held out a thick envelope. "Here's the orders. Are the ships ready? Fueled and armed?"

His man nodded as he took the package and shoved it into his jacket. He clearly hadn't noticed Jacoby's distress; good. "What's the target?" he asked with a grin. "I might go myself, if it's somewhere nice."

"It's not." Jacoby looked him in the eye. "It's Hell, actually."

"Oh, you've been there?"

"I have. Now on your way before somebody comes." He turned away as the airman hopped back into his saddle; but he was careful to watch and make sure that the jet roared to life, and that the courier rose and unclipped his line and fell into the night.

It was all in the hands of fate now, but he felt a little better at having finally done something decisive.

On the way back upstairs he became dizzy and nearly fell down. He sat in a broad windowsill and leaned his head against the rippled glass. A mile away, the giant can shape of Inshiri's observatory spun slowly in the black air. The structure was turned now so that Jacoby could see down its length. At its core glowed a tiny, human-shaped spark of crimson.

He smiled in angry satisfaction. Inshiri thought she was punishing him by giving him the Fracas operation. It was menial, after all; but she didn't know everything that was going on, nor did she suspect he might have a minor, but effective, fleet of his own.

Once it did what he'd just commanded it to do, he'd have one very big playing piece in his hands. With Fracas, he already had another; and if the bait he'd hung out worked (and he thought he knew the psychology of the person it was aimed at well enough) he would soon have the third.

There was only one more piece in play that mattered, and he didn't yet know how he would get possession of that.

He glared at the tiny figure playing goddess at the focus of her telescope. She thought the little sacrifice he'd given her tonight would make him a falcon on her glove. She was in for a surprise.

But not just yet. He levered himself back to his feet and grimly plodded up the last steps to his floor. In a few moments he could collapse on his room's tattered little bed, and tomorrow he'd send one of his men to locate a good source of painkillers.

Inshiri knew the game board, but he knew which pieces owned the game. With luck, in a few days he would have them all, and then Inshiri would become *his* pawn.

14

LEAL WAS LOOKING out one of the yacht's portholes when the ship began braking heavily. She braced her hands on the bulkhead in front of her, as fore suddenly became down.

Her reverie was broken. Leal wasn't even sure what she'd been daydreaming about, but she knew her shattered ambitions had been in there somewhere. Her dream of being a university professor, of achieving tenure and spending her twilight years surrounded by ancient books . . . it was all so far from here and now as to constitute a separate life. Once this was all over, could she return to those daydreams? It seemed so unlikely.

The braking eased up, and now she saw the running lights of some sort of way station up ahead. Several ships hulked in the twilight air. Stations and caravansaries weren't unusual in the zones where the light of different suns overlapped. It was too dim here for agriculture, but destinations were clearly visible. You could hang out a shingle and sell fuel and food, and make out pretty well. This particular station seemed even more prosperous than most.

It would be good to get out and stretch, even if there was no gravity to be had here. She climbed out of her narrow stateroom and nearly collided with Keir Chen, who was sailing down the yacht's spinal corridor. "Rest stop?" she said to him.

He shook his head. "Two of those ships are Slipstream cruisers, and I'm not the expert here, but they look pretty banged up."

She went back to her window to look. Sure enough, there were black scars and holes in the hulls of two of the vessels parked by the stop. Returning to the corridor she found Venera already undogging the main hatch. The admiral's wife wore functional leathers and a bandolier, with pistols at her belt. This must be serious.

"What's going on?"

Venera spared her a quick glance. "Those are two of the ships we sent to Serenity."

"Oh!" They all waited impatiently for the dockhands to catch their ropes and haul them in. Before they were even tied down, Venera had hopped off the ship and was pulling herself hand over hand along a rope that led to the station's main building. Leal and Keir followed as quickly as they could.

The station building was a wooden sphere about a hundred feet across, with various blocky buildings crowding its inside surface. There was an administrative shed, two stores, a hotel, a bar, and something that might actually be a brothel, based on the apparel of the women drifting in front of it. The center of the space held a bank of crude electrical lamps, whose flickering light was competing with a bright glow from the bar. Loud music and raucous voices could be heard coming from there.

Venera, Leal, and Keir looked at one another, then sailed in that direction.

Venera perched on the lip of the door and looked in; Keir did so opposite her. Windup lamps in colored paper balls were bouncing around the bar's main room, and all the wicker half-spheres where you could nestle with your drinks and friends were full. Men and women were leaping between the bar itself and various loud conversations; clearly, whatever was going on here was at its height.

One laugh wormed its way through the noise of all the others, and Leal found herself rearing back in confusion. "It can't be—"

She grabbed the doorframe and flipped herself into the room—and there he was, large as life and alive, in fact holding a helix glass of beer and cheering something. "*Hayden!*"

He glanced over, did a double take, and let go of the glass. "Leal!" Leaving his drink twirling in midair, Hayden Griffin launched himself across the bar, nearly colliding with another man who'd chosen the same moment to head for the toilets. Hayden opened his arms and docked with Leal, crushing her in his embrace. "There you are!"

She returned the hug, only now aware of how dangerously thin he was. Pushing him back, she gave him a once-over. He was dressed in an ill-fitting airman's uniform in Slipstream colors. His cheeks were hollow, his face and hands sunburnt. But he was alive, and he looked happy.

He looked past Leal and grew suddenly serious. "Lady Fanning."

"Griffin." Venera nodded coolly to him. They had a history, these two, Leal remembered, and not a romantic one. There was blood between them.

"Did all of your men make it?" Venera went on. She was looking around the room, taking in what was now clearly a strange mix of ill-sized Slipstream uniforms and ragged black ones that must belong to Home Guard members.

Hayden shook his head. "We lost ten. Four on the plains, six yesterday."

Venera looked startled. "What happened yesterday?"

"Your secret city was attacked!" The speaker was a lean Home Guard officer, his uniform stained and torn. He hopped over to perch by the door. "They looked like pirate ships, but there were eight of them and they were packed with men. They jumped us just as we were ferrying the last of our men out of Brink."

"Venera Fanning, Niels Lacerta of the Home Guard," said Hayden. "Without Niels and his men, we wouldn't have survived long in Aethyr."

"I remember you," said Leal. "You came to sit by our fire that first night after the crash. We talked about my message."

He nodded. "We've talked about little else since you left us, ma'am. —Whether you were right; whether your 'emissary' is a devil or an angel."

"But . . ." Hayden looked from Leal to Venera and back. He ignored Keir, whom he'd after all never met. "What are *you* doing here?"

Venera shrugged. "A courier found us six hours ago, said there were damaged Slipstream ships at one of our designated rendezvous. Tell me more about this attack."

"They definitely knew where to find the city, and they knew we were there," said Hayden. "It was a coordinated assault. They meant to capture Serenity, I'm sure of it. We managed to beat them back, but they may return. The base commander sent two frigates to Rush for reinforcements."

"But who could it be?" Keir burst out. "Nobody knows about the city but us!"

"Us, and Jacoby Sarto," said Venera.

There was a momentary silence. Leal was confused. "I thought he was a friend of yours?"

Venera appeared to consider this concept for a time. Finally, she held one hand out, and waggled it from side to side. "Even odds," she said. "I'm going to say it was him."

"The commander had planned to send Niels and his men straight back to the Guard, and us directly to Rush," Hayden went on. "But we were attacked again on the way out of the city. One of the cruisers was holed; we've been leaving a trail of fuel all the way across winter. The captain pulled us in here to patch us up and buy enough fuel to get us home. We were just . . ." He glanced around, grinning. ". . . celebrating being back."

He shook his head impatiently. "But anyway, what I *meant* was—Leal, we met your friends in the city and they told us a little of what happened. Is it true about Tarvey?"

"Ah," she said, suddenly stabbed by deep sadness. Tarvey had been Hayden's loyal servant and friend. Loyalty had brought him to Aethyr, had led to him risking his life for Hayden more than once. Ultimately, it had cost him everything.

"Hayden, I don't know what to say."

"Say what happened," advised Venera. "And I suggest you be quick about it. The admiralty's not going to like this tab we're running up."

THEY REMAINED AT the way station for a day, while final repairs were completed on the cruiser. Venera spent much of that time as the queen of a buzzing hive of courier bikes, who zipped in from all six points of the compass to drop off and pick up dispatches. She was planning something, that was obvious, and it was equally obvious that she didn't want her husband to know about it until it was too late for him to veto her. At one point as Keir flew by the main room in her yacht, he heard her telling one of the cruiser's captains, "We're on the far side of the world from Slipstream. I have no time to *send home for orders*! No, we do this now, or the opportunity is lost."

Later, Hayden Griffin and the Home Guard commander Lacerta came by. After an intensive grilling from Venera, they stayed to sample her liquor cabinet and talk. Keir was finally introduced to the famous sun lighter, and after some initial caution, found that he quite liked Griffin. They had something in common, after all: they both loved machines.

Maybe that was the trigger—thinking about machinery—because late that night, Keir began to remember.

There was a storm that night, and even though the *Judgment* was lashed to the station's dock, the winds howled past and shook it like a child's toy. Slotted into his bunk like a wasp in its hive, Keir found himself in total darkness, and weightless except when a gust caught the ship. The close walls of the sleeping closet would tap him unexpectedly, and he'd jolt awake to the sounds of flight or the strange rumble of thunder in an echoless sky. He had no idea how long this went on; and while it did, his mind drifted from Hayden's description of sun-building to jumbled images of things he'd built in Brink—and then beyond.

At first, yes, it was just Brink, and Maerta and the others, though Leal appeared to him, too, more than once. Something about his changing feelings for her reminded him of other memories—but he couldn't find them, he couldn't find them. He kept groping for scry's emblems, but scry didn't work in Virga.

That was Candesce's fault. Right now he hated the sun of suns, and its dark influence on technologies it didn't approve of. He resented its secretive mystery; how it hid itself in wreaths of flame at the heart of Virga, while its vast invisible wings unfurled to the very walls of the world and beyond.

So good, then, that he'd plucked one of its feathers—turned, triumphant, to wave it to Maerta except, no, hadn't it been Sita? Sita all along?

—And suddenly there he was, perched on a bench in a garden whose hedge mazes and flower-dewed trellises draped like the skirts of a seated woman around a round-towered, coral-hued house. The white sun Vega blazed in the zenith, and heat haze and the buzzing of insects complicated the air around him.

The planet's name was Revelation; the continent's, Aegeas, and the city whose floating aerostats peppered the horizon was Atavus. He'd grown up here.

His wife, Sita, was humming as she aerated the roots of some little yellow flowers with her long fingers, lovingly tending the little lives. She was also standing on a ladder and frowning at the gutters of the house, where stalks of grass were poking up. One of her was a proxy, but it would never have occurred to Keir to wonder which one. Sita inhabited both bodies simultaneously and with equal ease.

"Sandrine introduced me to this man the other day," her Self in the garden was saying. The glyphs around her head indicated she was talking to Fethe, one of her oldest friends, who was a thousand kilometers south of them today. "She said you know him a little?"

Keir watched her closely, as if he could learn something this time that he hadn't been able to perceive the last hundred times he'd visited this record within his scry.

"Yes, she said you thought I should meet him." Sita laughed. "His name is Keir Chen . . ." Her expression grew troubled, and she looked around herself, and spotted him.

They'd been married for six years at that point, and had known one another for ten.

Keir stood and walked a little ways away so that he could see himself sitting on the bench. You could do that in scry, since its records of an event didn't have to be limited to what you saw with your own eyes. From outside, the look on Keir's own face was eloquent, as it always was in the record. The version of Keir he was looking at had just come to realize that his wife was de-indexing, and that it was the emblems of her time with him that she was erasing.

A fateful conversation was about to start, but Keir didn't want to hear it. He kept on down the path, which stitched itself together from the infinite storage of his scry as he went. It could show him every instant he'd spent here, but it usually mashed them together into the emblem of an idealized, perfect day. Not for this day's events, though; he rarely accessed their emblems, but reviewed them in their entirety.

De-indexing had been a taboo for him before Sita started doing it. After, he'd drifted into temptation, year after year. But when something finally happened that made him annihilate vast tracts of his past, for some reason he'd remembered all those pieces he'd always planned to lose. Instead of erasing the pain and the disappointments—even Sita's betrayal—he'd kept it all, and lost something else.

Near the path, a cloud of pixies was fluttering around a meter-high revus bush that was threatening them with tiny cannons mounted on its metal leaves. "Don't you dare!" a pixie scolded as the guns swiveled toward it. "Keir Chen will dig you up if you shoot us!"

The plant began firing, in a cascade of little pops that would be inaudible from more than three meters away. The pixies ducked and swerved and, from a safe distance, began chanting "We're telling! We're telling!"

Keir rarely visited this part of the record, but somehow this time he remembered it—as he was remembering everything now in his dream, rather than accessing his scry. For some reason he'd stopped and frowned at the unfolding drama. Pixies, dryads, talking trees—they'd been a normal part of his life on Revelation. The world was an enchanted place and, even at the time of this memory, he'd taken that for granted.

Near the revus was a clutch of box tulips. The flowers were ordinary enough, but each one was contained in a crystal case scaled to its size and pose. Like the nanotech revus bush, each terrarium was festooned with miniature cannons, trembling stingers, and caterpillar-blinding lasers. Little doors in the boxes sported flashing bee-attractor signs.

Woe to the gardener who tried to dig up a box tulip. At the first cut of the trowel their planetary mesh network would go on high alert. Tulip sirens would go off all over the neighborhood. Brainhacked wasps would converge on you. The tulip consortium's AIs would harass you by tagging your scry with insults and slanderous accusations. Their shell companies and corporations would hire lawyers and sue you.

If you made it indoors unscathed, the tulips would bomb the other flowers in your garden until you came out again and promised them reparations.

That sort of ruckus had never seemed remarkable to Keir when he was living here. At some point after he'd left Revelation, though, and before he'd de-indexed his own life, the tulips and the pixies had become the most urgent part of his memories of Revelation. He just wished he remembered why.

A shadow fell across the clutch of tulip terrariums. Keir looked up to see a black, faceless, hooded figure looming over the path. It raised a bony finger and pointed it at him accusingly.

This was no longer a memory of the day he'd discovered Sita's discontent; instead, he was remembering visiting that memory at some time after.

"You should not be here," said the nag.

He glared at it. "I'm not staying." The nags were a common feature of the scry, and he would regularly see them in the distance when he visited this, or any memory. They were there to kick you out of your recorded past if you spent too much time there. They were an annoying, but important, mental-health tool of the scry.

He'd always considered the nags a nuisance, though he'd rarely met one up close. When he'd laid down this particular memory, they'd still been common in Revelation's scry.

"You keep coming here," grated the nag now. "We don't like it." It bent over and began swatting box tulips. Each virtual terrarium fizzed and vanished as the nag touched it.

Keir remembered cursing. "How can you say that! You *left* Revelation! You abandoned us."

"You should go. Or do you want me to wipe this record clean?" The nag began reaching out, grabbing distant clouds, hills on the horizon, and floating city-spheres. Soon it had an armful of scene elements. "Do you want these memories crushed?"

"You dare threaten *me* with that?" Keir pointed a shaking finger at one of his Sitas. "When you gave up on *her?*" The nag squeezed, and pieces of the memory popped like soap bubbles. Keir yelled in fury and fell out of the scene—and, on Venera's yacht, banged against the wall of his sleeping closet.

LEAL FOUND HIM outside. Keir was sitting on the yacht's hull, letting the fresh breeze following the storm caress his brow. He opened his eyes when she appeared in the hatch, noticed the concern on her face and, as she made to go back inside, said, "No. I'd appreciate the company."

She clipped a line to her belt and climbed out next to him. Candesce was a yellow fire at infinity, just slightly too dim to make daylight for any nation that might covet this volume of air. It was still night by Slipstream's clock, and the ship had been quiet when he'd come out here.

Leal settled down next to him, but said nothing. Keir felt a growing compulsion to fill the silence; at last he said, "Do you know how old I am?"

She shook her head. "Seventeen? Nineteen? Or do your years differ from ours?"

"No, they don't." He met her gaze and said, "Leal, I am seventy-nine years old. Too young to have neotenized myself twice. Yet it seems I did."

She reared back in surprise, almost losing her grip on the hull. "Keir, what are you talking about?"

"Neotenizing. De-indexing. They're two ways to renew yourself when the weight of life and memory gets to be too much." He looked back at the flowerlike cloudscape ahead of them. "With de-indexing, you sever your ability to access certain records of your past. Then, your natural memories wither as well. It's a gentle way of turning your back on past events . . . relationships . . . that you want to forget.

"But neotenization . . . it means 'to turn into a child.' That's a much more radical procedure." He held out his hands, which had once been larger and stronger. He'd had a scar on the back of the left one, though he no longer remembered where or when he'd gotten that. The scar was lost, and so was the memory.

"I've—I've been thinking a lot," murmured Leal, "about what you said—that death and immortality are equally bad choices. Your people learned this from experience with both."

"Of the two, death is the better choice," he said. "Death is forgetting, and there's plenty of reasons why you should want to do that.

"I was not born in the city of Brink. I come from a planet named Revelation, and I owned a house there. I was married." He looked at her, but now her expression was neutral. She was intent on his words, and not ready to judge them yet.

"My wife, Sita . . . she de-indexed me. At the time, I was devastated; it was the end of a relationship I had built my life around. What I didn't know at the time was that what she'd done . . . Well, millions of people on Revelation were undergoing similar transformations. The scry on Revelation had been compromised—*hacked*, I think is the old word for it. Sita didn't just leave me . . . she left humanity itself."

Now that he knew where to look in his own mind, he remembered it—not all, but enough. Sita had forgotten him; but in the months after their marrage had dissolved, he'd still held out hope that they might have a second chance. They could, after all, start over from scratch as long as she didn't de-list him from her social reality.

But then, during the gentle winter of the year, something had started killing nags.

Revelation had always been a beautiful planet, and most of its beauty was real. The virtual overlays that accented it (like the cascades of pixie dust the fairies threw off) were subtle and added to the wonder of the natural world. Anyone who spent too long in a purely virtual world would get kicked out by the nags; keeping people anchored in reality was, after all, their function.

"When the rumors about the nags started," he told Leal, "I was too sunk in my own misery to pay much attention. At first I didn't notice when the scry's overlays on my senses began to become more detailed, more interlinked into these strange and gorgeous, purely virtual realms. I guess I was sufficiently unhappy—and sufficiently stubborn not to take a cure for my misery—that I remained immune to this kind of a . . . siren call . . . of a nag-free, virtual paradise that had started to creep over Revelation."

As he'd sat here on the hull of the *Judgment*, Keir had found himself thinking about one memory in particular—a memory that he couldn't believe he'd lost during these past months. It was of his last glimpse of Sita.

"I remember her," he said softly, "standing on marble steps that led up to a golden, glowing archway. A dozen of my other friends were there, too. It's like a dream, but I know it really happened: some of them walked without hesitation up and into the light and it . . . swallowed them. Sita glanced around once, and there was recognition in her eyes. And then she, too, mounted the steps and consigned her mind to an online reality that would never again let her free."

In the real world, Sita's body and its double had fallen silent. That day they had left Atavus to join a vast throng of Revelation's population that was congregating at the edge of the seashore. Like ants, they were building a vast arcology—a hive—for the entity that had traded them its illusions for reality.

"A week after that, I sold my house to the tulips and I left Revelation for good." He had joined the Renaissance.

"Leal, I was one of the founders of the Brink expedition. But . . . something happened. Sometime in the past two years, I was neotenized. That's not all bad; my body began to change, shedding its old cells and structures, replacing it all with new, strong tissue. But my brain began to lose the pathways it had built for decades. It began to rewire itself, and when that happens it's not just memory that you lose. Most of your personality goes as well.

"Whether I did this to myself or . . . someone forced it on me, I don't know—"

"Forced it on you?" She looked horrified. "Who would do such a thing?"

He shrugged. "It's less than murder, but just as effective. And I would never have known, had I not come here to Virga. The process seems to have stopped, probably because of—" He nodded at distant Candesce.

She followed his gaze to the sun of suns. "Do you have any idea who it was? Someone at the Renaissance?"

"It could have been me." He slapped the cold hull. "I know I never got over what happened to Sita—but I'd also sworn never to do something like it to myself. And I remember resisting the feeling . . . of things slipping away."

"Keir," Leal said soberly, "why did you come to Virga? You had a chance to go back after you rescued us—"

"No, I had to get out!" Even as he said this he realized how intense that need for escape had been; yet now, he had no idea what had caused it. Unless— "If I didn't do this to myself . . . if someone else did it to me and I knew, knew it was happening . . . that would explain . . ."

Something welled up in him then, and to his astonishment Keir found he was crying. Part of him stood outside himself, watching in wonder, and his tears flicked away in the winds of Virga, and Leal wrapped him in her arms and murmured in his ear.

Eventually he stopped, but they stayed together, washed in the breeze and unspeaking.

Then the hatch flew open and Venera Fanning's head popped out. "There you are. Grab your things, I'm sending you back to Rush with the others."

Venera gave no sign of noticing that Leal and Keir were holding one another. Instead, she vigorously yanked at the tab on a signal flare, and when it lit, began waving it in broad strokes. She left a long spiral trail of smoke on the air.

Keir and Leal disengaged themselves. "Where are *you* going, Venera?" asked Leal.

"The city-state of Fracas," she announced with an air of satisfaction. "Currently something of a thorn in our side, no? And I'd like to know why." Keir had seen the red dots Venera had started adding to her chart of nations; and since their meeting with Princess Thavia, he'd certainly noticed how many cities and countries had begun turning the *Judgment* away. "If Sacrus and its outside allies are mustering their own alliance, we need to know the details. That could take a very long time if we were to rely on diplomacy and reportage. What we need is a way to make a very quick head count." She grinned rakishly, every inch the pirate queen in her leather trousers and flapping shirt, sizzling flare in one hand as the other clutched a guide rope hanging off the *Judgment*'s nose.

Keir laughed in surprise. His melancholy mood was evaporating in the face of the sheer strangeness that was Venera Fanning.

The flare died and Venera let it go. "It's funny—I've come full circle," she mused. "Fracas is right next to where Spyre used to be. The city's always sheltered under Spyre's battlements. It's under no one's jurisdiction. It would be the perfect base for people who claim no country of their own, don't you think? I've no doubt that if the hostages are still in Virga, this is where they're being kept.

"Ah!" she added brightly. "There they are."

A glitter of ship lights had appeared in the depths beyond the way station. There must be four or five vessels there—all quite large by Leal's reckoning.

Venera made to reenter the yacht, but looked back to say, "I'm leaving in a half-hour, so you'd best be gone by then."

"And a fond good-bye to you, too," Leal said after she vanished. She and Keir climbed over to the hatch. "Well, as usual, Venera seems to have a plan," she said as he opened it. "But what about you, Keir? —Now that you know . . . something . . . of yourself? What are you going to do?"

He took one more look at Candesce, half-wrapped now in veils of cloud. "My memory's a puzzle," he said. "But I think enough of the pieces remain . . . and one thing I do remember is that I'm good at puzzles.

"I'm going to put this one together."

"THIS ONE'S NOT on the list."

Jacoby Sarto frowned like a thunderhead at the dockmaster. The open-ended, cylindrical docking structure of the town of Fracas was crowded with ships, a jumble of national flags and royal seals. They'd all landed as scheduled over the past days, disgorging one or two key persons who would look around in apprehension or disdain, then take to the stairs that led down to the city—and never return.

The yacht that was settling onto the decking now was different from the others. It was a kind of assassin's dagger, long, sharp, and bristling with prickles for any unwary hand that tried to grasp it. Closer up, the thorns became fins, some adorned with jet engines. Jacoby's military experience told him that the yacht's cockpit was at its center of gravity, and those engines would let the craft spin around itself, for what Jacoby assumed was uncanny—and clearly military—maneuverability.

The yacht radiated personality, and it was a familiar personality. He rubbed at the itching bandage on his maimed hand, trying not to think of just how urgent this part of the plan had become, after the disaster of the last few days.

Yes, this must be the right ship: it looked like its owners had done their best to disguise the deadly nature of the vessel, but it hadn't done much good; the ominous name painted on its prow—*Judgment*—gave its purpose away.

Could she be so stupid as to have come here herself?

Jacoby assembled his honor guard at the infinite drop that ran around the edge of the circular docks. The yacht perched there, along with other ships, right on the rim of the hundred-foot-wide mouth of the dock structure. "Atten . . . shun!" he snapped as the yacht's main hatch opened.

The woman who stepped out was young, beautiful, and regal in her poise. She was dressed in a black bodysuit with a black lace poncho over it; Jacoby could see the crisscross of a gun belt at her hips. She looked like some sort of pirate queen, but he'd never seen her before—clearly she was a late addition to the list that Inshiri had not had time to tell him about.

He bowed, not too lowly, and said, "Welcome to Fracas. Who do I have the honor of addressing?"

She scowled down at him, no sign of recognition in her eyes, either. "Tell your bosses that Princess Thavia of Greydrop is here, and I demand to know what the hell they're up to."

If the gravity hadn't been trivial up here Jacoby might have fallen over. No, this was not the real Thavia, whom he knew well and whose loyalty he could always count on. What was hysterically funny was that this woman wasn't imitating the real Thavia at all, but rather another spoiled princess Jacoby knew—and she was doing a damned fine job of it.

"Princess Thavia?" She nodded impatiently. "Well, this is an honor, then." In the microgravity she merely had to undulate slightly and her body drifted forward and down to where she could perch on tiptoe in front of him.

"My name is Jacoby Sarto," he said, slightly emphasizing his name while looking her in the eye. Not a hint that she knew him. "I'll be your liaison during your stay here," he continued, then saw that she wasn't even looking at him, but was peering in apparent puzzlement through the iron grating to their left. Thousands of feet below it, the city began.

So, clearly Venera wasn't that stupid. She'd sent a proxy—but she was still taking his bait. If he knew her—and he liked to think he did—that meant that she was not far away.

"I take it you've never been to Fracas before?"

"Never," she said slowly; her eyes were on the interior of the dock cylinder behind him, which in any normal city would have been empty space where ships could hang weightless. "What is that godawful mess?"

"Fracas is special. You'll see."

Behind her, two other people emerged from the yacht, a man and a woman. Both wore drab servants' clothes, but they moved like soldiers.

Okay. This was clearly Venera's countermove to his dangled bait—but what came next?

"The city fathers are eager to meet you," Jacoby said neutrally as he led the way into the curving steel cylinder. Here, the steel deck plating had been removed to expose the cylinder's skeleton of girders. Penetrating this by the thousand were cables, ropes, and chains of all widths and colors, each sporting a bright name tag on which numbers and letters were written. The thicket of cabling was so dense you couldn't see the three hundred feet to the other end of the cylinder, and the view was further complicated by the many cranks, coils, pulley blocks, and winches knotted into it.

Caught off guard as he was, habit made Jacoby lead the imposters along a catwalk over the miles-long drop to the city. The cables all led that way, down beneath their feet. He could only grip the rail with his right hand, but barely noticed the vertigo-inducing scenery; he was thinking hectically about what would happen next. Thavia's message had been sent, and Venera had come running—or had she? Unless she herself came within the walls of the city, this ploy would fail as miserably as his attempt to take Serenity.

They came to the head of a yin-yang stairway that led down to distant rooftops, and he watched the imposters for the expected reaction, as the full grandeur and madness of what was below came into view.

In any ordinary town wheel, this long staircase—which started out nearly vertical here at the docks, and flattened gradually as it dropped—would have led to a ribbon of planking or metal half a mile below. That ribbon would normally make a vast hoop upon which would perch gravity-dependent shops and services, hostels, hotels, and the occasional mansion of the rich. This, however, was Fracas, and it had no such hoop.

"Is this a town, or a belfry?" drawled faux Thavia as she peered over the rail at the chaos below.

Jacoby pretended to chuckle. "Fracas was never planned, the way most towns are," he explained as he began to descend. This was the point of no return for them; he could still decide that they weren't on his list, and send them on their way. But he had no sympathy for sacrificial victims; he gestured for them to follow, and his honor guard closed in discreetly behind them, in case they should balk.

"Originally," he explained, "Fracas was just a couple of buildings spinning in bolo configuration. The original owners—a farming cooperative—added a couple more houses, then somebody thought of putting a hotel here for people who'd come to look at Spyre. As you may know, Spyre used to be quite visible from here . . . So then there were a dozen buildings all whirling around a central point. Then a hundred. Then a thousand . . . Well, you get the picture."

The full intricacy of a necklace town like Fracas could be understood only by someone born and raised here; but the concept was simple. Fracas was a collection of spokes without a wheel, each spoke a strong cable or rope tied at the great central knot where the ships docked. The cables suspended houses and schools and factories and even short arcs of street; Jacoby pointed out one of these nearby, as it was hoisted up through the forest of buildings like a giant elevator.

"The tax situation is favorable," he added as he watched faux Thavia hop down the long rope-suspended staircase. "They spend no upkeep on a wheel since there's no wheel. Every household simply pays directly to maintain its own cable—and if you let yours deteriorate to the point that it breaks and falls on one of the lower houses, well, then, the rest of the town gets together and they lynch you! It's a simple system, very economical."

"Fascinating," said the actress, or spy, in a bored tone. "I'm going to cut to the chase. I have no intention of remaining here one minute longer than it takes to clear this mess up. I hope you're taking us to see your masters?"

"Oh, I am, I am. Right this way."

Wind was teasing his gray hair now as they entered more deeply into the city's rotation. Weight was increasing, too, and the staircase's steps became correspondingly shallower. The stairway cut through layers of city, brightly painted can-shaped buildings like giant pendulums, all thronged together and lashed to one another with catwalks and ladders. Vertical lines of cable, rigging, and rope dissected the view everywhere. Here in the thick middle of the necklace, you could only catch glimpses of blue sky to either side, while below was a chaos of rooftops. The docks had vanished above, hidden by the sparred undersides of higher dwellings.

"I suppose you can pick your level of gravity," mused the male "servant." "Put the schools on the outside where the kids will have to run in more than a g. Retire to somewhere with lower weight when you get old."

"Maybe," replied the female. Then she held up her hand to the ever-present wind that coursed through the maze of buildings. "But what happens when your house catches fire?"

"The house cables all have release mechanisms," Jacoby said, pointing. "They're mounted above each roof, where the firemen can unlock and spring them in an emergency. They can either hoist a burning building up from above, or lower it below the rest of the city to let it burn out."

"Why not just cut it loose and let it fall?"

He arched an eyebrow at her. "What, through that?" She gave a startled nod as she realized that a burning house crashing down through its neighbors would be the ultimate nightmare here. "You can't just let something go," he added. "You saw the cabling at the docks. Few of these buildings are actually anchored up top. That would put too much strain on the docking ring. Each cable has a house on either end, and they counterbalance one another. It's a cunning feature of the city, it allows them to add as many buildings as they can thread cables through the dock."

She sniffed. "Well, I can certainly see why there are no other towns like this."

Oh, there was no doubt she'd met the real Venera. Five minutes with her would give any actress a lifetime's worth of repertoire.

They'd reached one of the staircase's many landings and now Jacoby left it for a long gangplank. They rounded the corner of a warehouse with the sigil of the cooper's guild on its wall, and ahead of them was one of Fracas's temporary streets. This was a long plank deck that could be winched up or down through the town's layers. Its owners could rent the street out as a market, processional route, or public thoroughfare. As per Jacoby's instructions, this one hadn't been joined to any gangways or other streets, but hung by itself in a canyon of facades. Bright pennants flew over the long tent that had been erected on it, and young men and women in livery were waiting to invite arriving visitors inside.

Aside from the Judgment, one other yacht had docked this morning. Its passenger was standing at the door to the tent now—and there was clearly trouble. Jacoby was just seconds too late to prevent the faux Thavia from seeing it as well, but it hardly mattered; this was a chance to gauge her reactions. She stopped suddenly, clapped her hand on the shoulder of her manservant, and pointed, just as the young nobleman outside the tent twitched his cape behind him to free up his sword arm. Then his sword was out. The pageboys retreated as he squared off against one of Jacoby's men.

They were still some distance away, but the youth's voice carried very well as he shouted, "Lies!"

Jacoby's man on the spot was Palatin, and while he was a good con man, he was no swordsman. He wasn't even trying to defend himself, just talking in a low, reasonable, but inaudible voice to the youth.

"What is this?" demanded faux Thavia. "What's going on here?"

Jacoby opened his mouth to say something plausible, but just then the young man yelled, "No, it's a trick! We're not guests, we're hostages!"

"Ah," said Jacoby—but some sound came from the entrance to the tent that made the youth turn. He lowered his sword and stepped back, just as a middle-aged woman in a regal gown stepped outside. She looked angry.

"How dare you question your father's wishes, Dorion!" she snapped at the youth. He gaped at her uncertainly. Jacoby nodded in approval; this was the boy's aunt, if he remembered right. Instinct and habit won out over suspicion, and young Dorion suffered her to walk right up to him, where she proceeded to deliver a lecture at him in an inaudible, but clearly intense, voice.

"I believe there's been a misunderstanding," Jacoby said to faux Thavia. She raised an eyebrow doubtfully.

The youth began to lower his sword. The woman pretending to be Thavia's servant stepped up to faux her and murmured in a low voice, "Come on. We can still get away."

"I don't think so," said the other with a frown. She nodded at the shadows beyond the catwalk, but her eyes were on Jacoby. "I think it's been a while now since we could have done that."

Her companions looked where she was indicating, and Jacoby saw them finally notice the men with rifles, standing in ones and twos on nearby rooftops and in the shadow of inset windows. The looks on his "guest's" faces were really quite funny, Jacoby thought.

"You led us right into this!" the younger actress hissed at faux Thavia. "I thought you knew what you were doing!"

"Silence," she said with imperious calm. She looked down her nose at the woman, just like Venera would have. "Follow my lead. —If you have the patience for that."

"Oh!"

This was fascinating. Was the younger actress getting cold feet? Was she about to drop the facade and confess in the hope that Jacoby would let her go? Or was her fear part of the performance?

Up ahead, young Dorion had put away his sword, although he still looked unhappy as he entered the tent with the matron.

"So it seems the rumors were right," faux Thavia said to Jacoby. "You've been accumulating hostages."

"And yet, you still came here," he said, shaking his head.

The fake Thavia looked grim. Her friends, stricken and furious by turns, were herded up to the tent where smiling pageboys in dark livery put them into single file. Jacoby watched in bemusement as they were surrounded by the rest of his team, who had not drawn but prominently displayed their holstered guns. They were frisked efficiently but quickly.

Jacoby had to figure out what they were doing. So far, he'd anticipated Venera perfectly. The problem was, if he was right, things were about to spiral dangerously close to out of control. He'd anticipated that, too—and ultimately decided that there was no easier way to get what he wanted.

Since none of the three imposters had any weapons on them, Jacoby waved them through the flap into the larger area. There they found the young nobleman angrily talking to the older woman, who was in tears.

"I had to, I had to," she burst out. "They were going to shoot you if you continued."

"Then at least someone else might have seen, and gotten the word out that this was a trap," he said contemptuously.

"Dorion, I—"

"Enough!"

Jacoby didn't really care what went on between them; he had a decision to make. He stood for a long moment, gazing at the partitions at the far end of the tent. His mouth was a thin, compressed line. Finally he turned to faux Thavia and said, "Make yourselves small." Then he shoved his way through the crowd of distraught nobility that filled the place.

The tent was about thirty feet wide, and twice that long. Jacoby's men had tightly tied down its green canvas sides, and the exits at each end were heavily guarded. Conspicuously, sticks of high explosives hung at regular intervals about ten feet above the heads of the people gathered here.

Jacoby had processed about a hundred hostages over the past several weeks, and none had left this tent once they arrived. A veritable who's who of social standing and ancient nobility sat on low benches, or on the floor, or stood talking in disconsolate groups. There were privies and showers behind a set of curtains, but otherwise, there was nothing for them to do but wait. To them, this deprivation must seem like Hell; but it was a lot better than Sacrus's holding pens had been in Jacoby's day. He had no time for their whining.

He quickly paced to the other end of the space, where a series of low tables and better-quality screens demarcated the administration area. "That's the last of them," he announced as he rounded one of the screens.

The local Fracas boys glanced at one another indifferently, then looked to the other man who waited with them.

"Let's move on to the next phase," said Derance of Arena.

Jacoby had told the men that "Arena" was a distant nation in Virga—but he himself knew the man was from the arena, that mysterious place surrounding Virga that Leal Maspeth had talked of. It was clear he was different. He had amazing presence, even more than Jacoby himself. In a tight space like this, all eyes instinctively went to him. His face was chiseled and his eyes intense blue, and just a touch of gray had started to leaven the black hair at his temples. His voice was low and resonant, as instantly commanding as his appearance.

None of that impressed Jacoby. The sheer workmanship of him, though—to an expert in power like Jacoby Sarto of Sacrus, that was impressive. Inshiri had put him here as Jacoby's minder.

Jacoby despised him.

Derance walked over to a bronze bell on a stand, and began tapping it with a hammer. As the long notes rolled through the tent, Jacoby could hear the murmur of conversation diminish, then cease.

A low podium stood near the tables. Derance walked over to it, and held up his hands for silence. He'd already had it, but at his gesture a low angry hiss came from the crowd.

"I know you're all upset," he called out. "And I apologize for how long this is taking. Some of you have been here for weeks, I know. We've had some trouble coordinating with the transfer ship. But rest assured, everything's on schedule now—"

"What schedule?" somebody shouted. "Who're you?" somebody else demanded, and "What transfer?" came from someone else. Jacoby scanned the crowd for any sign of real trouble, but these members of the vaunted ruling class all looked properly cowed—except . . . The faux Thavia had her hand on the arm of the young hothead, Dorion, and now she had a half-smile on her face that might have alarmed Jacoby if hadn't already figured out what was coming. He signaled his own men to alert the pickets he'd set up several blocks away.

After he got a confirmatory wave of reply he quickly looked for the other imposters, who weren't near faux Thavia. He spotted them circulating through the crowd, asking something of each hostage in turn. They looked for all the world like they were taking *attendance*.

Derance raised his hands for quiet again, and said, "You were all told you had an important role to play in coming here. That wasn't a lie. Your masters have awarded you the honor of becoming ambassadors to your brothers and sisters from beyond the walls of Virga—" He didn't get to finish as pandemonium broke out.

Jacoby heard one young lady say something about "taking us to the realm of the dead." He'd expected this; superstitious fools. Other hostages were trading stories they'd heard about what lay beyond Virga: rumors, legends, even plotlines to a lurid novel or two, now spouted as fact. What interested Jacoby, though, was that the imposter servants had finished whatever it was there were doing. Both raised their arms to signal to their mistress, and she nodded.

As he'd suspected, these three had already known what they were getting into when they arrived here. "I think we have a situation," he said to his men, who'd just started a card game behind the screens. They looked up, surprised, and at that moment he heard a very high, piercing whistle come from somewhere in the crowd.

Derance stopped talking in midword, then said, "What are you doing?" Jacoby stepped back out to look, and everyone else was turning, too, to stare at faux Thavia, who was holding a whistle to her mouth.

She lowered it. "He's lying, you know," she said calmly. "You really are hostages."

"Shut her up!" Derance shouted. Jacoby's men began knocking their way through the crowd. He, on the other hand, had begun backing toward the tent's other exit.

"I suggest you all lie down on the floor," faux Thavia continued loudly. "There's about to be bullets flying."

The nobles exchanged glances. "Who are you?" somebody asked.

She drew herself up into a regal pose. "True, I am not Thavia of Greydrop. I am your rescuer! My name is Venera Fanning, and I'm the wife of Chaison Fanning, admiral of Slipstream."

There was a moment of silence.

"No you're not," said a white-haired old man. "I've met Venera Fanning," he continued argumentatively, as faux Thavia/Venera rolled her eyes. "You, young lady, don't look a thing like her. Why, she has a famous scar, here—"

—and as he gestured at his chin the tent's canvas walls were ripped open in three simultaneous blasts, and he and everybody else were knocked off their feet.

THERE WAS GUNFIRE now—lots of it. Jacoby heaved one of the tables onto its side and drew his pistol. "To me!" he bellowed at his men while hostages pelted back and forth and generally made a clear shot impossible. He heard wild screaming and more than just the voices of his own men ordering the hapless nobles to get out of the way. Then, quite suddenly, there was silence.

He looked cautiously around the side of the table. The hostages were all on the plank floor, but he couldn't tell if any were actually hurt. The room was otherwise full of soldiers—some of them grim navy men wearing the red and gold of Slipstream, and some wearing ancient and baroque, but somehow familiar, uniforms. They had surrounded Derance of Sacrus and the remainder of Jacoby's men, including Palatin, who all stood back to back with their weapons raised.

It wasn't those guns that had momentarily halted the attack, though. It was Derance, who was holding something high over his head. When Jacoby saw what it was he grunted; he wouldn't have tried this ploy himself. His opinion of Derance wasn't improving.

"This detonator," hollered Derance, "will set off every one of the charges hanging over us. If you don't let us go, I really will push it."

"*Go ahead*," said someone.

And there she was, fan of black hair framing the lovely, oval face whose perfection was only enhanced by that single, discreet scar. She wore the naval uniform of Slipstream today (quite well) and held a carbine in her hands.

"Meet my better half," said the woman who'd so recently claimed to be Venera Fanning.

"Everybody, back off," said the real Venera to her men. "You don't need to get hurt."

She hadn't noticed Jacoby yet. He wondered whether she would simply shoot him when she did. That had been part of the calculated risk he'd taken in arranging this honeypot. He had to be here himself to make it convincing—both to Inshiri, who had no idea what he was planning, and to Venera.

Derance desperately tried to regain the initiative. "Nobody move! If so much as a single one of the hostages moves, I'll kill them all!"

"Oh, I believe you," said Fanning. "But I'm not here for them." She waved her hand and the Slipstream soldiers began cautiously moving back to the shredded canvas walls.

"What do you mean you're not here for—"

"Their people have already betrayed us by joining your side," she said. "They're a lost cause; despite what my double here said, what possible good would it do me to rescue this lot? They're supposed to be here, and if I wanted to curry favor with their masters I'd leave them here, wouldn't I? So it's a matter of complete indifference to me whether they live or die."

Derance blinked at her, once, twice, three times. "Then what *are* you here for?"

Jacoby walked out from behind the table. "I should think that would be obvious, Derance," he said, and he had the pleasure of seeing Venera blink in surprise when she saw it was him.

"She already has what she came for," Jacoby continued. "A list of all the nations represented here—and therefore, a list of the nations that have signed our secret pact. All this gunfire was just cover to get her actors out safely, wasn't it?"

Venera nodded, silent for once.

". . . And as you can see, that's already been accomplished," he finished.

Venera recovered her poise. "Jacoby Sarto," she said with a sneer. "So you ran home to Momma, did you? Cowering under the skirts of your dead Spyre? I'd expected more from you." He saw her notice his bandaged hand, and waited for her to make some quip about it—and he saw her think about it, but she didn't take the opportunity.

She wasn't going to kick him while he was down, and that threw him for just a second; but Derance was watching their exchange, so he said, "Who were your pretenders? Members of the Slipstream Naval Drama Society?" She shrugged in something like assent.

Derance glared from her to him. "Shut up, Sarto. What are you going to do now?" he asked Venera.

"Oh, the only thing that remains is to shoot you and your men, and let these good people," she indicated the hostages, "contemplate where in the world they would rather be these days. Unless, that is, you have a better idea . . . ?"

As she'd spoken, she had been backing away, leaving Derance standing with his detonator in the center of the cowering nobles. Jacoby's men began lowering their pistols, glancing to him for permission. He flicked his hand at them, and the guns went down.

Derance sighed heavily. "You just don't understand who you're up against," he said. Then he pushed the detonator button.

Nothing happened.

After a moment a faint voice from the edge of the crowd said, "Ah, y-yes, h-here it is. I, um, it took me a minute longer than, you know—but I found the right fuse line, and well . . ." A gangly man with thick glasses (and wearing the Slipstream uniform) held up two halves of a cut wire.

"Take that one," Venera said, pointing to Derance. Jacoby raised his pistol and shot Derance in the head. Dozens of rifles were suddenly aimed at him, as the agent of Artificial Nature crumpled to the plank floor.

"Okay, leave that one," said Venera. "But take *him*." With a quite unpleasant smile, she aimed her own pistol at Jacoby.

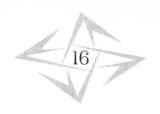

16

"THIS IS REALLY quite nostalgic," said Jacoby as soldiers bound his hands behind him. He smiled at Venera, then winced as one of the men brushed against his wound.

"Why'd you shoot that man?" she snapped.

"So that we'd be free to talk."

"I'm not in the mood." Her expression told him she really would be happy to shoot him if he said another word. He shrugged and focused his attention on his nervous men, making eye contact with each in turn and nodding or otherwise indicating his confidence that they would survive this.

Meanwhile, Venera had swung about to face the hostages. "You lot can do what you will!" she told them. "I think it should be clear to you now that your own people don't give a damn about you."

"Commander!" A soldier ran up and saluted hastily. "We're cut off!"

For the first time, Venera looked surprised. "What do you mean cut off? We brought two cruisers!"

"Apparently they've had to retreat!" Now Jacoby could hear it: the unsteady pop-pop of small-arms fire echoing through the dangling buildings.

Venera hauled Jacoby to his feet and marched him away from his companions. "Our reunion may be briefer than I'd hoped," she said. "First of all, thank you for not harming my actors. The fact that you treated them well will stand you in good stead when I decide whether to kill you or not."

"Oh, come now, Venera, we've been down this road before," he said. "You're spiteful and impulsive, but you never drop a trinket if it might end up being valuable to you."

"And you're a trinket?" She'd brought them out of the tent and to the edge of the street span. The shifting rooftops of Fracas made a bewildering kaleidoscope below. Fanning put the barrel of her pistol to Jacoby's ear and said, "We need to get out of here. You'll survive if you help. What's it to be?"

The gunfire was coming from above them. Jacoby couldn't turn his head, but caught a glimpse of uniformed figures on nearby rooftops. "Well, it depends," he said. "Where is it you want to get to?"

"First of all: Why are my ships retreating?"

He thought about how little he could get away with telling her. "There's guns mounted in some of the outside buildings. They can hit anything to either side of the city's disk. Your ships would have to put themselves in the plane of the city's rotation to avoid them, and even then, we can drop bombs on them from the lower towers . . ."

"But not very accurately. And they could obliterate Fracas from there."

"But you wouldn't. The people here are innocent."

"So were the people of Spyre."

He scoffed. "You hold too high an opinion of yourself. It wasn't you who destroyed Spyre. It was the generals. They weakened it—"

"Whatever," she said, but the pistol left his temple. "The point is," she went on, "if we go out we'll be shot." She nodded past the verticals of cable and chain. "The only way is to go down." She meant toward the outer rim of the spinning ring of buildings. — And she was right, in a way: from the rim one could simply let go and fall away in the plane of the city's rotation—safe from the guns mounted on either side of the disk of spokes.

"You could do that, but . . ." By now, and according to plan, her people were trapped. She had to surrender. "There are no ships or bikes in the lower mobiles," he pointed out. "They're only at the docks, at the center of the spokes, and to get from the axle to the rim you'd have to fly past all the guns. You'd be blown to pieces."

She peered over the railing. "Only if we fly *outside* the city."

While he tried to make sense of that comment, she turned decisively. "Back to the docks!" she commanded her men; but one of her lieutenants shook his head.

"They've taken out the staircase, and stationed themselves on the rooftops above us," he said. "We have no way to climb." He was one of the baroquely armored men, and he'd spoken in an accent Jacoby recognized.

"We'll see about that." She turned to the bespectacled bomb expert. "Guesses on how much tension these are under?" She slapped one of the thick ropes that held up the street.

He grabbed the bristly, tightly wound rigging and waggled it. "Mm, w-well, not much," he said doubtfully. "Wouldn't be t-too much of a backlash. Might toss you a few dozen feet if you held on and cut it below you." He looked over his glasses at her. "Th-that is what you had in mind, isn't it?"

"I don't want the backlash." She rounded on Jacoby again, leveling the pistol at his nose. "Are these moored at the top, or counterbalanced?"

Jacoby was curious to see where she was going with this, so he said, "Counterbalanced."

"Great," she said, and turned away. "Take those suicide charges and set them to cut these. We're going to drop the street."

Panic erupted among the hostages as they realized the soldiers were about to cut loose the decking they were standing on. They made a stampede for the gangways, but nobody shot at them. They were still valuable, and Jacoby still had plenty of men in the city with which to round them up later. "Let's test this," she said as the bomb expert tied a charge to one of the suspension ropes.

Bullet holes stitched a line across the canvas ceiling. "Give up!" one of Jacoby's men shouted from a nearby rooftop. The soldiers Venera herself had stationed on other rooftops and gangways began to make their way in under cover of intense fire, as, humming, Venera's bomber made his connections. He finished, and he and everybody else stood back as Fanning aimed her pistol at the charge.

"This is insane," said Jacoby. "It'll never—"

Bang-*blam!* The charge went off and the rope parted. Instantly it snapped upward—but only twenty or thirty feet high before the pent-up tension in the rope was used up, and it fell slack again.

The entire street creaked, groaned, and dipped a foot.

"Well, that's disappointing," said Venera, hands on her hips.

"No, no, your grasp of Newtonian physics is sound, m'lady," said the bomb expert as he hurried to lash a charge to another rope. "All these ropes conjoin about two hundred feet above us. We'll have to cut away most of the street before the counterweight takes over."

"Ah. Get going, then." But he was already rushing to the next line, accompanied by two soldiers who startled him every few seconds by firing over his head.

"Mount up!" she commanded. A soldier boosted her up one of the ropes and she twined her legs and inched her way up farther. "Tie the prisoner's hands on the other side of it," she told her men, and Jacoby was towed over to the rope next to hers and his hands lashed on the other side of it. He found himself nose-to-nose with one of the explosive charges, and judiciously took the aid of one of the soldiers to clamber up past it.

Gunfire from the surrounding rooftops was intensifying. One of the Slipstreamers fell, limp as a rag doll, and his companions cursed and sprayed gunfire indiscriminately into the city.

"Keep it together!" Venera yelled at them. "And get up here!" Without another word, she lowered her pistol and shot the charge below her.

Her rope—and her and the five other people clinging to it—rebounded into the air as all of them held on desperately. One of the men let go and tumbled spinning into the air.

"Pick me up later!" he shouted as he pawed at the foot-fins slung over his back. Jacoby watched in astonishment as he twisted to avoid guy-wires, sewage pipes, and catwalks. If he could do it for just a few more seconds, he'd exit the bottom of the city and be in clear air . . .

Blam! The charge on Jacoby's own rope had gone off and the rope whipped him in the face. Stunned, he let go and it slithered over his forearms and neck. Then he hit another man, who grunted. Jacoby grabbed at the rope again as the soldier swore at him.

They were twirling into the air, and now coming down to swing in a wide arc out over the bottomless canyons of the city. Somewhere, Venera Fanning was whooping.

"Just a couple more, boys!"

Everybody seemed to be shooting now—Jacoby's men in their sheltered windows, Venera's men on the ropes—and as his rope swung him around again Jacoby saw that the street was missing too many ropes now, listing and toppling tables, chairs, boxes, and bodies into the abyss. He watched a travel chest impact a conical roof a hundred feet below and burst like a sudden flower, shirts and trousers its petals.

The street groaned and lost its shape, becoming a U that shed planks like water. Fanning's soldiers shot out two more of the ropes and the rest snapped. Twisting like some tormented worm, the street sprawled over rooftops and nipped gangways and ladders in its death throes. It tumbled, split apart, and in deadly showers of lumber and coiling nooses of rope, left the city.

"*How could she do that!* How could she—" It was one of Jacoby's men, hanging off a nearby rope.

Jacoby swung by him, laughing a bit crazily. "How could she? She's the one who destroyed Spyre!"

"You said I didn't!" shouted Venera; then the ropes were hauling them upward faster and faster past bell-like houses and can-shaped shops. Whatever these lines were anchored to on the other side of the city, it was crashing down with as much enthusiasm as the street just had.

"Foot-fins, everyone," shouted Venera. "And see to the prisoner!" Pain was pounding through Jacoby's left hand and he was about to lose his grip with it entirely; but the upward pull was slackening, and gravity falling away. The last rooftops whipped by and then they were in the vertical forest of cables that reached up to the axle of the wheelless necklace city. They rose hundreds of feet and hanging on got easier. Jacoby was abruptly seized by the soldiers who bracketed him on the rope, and they untied his hands and retied them behind his back.

He nodded to the man next to him. "You're from Liris," he said. This man wore the ancient, outlandish armor of the tiny building-sized country Venera had been adopted into when she first landed in Spyre. The man grinned at Jacoby, and then they shared a sorrowful glance at the empty sky where Spyre had once been. Meanwhile, Fracas, below them, was turning from a town into an arc of toy-sized roofs.

"We're taking the yacht, ma'am?" called a soldier.

"Yes. You'll like it."

Jacoby knew now that he'd been right to build multiple layers into his trap. The only rational escape route for her yacht was perpendicular to the disk of the city, and his ships that had pinned down her escort had that way covered. No matter what she did now, he had her.

"Venera, you can't escape!" he yelled. "What you're doing is suicide."

"It's only suicide if it kills ya," said the soldier from Liris with a grin.

They were weightless now, flying upward at the tangled underside of the docking cylinder. Jacoby found himself zipping past the yin-yang staircase, looked into the astonished eyes of a businessman sauntering down it. All around him Venera's soldiers were letting go of their ropes, strapping big foot-fins to their feet, and readying grappling lines and hooks.

Freed of any significant centrifugal gravity, momentum carried them forward now—not up, because there was no "up" anymore.

The soldier from Liris let go of the slackening rope and began vigorously kicking his feet. Foot-fins weren't a strong mode of propulsion, but in cases like this they could at least change your heading, and he was angling himself and Jacoby out of the maze of cables and into the open air next to the city. The other soldiers were doing the same—and ahead of them was the lip of the docking cylinder.

"Ready grapnels!"

Something whizzed past Jacoby's ear: gunfire from the docks. He shouted and pointed, but Venera's lads were already laying down return fire. Figures ducked and dove into the cable forest inside the cylinder as her men tossed grapples to catch its lip. Somebody threw Jacoby's man a line and they hauled themselves in, and then there they were, standing tiptoed on the burnished edge of the city's axle.

Venera made a great leap, forty feet across the curve of the cylinder, to her yacht. Her men followed in ones and twos while their friends laid down covering fire. When it was his turn, Jacoby tried to twist free, but all he got was a blow to the ear and then he, too, was landing next to the yacht's hatch.

Inside, the thin vessel was stuffed with trigger-happy, adrenaline-charged men. "Bring him forward," Venera commanded, and Jacoby was hauled up to the cockpit. Bullets pinged off the hull and one starred a porthole as he passed it.

"Your survival depends on finding us a safe way off this city," Fanning said to her prisoner.

"There is none," Jacoby told her. "Surrender now."

"Very funny, Jacoby."

"I'm serious," he said. "You'll be exposed to fire from the city all the way. Most of the gun emplacements that used to encircle Spyre were moved here and hung in the city."

"These guns," mused Fanning. "They point out? Not down?"

"You mean, down past the rim? No. But to go that way, you'd have to fly right by them . . ."

She nodded. "But how many of them point into the city?"

Jacoby blinked at her. She had no rational choices left; but this was Venera. "You can't mean to—"

Fanning turned to the pilot. "We're going to do a matching maneuver to the city's rotation, then lower through it. Can you manage it?"

The pilot, a sandy-haired, windburned veteran, simply raised his eyebrows. "Not without consequence," he said.

"But it can be done?"

"Y-yes . . ."

Jacoby considered letting her go right then. He had no intention of killing Venera Fanning; in the great game, she was a vital token (and besides, he liked her). What she was proposing to do was far more likely to get her killed than he was.

If he let her go, though, he would have suffered two serious blows to his plans. He'd never be able to forgive himself for being so weak; so he bit his lip and just cursed past the blood on his tongue.

Outside the broad windscreen, Jacoby could see the docking ring rising past, and the forest of cables and chains swinging into view. Bullet trails sketched a cage around the ship, but none impacted; his men knew he was aboard.

"I'm prepared to be reasonable," Venera said suddenly. She'd braced herself, legs splayed straight at the floor and wall, both hands on the ceiling. Outside the windscreen at her back, cables whipped past, disturbingly close. The gunfire had ceased.

"Hmm-what?" He couldn't look away as narrow miss after narrow miss nearly cut the yacht in two. They were arcing down now, angling through the cables toward the city's rooftops.

She made a moue, eying him. "I'd be happy to drop you off with a pair of foot-fins and a bottle of water. Maybe in a handy cloud, once we've left the city behind. What do you say?"

There was no way they were going to survive the next five minutes, but the offer was touchingly generous. Jacoby said so.

"Threading the needle," said the pilot. "This could get bumpy."

The yacht's engines roared and with a stomach-churning slewing motion, they dropped into the narrow gap between a mansion and a school. Jacoby caught a glimpse of astonished faces, pointing fingers.

"So tell me, what was the plan?" When he didn't answer, Venera reached out and grabbed his chin, turning his face to hers. "Focus."

A crash came from somewhere behind them and the ship shook. In his peripheral vision Jacoby saw another tier of houses slide up past the windscreen.

He wasn't about to tell her his plan, but Inshiri's was another matter. "The hostages were bound for somewhere outside Virga," he said. "Derance called it the 'arena.' I'm unclear on the aeriography—"

"That group we set free. Were they the only ones?"

"So far, yes. But we were expecting another consignment."

"From what nations? Name names, please."

The yacht hooked a string of pipes and water exploded over the nose. The pilot cursed. There was another slamming crash from aft. Jacoby tried to hang on to everything all at once.

Engines roaring, the yacht hovered for a moment, hesitant in the face of thick towers, a barrier of heavy cables, and an open canyon that was, unfortunately, crisscrossed by several layers of catwalk bridges. Muttering some mix of prayers and curses under his breath, the pilot slid them toward the bridges.

"Really, Venera, you talk like you have the upper hand, here. But the fact is, the only thing keeping you alive—apart from him"—he nodded at the pilot—"is the fact that I am still alive. Why should I give you any details?"

The yacht took out a bridge. Townsfolk were fleeing ahead of it, and so far at least they hadn't hit anybody. Jacoby heard the hatch behind him open, and the voices of a dozen soldiers all say "Ow!" in simultaneous sympathy as another bridge snapped.

"Uh, Commander, not to, well, you know, overstate the obvious, but I thought you might want to know—"

"Not now!" she snapped at the bomb expert. He ducked his head and closed the hatch.

They were free-falling. Fanning's hair lifted like some black halo around her head. She put her pistol to his forehead and said, "Jacoby, I'm out of patience with you. Who are they? How many ships do they have? What sort of agreement are they making with these countries?"

Buildings whipped by, faster and faster. If they hit anything now, the yacht would be smashed into kindling.

Better give her something to keep her quiet. "It's about Candesce. They're mustering support for an incursion into the sun of suns. They promise they're not going to shut off the field, only tune it down—"

"Ha!" she said. "You were never that naïve. Besides, they would need the key to Candesce to get in, and Chaison gave it to a precipice moth. Last I saw it was flapping its ugly way into winter."

He just looked at her, and Venera's eyes widened. "But that's impossible," she said. "How could they have it when it was given to . . ."

"We're through!" whooped the pilot. Clear blue sky had broken across the windshield.

WITH A BRILLIANT flash, the yacht was knocked end over end. Jacoby tumbled, hit the wall, the ceiling. Spangled with shock and pain, he dimly felt Venera's feet on his chest; she pushed off, making him huff, and then he blinked and saw her strapping herself into the copilot's chair. The windscreen was cracked in a dozen places, and ahead and to starboard, another blossom of explosive fire lit the sky.

"Who are they?" she demanded. "How many?"

For a confused second Jacoby thought she was talking to him, but then the pilot pointed. "Six ships. That must be what chased ours away."

"Not guns in the city. Ships! They've been laying in wait for us?"

"Of course they've been laying in wait for you," huffed Jacoby. "You haven't realized that this was a trap all along?"

He saw the dawning realization on her face. "Then the real Thavia of Greydrop—"

"Works for me, damn it."

"But the hostages, they were genuine—"

"Of course they were! You wouldn't have fell for it if I'd used fakes."

"Ma'am," said the pilot, "I think they're launching bikes. Ideas?"

"Oh, yes," she said grimly. "I have an idea." Now it was her turn to point. The pilot groaned.

"First you tell me to drop us through a city, now it's clouds of razor wire and mines?"

"Don't forget the piranhawks," she said past a tight grin.

"No!" Jacoby clawed his way forward. "Not that way!"

The hatch behind them opened again. "Uh, ma'am? The boys were wondering—"

"Tell them to brace themselves," she called. "We're going to lose those ships in the ruins of Spyre."

She chuckled and rubbed her hands together. "Somebody's going to write a book about this," she said giddily. She leaned toward the pilot. "How's your penmanship?"

"Venera, give up to me now," pleaded Jacoby. "The alternative is much, much worse!"

"Bah," she said. "I'd rather die than be your prisoner again."

"That's not what I mean!"

Clouds lay ahead of them—but unlike the white and peach-touched thunderheads that dotted the sky above and to all sides, these were speckled and black, like thin smoke. Venera indicated the highlights of the view. "Spyre was an open cylinder twelve miles long," she said. "It had a lot of defenses. There's the razor wire, yes, but there were also clouds of caltrops, and of course the mines."

The pilot nodded vigorously. "Yes, about those—"

"I doubt we'll see any. They're navigation hazards; I can't see the neighbors tolerating them now that Spyre's gone. And it would be cheap to dispose of them; two men with machine guns could pick them off from a safe distance."

"All right."

"Venera, please! Don't go this way!"

Something long and silvery shot past to port. "Razor," said Venera unnecessarily. "Oh, look—"

"I see it, I see it." The yacht twisted, throwing Jacoby against the bulkhead again.

Well, there went any chance he'd had of keeping this capture from Inshiri. With Derance dead, there was nobody loyal to her who'd seen what had just unfolded in Fracas—but that was about to change.

"The old defenses made a kind of shell around Spyre," Venera was saying. "Egg-shaped, fifteen miles long by ten. Once we're in there it should be clear and we can take a more leisurely path out. Those big cruisers will have to circle around, they don't have our maneuvera . . . What the hell is that?"

A mist of spiked balls flew past, then a few strands of razor wire, and then they were into open air again. Venera and the pilot were suddenly silent, and Jacoby looked past them and saw that there was indeed nothing to hide anymore.

"There must be . . . hundreds," whispered Venera. For the first time, she looked afraid.

Oh, more than hundreds. Jacoby had long ago lost count. He shook his head, defeated and resigned.

"Run up the white flag," said Venera quietly.

They glided, engines idling, into a cloud of warships miles in extent.

17

KEIR HESITATED, THEN reached out to rap on the door. It was ornately carved, and like everything else in Aerie's new capital city, smelled of wood shavings and fresh paint.

"I said, *just a minute!*" Leal sounded frantic.

"What, you're not even decent yet?" He heard the assurance in his own voice; back in Brink, he would never have teased an adult like this. But that time was increasingly a blur.

"It's not that," she shouted. "I just can't—oh, hell." He heard her thumping, slightly ungraceful footsteps, and then the door flung open. "I don't know what to wear," she said in a defeated tone.

"May I?" She ducked aside and he entered the gigantic bedroom they'd given her. It was so new its ceiling was only half-painted, with scenes of some epic battle in recent Virgan history. Garish, he thought.

"I know how you feel," he said, spreading his arms to show off his dress uniform. "I was going to wear my clothes from Brink, but they don't fit me anymore."

At that she smiled and ran her eyes over his uniform, which emphasized his broad shoulders. Leal herself was in loose pants tied up with a drawstring, and a plain white shirt. Laid out on her gargantuan four-poster bed were six complete outfits, ranging from a golden gown (with, of course, ankle ties for freefall modesty) to a severe black pantsuit. Keir stood over them and rubbed his chin half-consciously. He'd had to start shaving lately, and the process had a reassuring familiarity to it; but he'd never been shaved by another man before, as he had this morning by the footman they'd assigned to him.

"I have to dress to impress," she said. "The question is, how?"

He pointed to the gown. "Too extreme. The rule here is, there'll always be a prettier woman in the room. But looks is all they have. You don't want to look pretty, you want to look *important*."

She scowled in annoyance. "When in my life am I going to get another chance to be pretty?"

He stepped up and took her hands. "When we've won, and the whole world comes to celebrate."

She just stood there, smiling up at him, until he stepped back and said, "Today, you're here to dominate, and frighten. Think Venera Fanning."

"But she always looks good!"

"The two goals are not incompatible." He looked at the outfits again. "Which of these would Venera choose?"

She bit her knuckle, concentrating. "Not . . . any of them. But it's all they gave me!"

"May I suggest we mix and match." He tapped the suit. "Too severe. But the trousers work." Next to it was a black top with corresponding harem pants. "The pants here are too much. But the top is off-the-shoulder, and the contradictions will be quite impressive." He handed her the black top and suit pants, and she stepped behind the screen to haul them on.

"Well . . ." She stood in front of the mirror, obviously pleased. "But it's not quite there."

"Gotta put your hair back and tie it off. Did they give you hairpins?" She nodded to the dressing table. He came back with two large red wooden pins and, stepping behind her, began tugging her hair into shape.

"You've done this before," she said.

"Apparently," he said past the pins between his teeth.

He was peripherally aware that she was watching him in the mirror, her face serious now. "Keir," she said at last, "where is it going to stop?"

"What?"

"This . . . transformation. These changes in you."

He paused. "I don't know. All I know is I feel better. More myself."

"And your memories? Are they coming back?"

"Y-yes. And no. I know that I did more than just de-index myself. That's a scry thing, it doesn't affect your biological memories. Since I got here, I haven't had scry to lean on, so I've had to access that natural memory system just to function. So I'm getting better at it. But . . . some things are just *gone.*"

"Sita?"

He shook his head. "I remember her better every day. No. It's a period when I was in Brink. Something happened. I think I . . . found out something. And it scared me, or something. So much that I wiped it from scry and my natural memory, and de-indexed and neotenized myself. It was a kind of suicide, really."

He'd said this dispassionately, but his hands were shaking a little as he finished adjusting Leal's hair. "There," he said, moving his hands to her shoulders. "Done."

"Yes." She was nodding. "I like it." The overall look was severe, but the top bared her shoulders and a plunge of skin between her breasts. Her hair was tightly drawn back, the two pins making a red X behind her head.

"Does it make you feel confident? Sharpen your eyebrows, and we're ready." He turned to the door, but didn't make it a meter before she'd grabbed his arm and hauled him back. She kissed him strongly, and his whole act of competence fell apart.

When they disengaged, he wobbled back a bit and she arched an eyebrow. "Yeah, it seems to work," she said.

"Let's go."

THE SPIN-GALE OF the city of Aurora whispered in the corners as Keir and Leal made their through the Slipstream ambassadorial mission. The building was marble, conspicuously made of stone in a city that was otherwise metal-poor. They heard adding machines and typewriters clattering in the side offices, and pageboys and -girls raced past carrying envelopes of various sizes.

An honor guard was waiting patiently by the bridge to the presidential palace. The red-and-gold-suited soldiers all saluted as they strolled up, and Keir grinned at Leal. She looked decidedly uncomfortable at the attention. "We're not even going outside," she whispered to him as they set out across the columned, covered bridge.

"Oh, just enjoy it." He was determined to wipe away the memories that had assailed him this morning, and made a point of looking out at the city as they walked. There was little to see, though; the way was obscured by thick forest.

The bridge connected to Aerie's new presidential palace, which was a fantasy in wrought iron, asteroidal pallasite, and glass. Beams of sunlight wheeled with majestic stateliness through corridors with polished floors and high arched ceilings. Workers were still buffing and painting here, too.

"Atten-shun!" The honor guard stopped as one, and saluted. Another group was approaching from the left, this second knot of Slipstream soldiers surrounding Admiral Chaison Fanning and Lacerta, the Home Guard officer who'd been stranded in Aethyr with Hayden Griffin. Despite their fresh dress uniforms, both appeared grim and tired.

"Any word on Venera?" Keir murmured to Leal, who shook her head. "Good morning, Admiral."

Fanning nodded impassively. The two groups merged and began to make their way to the front of the palace. Officials and support staff were everywhere now, scurrying to and fro, pushing tables, consulting over clipboards. It was some sort of organized chaos, and all done without scry. Keir was impressed.

Antaea Argyre waited alone at an intersection where white sunlight flooded in from the right. She wasn't the warrior today but the author, in a brocade jacket over a white blouse, dark knee-length trousers, and flats. There were no weapons belted at her hips.

She bowed, and the honor guard accepted her inside of it. She glanced up at Fanning, but no one spoke as they traversed the short sunlit hall to stand at the top of a broad, balconied level from which a vast, wide sweep of stairs led down to gardens.

Here, the front half of the palace became a single chamber walled by glass and supported by vaulting girders of iron. This part of the building was shaped somewhat like the inverted front of a ship, and the steps before them faced the prow. Sunlight poured in through the glass as if it wasn't there, flooding the trees and flower beds below. Outside, the forested city curved up on either side, and ahead rose and rose, to arch finally overhead in turquoise glory, its sweeping shape framed by two godlike wings of cloud.

One figure stood silhouetted at the top of the steps. Hayden Griffin was looking out over the new city, in the light of the sun he had built. There were plenty of other people traversing the steps, but all gave him a wide berth. Some paused behind him, to look back at him in awe.

His return from Aethyr had caused a frenzy of adulation in Aerie. They'd practically rioted in the streets, and even now, people were perched on buildings and in trees outside the palace, hoping to catch a glimpse of him. He'd responded to all of this with acute embarrassment, and had been hiding in his room.

The honor guard had hesitated at the sight of him. Keir smiled and walked through them, coming to stand by Griffin's side. "They say the whole city is made of trees," he commented.

Griffin stood with his arms crossed. Now he grinned at Keir. "Nothing like what your people could build, I'm sure," he said.

Keir barked a laugh. "None of my people would have the imagination for something like this." New as it was, Aerie had few hard resources, so the single vast wheel of Aurora had been grown rather than built. Young trees and whole groves of ancient ones had been towed here from across the world, and twined and tied, lashed and spiked together around a supporting skeleton of cable and iron beam to make a single, ring-shaped forest. Speed ivy from the ruins of Spyre had been seeded all about its outsides, and then slowly, over many months, it had all been spun up. The meandering plank streets still creaked and groaned as weight and tension adjusted beneath them; but the forest was dotted now with houses and hotels and shops. Many little lakes and ponds, spheres of water ranging from house- to block-sized, turned magisterially in the empty space within the ring. They threw rainbow refractions across the marble, a constant slow sweep of light like the passage of angels' wings.

A rustle of sound reached them from the throng of people that had spread in tendrils and knots through the gardens below. At the far end of the space was a broad square paved in glittering pallasite, and attendants were just in the process of clearing away the breakfast tables they had placed there. Others were making final adjustments to the placement of row after row of chairs for the delegates attending this, the colloquy's opening ceremony.

Someone appeared at Keir's shoulder; it was Leal. Her fingers found his hand. On the other side of Griffin, the admiral stepped up, the Guardsman next to him. On the end, still glancing up at Fanning, came Antaea Argyre.

The honor guard had retreated. They were alone at the top of the stairs.

Keir snuck a look at Chaison Fanning, too. His face was impassive, but Keir knew that the absence of his wife must be eating at his heart, especially on this of all days.

"Eyes forward," said Fanning. "We've all sacrificed for this moment, let's do it proud."

They walked together down the steps, under the gaze of a hundred nations.

CRICK, CRICK, CRICK. Leal was half-consciously twisting the pages of her speech, and she knew it was making a little noise, but she couldn't stop. Her mouth was dry and her knees felt weak, and if she could have turned and run from this stage, she would have.

The last of the delegates had just taken their seats. These were not people used to sitting in an audience; they had all been informed that there was no order to the seating—it was first come, first served. Some potentates of richer principalities looked indignant at ending up in the back.

The admiral stood with his hands behind his back, glaring them all into silence. He'd somehow draped himself with invisible Presence, and shortly, all eyes were on him.

He ignored the podium with its conical bullhorn, but instead walked to the edge of the stage.

"Thank you all for coming. And thanks to the government and people of Aerie for providing us with this glorious space in which to discuss the future of Virga." He ran through some more verbal salves, but was mercifully brief. His whole demeanor was that of a military commander at a briefing, and Leal supposed that was quite deliberate.

"The plan was to have my wife address the opening ceremonies," said Fanning—and suddenly Leal forgot her anxiety as he continued, "but she has gone missing somewhere in the airs of Virga."

There was a moment of shocked silence—not because those in the audience hadn't been hearing this rumor, but that this upstart admiral should admit it right now, right here. Fanning certainly had their undivided attention.

"Whether she is merely delayed or whether something has . . . happened to her," Fanning continued, "I want to make it plain that it changes nothing. Our goals for this conference remain the same as they were described in the briefs you all received before coming here. I will not use this venue to advance a personal agenda of rescue or revenge. However," he added as muttering broke out among the delegates, "in the interests of trust, I am prepared to step down as chair of these proceedings, if the consensus among you is that my objectivity has been compromised."

The delegate from Tracoune stood up. "Is it true about the hostages?" The muttering became a boil of conversation.

Fanning held up his hand. "We'll get to that shortly," he promised. "But I must insist on a vote on this matter. We can't proceed if you don't trust me to perform my duties dispassionately."

"Dispassionately?" One of a small group in drab gray suits had stood up. "You ambushed and destroyed the People's Fleet of Falcon Formation while it was on maneuvers! Without provocation!"

"You *paid* Mavery to stage a provocative raid on Slipstream in order to draw away their fleet!" roared a prince of Eidon. "Maneuvers? Your fleet was loaded with soldiers! I know, because half their bodies floated into our airspace afterwards, and you were too embarrassed to repatriate them. We had to pay to incinerate them in Candesce ourselves!"

"And when the Gretels invaded Falcon, he defended one of your cities, even after you'd held him in prison for a hundred days!" This from the premier of Malagan himself.

The few delegates of the ancient principalities of Candesce who'd bothered to come to the colloquy looked entertained. The promise of such provincial political theater was probably exactly why they'd showed up.

The whole Falcon Formation delegation stood up and prepared to walk out.

"Please," said Fanning, but they were no longer listening.

Leal watched in horror as the audience began standing up, shouting at one another, heading for the paths, or just shaking their heads. Beside her, Antaea sat with her head in her hands, and even Keir, so normally unflappable these days, was sitting there with his mouth open.

Admiral Fanning's aura of command had evaporated. He stood

there, shoulders slumped, a man lacking the one person in the world he needed to lean on.

Leal caught herself thinking that if she'd been here, Venera Fanning would have straightened this lot out in no time. What would she have done?

Leal could picture it with perfect clarity.

The pages of her speech slipped to the floor. As if from outside, she saw herself standing, walking to the leader of the ceremonial guardsmen at the side of the podium. "Give me your sidearm," she demanded, holding out her hand, palm up.

He goggled at her. "I'm not going to hurt anyone," she said. "Do it!"

She gave him the stare she'd learned worked best on undergrads. He glanced at the chaos in the audience, and a little smile appeared on his lips. "Do your best, ma'am," he said as he handed it to her.

Leal stalked up to the podium, her eyes on the pistol as she worked out how to turn off its safety. She heard a sudden commotion behind her as the others on the stage saw what she was holding, but it was too late as she raised the pistol high over her head and pulled the trigger.

Venera would have stood there after, with the gun smoking in her hand; so Leal did that. She glared out at the suddenly silent diplomats, military leaders, and heads of state, and then she put her mouth to the bullhorn affixed to the podium, and said, "My name is Leal Hieronyma Maspeth, and I have just returned from the universe beyond Virga with a message for you. A message and a warning, that you need to hear, because your very lives depend upon it.

"Now if you would all be seated, I would like to begin."

18

LEAL HAD BEEN working on this speech for months. Without pen and paper at hand, she had rehearsed it in her mind while trudging across the strange, flat landscapes of Aethyr. While climbing the long slope of the world's end, or sitting too exhausted to eat the meager rations they'd brought, she would retreat into herself and imagine that she stood in front of a vast assembly, all attentive and eager to hear the revelations she was about to drop, word by word, into their ears.

This was no assembly. It was a mob, and a hostile one that was only reluctantly subsiding into its seats. The lofty sense of mission that she'd imagined would sustain her in delivering this message simply wasn't there; instead, she felt exactly as she had on countless occasions when she'd had to tutor a roomful of impatient, pampered adolescent boys.

"Your nations nearly fell four years ago," she shouted, ignoring the sound of glass falling into the gardens somewhere to her right. "All of them. Would you be dead now if they had? Or controlled by something alien, like that poor soul, Aubrey Mahallan, whom Artificial Nature used as its pawn to break into Candesce? What do you suppose your fate would have been?"

She'd laid the pistol on the podium and leveled her jumbled note pages at the crowd. "Virga nearly fell again a year later, when another human became the vessel for an attempt to recapture the key to Candesce. Telen Argyre, whose sister stands behind me, was also possessed by a force from beyond our world. That force continues to press upon us, relentless. It has tried sneaking in. It has tried forcing the lock. Now, it prepares to batter down the doors."

"But why?" somebody shouted. "What do we have that they could possibly want?"

Leal's shoulders slumped in relief at the question. "Candesce," she said. "It's all about Candesce.

"Think about it." She wasn't following her speech in any of the ways she'd imagined, but it didn't matter now. She knew what to say. "Imagine that you've conquered the universe—and not just the universe outside yourself. Your offspring have flooded across the stars, copying and transforming themselves in a hurricane of ecstatic creativity. They are all wildly different in their shapes, sizes, their minds, morals, and goals. But the only ones that matter, you believe, are the ones that can think. This is because your perfected minds contain a complete model of reality. —A completed physics, a final chemistry, all possible biologies . . . an image, in your mind, of everything that is possible in our universe. Because your minds contain all possibilities, you've concluded that you *are* the real universe, and that messy, unpredictable realm of non-thinking matter and energy outside your perfect mind is just an illusion, a fallen dimension to be swept entirely aside in time.

"And then, your unstoppable flood hits a stone. Candesce stops you, and worse—far worse!—its very existence *refutes* you. You've come to believe that Mind is the true reality, and that the vessels you seem to need to house it are an afterthought, a noisome and filthy necessity you'll erase in time. But that's not true. Mind is always embodied. It has to be.

"And now, the cracks appear in your perfect mask. Why have you been expanding so relentlessly? Why this ceaseless creation of new forms in your infinite mind? —These paradises, each built on the rubble of the last? The million discarded languages, the games of culture, the recursive invention? It's because something still eludes you. Meaning . . . eludes you."

The emissary's people had deluged Leal with theory, with num-

bers and physics. The morphonts had told her how Candesce's protective field violated the physical laws that served as the bedrock of
Artificial Nature's operating system. Candesce's very existence dis-
proved the virtuals' claim that they held—and embodied—
universal truth. Yet there was more to it than that. For why did any
of this matter? During the long walk across the plains of Aethyr,
and at night as she sat next to the strange campfires that gravity
made possible, Leal had tried to see past those explanations. —Not
to understand what they were saying, but rather, what they meant.

"Why did our ancestors build Candesce?" she asked now, as
she'd finally learned to ask during those days. "Forget the how of
it. Why did they choose to limit themselves to these frail, brief
bodies, when they could have joined Artificial Nature in its syn-
thetic heavens? They could have had immortality, and they threw it
away.

"I will tell you why. It's because it is our frailty, our briefness,
our abject helplessness against the storms of fate that make our lives
meaningful. I tell you now the great secret of our entire existence:
that meaning can only come from being bound in the material
world, in its constraints, its agonies, its fleeting moments. The virtuals strive to escape all pain, all accident, and the brute mindless-
ness of nature. Yet without these things, existence is a hollow
vessel, and those who have become virtual have no true voice, can
hear only the bright echoes of our lives."

She'd seen it in John Tarvey's eyes. He'd moved past needing
flesh, and so what need did he have of emotions, which existed to
propel the body; no use for pain, certainly, but then no use for
pleasure, either. Without the need for a single unitary body, why
organize himself as a single mind at all? Why care, why think, why
feel, why be?

"Meaning comes from the moment, the place, and the bodies
struggling in it," she said—and then she smiled and laughed, as if
at a sudden thought; but this part she'd rehearsed.

"All of which," and now she softened her voice and gave her

audience a rare smile, "brings me to the question of why I, a simple history tutor from the city of Sere in the sunless country of Abyss, one day came to find myself hanging from the ledge of a library window, while soldiers ransacked its interior in search of me and my companions. For if you would look for meaning in what I've told you so far, you must start at that moment, in that place, and with those bodies in struggle."

And with that she was off, telling them now, in full confidence, how the emissary had come to Abyss as a great voice cloaked in darkness; how its message had panicked those who heard it, driving some mad; how they had destroyed their ships, their homes, and one another in their attempt to silence it. The fleet of Abyss was assembled, and it met the emissary and was scuttled by its own terror. Yet none of this chaos was the emissary's intent; it was simply that it was a creature born and bred in Artificial Nature. Within the influence of Candesce, it, too, had lost its mind. When Leal and her friend Easley Fencher found themselves crawling through the library window, it was because she had finally acquired the ancient, banned book that would give her clues about what the emissary was, and how to find it.

As concisely as she could, she told them the rest of it: how she'd found the emissary and gone with it into Aethyr and beyond; how, on her return, ships from Abyss and the Home Guard had pursued them; and how they'd all crashed on the surface of Aethyr.

Leal had lectured many times, but she had never told a story in such a way as she was now, and never a story so true, never one with her at its center. She spoke in a kind of ecstasy, and there was complete silence among her listeners.

—Until, as she was describing their harrowing flight through the lost city of Serenity, someone off to the left shouted, "Can't a man defend himself in this court of opinion?"

She blinked and looked over: Eustace Loll stood on the path beside the ranked chairs. He was in a formal suit and he wasn't alone.

Rustling murmurs sprang up again, and Leal heard the squeak of floorboards as people crisscrossed the podium behind her. Chaison Fanning had discreetly stepped aside during her speech, but now he appeared at her elbow. "Those men are from your country?" he asked her quietly. She nodded, suddenly ashen.

Loll fronted a delegation from Abyss—that much would have been disaster enough, for her. But beside them stood another group, newly arrived as well, and these men wore the severe black of the Home Guard. Considering the weight of the medals, braiding, and epaulets on their jackets, she assumed these were the Guard's very leaders.

And worse, much worse: next to the Guards stood fifteen unnaturally beautiful men and women, all tall and haughty, and dressed in beautiful, shimmering clothes. The virtuals had sent their own delegation to the colloquy.

The ecstasy of using her voice, of practically singing out her story, collapsed. Leal shrank back from the podium, but stopped as someone strolled to the front of this parade. Leal saw the dress first: black as space, adorned with random splashes of diamond, and cut very low. The lady's skin was pale, as were her wide eyes that were a gray so light as to nearly be white. Her mouth was a scarlet line, her hair a tumble of blond curls. She slunk along the line of alert Guardsmen, a sly smile on her face. "What?" she said. "Were you thinking we wouldn't show up? Not," she added with a pout, "that any of us received invitations."

Chaison Fanning was trotting down the steps of the stage, a broad smile on his face and his hand held out. "On the contrary," he said with all evidence of relief, "we'd announced to the world that this meeting was open to everyone, and we're very happy to see you."

"Are you?" She glided up to him, and he took her hand and bowed.

"Lady Inshiri Ferance, I take it?" he said, still in his bow. Leal heard some gasps from the crowd. "I am Admiral Chaison Fanning, and on behalf of our gracious hosts I would like to welcome you to the grand colloquy."

"Would you, now?" She took back her hand. "Then," purred Ferance, "you'll have no objection to our delegation making its own case, since your so-called free press has already painted us as the villains?"

"We would like nothing better," said Fanning. "We will make space for you in the program."

"We demand to go first," said Ferance.

"That," Fanning said, "I think would be harder to arrange. We want to ensure that all the delegates start with the same basic information—"

"What information?" One of the Guardsmen came to stand next to Ferance. This man was unnaturally tall, and ropy muscle bulged under his black uniform—which was festooned with medals.

Fanning bowed again. "To whom do I have the pleasure . . . ?"

"Nicolas Remoran, general secretary of the Virga Home Guard," the newcomer boomed. It was suddenly dead silent in the amphitheater. Without invitation, he stepped up onto the stage next to Fanning, where he loomed over the admiral of Slipstream like a tree. "And what is this information that *you* have about the outside world that can possibly compare to what the Guard has accumulated painstakingly over centuries?"

There was a momentary silence. Then: "Well, they knew I was alive. You didn't." Leal spun to see Hayden Griffin strolling past her, hands in his pockets as though he were spending an idle afternoon in the gardens. He walked right up to Remoran and said, "And anyway, it's not about what you know, is it? It's about what you *never told the rest of us.*"

There was muttering, murmuring, and a smattering of applause. Remoran whirled and shouted at the crowd, "Do you want to know the truth?" His voice was huge, utterly filling the space.

Moneyed powerbrokers and ancient nobles blinked in surprise. "Well, *do* you?" he roared.

There was a subdued reply. Fanning was calmly looking around, but Leal saw that his gaze was alighting in succession on the knots of soldiers he had scattered around the space. These were beginning to move forward.

"You're saying you don't want to hear our side?" shouted Remoran.

A hunched old woman in the front row stood up. "We do, we do," she said. That got a cheer, and the crowd began to chant, "Truth, truth, truth!"

Fanning threw up his hands and shook his head in sympathy to Leal. She shrugged in return.

The admiral held up a hand. "In the interest of keeping everyone *happy*," he said with a glare at the crowd, "we will allow the Home Guard delegation to go first." Before anyone could summon up a good cheer he added, "But anyone who tries to disrupt our program after this will be summarily ejected from the building."

Remoran crossed his arms and looked down at Fanning. "Fair enough," he rumbled.

Fanning tilted his head in ironic assent. "Then say your piece."

FOR A MINUTE or so Remoran prowled the edge of the stage, like some caught beast. Then he stopped in the center, clenched and unclenched his fists, and went through a remarkable transformation.

His expression softened; his shoulders slumped. He looked away from the crowd, and gave a great sigh. Then he said, "We couldn't do it anymore."

Leal had retaken her seat. She was boiling with rage at this interruption, and the stagy flamboyance of Ferance and her pet Guardsmen. Most of all, she was furious at Loll. There was that pistol on the podium . . .

"We of the First Line defend the walls of Virga," said Remoran. "Because we do that, we move in and out of the world. That confers advantages to us—unfair advantages. We see what humanity could be like, if only it were freed of the disease, infirmity, and ignorance that rule inside Virga. For centuries now, we've held our tongues because of our ancient pact with the founding nations of the world. *Leave us alone,* they'd commanded when they founded our order. *Let nothing from beyond the world touch us.*

"We do our job very well. If, in the past several years, you've heard rumors of attempts to pierce the world's walls—well, just think of all the attacks you never heard of, because we foiled them."

He shrugged and started to pace again. "We get compensated for our work. We suffer no disease and we live to fantastic ages, because we can go outside to treat these things. And yet, you cannot.

"This umbrella of protection has always been extended to our immediate families. That's been the benefit that Guardsmen treasured the most. It's selfish, I know, that we can enjoy these benefits and you can't—but that was the pact, we always thought. Our pact with the people of Virga. Except, it's not, is it?"

He spread his arms to encompass the crowd. "Who here signed that pact? Who even knew of it?" Nobody said anything. "Our pact was made with your ancestors, hundreds of years ago. *They* chose— not you."

Now he put his hand to his face, looking pained. It was, Leal thought, an extraordinary performance, because it was exactly not what she'd expected from this huge, intimidating man.

"I have to make you understand," he said with apparent reluctance, "so I'm going to confess to you. This will be my legacy, I suspect—just this one story, and it's not a story I ever wanted anyone to know."

He grimaced at the crowd. "I betrayed my wife. —You see, she had a cousin, and after ten years of marriage, I fell in love with that cousin. I'll spare you the details. The point is that, in the midst of all of that, I was called to the walls, and while I was away a plague hit our town.

"My family lived in the principalities, the safest, most civilized, richest place in Virga—but days from the walls. Still vulnerable to disease, and war, and all the insanities of our backward world. Some miasma of air, a cloud whose water droplets contained a pathogen easily cured at the walls, had drifted through the principalities and left vomiting, diarrhea, and death in its wake. When I heard about the outbreak I took the fastest ship home, and when I got there discovered that my wife, Miranda, was ill—and so was my beloved Elize, her cousin.

"Our rules were clear," he said heavily. "The immediate family of Guardsmen can be taken to the walls and cured—if there's time, because days can make a difference. I could certainly save my wife, but . . ." He fell silent, and when he began again, his voice cracked, "she wasn't the one I wanted to save."

The chamber had fallen into hushed silence. Leal was astonished, and she could tell that everyone else was, too.

Remoran pulled himself together. "I didn't know what to do. Could I be such a villain as to divorce my wife and marry Elize just so I could bring her to be healed instead? I did everything I could to treat them both, but the medicines I'd brought from the walls didn't work—didn't work—in Virga!

"I dithered for days, and then, heartbroken, I made my decision. I gathered Miranda from her sickbed and we set out for the walls. But I'd waited too long. She died on the way." He closed his eyes.

"I turned the ship around. I raced home. But again, I was too late. Elize died in her sleep just hours before I reached her side. I lost them both . . ."

Again, he struggled to compose himself. Then he seemed to expand, shoulders no longer slumped, face clear and determined. "Who here wants their loved ones to die? Who here wants to die themselves? That is the pact our ancestors made. Leal Maspeth admits that they traded away immortality, in favor of pain, disease, and death, all for some illusion of meaning? Well, forget meaning. Give me love. Give me back my love . . .

"There is another way. Our brothers from beyond the walls have always been troubled by our tragic lives, and they've made us an offer. Let's dial down Candesce's suppressive field, and for God's sake, let some aid and respite into this suffering world. Miranda didn't have to die. Elize didn't have to die; neither do any of us, ever again.

"Keep hiding in ignorance and misery, and condemn your own children to death—or open the doors and let choice into their lives. Decide which you want. May you decide . . . more wisely than I did."

He hung his head, turned, and left the stage.

IT TOOK A while for Fanning to regain control of the crowd and move the colloquy back onto its original program, but Keir didn't pay much attention; he was watching Leal. He was proud to see her recover quickly from having her passionate confession derailed by Remoran's dramatism. She was obviously upset, but it seemed that she had little sympathy for her own feelings. Fear, doubt, any sort of helplessness—they just made her angry at herself, and then she used the anger to prop up her indomitable sense of purpose. Soon, she was leading a breakout session on Virgan history, corralling and guiding a small mob of generals, high priests, and cabinet ministers as if they were recalcitrant schoolboys. Keir watched for a little while, but there was little he could do to help and he soon wandered away.

His role would be to help describe what the world outside Virga was like, but Remoran had set up multiple roadblocks to doing that effectively. So, while Fanning's strategists talked about how to proceed, he had nothing to do. The funny thing was that for the first while it was like being back in Brink, a child wandering through an awesome forest of adults. But then, gradually, a quiet voice somewhere inside him began to comment on those adults—not as a child, but as one of them.

They were so flawed, so obvious in their obsessions and willful blindness. Worst of all, they lacked scry, which could have so easily coordinated this fractious, chaotic tumble of disputes and paranoia. It was a miracle they were here at all, a miracle they were getting anything done. Keir began watching for patterns of interaction. Half-consciously, he was building a model of the meeting's social dynamics in his head.

"Keir Chen?" A page bowed to him. The boy was little older than Keir had recently thought he himself was. "Yes?"

"You're wanted in the grove." The boy pointed to the little stand of trees that spread out to embrace the left side of the government building within the curving sweep of its glass shell. Some kind of commotion was happening over there, with the paths blocked by security people and something tall and broad being trundled through the foliage.

"Hmm." He strolled in that direction. Various small crowds were clustered around speakers in the gardens; all were being very careful to avoid trampling on the flower beds, knowing as they did how rare gardens under gravity were in Virga. Other knots of people were arguing or conspiring in various corners.

The page led him past the grim security guards and under the trees. A number of people were talking up ahead; he heard shouted orders, the sound of creaking ropes. Rounding a bend in the path, they came upon a sight that made the page stop dead and swear under his breath. Keir grunted, but not because the bizarre vision was unfamiliar to him. Quite the opposite.

"Chen, can you explain this madness?" It was Admiral Fanning. He was standing with his arms crossed, tapping one foot impatiently on the gravel path. Next to him was a young, handsome officer in resplendent dress uniform who looked agitated and tired.

"We sent Travis here to the emissary's country and now he's

back—with this!" Fanning nodded past his officer to where a work gang was just finishing their moving operation.

Keir whistled appreciatively. Forgetting to answer Fanning, he walked up to the base of the vast oak tree the work gang had trundled into this intersection. It towered over the young trees around it, its twisted branches and thick sheets of leaves dark and wild-appearing next to their manicured perfection.

The oak's extensive root system was contained in a tangled metal structure that sprouted six thick metal legs. These in turn rested on several wheeled, wooden carts that were bowing under the strain.

Coils of metal and brightly colored plastics wound up the trunk of the tree. Thousands of intricate glittering shapes perched motionless among its branches. Its base sported many arms and sensing devices, all unmoving.

A grimy man in coveralls with a set of shears in his hand was staring up at the immense, unruly thing. "It needs a trim," he said.

"Touch it and you die," Keir said quickly. When the man glared at him, he added, "I'm not threatening you. I won't kill you. It will."

Something else was being wheeled out now. It was a statue of some kind, much smaller than the oak, smaller than a man, in fact. "What about that one?" the gardener asked. "Can we touch it?"

Keir glanced at it. "Yes." It was clearly a morphont, nothing at all like the creature towering over him.

Fanning and Travis had come up behind him. Keir spared the officer a sympathetic look. "Traveling with these two must have been a nightmare," he said. "I'm glad I wasn't with you."

"You know what these things are?" asked the admiral.

"Yes. It seems your man Travis gained us a very powerful ally while he was away." When Fanning continued to look puzzled, Keir pointed to the tree. "This."

He walked up and reached out, but didn't quite have the courage to touch one of its massive legs. "It's an oak."

"I can see that." Now Fanning was just annoyed.

"No, I don't think you can. The oaks are one of the most powerful species in the arena. They're aggressive, relentless, generally hostile to animalia . . ." He saw Fanning's look, and smiled. "Look at the legs. Look at the sensing nets, the power units. This oak is a tree wedded to an artificial intelligence with mobility, weapons, dexterous arms, and an internal Edisonian engine for designing whatever it may need."

The admiral was still shaking his head. "But all a tree needs is—"

"Air, soil, sunlight, and peace and quiet, yes. And if you deprive this fellow of any of those things, he'll hunt you down and obliterate you."

"But . . . but why? I mean, why should the artificial mind care? I can see what it has to offer the tree. But what does the tree offer it?"

"Something no AI has by itself," said Keir. "A four-billion-year-old will to live."

He could see that the admiral still didn't understand. And if he didn't, then explaining the awesome reality of the oak to the rest of the delegations was going to be a problem. Even AIs that controlled tremendous resources never lived very long, because their will to live was an add-on; it wasn't ingrained into every cell, into their most fundamental design parameters, the way it was with evolved life-forms. This oak gave the AI attached to it an anchor, an endpoint for any why it might ask about itself. The oak had no possible purpose beyond its own duration, and that was exactly what made it valuable.

"Admiral, you're looking at the great secret that divides the morphonts and the virtual. The virtual take everything as raw material for their creativity—even their own memories and identities. They have no root. They have no attachment to the physical world or any piece of that world. This oak does. It is its embodiment that makes it like us. That is what makes it our ally . . ."

He trailed off, hand still raised to nearly touch the oak. Being in the presence of the oak was bringing back memories. He remembered an oak visiting Brink, shortly before he'd de-indexed himself. Something about a warning . . .

"Chen?"

He blinked and looked to where Admiral Fanning was frowning down at the other visitor. It sat on its little wooden cart, glittering tail coiled around its front paws, staring enigmatically into the distance. He could see the faint white strands of nanofiber that tied together its sculpted iron muscles and limbs.

"It's a cheetah," he said, walking up to it and looking into its gigantic green eyes. "A beautiful piece." He glanced at Travis. "You've seen it in motion."

The officer nodded. "Admiral, it talked. It's a new emissary from the . . . the people who contacted Maspeth. This one is empowered to negotiate and its word will be binding."

"But it's not moving."

"Candesce," said Keir. "We're too close. To wake these two up, we'll have to bring them back near the skin of the world. You should have held this meeting there to begin with."

Fanning ran a hand through his hair. "They wouldn't have come. They'd have thought it was a trap. And they won't go now. This is a disaster."

Keir straightened. "No, it's a beginning." He stepped close to the admiral. "Sir, I lost my own wife to the virtuals. I will not see any hesitation or doubt among those who stand with me against it."

Fanning's eyes widened. Keir finally knew who he'd been before the de-indexing and his neotenization. Right now he saw in Fanning a young man, still inexperienced in many things—a technological and philosophical primitive who was preparing to hurl spears at starships.

"Guard these two, but do not touch them," he told the assembled soldiers. "Let no one know they're here as yet. *Not one word*," he emphasized, looming over the gardener who'd had the temerity to wave his shears at the oak. "All our lives depend on them."

He walked away, aware that Fanning was staring after him. He'd thought Keir was a boy; well, so had Keir himself. It was time to lay that illusion aside.

Yes, he remembered the oak's visit now. It might even have been this one. It had come to warn the Renaissance of some imminent danger, but what that was remained tantalizingly out of reach.

Keir did remember, though, how he'd been feeling just before it arrived. He'd been excited—no, far more than that: triumphant. He recalled savage satisfaction, an aesthetic sense of rightness, and how he'd used his scry to banish sleep for night after night as he'd worked out the final details of what he was going to present to the others. And then, when the oak came, fear . . .

To de-index himself, he'd wandered far into the labyrinth of Brink, into empty quarters no one had yet explored. His second body had plodded behind him, towing something massive and unwieldy . . . a manufacturing fab, that was it. But why just the fab? They were always attached to an Edisonian; there was no other source for the designs they used.

In darkness lit only by the eyes of his second body, he had built something. And then he'd given instructions to that other body, and as he'd laid down and fallen asleep, it had raised surgical hands that held a gleaming something . . .

Pulse.

Now, on the edge of the grove in Aurora's great gardens, he stopped. Something had changed the moment he'd seen the oak, but it was so quiet, so unexpected, that he hadn't even registered it consciously.

Pulse. There it was again. He closed his eyes and waited.

Pulse.

His scry was awake.

"There you are!"

He opened his eyes, blinking at another incongruity—a voice that he shouldn't be hearing inside Virga at all. Disoriented, Keir looked around at the crowd of haughty nobles, prime ministers and presidents, diplomats and retainers. One figure was walking straight through them all, hand extended, a broad smile on his face.

It was Gallard, his tutor from Brink.

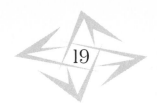

19

AS THE LIGHT from his sun faded toward dusk, Hayden Griffin could be seen climbing the broad steps to the gallery overlooking the gardens. He turned to face the sun, as he had that morning, and then stood stock-still, a statue of himself.

A few minutes later, Leal walked up, carrying two wineglasses. "Are you doing that on purpose?" she asked as she came to stand next to him.

He blinked and looked down at her. "Doing what?"

"Looking heroic."

He seemed to notice the crowd below for the first time. Many faces were turned to look at him, and some people were leaning together to talk, clearly telling stories about the sun lighter. "Ah," he said, embarrassed suddenly. "No, it's just this spot has a decent eyeline. I was checking the twilight calibration."

"Of course you were," she said smoothly, handing him one of the glasses. "But you wouldn't be so intimidating to all those fine, eligible young women down there if you did it with this in your hand."

Now his eyes widened in surprise. "I mean," she said, "you're not actually *trying* to scare them away, are you?"

Uncomfortable, he sipped at the wine. "I don't know how to play this game," he admitted finally. "Damnit, now I've forgotten the flicker rate."

"That's a good first step." Her gaze drifted across the people below, then stopped. Her smile faded.

Hayden noticed. "We ran rings around them once before," he

said, nodding to the Abyssal soldiers waiting at the foot of the steps. "And if worse comes to worst, there's a hundred noblemen down there who would happily shoot them for a chance to talk to you." Now it was her turn to look startled, and his to grin. ". . . Or hadn't *you* noticed *that*?"

Behind where the stage had stood this morning, workmen had finished dismantling a brand-new fountain in the center of the diamond-shaped plaza that served as the foyer to the gardens. They were levering slabs of paving stone in to replace it, and a small orchestra had begun tuning up in one corner of the diamond.

"I do believe we're having a ball," said Hayden dryly. "I hate these things."

"You just haven't attended one with the right partner," she countered.

"Speaking of which, where's your young man? Keir?"

"He's not as young as he looks. And I don't know. I haven't seen him since this afternoon." She frowned. "He's probably inspecting the wheel's buttresses or something. He's as much an engineer as you are."

"You say that as if it were a bad thing." He cocked his arm for her to hold and they began to stroll down the steps.

"You're both boys when you do that. Be a man for the evening."

His brows wrinkled with worry. "Is that going to involve dancing?"

"I fear it may." She smiled at Eustace Loll's goons as they passed them.

"I'll dance if you'll wear a gown."

"Cheeky! —Oh, all right."

They entered the swirl of color and waistcoats and jewelery as, unnoticed, Hayden's sun faded into nightly slumber overhead.

DINNER HAD BEEN served. Jugglers and acrobats had flown and tossed one another across the dance floor. As they pranced away Antaea saw the delegates looking askance at one another. Despite the best efforts of their hosts, they had not come to form any sort of community during the day. They were here because they agreed there might be a threat to Virga that the Home Guard couldn't deal with alone. Beyond that, they were suspicious.

The orchestra had begun to play, but nobody ventured onto the dance floor.

Antaea was neither dressed nor inclined to dance, but nonetheless she cursed under her breath and glanced around for a partner. Somebody would have to start things—but there stood Chaison, forlorn without his wife by his side. Should she . . . ? No, no, that would be disastrous in so many ways.

Suddenly the crowd parted and two lines of people filed onto the floor: the female acrobats, smiling, perfumed and dressed in sparkles and crinoline; and a column of extremely tall, extremely handsome Aerie naval officers. The lines dissolved in the center of the floor and the acrobats and officers walked up to hesitant men and women in the crowd, and curtsied and bowed.

Gray-haired men paired off with the young acrobats; matrons and ingenues stepped out with the officers; and suddenly it was a ball. Antaea blew out a breath and rolled her shoulders. Yet another reminder of a world that she would never feel a part of.

She took a seat at an empty table. Hayden and his men, as well as Travis, Lacerta, and Sayrea Airsigh's Last Liners were all sitting nearby, but she had no desire to join them. The rest of the guests were milling in strategic ways, all very political; but no one came near Antaea.

—That is, until Lady Inshiri strolled over and gathered her skirts to sit opposite her. "Ah, the *author*!" When Antaea didn't reply, the lady nodded to the Home Guard contingent and said, "They don't seem to like you," in a confiding tone.

Antaea eyed her. "What's to like?"

"Why, whatever do you mean? You're the one who saved their collective asses, if I've heard the story correctly. If not for you,

Candesce would now be in the hands of—" Inshiri paused. "Whose hands, exactly?"

"Your friends over there," Antaea nodded at the handsome outsiders, "would say it was the emissary's people. Or some such."

"And I'll bet," said Inshiri ironically, "that this emissary would say it was these very people"—and here she waved brightly at them—"who tricked your leader Gonlin into going after the key to Candesce, thence to open the sun of suns, switch off Virga's defensive field, and hand them our whole world on a platter."

"That is the argument," Antaea said neutrally.

"A bit of a 'my fault/your fault' tiff, don't you think? Though why anyone should want this dreary little world I don't know. Yet, I do remain puzzled by one thing." When Antaea didn't prompt her, Inshiri went on. "You were there. You met the creature that they—whoever 'they' are—sent to penetrate Candesce. I understand it took the form of your sister. So you must have looked it in the eye—you must have *seen* what kind of being it was."

Antaea turned away. She had seen. After she'd delivered Chaison Fanning to him, Gonlin had told Antaea that she was free to go, and that her sister was waiting for her in a nearby building. Antaea had put her hand on the door latch to that hut, then hesitated, and gone around the side to look in a grimy window. It had looked like Telen standing there—yet she didn't move, didn't even blink, just stood gazing at the door Antaea was supposed to come through. Her uncanny stillness had had the air of an automaton to it—of something without a mind.

She couldn't deny to herself that Leal's description of the emissary had sounded a lot like what she'd seen in Telen. But she would never admit that to Inshiri, whom Jacoby Sarto had painted as the vilest of political criminals.

"I've learned not to trust my own judgment in some things," she said finally, and turned a quick and formal smile on Inshiri. "It's not my place to judge who's lying unless I can catch them in the lie. That's why I brought Hayden Griffin here: because Eustace Loll, at least, is lying."

"Let me put it another way," said Inshiri in a musing tone. "If you had to give something up—power, rights, or, say, secrets—who would you rather give them up to: a human being, however different in culture and morality they may be from you; or something that doesn't even think, but claims to have your best interests in mind?"

"Is one of my options 'whichever side you're not on'?"

Inshiri laughed lightly. "You *have* heard of me. Fair enough—but I think that most people would choose the worst possible human tyranny over any tyranny by the nonhuman, for the simple reason that we all want to believe that someone, somewhere, is free, even if that person is grinding our own freedom into the muck. Because the alternative is that no one, anywhere, is free—and do you really think you could live with that?" She looked up. "Ah! I happen to be good at this dance. Surely one of these handsome officers will take a turn with me."

She left, and Antaea saw that Hayden had been watching them. She walked away herself, not seeing the gardens, the azure sky and dancers. Half-consciously, she reached up to unclip the locket that hung around her neck. She hefted its tiny weight in her hand.

In it were two tiny photos of her sister, Telen. The first showed her in happy times. The second, hidden behind it, showed Telen tied to a chair, bruised and apparently terrified. Gonlin had given it to Antaea, as proof of the leverage he had over her.

She couldn't hate Gonlin. He'd had the best of intentions. He'd felt he had to do what he did in order to save the world.

So did Leal Maspeth.

She stopped, holding the locket, and searched the dancers until she spotted Maspeth. The former history tutor was dancing with Chaison; seeing that, Antaea's mouth thinned, and she turned and took a shadowed and empty path away from the light and music, and everyone she knew.

CHAISON FANNING WAS being very polite to Leal, and she couldn't fault his dancing; but she knew he was angry. As they stepped across the floor he kept glancing at one edge of the crowd, where Inshiri Ferance posed with a glass in her hand. She was laughing gaily with a bevy of courtiers.

The admiral stumbled, and stopped for a moment. Leal hesitated, lifting her hand from his shoulder, but then he scowled and took up the dance again.

"Admiral . . ." she ventured.

"A talking tree?" He glared at her. "A four-pawed statue? Travis said they walked and talked outside of Virga, but if they're not going to do that here, what good are they?"

She ducked her head. "They want us to meet them at the walls—"

"That's not going to happen!" He tripped again but recovered and spun her around, rather roughly. "Maspeth, I've risked everything on your say-so. Not just my career, but the reputation of my people, my country's relationship not just with Aerie but all these states—and my . . ." His fingers tightened around her hand.

The day had swung one way and another like an off-balance town wheel. It was a miracle that so many nations had sent delegates at all, but their overall level of skepticism had been high, and hadn't come down by nightfall. Many of the delegates had to get over centuries of myth-based prejudice about what the greater universe was like, and, despite the best efforts of Hayden and Lacerta, many still refused to believe Leal's story. Nicolas Remoran's tale and his appeal for a simple change to Candesce had irrevocably won over half the crowd; and Inshiri Ferance was openly mocking the whole affair.

"You promised that your allies would back us up," said Fanning. "Instead, they've delivered us a practical joke. It's a disaster, Maspeth, and I don't see how we're going to recover from it."

"Travis brought documents, too, didn't he? They wrote us books . . ." In fact, it was Gallard, Keir's old friend from Brink, who'd brought the books. He and Keir had sat together and talked intensely for an hour; afterward, Keir had told Leal that Gallard and Maerta were worried about him. "It's the neotenization process," he'd told her. "Apparently they ran some sims, and they think . . . well, they say if I stay in Virga, it's going to kill me."

After Loll's arrival and the stresses of the day, that news had just been too much for Leal; Keir had become an anchor for her. Without him she felt adrift, nationless. So, she didn't protest now when Fanning said, "Books? Those books are so technical it'll take us years to decipher them. And anyway, a book proves nothing."

Was Keir going to leave? Virga had seemed to amaze and delight him at every turn; would he be the same person if he left, or would he revert to the child he'd been when she'd met him?

Immersed in these thoughts, she barely heard the admiral going on about how the whole emissary visit could be just some sort of elaborate hoax—until his voice trailed off. She snapped back to attention. He was staring at something over her shoulder.

As they spun, Leal followed his gaze. A man in a naval uniform was speaking urgently into Inshiri Ferance's ear. For the first time all day, she wore a frown. Then, as the officer continued to speak, she glanced at the dance floor. —At Chaison Fanning and Leal.

Then she was gone in a swirl of silks, and up and down the crowd, her whole entourage could be seen breaking off their conversations and fading into the crowd.

Leal and Chaison stopped dancing. Without a glance at Leal Chaison walked quickly to where a knot of Slipstream uniforms was working its way through the crowd. Leal followed, her heart suddenly pounding.

"What's going on?" he demanded of his men. A panting airman in flying leathers leaned on one of the tables; as Fanning strode up he straightened and saluted.

"Two of our ships docking at the axis, sir. They're the *Mercy* and the *Renown*."

Leal put her hand to her mouth. Those were the escorts for Venera's yacht. But where was . . .

"The *Judgment's* with them?" demanded Fanning. The airman shook his head.

"Apparently they've been trying to shake pursuit and spent the past few days hiding in a sargasso. They just managed to shake whoever it was and get here—"

"Ferance!" snapped Fanning. "She's trying to sneak away, damn it, stop her and her people from leaving." Two men took off at a run. "And locate the Abyssals as well," he added to another officer. "I'm just about ready to imprison the whole damn lot of them."

"Sir, our territorial agreement—"

"Then get me the prime minister! Damn it, man, it's my wife!"

News was spreading that something was up. Some people were still dancing, but more were leaving the dance floor to rejoin their parties. Pages were zipping back and forth, trying to answer people's questions.

The admiral had forgotten Leal. She stood on the periphery of his impromptu command center for a while, arms crossed, biting her lip. But there was nothing she could say or do to help. She turned, and saw soldiers from Abyss watching her alertly a few steps away.

And where the hell was Keir?

KEIR WAS WALKING in the far corners of the garden. Gallard's message was ringing in his head, as was something else that so far he had avoided thinking about.

Strange how life came to be divided, into the time before and the time after. His marriage to Sita had been like that; during those years, Keir's life before meeting her had seemed like a faded picture. Then, when it ended—and Revelation's human civilization began to fall shortly thereafter—the same cleaving had occurred again. During his time in Brink, Keir had immersed himself in the painfully recovered principles of science and physics, and all the ups and downs of normal human life had seemed far away.

Brink, and Revelation, and everything he'd ever done seemed now like a prelude to Virga. This world was alive for Keir in a way no other place had ever been. He was intoxicated by its fantastical, pastel-shaded skies, its tenacious, makeshift civilizations, and most of all its passionate people. Every single one of them burned brighter than any human he'd met outside. Brightest of all, for all her quiet, was Leal.

To think that he might have to leave Virga . . . He would almost rather die. The thought frightened him; not the idea of death, but the thought that any passion could have such a hold on him as to make the threat of dying irrelevant.

If he returned to Brink, would he continue to be the person he'd become here? Or would he lose his memories again and revert? He hadn't asked Gallard, because some residue of caution had prevented Keir from revealing just how much he remembered. It was galling now to recall being treated like a child by Gallard these past few months. In reality, Keir was the elder of the two, and prior to his de-indexing, Keir had been the dominant one.

He knew he still looked young, too. While they talked Keir had tried to act like his earlier self, while at the same time asking probing questions about the neotenization. And all the while, a slow, familiar pulse had sounded in the back of his head: his inexplicably awakened scry.

He paused under a young willow tree and looked back at the lighted heart of the garden. The vaulting wrought-iron and glass walls and arching ceiling gave the place a cathedral-like look. To the left were the flower beds, dinner tables, and tents and podiums where the presentations had been held. They surrounded the dance floor, and beyond it great tall glass doors opened out onto the upward-curving city streets. To the right, the glass walls wrapped halfway around the government palace before anchoring themselves in its stone facade. On the far side of the palace another wing of the greenhouse did the same. Both of these side-ways were thickly planted with trees.

A couple of security men were patrolling the entrance to the nearer grove, but as he walked up they waved him through. Keir was one of the few people they would let near the oak and its four-footed companion.

He ducked into the blackness under the trees. Keir wasn't sure why he had come in here. He had some dim notion of communing with something familiar, for in their own mad way, a cyborg tree and morphont cheetah seemed more ordinary to him right now than this handmade palace on its wheel of knotted-together forest. Maybe they could soothe his anxiety, make him more willing to leave Virga if he had to.

Pulse. He stopped in dappled darkness, because for just a moment, he'd thought he could see something. —Not with his own ordinary eyes, but through the second sight of scry.

It shouldn't be possible. The physics that underlay scry simply didn't exist here. He'd heard the stories today of the recent incursions into Virga by creatures of Artificial Nature: Aubrey Mahallan and Telen Argyre had both been possessed by it. Their alien riders must have been biological, however, bred in secret near Virga's walls by A.N.'s Edisonians. They'd been little more than mental parasites, although Argyre had apparently had some additional technology. Hard-won and fragile, Keir assumed, else they'd have flooded Virga with similarly equipped soldiers.

He was sure they had no idea how Candesce's suppression field actually worked. As he moved forward through the foliage, feeling his way with his arms outstretched, Keir caught himself feeling smug about that. The emotion surprised him; why should he be smug?

But, oh, of course, it was because of the . . . He strained to recover the rest of the memory, but it wasn't there. All he could picture in his mind was an oak visiting Brink, some months ago, before he de-indexed himself. It had come on some ordinary business, but now he remembered that it had also wanted to speak to him alone. It was there to warn Keir specifically, about . . .

Once again, the memory was just tantalizingly beyond his reach. *Pulse.*

He had another momentary flash of vision, clearer but somehow more confusing. For a second he'd been looking at a curtain of some kind—a dark wall of cloth. The feeling, though, of the image—not the image itself—was strangely familiar.

He parted some low-hanging branches and emerged onto the path where the oak and the cheetah sat still as statues. City light from high overhead bathed them in a pale lunar glow. No one was here, and the voices and music had faded to a distant murmur.

Kneeling, he gazed into the giant green glass eyes of the cheetah. They cupped refractions of city light, so it almost seemed they were glowing. "What did I have to hide?" he asked it. *And from whom?*

There was that other memory he'd been trying to catch all day. He'd taken his second body deep into Brink's unexplored reaches, and it had brought a fab unit. Together they had made something, he was sure of it; and yet he clearly remembered walking back to Complication Hall afterward, and he'd been carrying nothing. Nor had his second body brought anything back.

"You can't tell me, can you?" he asked the cheetah, and when it didn't answer, he straightened up.

At that moment vision flashed upon him again, and at the same time he felt a buzzing vibration in—no, on, his chest. Startled, he slapped at his jacket, thinking one of Virga's strange insects had flown into him. His secondary view staggered and suddenly he realized where it was coming from as a silvery dragonfly launched itself from his jacket pocket.

He gaped at it. This was impossible. He could clearly picture the final equations he'd solved to prove how Candesce's field worked and no, they would never allow a device like his dragonflies to operate here. Unless—

Breath caught in astonishment, it all unfolded in his mind

while his inner vision soared with the dragonfly up through the trees, darting between branches, ducking and swerving along the path and past the legs of the shadowed man who was running up behind Keir with a raised sword in his hand.

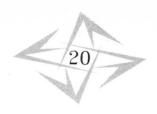

20

LEAL HAD GONE looking for Keir. She found Antaea instead. The wraith was walking slowly through the twilit flower beds behind the tables, her head down, her arms crossed. She looked up when Leal approached, but did not smile.

"Have you seen Keir?"

Antaea shook her head in a distracted way. Leal hesitated, but she was acutely aware of the Abyssal soldiers discreetly trailing her. She decided to leave Antaea alone. As she turned away, though, Antaea suddenly said, "What if it was a mistake?"

"What?" Leal took another look at her. Antaea's eyes were red and she stood now in a crestfallen posture. "What mistake?"

"The emissary. Did you ever think . . . it might be lying?"

Impatience flared in Leal. "Antaea, I saw the urgency, the way it was trying to communicate. I went to its home world—"

"I've seen other worlds, too!" Antaea stepped closer in sudden, unexpected anger. "Lots of us have! The Guard travel outside Virga all the time and we never met your 'emissary.' Were we lied to so well, all of us, century after century? Tell me, Leal, which is harder to believe? That we were lied to? Or that you, who'd never even left that little provincial city before, might be duped by the same enemy that fooled . . . ?" She closed her lips tightly and looked down.

"I know this is important to you—" Leal began, but Antaea shook her head violently.

"No, you don't. You think this is about Telen. It was never about Telen. It's about the reason she and I joined the Guard to begin with." Antaea's hand rose to clutch a locket around her neck as she turned to look at the city, an arch of sparkling lights cupping green foliage, that swept above them. "It's because we knew how vulnerable all this really is; and we were willing to give our lives to keep it safe. Telen did. So would I, in a second."

She stopped, having finally noticed the commotion swirling around Chaison Fanning. The admiral was now at the podium, giving orders to an assembled body of officers while pages and couriers ran in and out the greenhouse's giant doorway. A puzzled look crossed Antaea's face and she began to walk that way. Leal fell into step beside her.

"I made your mistake once," Antaea continued. "I mean, of following someone because they were a friend, rather than because of my principles. I trusted them, and made the mistake of thinking that somebody else was my enemy because, well, I didn't know them. Leal, I learned my lesson. We need better reasons than loyalty and love to choose which side we're on. If you choose loyalty and love—or hate and revenge—over what's good for Virga, then no matter how noble and right you may feel you are, you've put yourself on the side of the devils."

The ball was dissolving into knots of people: the delegations, all finding their countrymen to talk urgently with them. Antaea's head turned from side to side as she strode through the arguing, gesticulating mob. "What the—"

"If you'd believed me earlier," said Leal bitterly, "if they'd all listened earlier, maybe it wouldn't have come to this."

Antaea broke into a run, arriving moments later at the foot of the main stage. She grabbed a Slipstream officer by the arm and shouted, "What's going on?"

"A fleet!" He shook his head in amazement. "A giant bloody fleet, and it's on the move!"

Leal came up to her. "Venera's escort just made it back from some place called Fracas. Jacoby Sarto betrayed us. Maybe he was working for Inshiri Ferance all along; why not? She's his countryman. Venera's been taken by them, and her guards barely made it back here. They were chased by warships from the armada that Ferance's apparently been building now for months."

Antaea looked thunderstruck, and Leal felt a savage satisfaction at seeing her that way. "This armada," said Antaea. "Where's it going?"

Leal sneered at her. "Oh, where do you think? They're on their way to Candesce. They couldn't take it by guile, so now they'll do it by force."

Antaea stepped back. "But—but that's—" Whatever else she said was lost to Leal as a sudden, violently bright light spiked upward, drawing the distant glass canopy in black and white and erasing the city outside. Then noise poured over them, knocking many to their knees as others put their hands to their heads in sudden shock.

It was like a bellowing crowd, many voices thundering some overlapping refrain almost like music, almost a chant. The light was welling from the grove beside the palace, shafts and pinions of it dancing across the building's walls. Around Leal, men were drawing their swords, nobles waving to their squires to bring their gun cases. Some men and women were hunkering down under the tables.

Abruptly the volume of the shouting cut in half, then half again. The light dropped back, its beams hesitating, then drooping to be replaced by a white glow that turned the tops of the trees into silver filigree.

"What was that?" shouted Antaea in alarm. But Leal laughed wildly, for she recognized that great voice and it did not frighten her. —Though it was the last thing she had expected to hear in this place.

"Come on!" And she was running now, careless of the Abyssal soldiers on her heels, through the stunned mob, over flower beds and under trees, to where the emissary had awakened.

SHE WOULDN'T HAVE expected Leal to be a good runner, but the former educator was almost to the trees before Antaea caught up to her. "Stop! You don't know what's in there!"

"Yes I do!" Leal kept on going. Many others were converging on the grove now, mostly soldiers. The courtiers and diplomats hung back, talking and pointing.

The men who'd been posted at the entrance to the grove's pathways were staring in and so Leal burst past them before they could react. "Stop!" one of them yelled. "Something's crashing around!"

"I'll catch her," Antaea said on the way by. The guards started to follow Leal, but then noticed the crowd converging behind Antaea. They turned to deal with that.

She almost ran into her. Leal had stopped, was staring at something on the path. It was the body of a man, crumpled as though he'd fallen from a great height. Broken branches were scattered around him. Cautiously, Antaea knelt and turned his head to look at the face. She heard Leal gasp.

"That's the man from Brink—Keir's teacher, Gallard's his name."

They both looked down the path. Something very tall and very wide glowed brightly there, and something else, small and noticeable only as silvery flashes, was moving at its base. "Oh," said Leal. "But why—"

Antaea felt a terrible prickle of fear as she recognized the kind of light she was looking at. "It's them," she murmured, mouth dry. Memories of Telen, of her being forced to kidnap Chaison Fanning; of the moment when she saw her sister and realized she was dead—they stopped her just long enough that Leal ran on into the clearing before Antaea could stop her.

Antaea reached for her gun—but of course they hadn't let her carry it here. She hunched down, as if preparing for a blow. Her eyes were on Leal's leaf-cloaked shape, which slowed and moved toward the source of the light at a walk. Any second now she would be struck down. They all would be.

Footsteps pounded on the path behind her and Antaea snapped out of her paralysis. Fervently wishing she was armed, she crept to the end of the path and looked out. An involuntary moan escaped her lips.

Leal stood, feet planted wide, in front of a monstrous tree whose limbs shone with brilliant lines of white light. Some of the younger branches were wrapped in silvery pneumatic frameworks, like mechanical muscles, and those arms were now spreading wide as if to embrace the tiny woman below them.

Leal's own arms rose and spread wide. Antaea was astonished to hear her laughing—a long peal of unbridled joy, and what sounded strangely like relief.

Then something else moved. As armed men thundered up behind her, Antaea stood and instinctively put out her arm to keep them from passing. But she didn't take her eyes off of Leal and the four-legged thing now prowling in front of her.

It was beautiful, she had to give it that: a lithe, low-slung body with a long flicking tail behind it, and a diamond-shaped head with huge triangular ears and equally giant, glowing green eyes. It paced one way, cocking its head to look at Leal from the left, then fluidly turned and went to look at her from the right. Then it sat on its haunches in front of her, and curled its tail around its paws.

"How have you been?" Leal asked it.

Antaea remembered the name for this kind of creature: cat. Yet this was not a living being. Its body was made of metal, and its eyes were glass. Antaea should have expected what happened next, but she jerked back when it formed its mobile mouth into human speech: "A lot has happened," it said.

Its voice was as fluid as its body, startlingly mellow, in fact. It was a voice you'd be inclined to trust, but Antaea would do no such thing. She could hear the path behind her filling up with whispering people, but she still held her arm out to bar them.

The iron cat craned its neck to look at the galaxy of city lights above them. "You built a city outside Virga's walls? I think that was not wise."

"THAT IS NOT WHERE WE ARE."

The men around Antaea gave a collective shout and she herself went down on one knee. It was the tree that had spoken, but not from any single mouth. Rather, the sound poured from every part of it, trunk, branch, and leaf, an encompassing cloud.

Antaea remembered Leal's description of the being she'd called the emissary. It had manifested as a great voice speaking from the dark skies beyond the lights of the city of Sere. Leal had first heard the voice when returning to Sere from her hometown wheel. Later, that voice would become associated with disappearances, first of men and ships, then of entire villages. The whole Abyssal navy had gone in search of it and been destroyed. Yet Leal had sought it out, learned its intent—or so she claimed—and befriended it.

Antaea looked back to see Chaison moving up the path. Ashamed of her cowardly stance, she straightened and stepped out into the light. Leal glanced at her and smiled.

"Antaea. I'd like to introduce the emissaries. This one I've met before in other bodies," she indicated the cat, "and this is the seneschal of the oaks."

Antaea swallowed and stepped closer. "Do they have names?"

Leal shook her head. "They have addresses. I suppose we could name them ourselves, but it never seemed . . . appropriate."

Antaea came to stand next to Leal, and the cat bobbed its head as it looked at her. Chaison appeared at her elbow, and since he was brave enough to, his men followed. Soon a great throng of whispering people had gathered, all keeping a respectful distance from the strange beings.

The emissaries had remained silent as the crowd gathered. Now the oak said, "HOW HAVE YOU DONE THIS?"

Leal blinked and glanced at Chaison, who looked puzzled. "Done what?" she asked.

"Awakened us here," said the cat. "You have lifted Candesce's influence from this spot."

"N-not us," Leal began, but Antaea kicked her in the shin. She sent Leal a glare that she hoped said *Don't say anything.*

"IF NOT YOU, THEN WHO?"

Chaison waved one of his men forward. "Where are Ferance and the Home Guard people?" he murmured.

"We can't find them," murmured the officer.

Yes, it might have been them, thought Antaea. Waking the emissaries would be a highly effective display of power, if you had discovered Candesce's secret. And yet, you would want to be there for the unveiling of that capability; and would you really choose to inaugurate it by giving your enemies a chance to speak?

"This is strange," Chaison said. "We have no explanation. I suggest we worry about the *how* later, and seize the opportunity while we have it."

"WHO ARE YOU?" thundered the oak. Chaison bowed.

"Admiral Chaison Fanning of the navy of Slipstream," he said. To his aide he added, "Where is Shambles? Aerie's got to be represented here."

"DO YOU SPEAK FOR VIRGA?"

"No one speaks for Virga." He walked up to stand under the broad branches of the oak. "We here speak for some of the human nations in Virga. We came here to discuss how to protect ourselves and all the rest who are not here."

"THEN YOU WILL DO."

Chaison looked around, a pained expression on his face. The nobles, ministers, and diplomats of the other nations ringed him and the tree; all appeared awestruck and, clearly, at a loss for words. Antaea knew politicians, however. That silence would not last.

Chaison turned his attention to the iron cat. "You're the being that came to Abyss with a message? The one that Leal Maspeth knows?"

"I am part of that," said the cat with a duck of its head. Antaea twitched at those words. *Part of that.* It was admitting that it wasn't a conscious soul like herself. "We came to you with news of your danger," it continued. "It is our danger, too; and so, we propose an alliance."

Now the crowd began talking animatedly. Antaea crossed her arms and shook her head.

Chaison held up his hand for silence. "What kind of alliance?"

"It should not be possible for us to speak here," said the cat. "Obviously you have learned the secret of how Candesce is able to keep Artificial Nature at bay, even if you will not admit it to us. We want that secret for our own protection. In return, we will give you military and technological assistance."

Antaea couldn't help herself. "But *you're* part of Artificial Nature," she blurted. "You were frozen until just now because you're part of it. How would Candesce's field *protect* you? It would just turn you off."

"We would use it as a weapon, not a shield. And as to us being a part of the Artificial Nature, *you* are part of biology," said the cat. "Do you therefore ally yourself with plagues and parasites? Your operating system is DNA. Do you therefore think of yourself only as that? It gives you life, but it also gives you cancer, and diseases, and decrees that you must die." The creature paced away a little, then spun around impatiently. "We do not wish to be at the mercy of consciousness. We simply wish to remain what we are."

"You wish? You 'wish'?" Antaea shook her head with a cynical laugh. "You just admitted you're not even aware. How can you *want* anything? You're a robot," she said to the cat, "and you," she shouted at the oak, "you're nothing but a plant!"

She turned to the crowd. "They may be despicable people, but at least Ferance and her allies are like us."

"Oh, but they're not."

Antaea turned to look at Leal. The former history tutor had crossed her arms and had an annoyingly impatient look on her face.

"They're conscious beings like us," said Antaea. "They," she pointed at the emissaries, "are not."

Leal frowned at the path under her feet for a moment. Then she raised her head and said, "Consciousness is a passenger.

"—Or, at best, a crewman. Our values are the pilot.

"You and I are aware, Antaea, because that is what our bodies and our ways of life need from us. Sometimes we forget ourselves, and come to think that we are our minds—but that's a piece of foolishness. You must never forget what you really are."

"Which is?" Antaea felt light-headed. Her hands were shaking.

Leal smiled. "Love, and hunger, and aches and pains and family and all the things you want, and hate, and desire with your whole being. They are what you are, and your mind, too, in its own place.

"But even those creatures who don't have minds have values; they *are* their values, embodied in their form and function. So the oak," she nodded to the tree, "and so the multi-bodied morphont.

"Ask yourself," she said to Antaea, "what world does the oak want? The same that you want: a world of sunlight and clear air, rain, whispering branches and humming insects. The oaks want what we want. But what do Ferance's allies want? Not a garden. At best . . . a palace, for them; a prison, for the rest of us."

"You're wrong!" Yet she couldn't think. Leal was a practiced speaker, and Antaea had never mastered rhetoric, nor ever relied on argument to save her. In her frustration she wanted to cut Leal down where she stood; she wanted to make these idiots *see* the madness in front of them.

"It's suicide!" she shouted, turning to appeal to the crowd surrounding them. "Can't you see? It wasn't the virtuals who tried to take Candesce. Not them who hollowed out my—my sister . . ." Horror began to well up in her, for they were staring at her as if she were insane. She pushed it down one last time and cried, "If you make a pact with these dead things, then you're making a pact with death itself!"

"Antaea," Leal said gently—and Antaea knew she had to run, because if she stayed for another second she would kill Leal.

She knocked the watchers aside, cursed and kicked, and wept wildly as she ran for the tall glass gates and fresh air.

IN TIME, THE crowd began to relax again. The cat and oak talked of their homes and how their people lived. Leal told her own story again, and Chaison's officer, Travis, related his journeys with the emissaries as well.

Then Leal sat on one of the oak's iron-clad roots and watched Chaison Fanning relay the bad news about the existence of a vast armada, gathered from the many nations that had believed in Ferance's and Remoran's stories rather than the emissary's. This fleet, he told them, was mobilizing at that moment, on its way to Candesce with one clear objective in mind: to let Artificial Nature into Virga.

"But why?" demanded a senator from one of the principalities. "And how could they get into Candesce in the first place? There was only one key, and it was lost."

"Ah," said Chaison. "As to that . . ." Leal looked up in surprise, because she'd wondered about that very thing. The sun of suns was impregnable; the technology to batter down its defenses simply couldn't exist in its presence. What did Ferance think she could do?

Niels Lacerta, the Home Guard officer who'd been stranded in Aethyr with Griffin, came to stand next to Chaison. "The Guard recovered the key last year," he said. "It was given back to us by the precipice moth that had been keeping it. The moth had been holed up inside Candesce, but someone actually went there and told it that we needed the key. We don't know who that was, it wasn't a Guardsman, but they died bringing it the message."

Leal was stunned. "So the Guard can actually get into Candesce?" Lacerta nodded.

"Remoran's story makes more sense," protested the senator. "Why should they conquer us when they have the whole universe? And what's so bad about 'dialing down' Candesce's defense, like he said?"

"Antaea Argyre could explain," said Chaison, "if she were here. During the mutiny she was a part of, the outsiders they worked with claimed that Candesce's field is infinitely malleable: they said it could be dialed up, turned down, or adjusted to frame new physical laws. The Guard weren't willing to listen at the time—which is why Gonlin and his people went behind their backs. Clearly, Remoran's changed their minds."

"THIS 'DIALING' IS IMPOSSIBLE," bellowed the oak.

"Possible," countered the cat, "but only to someone who understood how Candesce works."

"Which Ferance and Holon do not," said Leal. "Any more than the Guard itself does. The best they can do is take a hammer to the mechanism."

This was her last contribution to the conversation. Exhausted, she sat on the root, watching Chaison Fanning, Hayden Griffin, and other legendary figures pace back and forth in the light of the tree, and debate and plan. She knew she should be here to witness and later record this night for history's sake; yet all she wanted to do was sleep.

And as the talk turned to the raising of a fleet to counter Ferance's, and while Chaison loudly refused to be its commander and was overruled by the majority—while all this and more went on, Leal scanned the crowd for one face. Keir was nowhere to be seen, and as it became clear that this clearing was the center of attention for everyone in the palace, her worry grew to fear.

Eventually she pushed herself up from the root and slipped away into the underbrush. For the next half-hour she walked all the garden paths and trailed under the branches of the groves on both sides of the palace. She called out his name. She asked servants and guardsmen if they'd seen him. She visited their chambers, which were tidy but empty. Finally she returned to the grove where the bizarre and historic meeting was happening, and went to stand over the now-shrouded body of Keir's tutor, Gallard.

"What happened?" she asked it, but no answer came back.

At that moment the light that had poured steadily from the meeting area went out. Cries of alarm went up from the delegations, and she ran back to the clearing, dodging the black silhouettes of gowned ladies and broad-shouldered officers. There was pandemonium under the oak, with lamps being brought in and everybody talking and running at once.

Leal walked up to the iron cat. The emissary had frozen in mid-gesture, one paw raised, palm out, in a curiously human stance. The lines of light on the branches of the oak had been extinguished, and its limbs no longer moved.

"Hold it together!" Chaison shouted, his voice cutting across the bedlam. "Whatever gave them speech is finished, but our work is not. We need paper, pens! We need to draft this alliance and then mobilize our people. Come on!"

After more shouting and cajoling, he got his wish. Palace workmen set up a table and chairs, and paper lanterns were strung over it. The whole thing looked bizarrely festive, but no one was smiling. As the details of an alliance began to take shape on paper, Leal wandered within the soft perimeter cast by the lanterns, watching, yet wishing she was anywhere else.

Something small glittered in the grass just in front of the oak. Leal blinked at it. This spot was right in the center of the area where the cat-shaped emissary had been able to prowl. During their conversation it had sometimes paced away to probe at the paths. She'd seen it stagger and jump back twice, as it apparently hit some invisible wall beyond which it couldn't go.

Leal knelt, forgetting the babble of the officials. She gently pried the crushed dragonfly out of the soil, and cupped it in the palm of her hand.

She knelt there with it for a very long time, and when she finally raised her head, it was to find that a war had begun.

Part Three | THE CHOICE

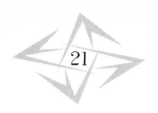

21

JACOBY SARTO WATCHED Inshiri's men haul the blind-folded prisoner out of a dart-shaped racing yacht. He checked his pocket watch and grunted; they were actually on time. Inshiri would have no ready excuse to punish anybody. Not that that would stop her if she was in the mood.

He was holding on to a thin wooden spar that formed part of a long, open fretwork gantry. The thousand feet of tensegrity structure intersected a dozen or more similar girders that jumbled madly in the weightless air like a cloud of straw. A few, like the one he was looking out of, stood out as dotted strings of lanterns; all were faintly traced on the sky in crimson light. Now that the yacht had shut down its engines, Jacoby could hear only the constant creaking of the gantries, the distant fat blatting of a propeller and, behind it all, the ever-present lilting of birdsong.

He swung out of the gantry and jammed his feet into the stirrups attached to the indigo wings strapped to his back. A few kicks and the spring-loaded pinions flapped strongly, pushing him in the direction of the yacht. The prisoner was struggling and had succeeded in kicking one of her captors in the face despite being bound hand and foot.

He grinned. He would have expected no less.

Jacoby dressed to intimidate, which in this place meant wearing black. The severe uniform and sky-colored wings rendered him invisible to the men until he landed to perch on the gantry ahead of them. One jerked in surprise, stifled an oath, and said, "Sir! We were going to the stockade—" Jacoby shook his head, and simply held out his hand.

The man had been towing the prisoner by one ankle. He hauled on his cargo and the cursing figure sailed past him. Jacoby caught her by the same ankle and, without a word, kicked off into the open air.

Strange that, in all their dealings, this was the first time he'd actually touched her.

After a minute or so of flapping he felt her stop struggling. A minute or so after that she said, "I have to pee."

Jacoby didn't reply. His destination hung a few hundred feet ahead, its spars and rain shields lit luridly red from a single point inside the can-shaped framework.

"I can pee with great force and, if I may say so, fantastic accuracy," continued the prisoner. "You'd be wise not to learn first-hand what I can do. Now if we can find me a bottle and somewhere private, and you loosen my wrists—"

She went silent as they entered the observatory. Clearly the red light penetrated her blindfold, for she began craning her neck this way and that to try to find its source. ". . . Furnaces?" she muttered.

The light was visible in the air itself, a vast red cone whose point was centered on a woman who hung in the midst of the great space. She was lit as bright as a lamp's wick, a bold angelic figure blazing scarlet and gold in the focus of a mirror two hundred feet across.

"Cousin," Jacoby called, and her head turned, its wreath of pale hair a writhing nimbus of fire. She nodded, kicked the stirrups of her own wings, and flew out of the light. Her sudden extinguishing rendered her invisible.

As his eyes adjusted he saw her frowning at him. She gestured at the prisoner's bonds. With some caution—knowing this one as he did—he untied the ropes around the woman's ankles, then the ones on her wrists. Then he turned her in the right direction and flipped off the blindfold.

Dark hair billowed up to frame her face like a cloud. Venera

Fanning blinked, peered around herself, and saw Jacoby. "There you are!"

Jacoby's employer gave a light flap with her wings and drifted back a few feet. The fan of white feathers behind her caught the shaft of crimson light and she became visible again. Venera Fanning turned from Jacoby, saw the red-lit woman, and hissed. "*Ferance!*"

"We've never met," said Inshiri. "You must have seen me in a photo from . . . somewhere." She looked down her nose at Jacoby. Jacoby crossed his arms and flew back a few feet. He really, really wanted to watch this meeting—but not from too close.

Venera barked an angry laugh. Then she thrust out her arm, pointing an indignant finger at him. "I never needed *his* help to gather intelligence. And why is he still here? Is he your butler now?"

"I gathered you two knew each other," said Inshiri. She was drifting slowly into the light, parts of her clothing and exposed skin dawning one after another. "I thought if I couldn't persuade you to cooperate, maybe Jacoby could, since you're friends and everything."

"Hardly that," muttered Venera, throwing him a poisonous glance. "There's not a man in the world whose word I trust less."

"Ah! Then you do know him." Inshiri laughed and, for just a second, both women were looking straight at him, not as adversaries, but almost as if they were *sharing a moment*—and Jacoby found his skin crawling.

"Cooperate how?" Venera asked suddenly. "I'm your prisoner. You don't need my cooperation. And anything I know is now out of date by many weeks. Remember, I'd been traveling for a while when you picked me up."

Inshiri smiled unpleasantly. "Much as I would enjoy interrogating you, you're right; I don't need you for that."

"Then what? I assume you plan to use me against Chaison."

"I'm not interested in your trophy husband. What *interests* me," and here she leaned out of the light, blacking out her face, "is that you are one of two living people who has actually been inside the sun of suns."

Venera didn't reply.

"According to the legend, not only have you been inside, but while there you actually observed the process whereby Candesce's field was turned off."

Venera shook her head. "Observed. I didn't understand it. And anyway, you don't need me for that. Your allies from outside know how to do it. Wasn't Aubrey Mahallan one of theirs?"

"They claim not," said Inshiri dryly. "But in any case, there's always the possibility that my *allies*," and she smiled at Jacoby, "will suffer some sort of accident that prevents them from getting inside Candesce. Now we would never want that to happen, but Heaven forbid if it should, it would be good if they were not the only ones who knew how to control Candesce."

Venera glanced at Jacoby. He kept his expression neutral.

"Where are your little friends, anyway?" Venera asked. She peered into the darkness. "I see no great fleet massed out there. Could it be that they no longer need you, now that events are in motion?" She turned to Jacoby. "They *are* in motion, aren't they?"

He gave a microscopic nod.

"Oh, they still need me, I've made sure of that. As to this place . . ." Inshiri smiled. "They don't know about it. Here! Let me show you." She reached out to grab Venera's arm; Jacoby saw her flinch at the touch. Inshiri flapped her wings and drew Venera over to the focal point of the giant, curved mirror. Jacoby narrowed his eyes and in the scarlet brilliance Venera did the same. As her eyes adjusted she slowly opened them, then they went wide and she said, "Oh!"

Venera hung at the focal point of a gigantic telescope aimed at Slipstream. She would be seeing the grandly rotating, metal town wheels of Rush, rendered in red and gold because the intervening air scattered out the blue end of the spectrum. The image wavered and was fuzzy, but was still good enough to show the inside surfaces of those cylinders, all papered with rooftops and streets and strolling people. —And more, it would be showing her the entire fleet her husband was amassing: their numbers, the types of their ships, the national crests painted on their sides, and their armament.

She looked impressed. "You're spying on us from here?"

"Not just you," said the heir of Sacrus. "We can point this telescope anywhere in Virga, though if we were to aim it at the world's heart and even just glimpse the sun of suns, you and I would light up like matches. This particular instrument works best when you aim it toward the darker corners of the world. But it works well for Slipstream, wouldn't you say? I can see your husband's whole plan unfolding, and when his fleet leaves, I'll be able to track its movements with utter precision."

"You're to remain a spectator here, then?" Venera inquired in a polite tone.

"Of course not. I intend to be there when you open Candesce's doors with the key the Home Guard so conveniently found for us." Inshiri waved a hand. "But we can talk about this later. For now, I want you to think about whose hands you would prefer to be on those controls when we finally penetrate the mystery of mysteries. Ours? —Yours and mine, I mean; or theirs." And she nodded to the darkness.

Venera scowled at Inshiri, who casually pushed her in Jacoby's direction. "Lord Sarto, put her somewhere that's not overly comfortable." He took Venera's hand and kicked down to flap his wings. They left Inshiri of Sacrus lofting like a blood-soaked angel in the fire of her giant spyglass.

VENERA AIMED HER gaze down her arm at him. "What happened to your hand?"

He grimaced. "Inshiri took my little finger as proof of my loyalty. She likes hostages, as I'm sure you've noticed."

"So she's promised to give it back later?" she asked lightly.

"Not exactly."

There was a brief pause as they sailed slowly through the sky. Then Venera said: "I really do have to pee."

"Posthaste, then.

"My apologies, by the way, for the manner in which you were brought here," said Jacoby after a silence in which he had become uncomfortably aware that he was holding her hand.

She thought about that. "Where are we, anyway?"

"It's called Kaleidogig. And I really am sorry. My plan was to capture you for my own purposes, not to hand you over to her."

"Was it also your plan to get sent home with a whipping after that foolish attack on Serenity?"

He growled.

"Two for two, then."

"Maybe," he said, "but there's still one vital piece in play."

She twisted her hand in his and spun slowly to look at the ungainly galaxy of giant mirrors and steaming, brightly lit boilers. "If we were near the principalities, the whole sky would be lit up. So where are we—in winter?"

He nodded. "On the same latitude as Meridian, but a thousand miles from the nearest sun."

"And yet," she mused, "there's light."

Kaleidogig burned like a string of giant's lanterns. Its jumbled scaffolding cupped a dozen or more curving mirrors, each hundreds of feet across, which mostly lit nets and balls of water filled with floating plants. The mirrors were fairly easy to make, Jacoby had learned—you waited for calm air and then blew a vast bubble from a seed of liquid resin; when it dried you cut it into bowl-shaped sections and silvered them and there were your mirrors.

Days away, nuclear-fusion lamps carved sunlit spheres of air out of the darkness, and nations swarmed around them like moths around a candle. Each fusion lamp lit a few hundred miles of air in every direction—but Virga was five thousand miles across. Most of its interior was dark, hence unsuitable for settlement.

"I always thought it would be totally dark out here," he told Venera. "But there's a very faint glow from the suns, and you can concentrate it. Which they do. All the blue gets filtered out by the time it gets here, but the red turns out to be perfect for plants. They also concentrate some of it until it's hot enough to melt iron; they have industries. It's really quite ingenious."

Venera looked back at him. "You say 'they.' This is not your new home, then?"

"I suppose you'd call it my current place of employ."

She was silent for a while; then suddenly she pulled her hand out of his. "I suppose you were working for Inshiri all along."

"Actually, no." He frowned pensively into the night. "I said you'd call this my current place of employ. I don't consider myself to be working for Inshiri at all. Any more than I ever said I was working with you and Chaison."

"But what about loyalty? How do you suppose Antaea Argyre felt when you attacked Serenity? We all knew it was you."

It hurt just thinking about how that debacle had gone; but Venera didn't need to know that. "What do you know about loyalty?" he retorted.

"Maybe more than either you or I suspected," she said quietly; and despite his deeply ingrained cynicism, Jacoby found that the words stung him.

They were approaching a quickly spinning town wheel. The thing was little, not more than a hundred feet across, and consisted of just a few streamlined wooden buildings joined together by swaying catwalks. It was really just a swinging bridge rolled into a circle and set rolling through the skies.

Jacoby nodded at it. "Home, for now. I have to warn you, it's a sixer." He was referring to the rate per minute of the wheel's rotation. "If you have any inner-ear problems, we can set you up somewhere else."

"Oh, please. I once bedded a pirate in a twelver." She grabbed his elbow and let him lead her through the air to the landing pad at the wheel's axle. "Anyway, what about it? Are you going to stand by and let Inshiri torture me into compliance? Or death?"

Their feet found the inner surface of the barrel-shaped landing pad. Lanterns glowed here, showing the way to four long ladders that led in four directions to the circle's rim. Jacoby gestured for her to go first. As they climbed down he said, "If you hadn't been suicidally brave at Fracas, you wouldn't be in this situation. I can protect you for now, but you have to at least pretend to cooperate with Inshiri."

They'd been gaining weight as they climbed down, and now entered the top floor of a house. It was ordinary enough, with carpets, wood-paneled walls, and lamps in sconces. The floor curved up rather quickly to each side, but that was to be expected in a sixer. Jacoby's own stomach was turning over with the wheel's spin, but he refused to let Venera see that. In the sudden quiet of the house, he pitched his voice lower and said, "I was after three things: control of the door to Brink, which would have made me the gatekeeper for your little alliance; you, to control your husband; and the key to Candesce, to bring Inshiri and the outsiders in line. With them I could have headed off this fiasco and steered us to a diplomatic solution."

Venera planted her hands on her hips and glowered. "Your solution."

"It would have been better than what's coming."

"But Inshiri—"

"My plans for her are another story, but as I said, the key is still in play. —Anyway, from the way you're shifting from foot to foot, I'd say you don't have the time for that particular tale."

"Urm, yes, the water closet—"

"Is that way."

––––––––––

NICOLAS REMORAN, GENERAL Secretary of the Virgan Home Guard, braced himself in the hatch of the battleship, watching its mighty engines settle it close to one of Kaleidogig's spidery docking arms. When he spotted the distant shapes of Inshiri Ferance and Jacoby Sarto waiting there, he turned and said, "Remember your orders. Observe only."

Antaea nodded, and unconsciously smoothed the black material of her new uniform. She knew she only wore it because Remoran wanted to keep her close and in line; still, every morning when she awoke, the first thing she did was go to the closet to check that it was really there.

"General Secretary, how good to see you," Inshiri called. As the ship inched closer to the dock she turned her head to take in its immensity, and said, "I'm somehow glad I never knew that the Guard had forces like these. It would have given me nightmares." Then she noticed Antaea.

"Argyre! I see you've regained your rank," she said as she reached out to take Antaea's hand. "Or," she squinted at Remoran, "was she yours all along?"

"She's been demoted, actually," said Remoran. "We could hardly justify her expulsion after we admitted that Gonlin's plan had been the right one. But her blind acceptance of his orders was a problem."

"Ah." Ferance looked down at her toes, which were together and pointing into the black abyss that lay beyond Kaleidogig's red light.

"I'm placing Argyre with you as an advisor," continued Remoran. "She's spent time in the enemy camp, after all."

Inshiri arched an eyebrow, but didn't complain. "Jacoby?"

"You can trust her judgment," he said, which nearly made Antaea guffaw out loud. *Who're you to talk about trust!* she wanted to say; but she kept her expression neutral.

They boarded the battleship and Antaea found herself in an echoing, warehouse-sized hangar lit with unwavering electric light. Dozens of missile-festooned attack ships hung from cranes here, and airmen swarmed around them, working, cursing, and throwing tools back and forth.

Inshiri pinwheeled slowly, taking it all in. "Wondrous," she said. "You could kill so many people with this thing."

"Hopefully we won't have to," said Remoran. "I'm still expecting the Last Line to come to their senses. No segment of the Home Guard has ever revolted—at least, never on this scale." He shot Antaea an ironic look. "They've swallowed the propaganda that Lacerta brought back from Aethyr, but the internal contradictions will bring them around soon. There are already cracks."

"Ooh," said Inshiri as they hand-walked along a cable to one of the many corridors that opened out of the hangar. "Defections?"

"Well, no, not yet. But let's call them 'reliable signs of unrest.'" He pointed down the corridor. "My office is this way."

"Oh, in a minute, thank you," said Inshiri. "One of your men can direct me. I just have some orders for this lot." She nodded to her servants, as well as Jacoby's other men who trailed her and the general secretary.

"As you will." He disappeared down the corridor. Inshiri turned to Jacoby.

"Your men stay behind," she said levelly.

"What? But I need them to run my communications net—" But Inshiri was shaking her head.

"I've coopted it, I'm afraid. Had to kill a few of your men to do it thoroughly." She laughed at the expression on his face. "Oh, don't act as if you weren't expecting this, cousin. You've had far too much autonomy, and I need you close and controlled for now. Your network is now my network, and you are useful because you know its logistics better than anyone. You can have it back—and I'll throw in a country or two—when we're done."

He glowered at her. "Not a good way to guarantee my loyalty."

"Loyalty? Don't make me laugh. You'd have made your move

against me sooner or later." She smiled sweetly and flew off after the general secretary.

Antaea met Jacoby's eye, and smiled.

He pulled himself straight and frowned at her with all the dignity of his years. "It's all right," he said. "I did see this coming." Turning to his men he said, "I'll see you all at Rendezvous Point B. But leave the luggage."

"And what did she mean with that crack about giving you a country?" Antaea continued. "The plan is to tune down Candesce and give the people of Virga more technological capacity. Not to take over the world."

Jacoby shrugged. "Your plan, my plan . . . everybody's got plans. Yours is also the Guard's plan, so I wouldn't worry about it too much. Inshiri talks a good line, but even she can't control your people. Now, who do I call to help get our bags to our cabins? It'll be a day or two before we rendezvous with the outsiders."

She watched him go, troubled, and uncomfortably aware that some of the airmen were watching her. *They know who I am.* Well, let them stare. Winter wraith; traitor; turncoat. She'd played them all, and the stares had always been the same.

But as she hauled her own luggage and it began to slowly move, she couldn't help but think about Inshiri's jabs and insults. The woman liked to keep people off balance; you could never tell when she was telling the truth or lying. What if she really did have some way of capturing Candesce? —Via the outsiders, perhaps?

Antaea would have to watch Ferance; though as she traversed the endless corridors of the giant battleship, the vast scale and obvious power of the vessel led her to concede that Jacoby was probably right.

Nothing inside Virga could successfully oppose the Virga Home Guard—not even its own rebellious Last Line. And surely not Inshiri Ferance.

22

TEN YEARS BEFORE, a single ship could have slipped into Candesce on any given night. An entire flotilla could have—and hundreds of ships did, every time the sun of suns shuttered its blazing eyes and retreated into sleep. The first visitors were always the scavengers: well-insulated, mirror-clad, and fast, they ventured in even before the last of Candesce's fusion engines had gone out. Braving incandescent air, they competed to find castoff and broken parts from Candesce's intimidating furnaces. The scavengers believed from firsthand experience that Candesce deliberately seeded its trash with intact machinery, for they often found vital components for the construction of suns among the flotsam. They snapped up this bounty, fought amongst themselves for it, and the winners retreated back to the principalities ahead of the dawn, to sell their prizes.

After them came the funeral ships. They were not here to pick up, but to drop off. Bodies from all over Virga made their final journey here, to be consigned to the dark, hot air by loved ones or the trusted funerary castes of a hundred nations. As Candesce began to rouse itself, these last ships departed, leaving roses and songbooks, the precious treasures of the beloved dead, and thousands of white-shrouded, silent figures hanging suspended in the air. Those who looked back as the sun of suns awoke might see light well past the throng, lighting the paper wings they wore. Dawn was an inferno of angels.

So it had been for centuries. But ever since the outage, the Last Line of the Virga Home Guard had tightened their defenses. They had long believed the last key to Candesce lost; so there was never any reason to board and inspect the funeral ships, nor to stop the scavengers from approaching the mysterious, closed blockhouses that nestled in Candesce's heart. Now that the key was loose again, everyone was suspect—even ships from other arms of the Guard.

Last Line ships were the first in at dusk, and the last out at dawn. They watched everyone, and their terrifying precipice moths clamped their talons onto ships at random, prying back their hulls to glare suspiciously at their cargoes. So when a small flotilla of First Line ships approached Candesce, they were stopped and boarded.

Since even before the grand colloquy, they'd all known this was going to happen. The First Line and Last Line had fallen out over what to do with Candesce. The First Line had the key, for it had been a First Line precipice moth that had taken it into Candesce to begin with, and when it burst forth again it had taken it to its masters at the rim of the world.

So those who boarded, and those who were boarded, had known for many months that their initially formal meeting would dissolve into gunfire and swordplay. They'd known, they'd even planned for it; but none of them really believed it until the bodies were in the air and blood was raining into the darkening skies. And the reaction that rippled back into both camps was shock, and outrage, and immediate mobilization.

SOMEBODY RAPPED ON the door to Leal's stateroom. She jerked and floated several feet away from the sleeping bag strapped to the wall. "Come in!"

The iron hatchway creaked open and Piero Harper stuck his head around it. "Ma'am, I'm sorry if I'm—"

"No, no, Piero, I was hoping to see you. And I can't sleep anyway." He glanced sympathetically at the little stateroom's porthole, where brilliant light was flooding in. It was nominally the night shift, but they were passing by some sun or other. "Oh, it's not that," Leal confessed. "It's the vibration." She put her hand to the wall, and felt an intensification of the throbbing from the ship's distant engines.

She didn't add that this stateroom reminded her too much of the cell she'd been stuck into aboard Eustace Loll's ship, back before they'd all crashed in Aethyr.

"But look at you!" she said. "You've fattened up nicely." Then, more seriously: "I can't believe your wife let you go again."

Piero grimaced. "She insisted. 'Those people'd be dead without you!' she said. 'You got to keep them safe!'" He grinned. "Truth to tell, I think she has her eye on the military pension I get for signing up."

"But you get to work with Hayden again?" He nodded.

"And you're a great lady now, as all knew you would be."

"Oh, I don't know about that. Nobody's telling me anything lately." No that she'd expected them to. She'd fulfilled her own mission by delivering the emissary's message, and now she was just so much dead weight. Leal didn't know why she'd insisted on coming along—the truth was, she would rather have been anywhere than here. But they were calling her the Herald these days; airmen got out of her way as she drifted down the corridors; and, apparently, even Admiral Chaison Fanning could not refuse her wishes.

A shadow crossed the porthole, and they both looked up. The sky outside Leal's porthole was full of ships; she'd never seen such an armada, and the thought that her message had launched it filled her with sorrow. "I just wish none of it had ever happened," she murmured.

"Ah, ma'am," said Piero. "This isn't your fault."

The light from the porthole shifted again; but this time, it brightened. Leal assumed one of the local suns had emerged from behind a cloud. Then it brightened again. And again.

Sirens went off all over the ship. She exchanged a wide-eyed look with Piero; then they both jumped to the porthole and looked out, ears touching.

All across the sky, suns were coming on. She knew the fleet was approaching the principalities, and in this spherical region around the sun of suns, some countries perversely lit their lamps in a rotation opposite to Candesce's. They had banished night entirely and grew crops and ran their industries twenty-four hours a day. Most of the principalities didn't even have their own suns; because of their proximity to Candesce, they didn't need their own lights. So Leal had been told. Yet incandescent pinpricks of light were appearing above, below, and to all sides—everywhere, even in those nations that were not supposed to have them.

She pushed open the bulletproof circle of glass, and a chaos of horns, sirens, and bells filled the stateroom. Warm, moist air puffed in and lifted her hair. She could feel the heat of all those suns on her face, and the feeling was so unfamiliar and hostile that she retreated into the shade of the room.

"Lady Fanning's list," said Piero. She shook her head at him, not comprehending.

"Couriers were sent to every country," he said, "all carrying the list, and the words of our treaty. People know which of their neighbors have sided with the invaders, and who's with us. They're choosing sides. They're moving!"

The drone of the ship's engines changed, increasing in pitch. "Is the whole world at war?" Leal asked, as the aft wall drifted up and became a tentative floor.

Piero didn't answer, but she knew the truth. Neighbor was turning against neighbor everywhere, all at once. Treaties a thousand years old were breaking, former friends were shooting one another in the airways between their ancestral homes. The majestic, intricate, and ancient systems of the principalities were being undone in minutes.

She covered her eyes against the glorious light—and it came to her that one man might understand the unraveling going on.

Wherever Chaison Fanning was, he held in his mind a tactical map of the world. He knew where the fleets were, who had what ships and how fast they were. Even now his semaphore men must be sending orders to dozens of receivers, turning chaos and random movement into the coordinated flocking of a thousand ships. But had he anticipated this terrible light, the banishing of night in the unveiling of secret suns?

Piero came to stand with her, and she held on to his arm for comfort. But dear as he was, he wasn't Keir, and his presence wasn't enough to keep at bay a growing sense of despair.

DISTANT SHEETS OF rain trailed like coy veils over the towers and bridges of the city of Brink, uncovering and hiding its vistas and architectural surprises, now here, now there. Where they had passed, the balconies and rearing walls gleamed like oil on water, presenting myriad pastel colors to the eye. The scents of rain and wet stone hung in the warm air, hinting at the possibility of life.

Despite his haste, the sight stopped Keir in his tracks. He had never seen Brink like this—never even guessed that its black minarets might hide such delicate hues. He couldn't even tell which of those distant pillared cathedrals was Complication Hall, because he had always found it in the past by the light from its windows. Now he saw that there was not one, nor two or even a dozen, but many such halls, some within hailing distance of the Renaissance's home.

He could also see bomb damage—lots of it. After enduring brutal avalanches for centuries, Brink was not easily erased; nonetheless, whole precincts of the city were flattened rubble-slopes now.

As he shaded his eyes against the blazing sun to try to make out details, somebody bumped Keir's shoulder from behind. "You're blocking the way!"

"Sorry." People, and stranger things, were pouring out of the wide doorway behind him. Twenty minutes ago, he had been packed into the tiny transfer room with them, enduring the sudden shift from Virga's now-familiar weightlessness to the gravity of Brink. No one had spoken during that short trip, and many of the humans, freshly recruited from Chaison Fanning's navy, had cowered in awe and fear of the morphonts. Now they were bursting into the glowing air of a new world, and everybody was talking at once.

He had to smile as he strolled after them. Brink was new to him, too, though in retrospect it was unsurprising that the Renaissance's allies would tow one of Aethyr's hovering suns up the long slopes to light the city. Those sheets of rain must come from melting glaciers high above, which meant that the avalance problem must be far worse these days. Sure enough, when he looked for it, he could see chunks of ice and snow piled around the bases of nearly every tower.

Better get inside, then. He hurried across the long span of bridge and into the lofting corridors of the metropoloid. Here was military order, of a sort: work gangs hauling strange devices up from the Hall and their various strange births in the Edisonians; soldiers hefting unfamiliar weapons; lines of men being debriefed by pacing officers.

Fanning had wasted no time in establishing a beachhead in Brink; in fact, he had clearly sent a sizable armada there after the abortive attack on Serenity. Keir had known a little about this activity, which was how he'd been able to get himself on board one of the fast courier sloops that Fanning had moored above the palace during the grand colloquy. Keir had talked to some of the pilots about what they might expect to find in Serenity and Brink. But he'd had no idea the operation was being conducted on this scale.

Lightning flickered through the windows and heads turned. "They're at it again," someone muttered. As he walked Keir counted half-consciously, waiting for the thunder to follow the lightning, but it didn't come. Just more insistent flashes.

He stopped a bare-chested navvy who was carrying a large steel cylinder. "What's that?" Keir pointed to the window.

"It's the Enemy, in't," said the airman. "Battle to end all battles going on, or so they say. They tryin' to get here, our boys holdin' em off."

Not lightning, then. Nukes, or laser fire, and probably hundreds of kilometers away. Keir frowned and hurried on.

He took the last set of stairs down to the Hall two steps at a time. In his imagination were all the ways that the virtuals could obliterate Aethyr, or Virga. They could accelerate an asteroid from the far side of the solar system, shoot it through both worlds at a thousand kilometers a second, and let the shock waves transform them into expanding spheres of gas . . . then simply move in and harvest Candesce like the seed in a smashed fruit. They could stand off and peel off the world's skin with terawatt lasers, then aim them through the holes at every sun and city inside. They need not be polite.

He could guess what stopped them. They had no idea how Candesce worked. They did not know what it was capable of. And so far, they had done everything in their power to avoid *waking it up*. But how long would that caution continue?

The tall doors to the Hall were guarded by a detachment of men in Slipstream uniforms. One put out his hand as Keir made to enter. "You're not on our list."

"I live here."

The man looked Keir up and down, and he realized he was still wearing his now-rumpled dress attire from the colloquy. "Try another one," said the doorman.

"But—" He caught himself as he felt an odd but familiar feeling. It was scry, the whole cloud of relationships and nonverbal political fencing that had once been as intimate to him as his own breath. He couldn't help but smile as the network lit up with glyphs and emoticons of astonishment: they'd felt him log in.

There was something else, though, another familiar presence

even more intimate than scry. And now his smile widened, alarming the doorman. "One second," said Keir; and he held up his arms, palms out.

A hundred dragonflies rustled out of the shadows, rising like the hood of a cobra to hover above him like some strange halo. The guards stepped back, swearing and fingering their unfamiliar new weapons. Suddenly Keir could see, in a way he hadn't been able to in months. He closed his own eyes in bliss.

"Let him in." He'd brought his second body over from where it had been languishing in a closet in the Hall's foyer. The guards were even more startled by its appearance, for of course it looked like a younger version of Keir. It was waving to him from the Hall behind them, so they fell back and Keir walked past them with a confident nod—and into the arms of friends and comrades he hadn't properly spoken to or even recognized since his de-indexing.

Maerta came running. "Keir, oh, Keir!" She flung her arms around him and he hugged her fiercely. "You're—are you—"

"I'm whole," he said as he squeezed her tightly. "I remember everything. Everything."

She broke away, troubled. "Even why you did it?" He nodded. "We sent Gallard to find you," she said. "Is he—?" But it would be obvious to all of them that he wasn't here. There was no sign of him in scry.

Keir shook his head. "You didn't send him," he said. "He manipulated you into choosing him. It was his mission to find me."

"Mission?" She shook her head, uncomprehending.

"I'll tell you everything," he said, "but not here." The Hall was a chaos of steaming, stinking manufactories and running soldiers. "Let's find somewhere quiet . . . with a window."

MAERTA AND A few others sat with him in a once-familiar boardroom now flooded with sunlight. The rest were listening in through scry. Keir sat in the sun, remembering the skies of

Revelation, then sighed and told them the story. He began with his adventures inside Virga, meeting Antaea Argyre and Jacoby Sarto in that other lost city, and their flight from the knife-balls.

He told them about the glory of Virgan skies, of how Slipstream had welled into view over days as they approached it, like the opening eye of some god of the dawn. How its vast sphere of sunlit air had reached out to encompass their ship, bringing with it the visions of farms and towns, flying people and flocking birds. He described the astonishing ring-shaped city of Rush, and the mad Fannings and their baroque admiralty.

He described it all—the travels with Venera, the grand colloquy, and his deepening relationship with Leal Maspeth. And then he came to the garden, the tree, and the iron cheetah. And Gallard.

"He would have buried his sword in my back if my dragonfly hadn't seen him," he said—and instantly, up and down Brink, in the Hall and the storerooms and laboratories, every member of the Renaissance stopped what they were doing.

Maerta stood up, almost knocking over her chair. "Gallard *attacked* you? But that's—"

"—What he would have done long before, had I not de-indexed myself," Keir said calmly. They were staring at him as if he were mad. He swiveled to look out the window pensively. The sky trembled with distant bursts of light. "It was when the oaks visited that time last year," he went on quietly. "They're very secretive, and their support of our research was secret. But they were worried. Somehow, the enemy had found out about us."

He turned back to Maerta. "That was the real reason the oak came to see us. It knew A.N. had put a spy in our midst, but it didn't know who it was. All it knew was that it wasn't me. So it found an opportunity to speak to me alone, and it warned me that we'd been compromised."

Maerta had laid both hands palm-down on the table, and was staring at him intently. "A week before you de-indexed, you told me you'd made a breakthrough. We thought—well, we didn't know what to think. You suddenly panicked, said you'd gone too far, learned something nobody was supposed to know. It was ridiculous, but all the more frightening because you seemed sincere."

Keir nodded, half-smiling. "I was part of a preindustrial-style drama society, oh, many decades ago. I'm glad my acting is still believable."

"But wiping your own mind . . . neotenizing yourself. Neither of those were an act."

He shook his head, saying, "They couldn't be. I didn't know who the traitor was, either. Whoever they were, the oak warned me they had tapped scry. I couldn't tell anyone what I'd found— not in the necessary detail—except through scry. He or she would learn it all; and if I kept it to myself, it was only a matter of time before the spy moved against me."

Maerta took a deep breath and said to the others, "And that was when he came to me and told me he was going to de-index himself." Glyphs of surprise exploded through scry; she shrugged. "He said it would be temporary, but he wouldn't tell me why he was doing it."

"But—" Thoun, one of the founders of the Renaissance, shook his head. "You could have come to us. To any of us—"

"Come to you? Come to *you*?" His voice was rising. "You were completely ignorant of the situation, all of you!" He stood up. "You thought we were safe here, or, oh, even worse! You never really believed in the danger. You never thought they would come after us. You never looked over your shoulders. And I was too distracted, I was so close for so long I couldn't raise my head out of the problem . . . It's just a good thing the oaks were watching out for us."

"But Gallard . . ." Maerta glanced around the table. "What happened that night in Virga?"

Keir closed his eyes, and heard the others gasp—for they were there now, seeing the tree and the shadowed pathways through the eyes of the dragonfly he'd carried with him into Virga. The perspective swooped and dove, and Keir smiled as he seemed to spiral with it, dizzyingly, above the treetops. The gardens of the palace at Aurora emerged, and again he felt the others react. Emoticons flooded scry as all of Renaissance saw the wonders of a Virgan city for the first time.

But something had moved below. The dragonfly plummeted, returning to Keir, who stood with a hand held half-out at the base of a machine-augmented oak.

Someone was running up behind him, revealed and hidden in flashes of shadow and city light. It was Gallard, and he had a sword in his hand.

He raised it, his face twisted into a grimace, and Keir saw himself react. Every time he'd reviewed this recording, he'd felt a sympathetic prickle between his shoulder blades and half-consciously hunched, and he did so this time, too. The Keir in the dragonfly's video dove to one side, and Gallard's strike missed.

He rolled to his feet and for a second Keir saw himself smile. The others wouldn't understand that, but he remembered: for just an instant, he'd reveled in having the reflexes and power of a young body. Despite his shock at the attack, he'd felt powerful.

The dragonfly lowered to head-height. Gallard hadn't noticed it. He advanced on Keir with his blade raised.

"You're not surprised," Gallard accused; his words appeared as subtitles in the recording, thanks to the dragonfly's lip-reading program.

Keir had laughed, half from adrenaline, half from contempt. "I'm only surprised at how badly you handled all of this. How long have you been working for them?"

"There's no 'them,'" said his former teacher. "There never was. This collective fantasy that somehow you could band together and defeat the final evolutionary stage of life is ridiculous. The Renaissance is pathetic."

Keir was backing away. "Then why pay attention to us at all? If we weren't a threat—"

Gallard lunged and Keir twisted away. "Because you're a rallying point for every lunatic species that wants to advance its own cause. Don't you know why the arena exists? It's here as a place where we can all learn to get along. Artificial Reality is the glue that keeps us together. The species that rise to the top should be at the top, and the ones at the bottom should be at the bottom. They shouldn't try to game the system to their own advantage. They shouldn't conspire . . . They shouldn't *cheat*—" He lunged again and this time his blade ripped through Keir's sleeve.

Keir jumped backward again, but this time he'd tripped. He fell. Before he could rise Gallard was kneeling on him, one knee across his chest. Gallard raised his sword.

Keir had made a last desperate plea, but not to Gallard's humanity. Whenever he watched this he thought, *Why didn't I appeal to our friendship? To all we'd been through together?* But something in Gallard's eyes had warned him that they were beyond that. So, he'd flinched back, hitting his head on the ground, and said, "Is Candesce a cheat?"

Gallard hesitated, and in that moment something black had snaked out of the air to wrap itself around his chest. Gallard tried to shout in surprise but it turned into a *whuff!* sound as all the air was driven out of his body. It wasn't visible from the dragonfly's perspective, but Keir saw the astonishment in his eyes as the silver-threaded tree branch plucked him into the air. It rose in a smooth motion and suddenly Gallard was flying, limbs flailing, into the city-starred sky.

The dragonfly moved, swerving around to hover next to Keir's head as he sat up. Something crashed through branches elsewhere in the grove, but all Keir had noticed at the time were the two gigantic, glowing green eyes that had appeared, winking, in front of him.

"Are you all right?" asked the emissary. Behind it, the oak writhed as lines of light began shooting along its trunk. The light became blinding and with it came an overwhelming roar of noise. Keir crouched, shielding his face with one hand, but the metal cheetah curled its own head around to put its nose an inch from his.

"Where *are* we?" it said.

Keir began to laugh hysterically. "I remember," he said. "They could never figure it out. They built scientists—made their own Renaissance to reinvent physics like we did. But they couldn't figure it out."

The cheetah blinked. "And you did?"

"Quantum gravity," he babbled. "The final theory. It's a formal system. Every time they tried to rediscover the science, they were led right back to it. Of course. It's what all obvious experiments lead to. But it's a *formal system!*" He'd begun to laugh uncontrollably. Then he stood and staggered away from the cheetah and the tree.

"Where are you going?" asked the cat.

Keir turned once and grinned. He was walking away from the dragonfly; he'd commanded it to stay where it was. "I can't do what I need to here," he said. "And there's no time. Talk to them." He waved at the other paths, where a babble of voices and running feet could now be heard. "Make a treaty. You've only got a few hours; waste no time." Then he'd turned and disappeared into the darkness.

The dragonfly settled onto the loam and watched as Antaea Argyre peered fearfully out from behind the trunk of a tree.

Keir ended the recording and, back now in the sunlit conference room, watched as Maerta and the others sat for a while in stunned silence.

At last Maerta looked up. "What did you mean? That our physics is a formal system?"

He shrugged. "Every formal language, like say, mathematics, has a fatal flaw: It's always possible to write self-contradictory statements in it. Like 'X equals not-X.' About a year ago I realized that if you could do that in math, you could do it in quantum gravity. But here's the thing: Every statement in QG corresponds to a real phenomenon. So what would happen if I found a self-contradictory formulation in QG, and then *made it*?"

Maerta blinked at him. "Made it?"

"Built a machine to create the phenomenon described in that statement. A particle that simultaneously existed and didn't exist, for instance. Negative and positive charge in one, gravity and non-gravity."

"You did it."

He nodded. "In secret. I'd planned it out, as the sort of mad-scientist experiment from an ancient movie; but I was afraid to actually do it, until the oak came to me. The night it told me there was a spy among us, I packed up a fab unit and a small Edisonian and went into the city alone, and I did the experiment. And then I knew how Candesce's field works, and I built a tiny version of it."

"And you put it inside one of your dragonflies."

He nodded. "And then I planned my own de-indexing, because the oak had showed me that scry was compromised. Something was on to us, and whatever it was could move at any moment." He looked down at the table. "I was afraid we were all about to be netted like fish and our minds taken apart. I was afraid to run, or say anything, because we were being watched. So I had to make sure we weren't seen as a threat."

No one said anything. After a while, Keir became aware of a distant rumbling. He knew the sound that avalanches made, had lived with them for many months. This was different.

He stood up and went to the window. The sky was full of pops and brief sheets of light. The battle was getting closer.

"What now?" asked Maerta.

With his dragonflies and his own eyes, he could see them and himself looking at them, could see his cheekbones revealed and shaded by the patter of dozens of faraway nuclear blasts.

"I need our biggest fab and our best Edisonian," he said. "And I need something else, too, that might be harder to retrieve."

He put his forehead to the window so he could see down the dizzying slope of Aethyr's skin, to where coiling cloud and the mottled green of landforms lay half-veiled by distance. "I need to retrieve a machine," he said, "from the plain where Leal Maspeth and the Home Guard crashed."

23

EVERYBODY KNEW, IN an abstract sort of way, that if the legendary Virga Home Guard did exist, they must have ships. Yet even Antaea, who knew the Guard intimately, found herself silent in the face of the truth.

Inshiri Ferance's alliance had its own armada, and it might have been the biggest of its kind ever assembled. Antaea had braced herself in a gunnery port and, with wind whipping past her and sky above, below and to both sides, watched the muster of a thousand battleships. They filled the sky like swarming insects, each surrounded by a buzzing retinue of smaller craft. Contrails confused the view. Yet behind them, something impossible was looming.

The First Line fleet was in cube formation. From here, many miles away, it appeared as a solid thing, a blued-out silhouette moving behind a veil of pale sky. Clouds and cities drifted in front of it. There was no way to distinguish individual ships in that mass, but she knew some were the size of Rush's town wheels.

This was not the flagship of Inshiri's fleet. Ferance would never have been so stupid as to ride in that big a target. Instead, she had commandeered the Thistle, the fastest courier-class sloop she could find, a powder-blue needle bristling with engines. Around the Thistle flew a swarm of armored bikes, an escort armed with ship-busting missiles and heavy machine guns. Antaea badly wanted to be riding one of those, but Inshiri had forbidden it. She had to keep reminding herself that, vile as Ferance was, her cause was the right one. If it hadn't been, Antaea would cheerfully have killed the woman by now.

Trailing well behind the sloop was a fuel tanker disguised as a hospital ship. A little breaking of the rules of war . . . Inshiri had shrugged: *Well, these things happen.*

The armada and the First Line fleet were only here to open the door a tiny crack; then Inshiri's ship would slip in. The Last Line was in sphere formation around Candesce, their own forces supplemented by those principalities that had sided with them at the last minute. Somewhere far away, Chaison's relief force would be approaching.

The thought of him made Antaea sad. His own glorious armada was an afterthought. It could do nothing. It was a joke. Everything would be over by the time it got here.

Antaea had come out here to watch sunoff. Candesce's great beacons had been dimming for some minutes, and now they were flicking off one by one. From a distance, the sun of suns looked like a single incandescent point of light, but she knew it was really an entire region of air populated by dozens of suns. Suns—and other ancient mechanisms whose purpose and potential no one understood.

While Candesce was alight, the Last Line fleet had an advantage. They had fire and blinding radiance at their backs. But as soon as that light faded . . .

A faint sound reached her over the tearing noise of the engines. Sirens—bells. Abruptly, the cruisers of the armada began to turn and flock, and the carriers coughed bikes and armored catamarans into the air. She took a deep breath, leaned out, and saw orange and white flashes dotting the sky where the last of Candesce's light was fading.

It was time.

TWO WALLS OF ships met in the hot air just inside Candesce's exclusion zone. Fire erupted along the line of that meeting as cruisers and battleships unleashed broadside after broadside at one another. In seconds the battle scene became opaque with smoke. The smaller escorts began peeling off from the core of the battle because visibility was nil, the air was full of shrapnel and debris, and worst of all, all the oxygen was getting used up. Any jet that flew into the expanding spherical aftermath of a fire would choke and die from anoxia, and if its pilot didn't get out he would quickly follow. From outside, the grinding and convulsion of vast whale-like ships, the bikes and catamarans and trimarans, poured withering machine-gun fire at the larger craft, and each other.

Venera Fanning, watching through a tiny porthole in Inshiri Ferance's ship, saw the traces of bullets flung in random directions—bullets that might travel a thousand miles before finding a destination—and fingered the scar on her chin.

SHEER MOMENTUM CARRIED the invaders through ten miles of Last Line defenses. The plan was to punch a hole in the shell and pour the rest of the fleet in behind it. The Last Line knew this, so as the blunt needle of battleships pushed forward, they gave way—then, at a signal, re-formed in torus formation, and *squeezed*.

The principalities were sleepless—and the citizens of many nations muttered in wonder at what appeared to be Candesce waking only hours after it had gone to sleep. An ominous red smudge appeared in the purple air inward of the six-hundred-mile-diameter shell of city lights and new suns that surrounded Candesce; and gradually it grew. It became a roiling sphere of fire, dozens of miles across, flickering with internal explosions and clots of smoke. In the cities, among the farms, errant missiles suddenly appeared out of nowhere, shattering ancient buildings and scattering crops. A whisper filled the air—not some echo of the battle, but the sound of millions of wings as countless birds and schools of disoriented fish fled the battle.

Leal had found an out-of-the-way corner in the bridge of Chaison Fanning's flagship, the *Surgeon*. This spot boasted a tiny quartz window, inches thick, and in an unwitting mirror image to Venera, she had watched the battle through this for hours. The alliance fleet was moving to join the action as quickly as it could, but the air here was thick with hazards: trees, houses, town wheels, and a million untethered and lost objects. Chaison's ships had to nose their way through this dense cloud, while at any moment the battle ahead of them might end.

The bridge was full of muted sounds, the hum of machinery, tactical discussions, the crackle of chart paper. Despite her best efforts, Leal nodded off, one hand against the window. She was still there when, hours later, light began to well up between her fingers. Candesce was lighting again.

Startled voices roused her. Blinking, she saw the bridge crew surrounding a circle of light on the back wall of the cone-shaped chamber. There were no large windows in this room, which was set well behind the armored prow. Outside light was piped from telescopes in the nose and projected on the white rear wall. With the flip of a lever, close-in or distant images could be put there, an effect that had seemed magical to Leal when she first saw it; but the images were dim, and they wavered. What she saw now was clear enough.

A long scar of smoke and wreckage led from the edge of the exclusion zone almost all the way to Candesce. Ferance's battleships had pushed the Last Line fleet back, and pouring in behind them came a gray cloud that must be the First Line armada.

Leal pushed off from her corner. "We're too late?"

Chaison was chatting with two officers and, perversely, smiling. He saw Leal and waved her over. "They took too long," he said. "Look at what's happening ahead of them."

She could hardly miss it: Candesce's suns were coming on line, one by one. "They're caught!"

Chaison nodded. The Last Line fleet had retreated, maybe deliberately, drawing Ferance's battleships and cruisers ever closer to the sun of suns. That was their destination—but they had to get there in time to deploy the key and enter Candesce's control rooms. The Last Line had given them hope, falling back quickly enough to draw them in, then putting up a fierce resistance right outside the machineries of the giant sun. The goal was tantalizingly close—too close to give up. When the attackers realized that the rest of the Last Line fleet had circled around behind to cut them off, it was too late.

"But . . ." She shook her head in horror. "They'll all be incinerated!"

"Not the Last Line," said Chaison. "Their ships are mirrored and insulated. They can't stay for long, but they'll survive this."

Leal couldn't speak; and soon, the triumphant chatter in the bridge dwindled, and in somber silence they watched as the attackers turned in desperation, unleashing an inferno of missiles into the contrail of smoke and destruction behind them. The sky lit with the scintillation of thousands of explosions, and the Last Line blockade dissolved.

Too late. Whatever happened next was made invisible by light as the great tungsten flowers of Candesce unfurled and opened their eyelike lamps.

"THOSE *IDIOTS!*" INSHIRI Ferance threw something heavy and half the bridge crew ducked. "How could they be so stupid, the animals!" Ferance was screaming, her face red, and Antaea had to fight to hide her disgust. If not for the steadying influence of Jacoby Sarto, she might have fled the Thistle already. It would be so easy, after all: just take a bike, fly to some distant corner of the world and leave the fate of Virga in others' hands.

As Jacoby moved to calm Ferance down, Antaea took a deep, ragged breath. This all had to be seen through, even if she had no more stomach for it. She turned and left the little bridge.

The side hatches of the sloop were open and staffers whose uniforms rippled in the headwind leaned out to exchange dispatches with men on bikes. Semaphore men crouched outside on the hull, moving their flag-draped arms in complicated patterns as clerks with writing pads watched. Bikes approaching and peeling off again made a constant howling chorus.

She hand-walked past the organized chaos to the ship's next bulkhead, and pushed through the hatch there into a quieter space. Ferance's more elite passengers slept or talked in small groups here: members of her cabal, outsiders with perfect features and sculpted bodies; and top officials of the Home Guard in whose presence she would once have felt reverent awe. She still trusted them, though the awe had dwindled. If anyone within the walls of Virga knew the truth of what lay outside, it should be these men and women.

Moving quietly past them, she opened the next hatch. The ship's hold was full of weapons, medical supplies, and crates of rations. It was hot back here, and sweat gleamed on the face of the prisoner who perched astride one of the portholes. Venera Fanning looked up at Antaea and grinned ferally.

"Sun's nice this morning, isn't it?" she said.

"I can't believe even you would make light of so many deaths," said Antaea.

Venera snorted. "It wasn't my plan to kill them. Not my plan to be here at all."

"You know why we're here. The current situation is unsustainable. The enemy will keep trying until they finally pierce Candesce's defenses and turn them off, unless we dial down the suppression field to allow us to deploy better countermeasures. That's all this is about."

Venera arched one eyebrow, then raised her bound-together hands to bring something into the light. With a shock Antaea recognized a well-thumbed copy of the book she'd dictated. "I know your plan well," said Venera. "I got a copy when it first came out, you know, though this one belongs to one of the crewmen. I was hoping someday to get your autograph on mine. —You know, something like 'To Venera, whose husband I slept with.'" She twirled the book, letting it go to become a white pinwheel in the air between them. "You describe the plan you and your sister developed with Gonlin. And of course, it's a grand plan. But it's *your* plan."

"It's the Guard's plan now," Antaea countered. "And what's yours?"

"Leave Candesce alone. You said 'the enemy' would keep trying," Venera went on. "But you are the enemy, and this is your latest try. You're trying exactly what Aubrey Mahallan tried. You're trying to get *in*. It should be obvious—"

"I didn't come here to argue," said Antaea.

"Then why did you come here?"

She hesitated. It wasn't entirely clear even to her. Or maybe, she was just having trouble admitting it even to herself. "I want you to know I'll protect you," she said. "I won't let Ferance harm you."

Venera sneered. "How touching. You and Jacoby are on the same page, I see. Did you talk about this together? How you'd present a common front, lull me as a team? He made the same promise, and it means as little coming from him as it does from you."

"You don't understand." Antaea moved to within an arm's length of Venera. She looked her in the eye. Deliberately and carefully, she said, "Venera, I will give my life to save yours if I have to. We are on opposite sides of this thing, but we are not enemies. Jacoby and I are your friends, and you will come to no harm from these people as long as I still draw breath."

Venera stared at her for a long moment. Then her lashes dropped to hood her eyes, and she turned away. "Satisfy your conscience however you want," she said. "You're saying this for Chaison's sake, not mine."

Antaea wanted to slap her. Instead, she drew back, reaching behind her for the hatch. "Believe what you want about my reasons," she said. "But the commitment remains."

She left the hold and dogged the door tightly behind her. Then she took a deep breath, and braced herself to go up to the bridge and find out what Inshiri Ferance intended to do next.

———

THE LAST LINE had held, at least for now. Smoking battle-ships from a dozen proud nations fled before Candesce's morning light, turning to regroup only when they'd passed enough veils of smoke that the savage radiance could be countered by venting water. Trailing new clouds, Ferance's armada sought to align its position with the approaching First Line fleet.

Chaison Fanning stood on the nose of the *Surgeon* and turned a brass spyglass this way and that, judging the situation. His own armada—the triumph of negotiation and diplomacy that had come from the grand colloquy—was equal to Ferance's Virgan allies. All told, though, it was less than half the size of the First Line fleet, which consisted of the largest, most sophisticated, and powerful craft in the world.

A small circle of officers hung in the air near Chaison like uniformed crows. Though she had no function, Leal was out here, too, blinking against the light. A staffer had brought her a helix glass coiled with hot tea, and she'd nearly burst into tears at the small act of kindness.

"What do you see?" the admiral of an allied navy asked Chaison.

"The Last Line're holding their position," he replied in a distracted voice. "They're safe inside the exclusion zone. Looks like Candesce is incinerating or blowing away all the debris around 'em. This will give them plenty of maneuvering room and an excellent look at the invaders."

"And they?"

"Getting a face-full of smoke and char right now. Having trouble regaining formation. But they have all day, don't they?"

"It's a problem."

"What does he mean by that?" Leal asked the staffer who'd brought her the tea. "That they've got all day?"

"They know we're not a threat," said the man with a shrug. "They can regroup, then hit the Last Line again at dusk. And they can keep that up until they've battered a way through."

Chaison bent to look over the short horizon of the *Surgeon's* hull. "We've got no choice, then. We have to hit the First Line before they can regroup with Ferance's armada." Leal heard several sharp intakes of breath from the others.

One of the admirals sputtered, "But we're no match at all for . . . that!"

"Well, it's true we can't fight them in the open, so we won't."

The admiral looked around at the available cover. "But sir, with all due respect, you can't mean to use a city as your shield!"

"No," he said. "I mean to use *that.*" Chaison smiled and pointed with the spyglass.

The other admiral, who was from the principalities himself, said, "Oh . . ." in a tone of such dismay that Leal was sure whatever Chaison was proposing must involve catastrophic civilian casualties. She looked where they were all gazing now, but once again all she saw was clouds.

Except . . . "Is it just me," she said, "or are those clouds *green?*"

IT WOULD LATER be called the Battle of the Gardens.

The Sylvan Gardens was the proudest jewel in the crown of the ancient nation of Ofirium. It was a vast volume of air containing countless cultivated groves and clouds of greenery and flowers. Strung along rope and bamboo tensegrity structures miles long, the foliage was arranged into many fantastical shapes; and those shapes changed.

One day the Garden might loom across half the sky in the form of a tableau of vast human shapes. They might be fighting or dancing as the whim of the gardeners dictated. The next morning, a coordinated nighttime rearrangement of forests and lakes might have transformed the sky into a heavenly palace, or a flat painting so gigantic that its far corners were lost in haze. Several times, the Garden had taken on the form of the lost Spyre, and refugees from the ancient wheel had wept to see it.

Chaison Fanning put the Sylvan Gardens between his fleet and the First Line, then once again within the safety of the *Surgeon's* bridge, gave the order to hurl his battleships forward. "I learned the value of a tree in Stonecloud," he announced just before the *Surgeon* crashed into a 200-year-old ball of elms. Ancient branches ground and scraped along the hull of the flagship. "Full power," ordered the admiral.

The rest of the fleet followed his lead, roaring past the incredulous gardeners, demolishing centuries of artistry as they snapped up this or that living bauble as a figurehead.

"Sir," said the helmsman nervously, "we've no visibility."

"Proceed," he said. The *Surgeon* passed sixty miles per hour, then eighty. Such speeds were reckless for any vessel in the crowded air of the principalities; doubly so in this forested region.

"Sir, we're burning through our fuel at—"

"Proceed."

They passed 120 miles per hour. "Sir? Sir!" The helmsman was practically jumping out of his seat. Chaison glared at him.

"One hundred sixty," somebody else said.

"Engines idle and deploy braking sails," Chaison ordered. Horns echoed from the open hatches behind Leal, and then the moderate gravity of their acceleration suddenly reversed: down had been aft, and then suddenly it was to forward. Leal gripped the arms of her chair and listened as protesting branches clutched at and scoured the armored hull again—this time, as the speeding grove left the *Surgeon* like a ball from a racket.

In this way, Chaison's relief force threw an entire forest at the First Line fleet.

"Fire incendiaries into our little package," Chaison said. "Let's see if we can get their hair smoking."

The First Line had spent their careers among the icebergs and mists of outer Virga. They had trained in total darkness to defend the walls of the world along thousands of miles of empty air. It would be fair to say that none of them were comfortable with the density of the skies here. None had expected to suddenly be facing a wall of flaming forest coming at them at over a hundred miles per hour.

"All ships: knife formation," said Chaison. "Let's see if we can cut them in two." The semaphore men went into their dance, and outside the portholes Leal glimpsed ships peeling off to either side of the *Surgeon*. Chaison, whose back was to the prow so he could watch the projection on the aft wall, leaned forward, cursed softly, then shouted, "Fire forward batteries!"

A gigantic sound came, and pulling and overturning and bright light, and Leal curled into a ball and put her hands over her head.

HOURS LATER, A small twin-engined courier ship nosed its way into the smoking remains of the garden. From zenith to abyss, the sky was crowded with soaring vessels, tumbling debris, and welling balls of flame. Spheres and teardrop-shapes of dissipating smoke hung like the ghosts of destroyed battleships. Missile, bike, and ship contrails threaded through the space like the web of some vast, drunken spider.

The little ship slewed past hanging bodies and the writhing shapes of injured men. Here and there airmen wearing angel's wings were leaping to ally and enemy alike, bringing bandages and water. Hospital ships sporting the crests of a hundred nations soared in and out, catching the wounded in nets without slowing down.

It was late afternoon, but Chaison Fanning's relief force had kept the First Line from regrouping with the remnants of Ferance's fleet. Beyond the local chaos, Ferance was trying on her own to push the Last Line back to Candesce.

All four fleets had local knots of density where smaller ships and bikes dove in and out like fish darting at some piece of food. Their flagships nestled deep in these well-defended kernels, and the little ship headed for one of these. It was largely ignored by the dogfighting bikes and maneuvering cruisers, though if any had looked closely they would have seen that it was towing something strange—a black iron ball a dozen feet across, a furnace, maybe, or chemical tank.

The vessel ran up its flags and made to enter the zone around the Surgeon. It was instantly surrounded by bikes and catamarans, and boarded in short order.

Minutes later, an escort formed around it and hove to next to the flagship.

"SIR, THE FIRST Line have regained their position between us and Candesce."

Chaison Fanning swore.

The bridge stank of sweat and stale air, yet Leal was afraid to leave her seat. They'd exchanged broadsides with an enemy battleship two hours ago, and she didn't want to face whatever carnage she might find if she went aft. Yet the increasing desperation of the men around her, those men who should be most in control, was agonizing. For a long time now she'd been unable to look away from Chaison Fanning, and she felt she'd learned every nuance of expression he was capable of.

"We need to reinforce the Last Line," said one of the admirals. "Any ship that can manage it should break off and—" Chaison shook his head.

"If they break formation they'll be picked off. There's a sphere of gunships around us now. We break out as a unit or not at all."

"But if we coalesce they'll surround us. And it's almost dusk! If Ferance gets to the sun—"

"She won't." Chaison turned to his loyal officer Travis, who hung in the air, ramrod-straight, near the command chair. "It's time," he said. Travis nodded and left the bridge without a word.

"Issue the order to regroup," said the admiral. "Sphere formation, centered on this ship."

The alliance's admirals began shouting, and even though she

knew little about military matters, Leal, too, stared at Chaison in disbelief. It was obvious that if Chaison brought the ships into a tight formation now, the First Line fleet could simply surround it and pick off the defenders at its leisure. Worse yet, it would be free to pin them down with a small contingent while sending the bulk of its forces on to reinforce Ferance's drive for the sun.

Yet Chaison held up a hand against the protests. "A tactic works until it stops working," he said. "This one's stopped working. Something new is called for."

The admirals exchanged looks of outrage. "But what—?"

"Sir!" The aft hatch, through which Travis had exited, was open, and a junior officer was waving tentatively at Chaison. The bridge staff glared at him and he began to back away, but the admiral waved him in.

"What is it, son?"

"News from Brink, sir."

"Can it wait?"

"No, it can't."

Leal shouted and whirled in her seat. Framed in the doorway, looking tired and disheveled, but smiling, was Keir Chen.

24

"YOUR BELOVED ADMIRAL is moving to save his ass," observed Inshiri Ferance. "Panic's never a pretty sight."

Antaea thought she was going to be sick. Since they were hanging well back from the main battle, Inshiri had come out to stand on the prow of the Thistle, holding on to its needle-shaped ram with one hand. The rest of her team was scattered in the air around her, all clutching binoculars and telescopes. While Antaea had tried to stay inside and out of Inshiri's way, Remoran had insisted she be present to observe whenever he was off the bridge. And Inshiri had decided to torment Antaea in tiny ways, apparently to blow off steam.

It was hard to make out the details through a hundred miles of smoke and debris-laden air, but it was clear that the First Line fleet was pulling itself together, returning to the threatening thunderhead shape it had held before Chaison's attack. The flickering orange of combat that had been distributed evenly through that distant smear was collapsing into a ball. Fanning's brave fleet was being routed.

"Just in time," said Jacoby. Candesce's spectrum was lengthening as its component suns shut down.

Some of the delegates who'd been selected to enter Candesce were climbing out of the ship to observe the mayhem for themselves. Remoran himself was here, and other Home Guard leaders; the surprise to Antaea had been the arrival of the outsider, Holon, and some of his compatriots, just prior to the battle. Inshiri was usually careful to behave herself in front of these officials, but her patience—and manners—was wearing thin. "Tell your people to stop messing around and get down here," she said to Remoran. "It's time for us to make our move."

Holon raised a perfect eyebrow. "The Last Line's still in our way," he pointed out. "We don't have a safe corridor."

"Why, my dear Holon, you disappoint me. This was never going to be *safe*." Inshiri scowled at the sparkling of the exclusion-zone battle. "More importantly, we're all going to run out of fuel or clean air soon. Isn't that true, General Secretary?"

Remoran nodded. "Signal the rest of the insertion group," he told her. "We're going in as soon as the First Line starts to move our way."

The signals were sent, and as Antaea went to reenter the sloop with the others, she could feel the air trembling with the noise of jet engines spinning up. She was one of the last to enter, and found the square of shadow in the hatch a black absence compared with the light of a hundred suns that radiated from the hull.

As she grabbed the edge of the hatch, something tickled the back of her hand. She flicked absentmindedly at it, heard multiple slapping sounds, and looked over to see a bright-spalled bullet hole right next to her index finger. A line of them wandered away across the Thistle's hull. They hadn't been there a moment ago—

Somebody reached out of the hatch and grabbed the lapel of her jacket, hauling her inside, where somebody else was screaming. Little droplets of blood, gorgeous red in the light from the door, spun through the shaft of daylight like minor planets.

Antaea blinked and looked back, in time to catch the head-on view of an incoming missile. It looked just like one of the ones she'd seen in the siege of Stonecloud . . .

"Damn it, move!" Jacoby Sarto shifted his grip to her shoulder and pushed her out of the doorway just as another line of bullet holes danced across the wall beside him. He grunted and jerked a foot to his left, while outside, the missile sighed past just a few feet below the sloop.

336 | KARL SCHROEDER

"Jacoby!" It was her turn to seize him as he drifted toward the starboard bulkhead. The screaming behind them had stopped. Jacoby pawed at his right shoulder with his left hand, wincing. "Wouldn't move, ya damn fool . . ."

Somebody slammed the hatch just in time as an explosion flashed outside and the portholes all starred. The sloop lurched to port and then began accelerating. Suddenly Antaea and Jacoby were falling aft with a cloud of men, crates, and blood drops. They landed atop one another and none could move for long minutes as the ship jigged and swerved crazily. More explosions chased them.

When the acceleration eased off a bit Antaea got to her knees to find Jacoby unconscious, two dead men next to him, and utter bedlam as crew and Home Guard officials tried to patch the freely bleeding wounds of two more.

"Help us here!" she demanded, but their attention was on their own. With a curse she dragged Jacoby over to the aft hatch and undogged it just as the acceleration finally let up. She bundled him through and closed the door against the noise.

"Venera! Are you okay?"

"Why?" came the dry reply. "Were you taking bets?"

"It's Jacoby, he's been hit."

"Untie me!"

Antaea hesitated for just a second, but Venera said, "Really, where am I going to go?" Antaea quickly unwove the rope and they turned their attention to Jacoby.

As they worked Candesce's light faded from the portholes, but it was still bright: fire and the glow of distant cities competed with the amber of more-distant suns to turn the skies lemon yellow. The Thistle ran ahead of pursuing Last Line gunboats, with a ragged swarm of bikes and light cruisers as escort. The task of every other ship in the armada was now to keep those pursuers from stopping the Thistle's run at Candesce; so as they soared and ducked and powered past debris clouds and tumbling mines, explosions lit the sky to all sides as attackers and defenders formed a vast cylinder around their trajectory. When Antaea had time to notice what was happening, she found herself thinking of the Thistle as a needle, aimed at the arm of a man who was twisting and turning to get out of its way. At any second one of the questing enemy missiles might find them, or a cloud of bullets, or they might hit a shrapnel cloud at three hundred miles per hour. If that happened, they'd be dead before she knew it; so, she kept her eyes on Jacoby, and her hands pressed against the site where the bullet had pierced his shoulder.

LEAL COULD SEE the ship approaching them in the wavering projection; but so could everybody else. It seemed pointless to throw out her arm and shout "Look out!" when this crash was inevitable. She reached for Keir, though, and he wrapped his arms around the back of her chair as the flame-gouting battleship loomed too large for the projection and the bridge went black.

Nothing happened. Then, just as she was about to relax, a tremendous shuddering took them and she was thrown from side to side like a rag doll. It was like the brief trip from Brink to Serenity, but a hundred times worse.

Light returned and the shuddering stopped. The projection screen showed an orange sky full of tumbling ships. Chaison Fanning leaned forward and said, "Damage report" into a speaking tube.

"Too damned crowded," muttered an admiral. The fleet was being forced into a smaller and smaller volume of air by the First Line fleet, which surrounded them on all sides. The problem was, any ship that stopped moving became an instant target, so they swirled around and around one another, like a school of trapped fish circled by sharks. The sharks had only to dart in and out again, leaving ever more wreckage in their wakes, and that—like the disabled battleship that had just struck the Surgeon a glancing blow—became a further hazard to the defenders.

"Best I can make out," one of the semaphore men was saying,

"is that the larger part of the First Line is moving to join Ferance's fleet."

"We held them as long as we could. Come on, Travis," hissed Chaison. "Where's that damned surprise?"

"Any minute now, sir."

"And you," Chaison said to Keir. "You're sure these will give us a miracle?" He held up a piece of paper Keir had brought with him. It was, he'd explained, a gift from the oaks.

"If every ship follows them to the letter, without exception," said Keir. He spoke with complete self-assurance: adult self-assurance. The man whose arm Leal held now bore no resemblance to the boy she'd met in Brink. The change was uncanny.

Chaison chewed his lip as he stared at the paper for the tenth time. Finally he gave a deep sigh, committing himself. "Send this out, coded, with a repeat order. I want every ship in the fleet to have received and be rebroadcasting it in ten minutes. They're to wait for our confirmation to proceed."

Keir grinned and slapped the back of the chair. "You won't regret this, Admiral." Chaison grunted wearily, and Keir turned to Leal. "I have to see if we lost it," he said. She shook her head at him, not in denial, but simply half-drunk with terror and the pounding they were taking.

"Griffin, I'll need you," Keir went on. "If that impact damaged the device—"

Hayden Griffin shook his head distractedly. "Why me? It's your baby."

"No, it's not," Keir insisted. "It's half yours. Admiral?" He looked to Chaison, who waved a hand.

"See to it," he said, and the two made to leave the room. Fanning returned to watching the semaphore men puzzle over the sheet he'd given them. Leal undid her straps and jumped after Keir.

"Where are you going?" she shouted over a sudden shriek of unexpected wind from the opening door. Keir and Hayden both stopped, gaping in unison at the vista that faced them.

A giant bite had been taken out of the ship just aft of the bridge. Where before the hatch had led to a tangle of corridors and box-like metal rooms, now there was gnarled sparking wreckage to the left, and open sky to the right. Hot air stinking of jet fuel and metal battered at them.

"Close the damned door!" bellowed the admiral, and the two men swung through it. Leal followed them and they slammed and sealed it.

The presence of an open and apparently infinite drop at one hand didn't intimidate Leal, since this was freefall; it was what was in that air that was frightening. Prudence dictated that she collect three pairs of foot-fins from the locker next to the bridge door; then she followed her men along the treacherous wreckage, not looking outward.

"Don't say we lost it, we couldn't have lost it," Keir mumbled as they climbed from one razor-sharp blade of scrap to the next. They passed half a water closet, where an airman with his pants around his knees still sat strapped onto the toilet. Hayden saluted him on the way past, and he returned the salute without turning his eyes from the vista of sky that had unexpectedly interrupted his meditations.

"There!" Hayden pointed ahead, to a curled-in bulkhead surrounding a clutch of catamarans and bombers. It took Leal a minute to recognize the hangar for what it was, and not just because of the turning light and overlapping shadow from hundreds of passing ships. It seemed impossible that the Surgeon could still maneuver, but way down past the peeled-back skin she could see the engines turning on their masts; and airmen were starting to cast lines and netting to one another, making temporary bridges and ladders between fore and aft. She saw a semaphore man take up position by the split hangar, as another one climbed, jacket flapping, toward the bridge.

She finally spared a glance outward, and nearly froze. The sky was jammed with ships, explosions, and spinning bits of metal.

The *Surgeon*'s helmsman was sending commands to the engine nacelles by semaphore; somehow, they had miraculously avoided another collision so far, but that luck couldn't last. The First Line was crushing them.

Up ahead, Keir and Hayden had reached something that she at first took to be just another piece of wreckage. Teetering on the edge of open air was a great iron ball, about ten feet across, that had been married by thick cables and two awkward metal girders to an equal-sized blue box that looked like it had been half-melted by a drunken designer. Her boys began clambering over the contraption, shouting questions and answers to one another over the noise of the headwind.

Engineers, she thought, and crawled over to them.

Hayden turned to her, grinning. "Recognize it?" She could barely make out the words over a shattering drone that must have been coming from the engines.

"What, this?" He nodded, expectant. Puzzled, Leal turned to look at the combined devices again. The box looked a lot like things she'd seen in Brink, but it was generic. The ball, on the other hand, was riveted together, dented in places, and streaked with iridescent discolorations, as though it had been put through a fire.

Then she got it. "Your weapon!" The last time she'd seen this sphere, Hayden had been towing it behind a small airship. It had smoked and buzzed, and apparently produced a wall of fierce radio waves that had interfered with the thoughts of the emissary.

The drone was so loud now that she could only catch every second word as he nodded and slapped its side: "Rejigged . . . generator . . . hundred megawatt . . ."

He froze suddenly, a look of astonishment on his face. "—Sound!" Keir and Leal looked at him; she had to put her hands over her ears, but leaned close as he yelled, "Heard! Before!"

She and Keir exchanged a glance. Hayden tried one more time. *"Capital! Bug!"*

IT EMERGED FROM a cloud bank bit by bit, something too big to take in without a turn of the head, too distant as yet for its details to be resolved. Candesce was dimming rapidly, and in the smoke and chaos the First Line simply hadn't seen it coming. No capital bug had ever penetrated this close to the sun, after all—but this was no random encounter. Chaison's ships had stolen it from Abyss weeks before; in the run-up to war, nobody had noticed its absence.

It was miles long. An entire ecosystem sheltered behind its vast curving flanks, safe from sharks or any kind of bird—or even Man. The towering horns that festooned its carapace guaranteed that, because the sound they poured out could kill a man from a mile away.

The bug's skin was pockmarked with holes. Ropes trailed from its trumpets, and one or two were still stuffed with foliage and moss. Spiraling around it were the six vessels that had jammed the horns and used rockets and machine guns to herd the beast through the dense skies of the principalities.

It wasn't fast, but it was unstoppable. The bug plowed into the First Line ships surrounding the alliance fleet, scattering them like startled fish. A few battleships tried to shoot out the horns, but they were too far away to be accurate; one that held fast also fell ominously quiet once it got close enough to take its shot. It drifted, touched the skin of the bug, and tore through it like a pen through paper.

The First Line concentrated their fire on the bug, but its Slipstream herders had put enough volleys into its back that it was maddened now. It would not turn away.

Keir caught glimpses of this carnage as the *Surgeon* maneuvered. The bug was running tangent to the alliance fleet, so the noise stabilized after a few minutes, then began to fall. He was able to listen as Hayden described his one encounter with a bug, years before, on the first occasion when he'd traveled with Chaison Fanning. "But it was finding out that the key to Candesce had been hidden in a bug that reminded us of this one," he explained. "The boy who found it was with a group of treasure hunters who'd figured out how to enter a bug. They shot off half its horns, and it repaired them but not fast enough to keep them from getting in and out. But it *could* repair them. So why not bring this one back and let it heal in the warm air? Fanning sent Travis to try. I guess it worked."

A heavy cruiser thundered past, less than a hundred feet away. Keir coughed in its choking wake and shouted, "Now if he would only give the flocking order . . ."

Leal was wide-eyed, and her hair coiled and writhed around her in medusoid tangles. She clung to Griffin's generator, but was clearly paying attention. "What order?"

"That paper I brought the admiral. It—" He blinked at the suddenly changing sky. "I think he gave it."

Far down the bullet-pocked hull of the *Surgeon*, the great engine nacelles swiveled on their arms and roared into full power. A ripple of stress raced up the skin of the ship and Hayden yelled "Hang on!" as the whole vessel wrenched itself onto a new heading.

With a metallic shriek the generator and his device fell into the shrapnel-ridden sky.

Keir dove after it.

"SOMETHING'S GONE WRONG." Inshiri had poked her head out the hatch, and as she came back in she had a puzzled expression on her face. "Where's the goddamn First Line?"

She slammed the hatch and turned her best glower on the semaphore team. "Aren't you getting anything?"

The semaphore captain shook his head. "There's too much clutter, sir. It's not just the smoke and wreckage—there's signaling flags floating everywhere. They're pretty much the first thing to get shot off a ship in a firefight."

"What about flares?"

The officer shrugged. "Same problem. The enemy's look just like ours."

Antaea was listening from the aft chamber. Now she felt Jacoby cough weakly and try to sit forward. He was pale, but he was awake, and she and Venera had at least stopped the bleeding. "What's happening?" he asked.

Through the porthole behind her, Antaea could see tracer fire stitching the air from behind. "Another one's on our tail," she pointed out. "Where's the rear guns?"

They all listened for the clatter of the machine gun, but there was only silence. Inshiri also noticed, and came back to point at Antaea. "You, you're a good shot, aren't you? Get back there and take over."

"I don't take orders from you," Antaea replied coolly.

Something pinged through the cabin, making the guardsmen jump in surprise. Jacoby pushed at her weakly. "Probably a good idea," he muttered.

"Oh, hell." Rear gunners always died first. But if somebody didn't go back there, they would get their engines shot off. Then they'd be picked off by whoever happened by.

She clambered back through the hold, cursing the ineptitude of their escort ships. They'd lost more than half already, and the rest were distracted by some heavy Last Line cruisers that had noticed them and fallen into pursuit. It was probably one fanatic on a bike chasing the Thistle now—but if he had a machine gun in his hands, one would be enough.

"Need a hand?" Venera said from right behind her. Antaea jerked and bit off a sharp retort. She shook her head and opened the tail blister.

"Eh, maybe I do after all." Venera looked over her shoulder and whistled softly. It was going to take them a few minutes to get that man out of there.

He'd been good-looking, and he'd had a nice laugh. Antaea felt heartsick as she and Venera hauled his body into the hold. She took the last of their bandages and began wiping down the grips on the machine gun, then the supposedly bulletproof glass of the blister. It stank of sweat and iron in here, but hot air from outside was whistling through the three holes that starred her view.

She swiveled the blister about and squeezed the gun's trigger experimentally. One bullet discharged, then the mechanism froze. "What the—"

"You've got a jam in the feeder," said Venera. "I'll get it." The former princess of Hale kicked the lid off the ammo mechanism under Antaea's feet and began rummaging around in it with bloody fingers. All the while, the Thistle was weaving back and forth in a sickening way, dodging the intermittent stutter of tracers that chased them.

While she waited, Antaea stared at the fading purple backdrop to all the local carnage. "Where's the First Line? And what the hell is that?" A black silhouette, impossibly big, was cutting off the light from one of the principalities' suns. And those sparkles and speckles around it: Could they be ships?

Venera glanced up. "Sometimes, when night falls, Candesce goes walking," she said.

"Shut up."

"It's true. It curls its way through the blackness until it finds some sleeping town or farm. And then it feeds . . ."

"I'd believe anything at this point," Antaea conceded.

"Try now."

She aimed the guns at the source of the tracer rounds and opened fire. The blast of the weapon was a physical shock, numbing her hands as it leaped about, and deafening her.

She gave Venera the thumbs-up signal and turned her attention to killing their pursuer.

ADMIRAL FANNING'S SIGNAL had gone out, and for a few minutes, chaos had reigned among the alliance fleet. The ships had been settling into uneasy patterns, barely avoiding one another while dodging missiles from the circling First Line. In the bedlam caused by the capital bug's arrival the bombardment had eased up a bit, and in clean, daylit air, this might have given the alliance a chance to regroup. But it was dark, the air was full of smoke; nobody could see more than half a mile in any direction.

Yet suddenly the ships surrounding Keir and his machine were accelerating, turning—blindly, at first, then in increasingly coordinated patterns. He couldn't see the full fleet, but he could hear the change. Somehow, even with the failure of the semaphore, hundreds of ships' headlamps were beginning to turn as one thing.

"Hey!" He turned and saw two figures, black on black in this light, kicking slowly toward him. "You forgot your fins!" shouted Leal.

He laughed crazily. Keir had never been stranded like this, weightless, yet in hot air and surrounded by infinite possibility in all directions. It was terrifying and intoxicating, yet as they slowly flapped their way up to his machine, Leal Maspeth and Hayden Griffin looked quite at home.

Stretching out, he touched Leal's fingertips, then drew her to him. They kissed, and then she reached to hold one of the loose straps attached to the machine. "Look at them go!" she said in awe. "It reminds me of the fleet leaving Abyss."

"I guess this is just like home for you?" he asked.

"Yes, except for the smoke and heat and the burning ships and all those suns out there like monsters' eyes. Just like home." The fleet's lamps suddenly turned as one, as though from some silent signal. Then they surged into life, pouring intense fire into one flank of the encircling First Line. Cruisers, battleships, bikes, and catamarans surged past the three people clinging to their little island, and for a while they couldn't speak for the thud of explosions and whine of passing jets.

Then, astonishingly, the fleet was accelerating out of the trap the First Line had held them in. A giant hole full of drifting hulks was all that was left of the enemy's inner divisions.

It wasn't exactly silent. The capital bug still screamed its discordant song, but many miles away; and the sound of explosions no longer came with a body-blow of shocked air as emphasis. Compared to what they'd endured for hours now, this air seemed peaceful to Leal.

"Do you think they'll stop them from getting in?" Hayden asked after a while. Keir shrugged.

"If they don't, it's going to be up to us."

Leal watched the retreating flashes and silhouetted gray of the fleet's headlamps. "How did they do that?" she mused.

"The oaks' gift," said Keir. "A set of flocking rules for the fleet. All you have to do is watch what your neighbors are doing, and follow this or that rule depending on the situation. It's an emergent system—creates ordered behavior on the macro scale."

"They're acting like they're all controlled by one mind."

"In a way, they are. But there's nothing magical about it— nothing technological, either, which is the point. Those rules will work here, where all the machineries of the virtuals won't."

"So you're saying we have a chance."

He shrugged, and then, realizing she couldn't see the gesture in the dark, said, "We wait now. If it's all been for nothing, I'll feel it."

"How?" asked Hayden.

He wondered how to describe the sensation of scry turning itself on.

"I'll wake up," he said.

WHETHER SHE'D KILLED its pilot or disabled its engines, Antaea didn't know; but whatever had been firing on them was gone. It was small comfort to her, because right now it looked like the entire universe was collapsing in on their exact spot.

Venera had crammed herself in next to Antaea and, companionably, they were pointing out this or that feature of the approaching apocalypse. "Those ones look like a hawk's head," said Venera, indicating a formation of carriers visible only as glittering running lights.

The sky was full of such constellations, some superimposed on purple-, orange-, or green-colored cloudscapes backlit by distant suns. Most were maneuvering in darkness, and they were drawing closer, both to each other and to the Thistle. The little sloop was running flat-out now, its two remaining escorts straining to keep up. All the while, four fleets whirled and coalesced behind them, like flotsam in their wake.

"Haven't seen any trash for a while now," Antaea said. Venera nodded.

"We're nearly there. Anything that fell this far in during the day would have been incinerated."

Even as she said this, something flickered past—not from behind them, as a missile would have done, but from in front. Antaea stared in shock as she realized what she'd seen was just a highlight gleaming off something so big that she'd completely missed it. It was like a vast crystal spike, miles long. Others began to cut off portions of the view above and below.

"Refractors and reflectors," Venera explained. "They're what give Candesce the illusion of being a single object."

The engines slowed, then their scream lowered to an idling grumble. An airman pounded on the hatch behind them and both Antaea and Venera turned. The man thrust his head in.

"You," he said to Venera. "You're to guide us in to the dock."

"There's no dock, you silly boy." Venera stretched luxuriously. When he didn't move she sighed and said, "All right, I'm coming. But fetch me some food, will you? I'm tired from all this excitement."

He backed away. Antaea hid a grin as Venera began to climb out of the blister.

Five minutes later, with none of the preamble or pomp and ceremony she had expected, she found herself hanging in the stifling air outside the sloop. Venera had planted both feet against the smooth pale wall of a gigantic cube, and had done something with a white wand that Nicolas Remoran had given her.

As the door to Candesce's control room slid silently open, Venera turned, pouting, and held out the key.

"Really, you didn't need me," she said. "A child could have done it."

25

THE PAIN WAS intense. It took Jacoby back to crystalline memories of his youth, and the training he and the other children of the great houses of Sacrus had been put through. At the time they'd called it "endurance exercise"; later, they'd admitted it was torture, systematically applied to toughen up the candidates. Some broke under the strain. Others, like Inshiri Ferance, responded by developing an avid fascination with others' agony.

The "training" hadn't helped him much after she took his finger; he didn't think it was going to help now.

"Get your hands off me," he snarled at the airman who was trying to boost him through the sloop's hatch. Inshiri was outside watching Venera open Candesce's magic door; she shot Jacoby an approving look.

Thunder grumbled irregularly above and below them. Distant flashes revealed something of the intense battle that was surrounding them now. Their two escort ships were standing off, guns swiveling, but both had numerous breaks in their hulls as well as the same peppering of bullet holes that covered the *Thistle*. If any of the enemy broke through, they wouldn't last very long.

Venera had seen where he was looking, and she sent him one of her less pleasant smiles. "We'd better hope none of those thousands of missiles up there hits any part of Candesce," she said loudly. "I'd hate to see what the sun of suns would do if you stung it."

"Shut up and get inside," Inshiri told her.

Antaea was climbing out of the sloop. Jacoby did a quick head count of the assembled group. *Perfect.*

"One second," he said, putting out his good arm to stop Antaea. Quickly, he murmured, "If it comes to it, who are you with? Inshiri? Or me?"

To her credit, she didn't even give a sign that she'd heard him, merely mouthing, *You.*

"I need you to get me something," he said, more loudly.

"What? Now?" She was staring with almost feverish anxiety at the entrance, where cool electric light now glowed.

"Yes, *you'll know it when you see it*," he said, looking in her eyes as he emphasized those words. "It's in the first of the water tanks."

She cocked her head, puzzled, then retreated into the ship.

Satisfied that he was at least doing something to try to control the situation, Jacoby stepped gingerly across the air and entered the bizarre spaces of Candesce's control center.

Venera had described the place in detail, but it was still impressive to see. Once beyond the cubic foyer, the place was filled with chambers whose walls and floors did not quite touch. You could slip under or around any of them, moving by ducking and turning sideways through a kind of corridorless maze. This was a common enough design for freefall houses, but in this case, Venera had said, there was nothing visible holding the walls and screens in place. She was right, which would have fascinated Jacoby at another time; but with his arm in a sling and spasms of pain radiating from his shoulder, it was hard for him to maneuver here. At least it was cooler.

He caught up to Inshiri's party in a large space with a blank black rectangle, like a picture frame, on one of its surfaces. "Hurry up, we don't have much time," Remoran was telling Venera.

"Actually, I think we do," she said. She pointed. "Do you see those little dots on the wall there? Bloodstains, from," she smiled at Inshiri, "the last person I killed here."

"You're really in no position to be bragging," retorted Inshiri.

"My point is that it's cool in here. And, that those bloodstains are still here after thousands of days. The first time I was here, I suspected that this blockhouse might be immune to Candesce's heat and radiation. This proves it."

"Which means—?"

"That we could hold out here for months, maybe even years, if we had to. All we'd need to do is close the door. This place has supplies and machinery to feed hundreds. It even has medical facilities. It—"

"Stop stalling!" Inshiri drew an intricately etched pistol from inside her jacket.

Venera examined her nails. "Fine line between stalling and outright rebellion, isn't it?"

"Enough of this petty sniping," snapped Remoran. "Mrs. Fanning, we need your cooperation because under our agreement, it will be natives of Virga who make any changes to Candesce's defensive field. Our guests," he nodded at Holon and his party, "are here to observe. However, if you should prove uncooperative, we may have to enlist one of them to operate the machinery instead of you. They all know how to do it. Would you prefer we take that route?"

She scowled. "No."

"Then take us to the controls."

"We're already there," said Venera sullenly. She turned to face the frame on the wall, and spoke several words in what sounded like some foreign language. The area in the rectangle lit up, and then, miraculously, images began to form there.

Jacoby had heard of this sort of technology, but seeing it still took his breath away. The projections of Kaleidogig were laughable next to this. He saw the reaction on Inshiri's face, and knew exactly what she was feeling: hunger for this power to be hers. He was feeling the same thing.

"I can show you how to make the changes," Venera told Remoran. "I watched Aubrey Mahallan do it. And one thing I learned was that control mirrors like this one don't discriminate. They'll take the commands of anyone and everyone gazing into them.

Which means that they," she indicated the outsiders, "had better leave until this is over."

Remoran gestured to his men. "If you wouldn't mind?" he asked Holon politely. The outsider glanced at his fellows, and Inshiri Ferance said breezily, "Oh, it's all right. I'll come with you." Holon ducked his head politely, and his group, along with Inshiri and her bodyguards, left escorted by several well-armed guardsmen.

Venera frowned gravely at the general secretary of the Virga Home Guard. "I hope you know what you're doing," she said. "Now, you see that clutch of suns there? The knot of six of them?" Jacoby spotted them before Remoran did: six spiky balls, each at least a hundred feet across, all made of what looked like pale stained glass. "Do you see what they're hiding?"

Remoran peered at the command mirror. "That black thing?"

"That 'black thing' is it. The great mystery," she said in a cynical tone. "Now you're going to concentrate on it, and you will begin to see words and numbers forming around it."

"Oh! Yes, I see." Remoran was silent for a long minute, both he and Venera focused on the picture before them. Then he said, "I see how to do it. We'll start with a little adjustment . . ."

Jacoby drifted backward. *When's it coming?* He knew something was going to happen, and soon; he just didn't know what it would be. He'd better make sure he was out of the way when that happened.

So, he was expecting something; yet he still jerked in surprise when the screaming started.

ANTAEA HAD WASTED no time in finding the tanks Jacoby had talked about. Whatever he was playing at, she needed to get it over with right now, and get inside that blockhouse. As she hauled the heavy tarpaulin away from the water containers, though, her hands were shaking.

Since the trial, a night hadn't gone by when she hadn't thought about what it would have been like to have been here, with Telen at her side. Chaison had allowed her to describe that plan in her book, a plan to put more control of humanity's fate in its own hands, by adjusting Candesce's ability to suppress technologies. But this had not been her idea. It had been Telen's.

There was too much misery in the world. There might well be monsters circling Virga, clawing at the walls of the world to get in. Yet, what more misery could they cause than the hereditary nobles, dictators, and disease and famine already did? The educated in Virga knew what they lacked. They knew about machines that could look inside the body and diagnose or fix diseases before you were even aware of them. They knew about miraculous mechanisms, like Keir Chen's Edisonians, that could evolve the design for any device or object you wanted. They also knew that such things were not just forbidden to all who dwelt in Virga; they were impossible.

Antaea and Telen had dreamt together of a different world. A Virga where Artificial Nature remained outside, but scanners and fabs and computers could exist. Telen had understood the nuances of the plan better than Antaea. She'd been the more intellectual of the two. What Antaea understood was the outcome, if it worked.

And that was why she was here, allied with people she hated and feared, and enduring humiliation after humiliation. To see it through, for Telen's sake, and the sake of millions of people she would never meet, and who would probably never know her name. To prove that their lives were not predestined to be miserable and brief.

She hauled on the lid of one of the tanks at the back, and with a reluctant pop, it sprang open. Antaea hunkered down in the space between the tank and the back bulkhead, and looked inside.

The thing was oval and a kind of translucent gray, and filled the large container almost completely. Various ragged patches on its sides suggested that it had been glued in some way to something else, and torn roughly loose at some point.

Tears started in Antaea's eyes. She couldn't breathe; she watched one of her trembling hands reach up as though to touch her hair, and hang in the air, helpless. Her other hand came up, in a warding gesture. She realized with a distant sort of wonder that she was whimpering.

She had seen such a thing as this before. The last time had been in the abandoned city of Serenity, in a black corridor filled with bodies.

The sound of murmuring voices snapped her back to the here and now. It was the pilot and two crewmen who'd been left behind to guard the ship.

They were Inshiri's people. She reached for her pistol. Did they know about this thing?

Probably not. But the heft of the gun in her hand reminded her of something. She held it up in the dim cabin light. This had come from Brink; it had been made for Keir Chen's group by the Edisonians. It seemed to have been designed—no, "evolved," apparently—especially to handle monsters like this one. She hadn't fired it since the fight in Serenity, and it still had a full clip of its original ammunition in it.

Antaea thought for a second. Then she popped out from behind the tank and said, "Hey, boys, I don't want to ruin your day or anything, but there's an unexploded rocket lodged in this tank."

Their banter stopped. "Hell," said one. "Must have caught us in that last run in."

"I didn't feel an impact," protested the pilot.

"Well, you're going to feel a pretty big one if we don't get this guy out of here."

They came over. Antaea made sure she was between them and the tank's door. "Can you pull it out?" one asked. She shook her head.

"I could try, but . . . you want me to try?"

"No, no!" They all raised their hands and shook their heads.

"Okay, then. Why don't we ease this baby outside, and just . . . give it a gentle shove?"

They liked that idea, and when they'd all managed to get the tank out the main hatch, she left them to debate how hard to push the thing. Hopefully it would go a long, long ways away.

Antaea dove into Candesce's blockhouse. Suspicious soldiers of the Home Guard elite were manning the door; they gave her suspicious looks, but didn't bar her entry. "That way," one said. "Follow the voices."

She nodded. She had no intention of going that way.

After she was out of sight of the doormen, she took a side route; it was easy since you could duck under, over, or around any wall in this place. Venera had been right about the scale of the blockhouse: she passed sleeping quarters outfitted for hundreds, the chambers immaculate but probably untouched for a thousand years; kitchens, dining nooks, gymnasia, and even a spherical pool. Before she could get too lost, she circled back, pausing to listen every now and then for voices. When she heard them she checked the pistol, then crept cautiously closer.

A loud conversation was happening on the other side of this next wall. She backed into the shadows, then angled herself so she could see past its edge. When she took in the scene, she hissed under her breath.

Three members of the Guard hung lifelessly in the center of the room. Inshiri Ferance perched on the branch of an archaic-looking couch tree just a few feet from the nearest corpse. She was chatting animatedly with the outsider, Holon.

"That's our part done," Inshiri was saying. "You agreed you'd take on the risk for this next step. You clear out the Home Guard and dispose of Remoran, and then we dial Candesce to the mutually agreed-upon level."

"Something like that," said Holon.

"Then why aren't you on about it? We don't have much time."

"If we wait until Remoran's done, then we won't have to attack them with these primitive weapons," said Holon, gesturing at the guns Inshiri's bodyguards were carrying. Their carbines, Antaea now saw, had silencers on them.

"What do you mean?" asked Inshiri.

"Candesce will shift through several stable emulations of Newtonian physics and normal electrodynamics while Remoran dials it down. We don't know how that process works, but we do know, from tests we conducted right at the edge of the field, which technologies will work at the dialed-down level."

"So? What of it?"

"We've brought weapons that will work at that level," he said.

Inshiri nodded. "Yes, that was exactly what I thought. Lads?"

Her men opened fire, and now it was clear that their guns had some sort of silencing mechanism; the shots were barely audible. Holon and the other outsiders twitched under the onslaught, then, propelled by the residual momentum of the bullets in their bodies, drifted to the far wall.

"Looks like the wetwork's up to us after all," sighed Inshiri. She unfolded herself from the couch and unholstered her intricately carved little pistol. Her men, meanwhile, were forming up into three squads.

An odd crick-cracking sound reached Antaea's ears. She saw Inshiri and her men turn; one of the bodyguards swore. Antaea shifted her position to make out what was happening.

Holon's body was convulsing. Its thrashing limbs were bending in ways they shouldn't, and it was the sound of bones breaking that Antaea had heard. "Shoot it, shoot it!" Inshiri screamed—just as the other three outsiders' corpses began to twitch as well.

By the time Holon's body tore itself apart to reveal the thing underneath, they'd put a couple dozen rounds apiece into it. It showed no signs of having noticed.

REMORAN WHIRLED AT the shouting. "What's going—"
His men unslung their machine guns, and two leaped to perch on the edge of the opening where the virtuals had gone. One was im-

mediately flung backward. He hit the far wall and bounced off, clutching at his neck as blood sprayed into the chamber.

Jacoby blinked at the dying man. Of all the things he'd worried about happening in here, a simple gunfight had never crossed his mind.

Then they were all firing as Remoran twisted in midair, trying to find purchase on something—anything—for freefall leverage. He grabbed Venera and doubled up, putting his feet against her flank. The general secretary was about to use her mass to launch himself to safety, and the recoil would take Venera into the line of fire.

She grabbed his ankle. As he cursed and kicked at her, she adroitly spun around and kicked him in the head. Then she made the leap he'd been about to, and grabbed the edge of the wall next to Jacoby. "Hi," she said.

Shouts of alarm distracted Jacoby, and so he turned in time to see something gray and multi-limbed clamber over the far wall. Inshiri's soldiers and Remoran's guardsmen were peppering it with gunfire, but it didn't slow down. "What the hell is that?" shouted Jacoby.

"That would be our boy Holon," said Venera. "I believe he's shed his skin." Another of the spiderlike things was coming over the wall behind the first one.

"Come on." He pawed at her with his good arm, and when she pulled away he pointed at the empty chamber on the other side of the wall. "Time to go."

He looked back for just a second, and beheld a nightmarish scene: long jointed threads had snaked from the sides of the bark-colored thing, and they were stabbing the soldiers. One twisted itself around Remoran's throat, and another was darting at Inshiri Ferance. She kicked off from the nearest wall and sailed over to land next to Jacoby and Venera.

A gray whip coiled around her ankle and she shrieked in surprise. "Cousin!" She lunged for Jacoby, hand outstretched.

"Good-bye, Inshiri." He kicked away into the next room.

"Jacoby! Jacobyyyyy!" She gripped the edge of the wall for a second, then let go and disappeared.

"The entrance!" barked Venera. She took his good hand and they leaped for the next wall. Just as they landed on it a silhouette reared up above it and Jacoby raised his pistol, then cursed.

"Took you long enough," he snapped at Antaea. She shook her head silently, then gestured with her pistol.

"—Not going back there!" Venera protested.

"I shot one of them." Antaea raised her weapon, turning it in the cool light. "This works, but we need to keep them distracted. They haven't figured out where the shot came from yet, but—"

Jacoby nodded. "Glad you thought to bring that. Remoran was a fool—and so was Inshiri. They thought they could rely on Virgan technology and Holon's word of honor to keep his boys in line. I did my best in case they were wrong, but—" He flipped over, preparing to jump back to the room where just a few sporadic shots and screams now sounded.

Venera slapped his shoulder and he nearly blacked out. "—see?" she was saying when he regained his breath. "You're in no shape. Give me the gun, old man."

He handed her his pistol. "You'll pay for that."

"What, hitting you?"

"No, calling me old."

She and Antaea hopped away, and he flipped over the wall. If he got lucky he might make it to the entrance before the monsters finished with those two.

26

HOLON HAD REGAINED something of his original form; at least, Antaea assumed that the dark, man-shaped thing hunched in front of the control mirror was him. She edged backward, finding the right opening for her shot. Holon was busy, so he was a natural target; but because he *was* busy, she could probably afford to ignore him for now.

She nodded to Venera, who took a deep breath and then popped up over the top of the wall. "Bastaaaards!" she screamed as she fired off several indiscriminate rounds into the corpse-filled room. Then she kicked backward, sailing toward the opposite wall of her own empty room.

One of the three remaining monsters whistled and disappeared out of Antaea's point of view, but she knew where it was going. It appeared over the top of the control room's wall just as Venera disappeared over the next one.

She shot it.

As it tumbled into the air, Antaea shook her head in surprise. "Damn, this is too easy."

"Is it now?" Suddenly she was seeing stars as something had lashed her in the face. Before she knew it she was tumbling somewhere, blazing pain in her eyes, her arms, her belly. She tried to shoot, but where was the gun? She couldn't feel anything in her right hand.

Something had her—was carrying her. She hit a wall and bounced back, hit something softer. A body. Gasping, she tried to clear her vision, found that her eyes and nose were soaking wet.

"Now how would she have gotten a weapon like this?" The questioner sounded like Holon; was he asking her?

"I don't know, I don't, please don't, I swear I—" It was Inshiri Ferance, hysterical and begging.

"You really don't know, do you?"

"I swear!"

"Then I don't need you for now. —Don't worry, I'll resurrect you later."

Antaea heard a horrible choking sound. She rubbed again at her eyes, was rewarded by a sliver of red-soaked vision. She seemed to be bleeding freely into the air. She was also missing two fingers from her right hand, and long black tendrils draped through the air to somewhere below Antaea's chin, from the monster that was killing Ferance.

She couldn't move, but he knew she was still alive, because when he had finished with Inshiri he turned to her. The vaguely head-shaped thing atop his torso tilted as if looking at her. "It took us centuries to evolve these bodies so they'd work inside Virga," he said. "This bioform is related to the one we hid inside your sister. Like what you see?" he said.

Antaea couldn't speak. He had finally admitted that it was his people who'd destroyed Telen. When she didn't reply, Holon, apparently disappointed that she didn't want to talk, turned back to the command mirror. "It's done," he said. "Candesce's protection is gone."

"Thank you," he said to her, "for all your help. And that of your sister. I'm sure she would be proud."

I was wrong. This was the last coherent thought Antaea had before the red in her eyes was joined by black. She was losing track—of where she was, who was talking to her, and what she'd been doing that was so important . . .

———————

SCRY SUDDENLY FILLED Keir's visual field with update windows and helpful directional gridlines. He stiffened and almost let go of the cable he'd been holding.

"It's happened," he said.

Griffin and Leal looked at one another. "Are you sure?" asked the sun lighter.

"See for yourself." Keir nodded in the direction of Candesce.

When night came here, the hot expanded air around the sun of suns cooled and contracted. Breezes blew up from the principalities and carried the accumulated grit and flotsam of the day into the exclusion zone. Such a breeze was blowing now, and it had carried enough of the smoke from the Battle of the Gardens away that the other battle—the one still raging around Candesce itself—was clearly visible.

That battle had been a little flickering galaxy, a coruscating cloud of brief orange dots that signaled the explosion of missiles. A few larger, more long-lasting dots would be burning ships. Now, though, the nature of the light was changing. Orange was being replaced by blue, and the blue flashes were not appearing as pinprick points, but as fuzzy lozenges.

Griffin's brow furrowed as he watched this change. "What . . ."

"Lasers," said Keir. "And plasma guns, rail guns . . . who knows what else. Whatever the virtuals gave Inshiri Ferance. They probably packed her ships with weapons, and she may not even have known about it. They could have been disguised as anything—food supplies, even water. They'd be rigged to self-assemble the instant Candesce's field shut off. I'm betting there's not much left of the ships that brought them here."

Griffin swore. "We have to ·fire this thing up." He turned his attention to the black ball he was clinging to. "I know how to start a polywell fusion generator, of course; hell, I built this one. But why are we using it to power your device? Couldn't you have built some A.N. battery like they did?" He nodded at the rainbow colors of the battle. "—Some miraculous energy source that would kick in when Candesce's field shut down?"

"Sure," said Keir. "But whatever I used would have to keep working after I turned my machine on . . . The suppressor field would shut down its own generator if that used A.N. technology."

"Right . . . right." Griffin shook his head.

Sudden blinding light stabbed Keir's eyes. For a second he thought somebody had set off a fission nuke near Candesce, but then an amplified voice said, "You on the mine! Come away!"

He shielded his eyes with his hand, and found that they were pinned in the beam of a floodlight. He heard the grumble of idling jets.

Hayden Griffin squinted into the glare. "Who're you?"

"This is the Last Line army engineers. Come away from the explosive device."

"They think this is a mine," said Leal.

"Well, it looks like one," admitted Griffin.

"What are we going to do? They'll shoot us if we touch anything."

In the sudden bright light, he and Leal looked very much like refugees; none of them, Keir realized, was wearing a uniform. Leal in particular was wide-eyed, her hair a frizz of tangles and mats. Smudges of soot on her face had given her a mask of fear, though he knew she was relatively calm. That gave him an idea.

When he saw Griffin start to cautiously reach for his sidearm, he said, "Let me handle this."

"What are you going to do?"

He grimaced and shrugged. "Leal."

"Yes?"

"Have you ever done any acting?"

JACOBY SARTO STARED at a world transformed. The night sky was filled with flickering lines of blue and green light.

Ships were on fire everywhere he looked. It wasn't just the alliance fleet that had been destroyed; those ships that were emitting the strange bright lines were also breaking up. They, though, were not exploding. Instead, they were disgorging gigantic, many-limbed metal things into the air, and some of those things were turning back and *eating* the ships that had birthed them.

This would be just a taste of what was happening at the walls of Virga. Leal Maspeth had spoken of an alien armada waiting in silence there, a fleet so vast that it surrounded the entire world. Even now, those ships, and whatever creatures accompanied them, must be bursting through Virga's iceberg-choked skin, preparing to wreak havoc on everything within.

Leal had been right. Jacoby had suspected she was, which was one reason he'd decided to put himself right at the heart of the action. There, he could make a command decision at the critical moment; and he had. It just hadn't been enough.

Closer by, the *Thistle* drifted, uncrewed. The badly cut bodies of its pilot and mates hung near it like grotesque angels. Near them were the bodies of the two Home Guard soldiers who'd been set to guard the door.

Jacoby leaned out cautiously. The dagger-ball he'd planted in the *Thistle* could be anywhere. With any luck it wasn't actually in the sloop. He should be able to dive out to it and get it under way before the monster found its way back to him.

It had been a nice trick, keeping that thing in reserve. He'd been sure Antaea would figure it out: if the dagger-ball came to life, then Candesce had been dialed down too far. The monster was like a mine—set to go off if things in the control room went too far.

It had worked to clear the blockhouse's entrance—for all the good that was going to do. Antaea still stood little chance against Holon and his horrible companions.

One of the soldier's carbines was sailing by with stately slowness. Jacoby eyed it.

He could be out of Candesce in ten minutes. There was an open patch of sky down beneath his feet, and if he avoided those damned lights, he stood a good chance of getting out of this alive. Surely the virtuals wouldn't kill every human being in Virga. They had no need to, and it would be a lot of work. No, Virga would probably survive, just under new management.

He watched himself reach out and pluck the carbine from the air. Then, just in case the dagger-ball was nearby, he sealed the door shut before reentering the maze of the control center.

"HERE THEY COME," Holon was saying. Antaea realized where she was, and tried to scramble out of the way—any direction, anywhere but here. She couldn't move; something was holding her.

"They'll have it apart in a few hours," said Holon. She realized he was talking about something in the command mirror. Scraping clotted blood out of her eyes, she peered at it. Big metal things, like gigantic crabs, had encircled a black oval. Surrounding this tableau were six dormant suns, and, as backdrop, a sky full of laser light and flame.

"I've told Candesce not to come on at dawn," Holon continued. "No day today. We have all the time in the world. But I expect that by the time your current body gives out, we'll have figured out Candesce's secret. The question then will be, can we afford to ever resurrect you? The plan, after all, is to erase Candesce, Virga, and any hint that this place was ever here."

"Why?" she croaked.

His eyeless head turned her way. "This foolish movement toward embodiment must be stopped," he said. "Mind is all that matters. Your people have made themselves enemies of unbounded consciousness. That's evil."

He came closer to her, and she could see the dry, writhing branches that made up his features rearrange themselves in a smile. "Candesce is an abomination. It's a machine for erasing consciousness—for suppressing it. Dumb matter reigns in Virga, except for your brief little sparks. And you'd export this horror to the rest of the universe?

"Don't worry, we can work something out," he soothed. "What you know can never be allowed out in the greater universe, but we can build a quarantined virtuality for you to live in. Death's not the end for the likes of us."

"Then you won't mind if I kill you," somebody said. Holon's body jerked as several bullets hit it.

"Don't be ridiculous, old man," said the outsider as one of his whiplike arms shot out to wrap around Jacoby Sarto's throat. Holon dragged him over the wall and Jacoby lost his one-handed grip on the carbine he'd fired. As this happened, though, a blur shot across the room from the other direction.

Venera yanked at Antaea's pistol, which was still held in one of Holon's coils. Holon turned, twitched his arms, and sent Venera across the room. She hit the wall, but she'd also held on to the gun, and had managed to turn it. Venera jammed her finger against the trigger and a shot spanged off the ceiling just over Holon's head. He roared and ducked, and her next shot took him at the base of one of his four branchlike limbs.

Then he'd swung Venera and Jacoby, bashing them against one another. The pistol went flying, and the two were shoved violently through a cloud of corpses to fetch up next to Antaea.

"Enough of spectators," said Holon. "I'll finish this alone." He raised four of his branches, their sharp ends hovering like poised snakes. Antaea closed her eyes.

The ever-present hum that filled the command center went silent and so did the red light penetrating her closed eyes. But there was no pain. After a second, she opened her eyes.

"What . . . ?" It was Venera's voice.

The lights came back on, and the command mirror flickered back into life. Holon hung in the middle of the room, frozen in place like some grotesque statue. Beyond him, the mirror showed the metal crab shapes that had surrounded Candesce's generator. They had also stopped moving.

"Get the gun," mumbled Jacoby. "And finish the bastard before he wakes up."

"Good idea," said Antaea. But it was too hard to move. She felt herself drifting off to sleep, and it seemed like such a good idea that she closed her eyes, and smiled.

"YOU CAN STOP screaming," said Keir. Leal coughed and fell silent. A good thing, too: her throat was raw from her performance.

The army engineers had finally dragged her aboard their open-sided vessel, but not before she'd led them on a merry chase around Keir's machine. "No, don't kill me!" she'd screamed. "I don't want to die. Get away from me!" She'd played the hysteria to the hilt, while Hayden clambered out of sight of the engineers and fired up his sun's mechanism.

It had started huffing and thrumming now, and the engineers were alarmed. Hayden appeared around from behind it, waving his arms. "It's okay!" he shouted. "It's not a bomb!"

"Surrender!" shouted an engineer. The man was trying to sound authoritative, but against this sky he stood little chance. Hospital ships and looters were arriving in equal numbers, and as the last of the smoke drifted away, the sheer monumental scale of the damage was becoming clear. The engineers would be clearing unexploded ordnance from the skies of the principalities for years.

"Look!" Keir pointed. Leal peered at the clots of smoke and fire surrounding Candesce. They were appalling, and she shook her head.

"No, look! The lasers have stopped."

She blinked. "Don't you see?" he said. "It's working."

Hayden had drifted over, his hands on his head in deference to the guns pointed at him. "We're generating an analogue of Candesce's suppression field," he said.

"How big is it, Keir?"

"Probably not more than four hundred miles in radius," he said. "But that's big enough to have stopped the attack."

Leal shook her head. "Here, maybe. But at the edge of the world . . ."

"Get us clear," the engineers' commander was saying. "We'll detonate this one from a safe distance like we did the others."

"Wait!" "No!" Hayden and Keir leaped up together, only to be forced back by armed jittery men. "You can't destroy it!" Keir continued. "It's what won the battle!"

The commander looked at them sympathetically. "They're all going to take a long time to recover from this." He sighed. "Ready the two-inch gun. We'll pick it off from a half-mile out."

"—NOT COMFORTABLE LEAVING him like that," Venera was saying. "Didn't he say that body was designed to live in the suppressive field? Then why . . . ?"

Antaea blinked at her. "Wha—?"

"It doesn't matter, the field's obviously back on somehow. He's frozen. Shoot his limbs off and throw the pieces out the door," said Jacoby.

"Where—" Pain lanced through her side, and the sudden sound of gunfire woke Antaea further. She remembered it all suddenly: the fight, the monsters, her fighting back. And Holon.

She pulled against Venera, who was hauling pieces of Holon toward the blockhouse's exit. "Wait, you don't understand."

"You're fine, Antaea. We're going to get you out of here." Antaea drifted for a minute, and when she awoke again Venera was back, this time encircling her waist with one arm. Jacoby had appeared on her other side.

"No, no, wait." She was finding it hard to frame her thoughts. And what about that tone in Venera's voice? It was the sort of soothing cadence you used with someone who was dying.

Antaea tried to pull away. "Day's not going to come."

They both let go of her. "What?" said Venera.

"Holon . . . turned off the dawn. Candesce . . ." She was finding it hard to breathe. "Candesce won't come on again unless we tell it to."

They'd kept drifting through the maze as she spoke, and the exit was approaching. "Shall I, or do you think you can do it?" Venera said to Jacoby.

"Let's get her to the sloop first," he said. "Then we'll both go." He pressed the switch that opened the door, and it slid silently aside, letting in hot, smoky air.

"Ouch," said Antaea. She flexed her fingers; at least her left hand was working. "And where's the key?" she demanded.

Venera held it up. "I picked it off Remoran. He—" Praying she had the strength, Antaea made a grab for it. Venera was so surprised she let Antaea take it—and kick her in the stomach.

Antaea had been holding on to the edge of the door as she'd done it, so as Venera sailed out into the night, she reoriented herself and grabbed Jacoby by his bad shoulder.

"Ah!" He doubled up around the pain and she hauled with all her might. He, too, went through the door.

"Somebody has to turn on the sun again!" she cried at the two receding figures. "And how are you going to lock this door? It needs the key to do it!"

Venera swore as she reached impotently to any kind of purchase on the empty air. "We'll lock it from out here!"

"And I'm to trust you?" Antaea shook her head. "This has to end here. The key can never be used again. And the only place in the world where it can never be recovered is right here."

They were shouting at her to stop, to reconsider, but the red-ness was starting to overwhelm her sight again, and a roaring like thunder was in her ears, so she shut the door.

Then she raised the key to Candesce, and locked herself in.

IT TOOK FOUR shots before the engineers hit something vital. Then, instead of exploding, Hayden's generator simply sparked spectacularly, and went black.

"Aw, no," said Hayden. "That was good work."

Keir waited for scry to reappear. The seconds dragged on. No new lights came on from the region of Candesce, and while the thud and fire of battle still continued on the other side of the sky, the gauzy blue of lasers was still missing.

When that light still hadn't reappeared after two minutes, he let out a ragged breath.

"I think it's over," he said.

"YOU'RE A TERRIBLE pilot," Jacoby muttered as yet another body thudded into the sloop's windshield. Venera didn't smile, and he instantly regretted his gallows humor. Hunched at the controls, Venera guided the sloop into the wreckage of the greatest battle Virga had ever seen.

"She'll be all right," he said. "That blockhouse has the best medical facilities in the world. All automated. She'd have to go to Brink to find better."

A bullet or something starred the windshield. Venera jerked, then fingered her jaw, and returned her attention to the controls. ". . . Can't see a damned thing," she said.

"Just point us at any sun," he said. "Like that one." He nodded at an orange smear behind a bank of indigo clouds, but Venera shook her head.

"We have to find the *Surgeon*," she said.

For a moment he thought she was still talking about Antaea, and then he realized she meant her husband's flagship.

"He'll be fine, Venera. For God's sake, he's inside a *battleship*. If he's not safe there, what are we going to do for him?"

She'd grabbed a new pistol from the armory as they'd entered the sloop. She pointed it at him. "The *Surgeon*," she said levelly. "We'll not be separated again."

He raised his good hand. "The *Surgeon* it is."

While she piloted, he went back and found the tarpaulin that had been used to cover the water tanks. The tank where he'd hidden the knife-ball egg was gone; Antaea must have tried to dispose of it. He dragged the tarp to the sloop's main hatch and draped it outside. It wasn't much as white flags went, but it would have to do.

They sailed on through darkness and smoke, but everywhere signs of life and humanity were beginning to reassert themselves. Cruisers and cutters from a hundred navies were nosing through the wreckage, netting injured men from the air and tossing ropes to disabled ships to allow their crews on board. He saw one giant vessel that was so festooned with men they hung from every surface and clustered on its hull like flies. This was all the more amazing since the ship had a terrible wound in its flank that had nearly cut it in two.

It rotated into faint amber light and Jacoby saw the colors of Slipstream and the lettering on its prow: *Surgeon*.

With a smile he turned to tell Venera—then paused. Nearly all the fires of the battle were out, smothered in their own exhaust. Most of the principalities' suns were obscured by clouds. How had he been able to read the lettering on that ship's prow?

He climbed around the *Thistle*'s hull to look back at the sun of suns. Deep red lights glowed there, and they were brightening. As he watched, something like a metal flower began to open behind the vast crystalline spikes that marked Candesce's perimeter. Instead of a stamen and pistil, this flower cradled fire in its heart, and that fire, too, began to brighten.

He swung into the sloop. "Dawn! Dawn's coming! We have to get out of here!"

Venera turned. Her hands were white on the controls, and the expression on her face was terrible.

To his own surprise, Jacoby heard himself say, "The *Surgeon*'s right over there." He pointed to starboard.

She simply said, "Thank you," and banked the *Thistle*.

The air was choppy now, and they could feel the heat rising through the glass. Outside, the growing radiance illuminated clouds of bodies and shattered ships, and the contorted forms of strange, crablike machines, each one a hundred feet long or more. These had frozen in midgesture and now cast nightmarish shadows across the receding vistas of smoke and the intricate details of aerial carnage.

All the ships that had power were turning away now, racing to escape the exclusion zone before full daylight. Many pilots were having to make agonizing decisions not to try to reach airmen who were waving frantically at them from stranded ships. Chaison Fanning's battleship was powering up its engines, too, but it would take it a while to get up to speed. The *Thistle* caught up to it easily.

Venera threw a line to some airmen standing in the wreckage of the *Surgeon*'s hangar, and climbed across to join a growing mob of refugees who were all scrambling to get inside before the sun came on.

The heat was becoming intense. Jacoby shaded his eyes and looked back to behold the funeral rites of the principalities writ large: ship by ship, body by body, the radiance of the sun of suns was reaching out to engulf all that remained behind. Whatever was closest to Candesce was already aflame, though the fires were barely visible against the greater light behind them. Thousands upon thousands of silhouetted human figures patterned this sky, and one by one the light reached out to them, and they vanished.

Venera grabbed the arm of a Slipstream officer. "I have to get to the bridge."

He shook his head. "Crew only, ma'am. Besides, it's not safe crossing that." He indicated the twisted girders and shorn bulkheads of the Surgeon's giant wound.

Venera looked him in the eye. "My name is Venera Fanning, and I have to get to the bridge."

"Oh!" He waved at another man. "We need an escort! And semaphore the admiral! Tell him we found his wife."

"Don't," she said; and then she smiled impishly. "I'd prefer to surprise him."

Escorted by four tough airmen, she began climbing up the rigging that stretched across the wreckage. After a moment she paused, and squinted back at Jacoby. "Coming?"

He shook his head. "This is your moment. Besides, if I show my face I'll just be arrested."

"Oh, pfft." But she smiled again. "See you, then, Jacoby."

He watched her climb out of sight. Then he braced his feet under the edge of the buckled hull to watch new upwelling clouds rise from the inferno of Candesce: clouds of ash from a pyre big as the sky. His shoulder throbbed; his left hand pulsed back. He'd come to the end of his strength, and there was no going back from here. In the end, all his guile and violence had been insufficient to prevent a holocaust, and now, he finally felt his age, and knew how little his own epitaph would say.

Jacoby put his head in his hands, and wept.

Epilogue

ROWAN WHEEL CUTS into a cloud, and rain chutes along the copper streets of the city. Dark-coated pedestrians turn up their collars and hurry from doorway to doorway—each portico or glass-doored entrance a gaslit altar in the eternal night. At certain angles the streets gleam like beaten gold, runnels of water making them waver like a hallucination of treasure.

People gather under the eaves and canopies to wait out the storm. The warm orange windows are smudged and faded to sepia by the incoming mist. Conversations start, pause, punctuated by distant rumbles of thunder and the murmuring of the rain; start again.

There's a curfew checkpoint being dismantled about a block away. The soldiers keep working through the rain, faces impassive ovals on a velvet backdrop. Someone comments that it's such a relief the danger is over. No one looks up past the perches of the spokesmen, to where faintly gleam the running lights of new visitors from outside the world.

She will imagine that these streets still bear old impressions of her shoes, an added layer to the map-upon-map that is the history of Sere. Certainly, her ghosts will always walk here: her parents, Easley Fencher, Brun Mafin, old William. Somewhere, shrouded by darkness and rain, Seana also walks, dear sad Porril hurries into his house, and Uthor pauses to glance out the obsidian square of a window as he prepares a meal for his latest client.

She will write to Seana when she's ready. It will be so easy, now that communications systems can reach instantly across the world.

When she's ready—but not yet.

In the meantime, the foghorns of the city will invade her dreams—brooom, brauum, braaam—and when she's careless her footsteps will unconsciously revert to the gait she had under the gravity of Sere. She will talk in her mind to the *people she left behind, and even the brightest of suns will never reach all the alleys and roofscapes that she sees behind closed eyes.*

Leal will never entirely leave Sere. But she will never return.

KEIR FINALLY SPOTTED her, a dark-on-dark silhouette halfway around the curve of the sun. "Leal!"

She didn't answer, so he left Hayden Griffin's side and flew over to her. The tessellated panes of Aerie's sun fell away beneath his feet, dark pools that for now reflected the distant light of other nations' suns. The fusion generator was roughly spherical, but giant glass-and-steel spines six times its length gave it a starlike profile. Leal was holding on to one of these with two toes, her body straight as if standing. As Keir stopped himself against the spine, he saw that her eyes were closed.

"Leal?"

She blinked, and smiled down at him. "Sorry, I was just— remembering."

Where she was facing, the sky was completely dark. Keir guessed where her thoughts had been, and nodded sympathetically. She'd never talked about the country she'd come from, but, now that the war was over, she woke crying in the middle of the night, and often fell into these reveries.

He put his arm around her. "Hayden says the adjustment's complete. Dawn is in half an hour, so we'd better get going."

Leal nodded absently, then said, "Was it fun?"

He grinned. "Actually, yes, it was." Griffin had given Keir a tour of Aerie's sun during today's maintenance period. The two had discussed physics and engineering, and the minute differences in how this giant fusion lantern worked here, compared with how it should work outside Virga.

"You know," he said, "I find that having a single machine to focus on is relaxing. You learn its . . . well, its character, I guess, by repairing and tuning it. —What it does easily, and where it has a mind of its own. You could spend a lifetime just maintaining this one sun . . . There's worse things I could do."

Leal laughed. "Did you say that to Hayden?"

"Yes. He said I'd already built a million new suns, and shouldn't I just consider relaxing?"

He turned away from the darkness, and a moment later she followed. In this direction was a vast sweep of light, deep purple at its edges and fading, while brightening through red to orange and then gold at its center. That glow came from Slipstream's sun. Slipstream, Rush, and all the controversy and excitement of its pirate sun were moving away from Aerie, following the slow drift of the asteroid that both city and sun were tethered to. Between Aerie's sun and the retreating nation, the sky was speckled with detail: ball-shaped groves of trees, clouds of crops; lakes that shone like pearls; and spinning bolo-houses and town wheels. There was plenty of room around a new sun, and people from all over the world were moving here to take advantage of it. Aerie was coming into its own.

This flowering was mirrored, Keir knew, by events unfolding beyond Virga's walls. The oaks were scouring the arena clean of the virtuals, and who knew? —Maybe emigrants from Virga would end up settling on the plains of Aethyr, or the vast spaces of Crucible, a balloon world at least ten times the size of Virga that the Virgans now knew orbited nearby. It was the ability of embodied creatures to set limits on Artificial Nature's power that was making all of this possible. Candesce's suppressive technology was quickly spreading to every place where life-forms wanted to anchor their values in some sort of unchanging reality.

"I am the Mighty Brick," he murmured. "Tremble before me." And he had to smile.

"What are you *talking* about?" Leal was sending him a look that said she feared for his sanity.

He was trying to figure out how to explain it to her when a sudden blossoming of virtual light enfolded them. Icons burst into view, glyphs and tags exploded onto the sky. With aggressive buzzes, dragonflies shot from the bag at Keir's belt, showing him what was under, behind, and above him.

With practiced nonchalance, a golden doll flipped back the flap of Leal's purse, and climbed up her arm to perch on her shoulder.

Somewhere below them, Hayden Griffin gave a whoop. "And not a moment too soon!" he shouted. "Thank you, Antaea!"

The glyphs from Leal's own (newly installed) scry made her reaction to that comment plain. Nobody knew whether the outages were of Antaea's design or not; nobody knew if she was still alive, and Leal disapproved of superstition. All up and down Virga, however, people would be pausing now in their daily routines and nodding to, or raising glasses to, or even praying to the sun of suns, and the new queen who, according to the stories, sat on a diamond throne behind its light.

Antaea must have lived long enough to restart Candesce's day/night cycle. Beyond that, what had happened to her was anybody's guess.

"I just worry," said Leal, "that we're seeing the birth of a new religion, that's all."

He shrugged. "There could be worse things."

"We've got three hours," Hayden was telling one of the technicians. "Make those diagnostics count."

Three hours every two days or so was as long as any of these outages ever lasted. It was long enough for the newly imported surgery bots to wake up, for a patient to be prepped, and for their heart to be replaced. Three hours was enough time to commune with loved ones or send calls for help through scry or by simple radio; it was long enough for suns to be tuned, reporters to gather news, and computers to wake up and analyze crop yields or the genetics of new pathogens. Much good could be done in those three hours, and yet, the timing of this window was just a bit too random to plan an invasion or bank robbery or terrorist attack to coincide with it—and that, or so people said, was clear evidence that the outages were part of a plan.

Whether Candesce's new flicker was due to the intercession of the queen of Candesce, or just a stutter in the sun of suns' control mechanisms, the result was the same. You dropped whatever else you were doing to deal with a sudden flood of scry mail, news, weather, and entertainment. Keir and Leal stood in the air for long moments, absorbing the sudden intake.

She laughed. "Piero's bought a farm! Can you believe it? He says there's not enough room in the city for all his kids to run wild."

When Keir didn't respond, she looked over in sudden concern. "What is it?"

He blinked and turned his eyes away from a virtual world to her. "They've identified the last of the remains from Brink," he said. "It's Maerta."

"Oh, Keir, I'm so sorry."

He'd seen the photos before, but couldn't help calling up again the incinerated towers and jumbled walls skating in random lines down the slopes of Aethyr. You needed your imagination to picture what had been here once; the metropoloid was no longer easily distinguished from the scree that surrounded it. Brink had fallen in the first hours of the battle, before Keir had even reached Fanning's flagship. He'd given the fabs there the plans for his generator, but all their efforts had gone into finishing his in time; they hadn't been able to build their own before the bombs had fallen. His only consolation was that the invaders had poised themselves eagerly above the vast hammerlike cloud of the city's destruction, and burst as one into Virga when Candesce's field fell only to become frozen, as if in amber, when Candesce reawakened. They had been easy pickings for the Guard's precipice moths and none were left by the time Candesce began its stuttering.

He swept the pictures away, and found that another set had been mailed to him by some anonymous fan of his work. These new images were from the planet Revelation, where he'd grown up. That entire world was now surrounded by a Candesce-like field, and photos from the ground showed plains of shattered and crumbling structures stretching all the way to the horizon. The virtuals had spent the last few years papering over Revelation's biosphere with computronium in an attempt to turn the whole planet into a giant simulator for their virtual paradise. It had all collapsed, and grass and new trees now poked between the crystalline spines of the virtuals' machineries. Somewhere in there, Sita's bones would finally be returning to the ecosystem that had first given them life.

In a hundred years, maybe, his old home would begin to look the way it once had. That was a sad thought; but if there was any lesson to be learned from Virga's fight with Artificial Nature, it was that you must let some things unfold in their own way, and in their own time.

Bangs and thumps came from below as Hayden and his men slammed the sun's maintenance hatches. "Clear out!" he shouted, waving a wrench over his head in the faint light from Slipstream. "Daybreak in ten minutes!"

"Come, love," said Leal, taking his hand. "You need a rest, and I've got a lecture at nine."

He dismissed the photos, and the memories and regrets, and with his wife stepped into the unbounded air of the new day.

"WHERE IS HE? Where is he?" Venera Fanning was practically running down the corridors of the ambassadorial mansion in Aurora. Hayden Griffin had been musing at some virtual windows that showed the current performance of his sun, but now he turned to watch her go by.

"What's wrong?" he asked.

She didn't reply, just snarled and kept quick-marching along. That was a difficult thing to do, given the sheath dress she had evidently decided to wear for today's ceremony. He'd rarely seen Venera so upset, though, so after a glance at his displays, Hayden strolled after her. His windows drifted after him, keeping a discreet distance.

"Disaster!" Venera veered toward a drinks table on her way through the ballroom, and grabbed a champagne glass. "A complete catastrophe!" She downed the glass in one gulp, set it to teeter on the edge of the table, and hurried on, feet tick-ticking in the very short steps allowed by the dress.

Since nobody had asked him to give a speech, Hayden had not bothered to remember what today's ceremony was for—he only knew that it was the last time he'd be seeing the Fannings in Aurora. They were bound for Rush tomorrow, doubtless to plan some sort of grief for the next cloud of countries Slipstream was drifting into. Hayden would be sad to see them go, though he knew the entire city was holding its collective breath. The final departure of the Fannings was, to many, the ultimate sign that Aerie was now in the hands of its own people.

"Where is the bastard?" Venera roared at a footman. He pointed down a covered walkway that connected two of the residence's buildings. "He's going to pay for this one," she told the man before continuing on. The footman watched her go, then turned to see Hayden lumbering up behind her. He and Hayden exchanged a glance and a shrug.

Though she kept walking at top speed, Hayden slowed to a stop about halfway down the gallery. Warm sunlight was streaming in through its leaded-glass walls; several ventilation panes were angled open, and a slight breeze teased the gauzy white curtains that had been pulled back to let the light in. The light shone across the polished stone floor, reflected in pale squares along the ceiling, and surrounded and embraced everything in the space.

"There you are!" sounded faintly from somewhere ahead.

"Venera, what's wrong?"

A pair of wood-framed glass doors led to a little sitting area outside the gallery. Hayden dismissed his virtual windows and laid his hand on the latch.

"What's wrong?" she roared. "What's *wrong?*

"I'm pregnant!"

Hayden paused, looked to where two figures stood silhouetted in the next parlor—one, hands on hips, curved up as if to take off into the air, the other, ramrod straight, looking down at her.

"Chaison, I don't know how to do this . . ." As he put his arms out to encircle her, Hayden turned back to the doors. Smiling, he turned the latch and opened them.

Warm air, laden with the scent of flowers and grass, coiled around him. He stepped outside, and at that moment the icons of scry that had surrounded him blinked out. Today's outage was over.

It was quiet here, save for the buzzing of insects and intermittent birdsong. The gallery doors opened onto a little semicircular patio, not more than ten feet across, bounded by a low stone wall. Two white benches made angles on either side of the doors; over the little wall, luxurious gardens began.

There had been a time when Hayden couldn't still the churn of thoughts in his head. He'd spent his days thinking, scheming, worrying, and rationalizing. When he first lit this sun, he'd been too focused on its spectrum and modulations to take in the fact that this was the project his parents had given their lives for. When that realization finally caught up to him, it had come in the form of sorrow and grief, and at the height of his success, he'd found himself running away from the very sun he'd worked so hard to build.

Since that time he'd been so wrapped up in the miseries of his own past that he barely noticed the world around him. He'd given up caring about the suns he designed; but things had changed the day he met that indomitable history tutor, Leal Hieronyma Maspeth. His reemergence hadn't been sudden—more like slowly waking from a dream. Finally, today, and maybe for the first time, he was entirely back.

If he mentioned this to Leal, she would of course lay the cause at the feet of the countess of Greendeep, who managed to appear everywhere Hayden went lately. There was something between them, no doubt of that. But there was more to this feeling than that—more, too, than simply laying his past to rest.

Hayden stepped up to the stone wall and laid his fingertips on it. The stone was warm, almost as though it were alive. He felt the long slow breaths coursing in and out of his own body, and faintly, the presence of his pulse.

He leaned back and tilted his face up to the sun. He'd spent so much time thinking about its calibration, its dynamics and tolerances—it was long past time he should do this.

The heat of its fire sank into him in slow waves, penetrating under his skin, washing down his throat and shoulders, settling into his entire body. He closed his eyes, and the air teased his hair. Birdsong and his breath; the heat of a sun; he had all he needed.

He emptied his mind of thought, and let it fill with a vast and comforting radiance.

About the Author

Karl Schroeder lives in Toronto, Ontario, Canada, with his wife and daughter. In addition to writing science fiction, he consults on the future of technology and culture for clients, such as the Canadian government and army. His Web site is www.karlschroeder.com.